> *She looked in the mirror.*
> *A stranger gazed back at her.*

Short blonde hair and a neck that was exposed, vulnerable. She donned the oversized sunglasses, blinking to get used to the dim light.

She checked her watch for the thousandth time. She was on schedule.

By now, he knew.

The thought sent a jolt of fear sizzling through her like an electric current, robbing her breath and making the stall spin dizzily. Caroline squeezed her eyes shut, reached out, and grabbed the cold porcelain sink for support. She took a deep breath, licked her lips, and tried to swallow. Because she knew as sure as she stood there that his search had begun.

She had made up her mind. Today would be the day. And now it was happening.

Tears sprang to her eyes as the full imp____ __ ____ _____ ne. There was ___

He

By Margaret Carroll

A DARK LOVE

Coming October 2009

RIPTIDE

MARGARET CARROLL

A DARK LOVE

AVON

An Imprint of HarperCollins*Publishers*

This is a work of fiction. Names, characters, places, and incidents are products of the author's imagination or are used fictitiously and are not to be construed as real. Any resemblance to actual events, locales, organizations, or persons, living or dead, is entirely coincidental.

AVON BOOKS
An Imprint of HarperCollins*Publishers*
10 East 53rd Street
New York, New York 10022-5299

Copyright © 2009 by Margaret Carroll
Excerpt from *Riptide* copyright © 2009 by Margaret Carroll
ISBN 978-0-06-165278-3
www.avonromance.com

First Avon Books paperback printing: September 2009

Avon Trademark Reg. U.S. Pat. Off. and in Other Countries, Marca Registrada, Hecho en U.S.A.
HarperCollins® is a registered trademark of HarperCollins Publishers.

Printed in the U.S.A.

10 9 8 7 6 5 4 3 2 1

For Mom and Katie Mae

ACKNOWLEDGMENTS

My fabulous and daring agent, Stephanie Cabot, and her team at The Gernert Company, who took a chance on me. Carrie Feron and her brilliant team at Harper-Collins, especially Tessa Woodward. Trish and cousin Maggie, world's greatest cheerleaders. Aunt Kay and Uncle Joe, for a sunny place in winter to dream up this book. Kate, the world's greatest camper. John, for teaching me what it looks like to never quit, never give up. Jim and Dore, for helping me on my way. Jeannie Arlin Koster, for fluency in French. Therese McGratty, world's best neighbor. John Fundukian, who knows about handguns. Andrew Baxley, who knows his way around Washington, D.C. Dr. Swami Mamboni, who dreamt up a cocktail with a heckuva kick. Chip Berschback, Jenny Emmons, and Dr. Kathleen Moore, who do heroic works. Tim and Jodi (you know why). Rand, for showing me Pagosa Springs (heaven on earth) and making all my dreams come true. And Buddy, just for being my buddy.

CHAPTER

1

WASHINGTON, D.C.
MONDAY

Caroline Hughes left her husband on a scorching Monday in September. It was just after nine o'clock in the morning, but already the cobblestone streets of Georgetown shimmered under a heat so intense it made breathing difficult and thinking almost impossible.

She stepped outside and paused, as though she had nothing more important to decide than which direction to take the dog on his morning walk. She had rehearsed this moment in her mind a thousand times.

Porter was watching from his office window.

The heat from the red brick sidewalk worked its way up through the thin soles of Caroline's Keds and beyond, to the thick layer of currency she had stashed inside. Mostly hundreds, with some twenties mixed in. Four thousand dollars in all.

She looked right and then left. Pippin tugged at his leash, dancing around on the hot sidewalk.

"Okay, handsome, now or never," Caroline spoke softly to the dog. Her hands shook so badly she nearly dropped the leash. She glanced at the ground-floor window of their townhouse. Inside, she knew, he had a good view of her from his leather wing-backed chair.

Caroline forced a smile to her lips and gave a quick nod. It was their signal. Which meant she had twenty minutes. She forced herself to saunter the short distance to the end of the block. She turned left onto Wisconsin Avenue, Georgetown's main thoroughfare. Once around the corner she quickened her pace, walking more swiftly now but not fast enough to attract attention.

The Yorkshire terrier trotted, ears erect, happy to be out.

Reaching into the slender pocket of her Capri pants, she pulled out her and Porter's passports. She pushed them deep into an overflowing waste can and kept walking. If her passport was missing he might think she had traveled overseas. Keeping it with her brought a risk of identification that she could not afford. Tossing his bought her time.

Caroline Hughes had just made herself disappear.

The bills inside her sneakers slipped against her bare feet, and bunched around her insteps. Halfway down the block, she hailed a cab, her breath coming in shallow, uneven bursts. She had gone far enough that he wouldn't see brake lights even if he walked out onto the front stoop right now. Not that he would have reason to do so.

She reached for the door, half expecting Porter to grab her from behind before she could get in. Her sweat-slicked hand slipped from the handle. She tried again, heart pounding so hard blood roared in her ears. She scooped Pippin up and climbed in, her arms and legs shaking like rubber. She exhaled as her cab headed down Wisconsin to M Street and into Foggy Bottom, a short distance she had walked many times. Every second counted now.

Caroline ducked her head, letting her long brown hair fall forward like a curtain around her face. The driver paid her no attention, speaking rapid-fire Farsi into a walkie-talkie mounted on the dash.

Pippin scrambled to find his footing on the seat beside her. He let out a small whine, as though he, too, was afraid.

From her pocket, Caroline withdrew a small package of aluminum foil and unwrapped a wad of cream cheese. It contained a pill from the vet, left over from a supply given last year to help Pippin sleep on an airline flight. She had six more in reserve.

"Bottoms up, friend," she whispered. "We're free."

The Yorkie took one sniff and gobbled it down.

She peeled two bills from the stack inside her sneaker as the cab slowed to a halt. Two twenties, already damp with sweat. Head down, she pushed a twenty over the seat and placed the other in her back pocket. She counted the change and gave the driver a good tip. Not too big. Nothing that would attract attention.

She scooped the dog into her arms and entered CVS. Collecting a basket, she made straight for the hair care aisle. She chose a box of hair dye and added scissors, a comb, and a small bottle of shampoo before moving on. Next she picked up toothpaste and a toothbrush on her way to the sundries aisle, praying the zippered beach totes would still be on sale. They were. She grabbed one, along with a pair of oversized sunglasses and a floppy hat before heading to the baby aisle to get a small bowl for Pippin's food. To this she added a package of dog food, bottled water, and several packs of cheese and crackers, even though the thought of food nauseated her.

She waited in line to pay, hoping the other customers couldn't hear the pounding of her heart. Despite the soaring temperature outside, her hands had turned cold and clammy. Her mouth was dry, making it difficult to swallow. She hoped she wouldn't faint. At least there wasn't much worry of seeing anyone she knew. She had no real friends in Washington, D.C. Porter's business acquaintances would be working at this hour.

But she was wrong.

"Well, howdy neighbor."

Caroline's heart sank at the cheery greeting. The one and only neighbor Caroline called a friend had just entered the drugstore.

"Don't mind me, I'm out for my morning power walk, and right now, I'm a sweaty mess," Lindsay Crowley exclaimed in her deep Southern twang.

Which was so not true that Caroline couldn't hold back a weak smile of her own, despite the fact that she was in the biggest crisis of her entire life and had no time to stop and chat. Even in hundred-degree heat with humidity to match, not a single strand of Lindsay's perfect coif had come undone. Lindsay was from Houston, where, Caroline supposed, they made a science of taming frizz. The thought made her glance involuntarily down at the box of hair dye in her basket.

Lindsay's gaze followed. "Now, honey, don't tell me you came all the way down here to run errands in this heat. And dragged Lover Boy with you." She reached down to pat Pippin, who wagged his tail.

Caroline glanced nervously at her watch and shifted her basket from one arm to the other. She'd met Lindsay Crowley on M Street one day when she was out taking Pippin for his walk. The older woman was dressed in designer coordinates, was perfectly made up, and practically fell out of her dainty mules at the sight of the Yorkie.

Caroline had liked her on sight.

But every second counted now and there was no going back. Caroline cleared her throat. "Um, we have to get going."

Lindsay straightened, bouncing on to the balls of her cross-trainers. "If you've got a minute, I'll grab a bottle of water and we can go back home together." She dropped her voice a notch and leaned in, a mischievous twinkle in her eye. "In fact, let's share a cab. My treat. Who can exercise in this heat?"

Caroline took a step away. "Thanks, but we're headed . . ." Her voice trailed off as she cringed inside. Where on earth would she be going with the dog in this heat first thing in the morning? Stupid, stupid, she thought, hunching her shoulders and edging away.

But Lindsay was either too polite or too thirsty to press the offer, giving Caroline a cheery wave before turning to scan the signs above the aisles for bottled water.

She didn't have to wait long for a register. When she reached the front of the line, Caroline placed her items on the counter, careful to avoid eye contact.

The clerk's voice came out loud, booming. "Time for a whole new you, I guess."

Caroline flinched.

Smiling, the clerk tapped the box of hair dye.

Flustered, Caroline had visions of private investigators passing themselves off as D.C. cops, asking the counter clerks if a young woman had recently purchased items of interest. She wondered whether Lindsay was nearby, within earshot. She didn't have the nerve to turn and look. She forced herself to smile. "It's for a friend, not me." She licked her lips and tried to swallow, aware that it sounded like a lie. "My best friend sprained her wrist. I'm helping her touch up her roots." Best friend. It sounded so normal.

"You're a good friend," the cashier said, counting out change. "You tell your friend to stay out of this heat now till she's feeling better."

"I sure will." Caroline took the bag and left. The sidewalk pulsed with a heat so intense the top of her head ached. She tore the tag off the sunglasses, put them on, and looked around. She half expected to see Porter, waiting to take her home. But the only soul braving the heat was an elderly man in a straw bowler, taking slow, deliberate steps down Pennsylvania Avenue. She donned the hat, tucked her hair up inside, and rearranged the contents of the CVS bag so there was enough room on top for the dog.

"Sorry, friend," she said, scooping him up and piling him on top.

She hailed a cab.

Within seconds a taxi appeared, swerving across two lanes of traffic to reach her. Caroline clambered in, directing the driver to First and L streets. She checked her watch as they headed east. Twenty-three minutes had passed. She'd been spotted by a neighbor, and that put her a few minutes behind schedule. But there was nothing she could do about that.

Porter would be growing impatient. Staring out his office window. Rubbing his jaw. Twenty minutes remained until the end of his patient's session. Then he would have just fifteen minutes free until his next patient arrived.

Caroline tried to push the thought away and hunched

lower against the backseat. She put Pippin on the floor of the cab, pulled the cheap tote out of the CVS bag, removed the price tag, and placed all her purchases inside. Plenty of room left for Pippin.

The Yorkie panted, watching her. The drug was taking effect. She was tempted to offer him water, but knew better. Greyhound didn't allow pets.

Dr. Porter Moross stared out his office window, his sense of unease growing with each moment. His wife was allocated twenty minutes to walk her dog. That was the amount of time they had agreed upon. Today she was late. Ten minutes already. That never happened. A woman with long brown hair walked past, and for an instant his heart leaped. But the woman was not his wife. His stomach curled and contracted until it twisted into a tight ball, leaving him nauseated. The feeling dated back to his childhood, and Porter's knowledge of that didn't help.

His first patient was lying on the couch. There was no sound from the upper floors of the historic townhouse he shared with his wife and her dog. Caroline was gone. His wife had left him. Porter knew it with absolute certainty. The knot in his stomach didn't lie.

The man on the couch fell silent. The sudden stillness in the room startled Porter, and brought his attention back to his office. Keeping the window in view, Porter glanced at his desk clock. This never happened. She understood very well what it meant. Now he'd have to punish her.

"So?" The tone was plaintive, demanding. The man on the couch was a second-term U.S. senator.

Porter frowned.

The senator fluttered his hand for emphasis. "I know this isn't about you or what you think, but I had to ask."

Porter had no idea what the senator was talking about. A figure appeared in the window, and Porter's heart leaped like a small child awaiting the return of his mother. But the woman on the sidewalk was not Caroline.

Porter's stomach clinched even tighter. She had betrayed him. He took a deep breath to stop the wave of panic. He gripped the edge of his wing chair and shifted in his seat. "You're right," he said carefully. "This isn't about me."

The senator glanced at his watch.

"We have three minutes remaining," Porter said in a well-modulated voice. "But I'd like to explore this further and we're almost out of time. I want you to hold that thought and we'll pick this up tomorrow."

The senator considered a moment before swinging his feet over the edge of the couch. He sat up and donned his suit jacket.

Porter kept a steady watch out the window. "See you tomorrow." Outside, he knew, the man's chauffeur waited to whisk him back to Capitol Hill.

Once Porter heard the street door click shut, he bounded up the steep staircase to the living quarters above.

He quickly searched the residence, even though he knew she was gone. His heart labored under a great weight as he walked through the place, deserted except for the antiques he had spent years collecting at private auctions. All for the purpose of making his home, their home, beautiful. The polished pieces of pecan and walnut, the horsehair sofa, mocked him now. The only sound was the hum of the air-conditioning pack they had installed last year, at great expense, in the crawl space at the top of the old house.

He stamped his foot and let out a low growl of frustration. But these sounds somehow made it worse by confirming his fear. She was gone and she wasn't coming back. Porter shook his head in a useless attempt to quell the panic rising in his gut. He checked his watch again. His next patient would arrive in twelve minutes.

In the entry hall, he removed the phone from its charger atop a gleaming mahogany secretary's desk. He speed-dialed their private voice mail. No messages. He speed-dialed the garage where they kept the Saab.

"Dr. Moross calling. Has my wife been down today?"

"Haven't seen her, Dr. Moross. Shall I bring the car around for her?"

"No," Porter replied quickly. "There's a problem with the car." He paused. "A safety issue."

"I see, sir."

"I don't want to alarm my wife. If she comes in to get the car, you need to call me at once. It's urgent."

"Yes, sir."

"Or if anybody comes in with her. Is that clear? Under no circumstances are you to release the vehicle." Porter was aware of the edge in his voice. But he couldn't help himself.

"Very good, sir. As you wish. I'll make a note of it for the afternoon shift, sir."

"Thank you. And be sure to call me if she comes in."

"Very good, Doctor."

Porter hung up. Caroline's Louis Vuitton purse was in the sitting room. Her scent drifted from it. Gardenia, mixed with the mint smell of chewing gum. He found her wallet inside, plus tampons, brush, lipstick, gum, and several crumbling dog treats. He wrinkled his nose in disgust. He had explained to her many times the dog treats would ruin the lining. He dumped the contents of the wallet on the floor. Seventy-one dollars in cash fluttered out, along with her ATM card and credit cards. Her driver's license was there as well. All of which should mean she had gone for a long walk.

But he didn't believe it. She was gone. He knew it. He tightened his grip on the change purse until the metal hasp hurt his hands.

He ran back down the stairs and outside, stepping into a heat so stifling it took his breath away.

He looked toward Wisconsin Avenue, which would be filling with tourists at this hour despite the ungodly heat. Caroline avoided crowds. She had, he was pleased to note, brought her habits into alignment with Porter's and had come to share his preference for spending time alone with him, just the two of them, without the distraction of other people.

Porter turned and walked quickly away from Wisconsin, to the Twenty-ninth Street Park at the end of the block. Heat hung like a thick layer of molasses over the row of immaculate townhouses dating to Thomas Jefferson's presidency. Porter's breath burned at the back of his throat.

The park was nearly deserted except for a handful of students lying in the shade. There was no sign of Caroline or her dog.

Swearing under his breath, Porter checked his watch. The air weighed in his lungs like burning ashes. He reached his front stoop and paused, one foot on the antique brass boot scraper.

Why, Caroline, why?

He squinted one last time toward Wisconsin Avenue. It was no use. She wasn't there. He shook his head and tried to clear his mind. He needed to concentrate now.

He reached for the polished brass doorknob, hot to the touch, and stepped inside.

His next patient was seated on the deacon's bench under the stairway. "Dr. Moross? Is everything okay?" She was the wealthy, American-born second wife of a former aide to the late Shah of Iran.

Beads of sweat rolled into Porter's eyes. He pushed his steel-rimmed glasses aside and rubbed. "Fine," he replied. "Go inside and get settled. I'll join you in a moment."

She hesitated. Her abandonment issues had no doubt flared at Porter's unprecedented tardiness. Porter insisted on punctuality and perfect attendance. It was the most basic component of the patient-therapist relationship. He refused to treat anyone who could not abide by his rules. Nor were his sessions covered by health insurance. In spite of this, Porter Moross had a reputation for being one of the best Freudian psychoanalysts in the nation. His roster of patients read like the venerable Green Book of Washington's social elite.

The woman on the bench tugged anxiously at the hem of her Chanel summer suit. She looked down at the blue carpet with its gold fleur-de-lis pattern. Beneath her abandonment issues was a desperate need for security. She liked being told what to do.

"I'll be right in," Porter said more forcefully, mopping at the beads of sweat that lined his brow.

With a meek nod, she collected her belongings and went.

Porter took the stairs two at a time up to the residence. He went directly to the desk, opened his BlackBerry, and obtained the private cell phone number of his third and final patient of the morning.

The phone was answered on the first ring by the editor-in-chief of one of the world's largest daily newspapers.

Porter canceled their appointment and offered to reschedule.

The editor, six years into his treatment, thanked Porter for the call.

Porter entered another name into his BlackBerry as the brief exchange took place, found the next number he wanted, and dialed. He left a message requesting a meeting at his office in one hour's time. He knew his request would be given the highest priority. Porter Moross was a steady customer of Beltway Security Investigations.

The cab dropped Caroline in a seedy part of town, one block from the Greyhound bus station. Pippin let out a small whine of protest when she hoisted the tote onto her shoulder. Her destination was a fast-food restaurant she had visited several times in preparation for this day. The lunch crowd hadn't arrived yet, and the staff behind the counter didn't even glance up when Caroline entered. She made a beeline for the bathroom.

The place reeked of cigarettes and homeless people, perfect for her purposes. It was, thankfully, deserted. With her heart hammering inside her chest, she made for the roomy handicapped stall at the end. Bolting the stall door behind her, she set the tote down. Pippin stuck his nose out, sniffed, and yawned before curling into a ball and drifting back to sleep.

She pulled out the scissors and comb, looked in the mirror, took a deep breath, and began snipping. Her thick brown hair drifted to the floor like leaves from a dying tree.

Caroline cut in a line around her neck, just above her chin. Pulling the ends straight up in sections over her head, she jabbed straight down in short strokes, the way her hairdresser did. The result was passable, she decided.

She swept the loose hair from the floor and flushed it. Tearing open the dye, she mixed it up in the sink. She knew exactly what to do. She had purchased a box several weeks ago and memorized the instructions before tossing it into a public trash can on the way home.

Porter didn't approve of women who dyed their hair.

She lined the neck of her T-shirt with paper towels before donning the disposable gloves and applying bleach beginning at the roots, all the way through to the ends. She took care not to drip any on her shirt.

She needed to wait twenty minutes. Ammonia stung her nose and eyes. Her shoulder and back muscles ached. She had spent the night locked in the bathroom, curled on a bath towel on the cold tiled floor. Praying Porter wouldn't try to break the door down. Too frightened to sleep. Tempted to unlatch the window and climb out, taking her chances in the narrow airshaft that separated their house from the one next door. But she was afraid the noise would attract Porter's attention. She had made up her mind. Today would be the day. And now it was happening.

Tears sprang to her eyes as the full impact of her actions hit home. There was no going back.

He would kill her if she did.

Caroline tried to push the thought from her mind. She didn't want to lose her nerve.

The door to the ladies' room swung open, making her jump. She prayed it wasn't anybody requiring use of the handicapped stall. But luck was with her. She listened to sounds from another stall as the minutes ticked by, trying not to think.

When twenty minutes had passed, she stood stiffly and rinsed in the sink, blotting her hair as best she could with paper towels. She ran the drugstore comb through her new short locks and surveyed the result.

A stranger gazed back at her. Short blond hair and a neck that was exposed, vulnerable. Her eyes were hollow, haunted. She couldn't bear the sight of them. She donned the oversized sunglasses, blinking to get used to the dim light.

She checked her watch for the thousandth time. She was on schedule.

By now, he knew.

The thought sent a jolt of fear sizzling through her like an electric current, robbing her breath and making the stall spin dizzily. Caroline squeezed her eyes shut, reached out and grabbed the cold porcelain sink for support. She took a deep breath, licked her lips, and tried to swallow. But her throat refused to close around the ball of solid fear inside her. Because she knew as sure as she stood there that his search had begun.

She opened her eyes and reached with unsteady hands for the CVS tote bag, which now held all her earthly belongings. She took one last look in the mirror at the frightened stranger.

"Alice Stevens," she whispered. "Good luck."

CHAPTER

2

Caroline didn't doze despite the rhythmic motion of the bus as it headed north and west, the engine working overtime whenever they left the Interstate and downshifted across blacktop roads that coiled through the mountains of West Virginia and then, toward evening, Ohio. The edge of the Great Plains. She was too nervous even to get carsick.

She willed the bus to roll on. Each mile should have been a victory but she couldn't think that much about it. She was grateful just to sit in the back as the bus rumbled through a time and place that did not have Porter in it. Her world consisted of nothing more than the inside of the Greyhound bus, and she could manage that.

Passengers got on and off. A baby squalled. Children fought over an electronic toy. A heavyset woman mouthed words from a well-worn Bible. Tinny sounds of hard rock drifted from the headphones of a young man sprawled across two seats.

Dread settled over Caroline like a heavy blanket, stealing her breath, each time the bus pulled off the highway. She scanned the people waiting to board, looking for . . . what? Whom would he send? She didn't know.

Relief flooded through her at the sight of mothers with children in tow, old men smoking cigarettes, a young German couple with backpacks.

They made a scheduled stop for a meal break as the sun dipped below an impossibly flat horizon. They had left the mountains behind and now they were in farm country, a landscape that could have been the background for Grant Wood's *American Gothic*. The solid smell of earth hit her when she left her seat for the first time all day. She stepped off, legs stiff and cramped, into air that was hot and humid, buzzing with the whine of traffic on the Interstate.

"Departure in twenty-five minutes," the driver called.

Caroline didn't follow the others inside to a plaza where the signs promised showers, a Laundromat, and twenty-four-hour dining. She couldn't risk being remembered for having traveled with a dog, not to mention the fact she didn't want to be kicked off here. She hadn't gotten far enough away.

She walked on shaky legs to the far end of the parking lot, where dusk was already settling in a grove of trees. Pippin wriggled from the tote and shook himself. He sniffed the grass and lapped at the water, gobbling the cheddar cheese snack she offered. A second pill was buried inside.

Caroline finished off the bottle of water in a single swig and forced herself to eat the remaining cheese snack. Her stomach made loud rumbling noises. She hadn't eaten since early this morning, at the small round oak table outside the galley kitchen of the townhouse. She had prepared the brand of Irish oatmeal Porter preferred, served with unrefined brown sugar and sliced bananas the way he liked it. She had forced herself to chew quickly as though she was hungry, although fear had robbed her mouth of saliva so the oatmeal stuck to her lips like glue.

Porter watched her over the rim of his cup as he sipped his coffee. He swallowed, his lips pursed into a thin line, and shook his head. "I don't know how you can eat after what you did."

Caroline nodded silently. She had apologized, and her apology had not been accepted. But she was afraid to decline breakfast. She didn't want him to see how nervous she was.

He patted his mouth with his napkin and tossed it onto the table. He checked his watch and shook his head. "We need to talk about this," he said wearily. "But I don't have the time. My first patient is due any minute. We'll talk tonight. I think you need to consider the source of your behavior. What's driving you, Caroline? I mean, if you could just see yourself." He slammed his fist against the side of her head so hard it banged against the wall and bounced back off. He flexed his hand a few times and shook it where it was sore. Pushing his chair back, he stood and let out a sigh. "We'll talk later, Caroline."

That had been thirteen hours ago. She drew in a deep breath of air that smelled of cornfields and held it in her lungs as long as she could. As though it could anchor her, steady the shaking in her limbs. It did not.

She gathered Pippin in her arms. "Sorry, pal," she murmured, planting a quick kiss on his head before setting him back inside the bag. She went inside to the ladies' room, where she used the toilet and splashed water on her face. The water felt good and cold on her bruised skin.

She boarded the bus and found her way back to her

seat, her cocoon. The last rays of daylight faded on the horizon as the bus picked up speed and merged back onto the Interstate.

The smell of French fries drifted from across the aisle. The woman had set her Bible down to focus on her take-out dinner. Still chewing, she offered Caroline a French fry. "Help yourself, dearie," she said in a mountain accent.

Caroline shook her head and gave a small smile but the woman was undeterred. She leaned closer.

Pippin stirred inside the tote.

"You look like you missed a couple dinners, and some breakfasts and lunch while you were at it." The woman grinned.

Pippin let out a small whine and the tote began to move.

Caroline placed a hand on top of the mound that was Pippin and held it, willing him to be quiet.

One of the kids with the Game Boy peeked around the edge of her seat and gave Caroline a curious look.

Not willing to risk more turned heads, Caroline accepted the limp fry and bit it in half.

The woman across the aisle smiled approvingly.

Caroline waited till the woman glanced away before slipping the remainder of the French fry inside the tote. Pippin's mouth closed around it, licking her fingers eagerly.

The woman smiled. "That's it. Girl, you're too thin. Take some more." She shook a white Styrofoam container in Caroline's direction.

Caroline took another, forcing herself to chew and swallow. Grease coated the insides of her mouth and lips, making her stomach heave.

"Where you headed?" The woman shifted in her seat to get a better look at Caroline.

Another kid at the front of the bus poked his head around the seat and giggled. It was a game now.

Caroline searched wildly for a phrase in a language the woman wouldn't know. She remembered only a few words from her semester abroad in St. Petersburg. She spoke them now, soft and low so the children wouldn't hear. "Happy Easter," she said in Russian.

The woman's eyes widened.

"Happy Easter," Caroline repeated in Russian. "Christ is risen."

"I get it." The woman across the aisle smiled and spoke slowly, louder now. "You're on vacation. Well, you just enjoy yourself then." She pushed the Styrofoam container once more in Caroline's direction before returning to her meal.

The miles rolled on beneath the wheels as the coach carried them west into the night.

John Crowley turned his full attention to the tiny television that was always tuned to CNN. Lou Dobbs was interviewing a government spokesman about the latest attempt to breach security at one of the nation's airports.

"That young man handled himself nicely," John's wife remarked when the piece ended.

John nodded, satisfied. He had personally signed off on the statement for the Lou Dobbs show and seen to it that the spokesman was fully briefed on the incident. John Crowley had resigned as CEO of a Texas-based airline after 9/11 to take the helm of a brand-new federal agency charged with airport security. Crowley turned his attention back to the low-fat, low-cholesterol dinner his wife had prepared. Grilled seasoned chicken breast, fully trimmed and skin removed, with steamed vegetables, brown rice, and sesame crackers on the side. He picked one up and crunched loudly, to prove a point.

Lindsay Crowley fluttered her eyelids mildly. "Now, this isn't so bad. We'll get that ol' cholesterol back down to where it should be. You'll see."

She meant every word. Once his wife had made up her mind about a thing, well, that thing was settled. John took a bite of chicken and smiled to show his appreciation for her efforts on behalf of his diet.

Lindsay smiled back sweetly.

The Crowleys had been married for more than thirty years and their union was, by any measure, a success.

"As I was saying, I ran into little Caroline today."

"Mmmm, hmmmm." John surveyed his plate. He had already devoured his six ounces of lean chicken and rice. All that remained was steamed broccoli and julienne strips of something he didn't recognize. He pitched in his fork, resigned.

"Don't you think?" His wife was frowning at him from across the tiny round glass-topped antique table the decorator had insisted they buy after their kids had left home. John hadn't seen what was wrong with the old one, but Lindsay had been happy with it and that was the important thing.

"I mean, it's not like there's any law against shopping in the Foggy Bottom CVS," Lindsay said. "But why go there first thing in the morning when there's one right up the street? And in this heat?"

"It's a mystery," John observed mildly. He knew from

long experience to let Lindsay run her mind over something till she got it settled one way or the other.

She easily spotted the twinkle in his eye, and made a face. "It wasn't anything you could put your finger on," she protested. "But there's something with that little gal and her husband."

Their newest neighbor was an odd duck, no doubt about it. One of those skinny New York intellectual types dressed head to toe in black. Way too interested in the artwork Lindsay had chosen with the help of her gay decorator. But John Crowley was not a gossip, a fact that sometimes put him at odds with his wife, who was a social being all the way to her very innermost core. He harrumphed now, signaling he was finished with this conversation.

Lindsay, he knew, was not near half done and would have liked to discuss the odd pairing of the couple who had moved into a row house across the street. But she began clearing the plates away instead. His wife knew when to let a subject drop, a fact John appreciated more the longer he lived with her. Although she had another trait, one he had also come to respect.

Lindsay Crowley always evened the score.

She did so now, flashing a sweet smile his way before heading to the kitchen. "Get your sneakers on, my love. Time for your fitness walk."

CHAPTER

3

*H*is wife's disappearance brought on a panic attack that was so intense that Porter was not sure he would survive. It was, he knew, a harbinger of the pain that was to come. The scorching heat wave didn't help. It only intensified the air of unreality that settled over his life. He waded rather than walked, his movements slow and heavy, through air that was hot and thick like car exhaust. His muscles protested every movement. Voices were tinny like old phonograph recordings. Speaking required tremendous effort. He knew from his medical training that he was suffering classic symptoms of shock.

The shock eventually passed and would be replaced by a grief so profound that it would etch new contours on Porter's face, squaring his eyes and settling in lines around his mouth.

When the Iranian VIP's wife finally left that first morning, Porter sprang into action. He knew there was no time to waste. He canceled all his sessions for the remainder of that day and the next. His patients would retaliate in small ways by showing up late for their next session, manufacturing conflict with him, or simply missing their appointments altogether.

The investigator from Beltway Security Investigations was prompt as always, waiting outside Porter's office at the designated time.

He greeted Porter with a curt nod and followed him inside. He gave the place an appraising look, his gaze lingering on the couch and Porter's framed Ivy League diplomas. Their previous meetings had been held in Beltway's suite of offices near McPherson Square or in a coffee shop just across the Keystone Bridge in Virginia. Places Caroline would never venture.

The PI settled into a chair, flipped open his notebook, and waited.

"My wife left." Porter's nostrils flared and his mouth hardened into a tight line.

"When?"

"Almost two hours ago." Porter ignored the way the investigator's brows rose on his forehead.

"Maybe she went shopping."

It occurred to Porter that the man disliked him intensely. Porter shook his head, rubbing his jaw until the wiry white hairs of his beard dug into the tender flesh of his chin, inflaming skin that was already ravaged by a chronic condition that was made worse by cortisol, the hormone released in times of stress. Porter's face felt like he'd been stung by a horde of angry bees. He cleared his throat. "She wouldn't have done that without telling me."

The investigator's eyebrows hiked another notch but he said nothing. He checked his watch, his face impassive. "So, she left here at nine?"

Porter nodded. "She took the dog for its morning walk." Porter had worked with Beltway Security Investigations for the last two years, building a portfolio, complete with photographs, of Caroline's daily comings and goings.

"Have you tried calling her cell phone?"

"She left it here. Along with everything else, even her house keys." Porter shook his head slowly in frustration, his shoulders collapsing.

The PI scribbled notes. "What about her wallet? Cash? Credit cards? Any large withdrawals lately?"

Porter shook his head. "I checked. Nothing." He had positioned himself in the Eames chair at the desk during his last patient's session so he could scan their bank accounts online. It was another break with routine, one that had garnered a nervous reaction from the Iranian politician's wife. She had fidgeted, jumping from one subject to the next, seeking assurances from Porter that everything was okay. But she had stopped short of questioning him outright, and Porter considered this fact a testament to the years he had invested in this particular patient, building a relationship of confidence and trust. Something he had failed to establish in his own marriage. Bile rose in the back of his throat, making him gag.

"What about jewelry? Her passport?"

An icy tingle snaked across the back of Porter's neck. He hadn't thought to check the safe. Caroline wouldn't have access to it. But the hairs on the back of his neck, not to mention the smug look on the PI's face, told Porter anything was possible.

He removed the gilt-framed map of Colonial George- town that hung behind his desk, revealing a safe mounted in the wall. He spun the dial, whirling through a short series of numbers. Their wedding date.

The tempered steel door sprang open. Inside were sev- eral manila envelopes and a jewelry box. Porter opened the jewelry box first and stared, stunned. The platinum- mounted diamond stud earrings he had given her on their wedding night were gone. Also missing was the strand of AA Mikimoto pearls he had given her when they first met. So was the thick eighteen-karat gold panther bracelet he had bought her on their first wedding anniversary. All gone. Other more costly items, plus a brooch that was the one and only thing Porter had from his own mother, were stored in a safe deposit box at a bank that only Porter could access.

A terrible dread settled over him, dark and bleak, unlike anything he had ever known, and he was filled with an impulse to use the revolver he kept in case of emergency and blow out his brains. Aware of the PI's watchful gaze, he reached for the envelope containing their passports. He knew before he felt its weightlessness that it would be empty, and he was right.

Porter tossed the envelope to the back of the safe and slammed the door shut. He raked his hand once more through his beard and struggled to stay calm. When he spoke, his voice sounded brittle to his own ears. "Both passports are gone. So is her jewelry."

The investigator nodded, his face impassive with its network of smoker's lines, as though he had heard it all before. Porter wondered if women did this all the time. But he didn't ask, couldn't bear to. It would be too much of an admission. So Porter sat, trying to ignore the buzzing in his head while the investigator did his work, gathering approximate values for each item of jewelry and jotting the figures down in a worn notepad he balanced in one hand.

Porter's mind reeled. Caroline took her passport so she could go far away. She took his so he couldn't follow. An image came to him. Caroline, her hand wrapped tightly inside his on a damp morning in Knightsbridge where the streets smelled of diesel. "I could live here," she murmured, leaning in close to him on the second day of their honeymoon. His heart had swelled with tenderness. Someday they would, he'd vowed.

Porter ran through the most likely course of events. She could have guessed the combination to the safe easily enough. Choosing their wedding date had been an obvious mistake on his part. But this room was kept locked. She could have copied his key, but that still wouldn't have gained her access. The townhouse was equipped with a state-of-the-art security system, divided into zones that could be activated only by punching codes into keypads that were mounted on walls throughout the building. Caroline knew the codes for the main entrance, the residence, and the door to the tiny garden, but not the office.

Only the cleaning woman knew that.

Porter closed his eyes. Akua, his cleaning woman of ten years, had quit without warning two weeks ago. With a face as broad and open as the African veldt where she was born, she had started out cleaning his tiny studio in Foggy Bottom and stayed with him when he purchased his luxury condo in Dupont Circle. She had earned Porter's trust and he had rewarded her with a bonus each Christmas, including one big enough to purchase an airline ticket for her husband, whom Porter suspected was here illegally.

He gave Akua a raise after Caroline moved in with her dog, and nearly doubled her salary again when they moved to the townhouse in Georgetown, even contracting with a car service to bring her home on nights when she stayed late to clean his office. Lately, though, something had changed. Akua chatted about the weather, still laughed at Porter's occasional jokes. But the warmth was gone from her eyes, her face was closed against him. And then she quit, saying she needed to go to Tanzania for her sister's funeral. There had been no funeral in Tanzania, Porter now realized.

The investigator tapped his pen on his notepad. "Any chance somebody besides your wife got at that safe?"

They both knew the answer to that.

Porter shook his head.

The PI let out a long breath. "Based on these estimates, I'd say if your wife hocked the stuff she got somewhere around forty-five hundred dollars. Give or take a few hundred."

Less than a quarter of the jewelry's value.

More than enough to reward Akua for the office access code.

Despair turned to rage, heating the bile in Porter's stomach. "Excuse me," he muttered, stumbling off to the tiny half bath he'd installed for his patients' use.

The investigator was finishing a call when Porter returned, hollowed out and empty.

"We're on this," he said. "I'll walk you through the preliminary game plan now. I'll have something faxed over for your signature later today."

Porter nodded wordlessly.

"We'll start by monitoring your accounts for unusual activity."

Porter nodded again.

"We'll post men at Union Station, Ronald Reagan Airport, and the Greyhound terminal. We've got plenty of photos on file. I can assign a guy to stay outside and keep watch here in case she tries to gain access."

Porter remembered Caroline walking at his side along

the River Thames, approaching the entrance to the Tate. "Someday, let's rent a flat and spend a whole month," she'd said. Happy. Hopeful for the future. And it had come to this, piecing together bits of information with a man who sifted through other people's trash for a living. Porter shook his head in disbelief. "We need to scan the international flights," he said dully.

"No can do." The investigator shook his head. "Not since 9/11."

Porter paused, considering whether there was a way around this, a way to get what he wanted. Sometimes getting what he wanted was as simple as letting silence take over and fill a room, as now.

After several beats, the PI flipped his notebook shut. "Unless you know somebody at the TSA . . ." He shrugged, leaned back in his chair. His body language announced he was prepared to walk away and lose Porter's fee.

The surveillance business in Washington must be booming, Porter thought. Moistening his lips, he struggled to get his mind to focus on his options. In fact, he did know somebody with access to the nation's database of commercial airline flights. Whether the man could be persuaded to do Porter's bidding was another matter, one that did not involve the PI in any event. "Okay," Porter said, settling on what he considered to be his best course of action for the moment. "Go ahead and post men at the locations you've suggested."

"It'll cost you. Sixty per hour, per man."

Porter didn't flinch. Beltway's staff consisted of ex-CIA types and students studying forensics at local colleges. "Do it."

"Okay." The man stood to leave. "Make sure I'm your first call if she comes back."

The guy still didn't get it. Caroline was gone. Frustration tightened Porter's lips into a thin line. Nodding, he extended his hand.

The investigator shook Porter's hand and released it too quickly. "After twenty-four hours, you can file a missing persons report." He looked away as he said this, as though he knew Porter would never do it.

On a very core level, Porter knew that all his efforts were in vain. Caroline was long gone, far away, beyond his reach. He knew it deep inside, just as in some way he had always known she would go. Maybe not always, he decided, but soon after they'd met. He'd managed the fear the only way he knew how, doing his best to control the events of their shared life, but it had come to naught. The inevitability of this realization now burned in his gut like hot coals at the bottom of a fireplace.

He busied himself in the days to come scouring train, bus, and airline schedules for connections to places she might have gone, but the list was endless. He dug through her belongings for clues but found nothing.

His mind reeled as he struggled to accept the basic fact of his existence from this moment forward. Dr. Porter Moross was a realist. He liked to think of himself in this way, and took great pride in the fact that he had dedicated his life to helping others learn to accept their reality as well. But now he learned why most patients resisted psychotherapy.

The truth was reality sucked.

He refused to comfort himself with the fantasy that his wife might reappear on their doorstep, teary-eyed

and contrite, begging to try again. Dr. Porter Moross
was not one to indulge in emotional thumb sucking of
any kind.

Porter gave himself over completely and fully, in private,
to grieving the loss of his wife. He realized he could keep
the most options open for himself by avoiding all discus-
sion of his wife, except in such cases when he judged it
to be to his advantage.

The first opportunity presented itself the first night on
the day Caroline had left, during a chance encounter
with his neighbors. Lindsay Crowley was a loud, crass
Texan possessed of a deep-seated desire to be the center
of attention. Porter had disliked her on sight, and had
been disappointed that Caroline hadn't seen her for
what she was.

But now, more than anything, Porter hoped his feelings for Lindsay Crowley were not mutual.

That first night the walls threatened to close in on him
and Porter stumbled outside into a heat so intense it was
causing the tar seams at the edges of the sidewalk to
melt. But Porter didn't notice. Pain squeezed everything
else from his mind, weighing on him like an acid fog,
erasing all color from his world and rendering everything gray.

His wife had left him.

He wore his cell phone clipped to his belt. He had
programmed his computer to place a call automatically
if he received any e-mails from Beltway Security Investigations. He took the pager along as backup. He turned
in the direction of Twenty-ninth Street Park, not as the
result of any conscious choice but as a way to avoid the
lights and noise of Wisconsin Avenue.

The simple act of putting one foot in front of the other required all his concentration, and he shuffled along, head down, trying to keep his panic from swallowing him alive.

"Howdy there, stranger."

Lost in his emotions, Porter did not instantly recognize the voice. He just knew it carried a negative connotation. He hunched his shoulders deeper.

But it was no use. He'd been spotted.

"You see, John, I told you we're not crazy for taking our power walk tonight. Porter's out, and he's a doctor."

John. Recognition flashed, and Porter lifted his head, sensing opportunity. He arranged his features to hide the irritation he felt for Lindsay Crowley and her endless chatter. "Hi, Lindsay, John."

They stopped in front of him, John Crowley standing quietly while Lindsay bobbed up and down, to and fro on the balls of her feet, like a jogger waiting for a traffic light to turn green. Annoying.

"Where's Caroline? Don't tell me you left her home cleaning the dishes all by her lonesome?"

Porter knew they were taking it all in, from his dress shirt and slacks despite the suffocating heat to the misery that showed on his face. Reaching a quick decision, he didn't try to hide his emotion. "No," he replied. "Caroline's not there."

Lindsay stopped bobbing and raised both eyebrows. "Where'd she go?"

Satisfied that Lindsay was already on the right track, Porter drew in a deep breath, letting it out slowly before he made a reply. "God only knows." Slowly, he slid his hands into his pockets and looked down at the sidewalk. "After last time . . ." He shook his head.

"Is she all right?" Lindsay's accent, combined with the emphasis she placed on the second syllable, caused the words to come out sounding like *all raaht*.

Which clearly indicated that Lindsay had already made up her mind that things were not all right, a fact Porter intended to use to his full advantage. "Not really. She stopped taking her medication. She's done it before." Porter allowed his sorrow to show in his eyes. "People think because I'm a psychoanalyst, that I can control things, but there's only so much I can do."

Lindsay Crowley's eyes grew round, questioning. She settled on the simplest one. Saving the biggest ones for later, Porter thought. "So, she just up and left?"

Porter nodded. "She could be anywhere." He pulled his hands from his pocket and spread them in front, palms out, in slow motion. "Her passport's gone."

There was silence as they all considered this fact.

Porter waited a beat before seizing the moment. "Now we just have to wait and hope." He snuck a glance at John Crowley, who was frowning at a point in the darkness.

Crowley cleared his throat, which Porter took to be an encouraging sign. He waited, hardly daring to breathe, keeping his eyes on Crowley's face in a silent plea.

But it was Lindsay who spoke next. "When did she go?"

Lindsay was digging for information, not yet ready to assist him. Porter evaluated her question before settling on the truth. If Crowley did take the bait, he'd need to know which flights to scan. "This morning, around nine."

He watched Crowley, silently urging him to speak. Like all of Porter's patients, John Crowley had risen to the top of his field. Not without doing favors when it suited him, Porter reflected.

Crowley perked up at this bit of information, turning his gaze on Porter. Interested now. "You mean, she left at nine o'clock today?"

Porter nodded as Crowley threw his wife a questioning glance.

At which point Lindsay Crowley resumed bobbing up and down on the balls of her feet. But not before raising one laced cross-trainer and dragging it down the back of her husband's heel.

Crowley did a quick about-face. "That's a shame."

Porter's single ray of hope sputtered and died. Caroline could be on a flight to Heathrow at this very moment, or Charles de Gaulle or fucking Beijing for that matter. And his neighbor, who headed up a special post-9/11 agency to oversee airline security, and his busybody wife were not going to lift a collective finger to help.

Porter watched Crowley work to maintain his footing, shifting his stance so the toes of his brand-new cross-trainers were now pointing squarely across the street at his own front door, signaling this get-together had come to an end.

Lindsay murmured something about keeping Porter and Caroline in her prayers. She did not ask if there was anything she could do to help.

"What was that about? You nearly took my ankle off." John Crowley basked in the air-conditioning as he locked their townhouse door behind them and kicked off his costly new exercise shoes.

"That man," Lindsay muttered, bending down to

untie her laces before removing her exercise shoes one at a time.

"He's worried about his wife, who seems to have taken off," he pointed out. He had met Caroline just once and she had seemed shy and ill at ease. The memory tugged at him. He made a mental note to call their daughter at college in Austin tonight before he went to bed.

John Crowley had a well-earned reputation for being tough in business, but fatherhood had mellowed him. "Sounds like she's in trouble." The truth was, Moross seemed in need of help.

"No." Lindsay's tone was sharp. She pulled off her socks and straightened up, wriggling her toes against the cool floor. "She's not in trouble. She just got herself out of trouble."

John pulled his socks off and followed suit. It felt good.

"I thought you said you saw her this morning at CVS drug store, and something seemed wrong. If it was nine o'clock that would be just about the time she walked away. The guy seems upset."

Lindsay jutted her chin into the air and blew a breath out through her upturned nose, a move John had come to know over the years. It showed his wife cared little for the facts surrounding a situation because her mind was made up.

"I know he's upset," Lindsay said, meeting her husband's gaze. "But there's something about that man I just don't trust."

"Yeah," John said, reaching down to tuck a piece of Lindsay's hair behind her ear. It was something he did out of habit as he reflected what he had learned during a career spent negotiating deals with Wall Street investment bankers, union lawyers, and even the president of the United States.

"But if that girl walked out, it's not because she's crazy. It's because she needed to get away from that man."

That man. Lindsay had made up her mind, no two ways about it.

"It would be good to stay in touch with that girl," Lindsay said thoughtfully. "But that man is someone I would not trust even one little bit."

John Crowley generally made up his mind after careful consideration of the evidence and all the facts, while his wife went with her gut in an instant. Ninety-nine times out of one hundred they reached the same conclusion. His wife had the sharp instincts of a jackal, a trait that had served team Crowley well over the years. "You know," Crowley said now, "I don't trust him, either."

Caroline must have dozed sometime during the night. She had wanted to stay awake, so as to savor every minute of her life here in the eighth row from the front of the Greyhound bus, where it didn't matter that she had no identity, no home, no family, no friends. Just her and Pippin, safe inside their cocoon.

As the morning wore on, the bus slowed, weaving its way through traffic. By eleven A.M. Chicago's famous skyline came into view.

The first leg of Caroline's journey was coming to an end.

The bus rumbled through downtown to the terminal. She followed the crowd inside, her eyes aching with lack of sleep, jumpy with nerves. She expected someone to grab her at any moment and force her to go back home. She waited in line at Amtrak and purchased a one-way ticket to Denver on the California Zephyr, departing that afternoon. She stowed the ticket carefully inside her tote before heading out into the searing midday sun. She had three hours to kill.

A stiff breeze blew off Lake Michigan, whipping bits of trash around in tiny eddies. She released Pippin and the little dog stood, unsteady after so many hours in the tote. He shook himself top to bottom, panting heavily.

"C'mon, fella." Caroline gave the leash a gentle tug and was relieved to see him prance along beside her, his usual self, none the worse for wear. She made her way quickly along the unfamiliar streets, checking signs to get her bearings. She had charted it out beforehand on MapQuest.

Within a short while, she reached her destination. A pawnshop. She was becoming schooled in the business of hocking jewelry, trading it for the cash she had smuggled out in her Keds. Just yesterday morning. It already seemed eons ago. She was already growing wise in the ways of her new life. Pawnshops, she now knew, were conveniently located near bus stations and train depots.

She got buzzed in and deposited her wedding and engagement rings on a worn velvet mat of midnight blue. She waited while the man behind the counter studied them with the aid of a jeweler's loupe.

He named a price.

Giving a quick shake of her head, Caroline named a price that was nearly double and waited, unsmiling. She had already learned the first rule of survival on the streets. Smiling was a sign of weakness.

A short time later, she was six hundred dollars richer. She dined on a park bench overlooking Lake Michigan before heading back to Union Station to board the westbound Amtrak express.

She collapsed against the upholstered seat, reciting a silent prayer as the train pulled out, carrying her from the Midwest and into her new life.

* * *

Porter awoke to the persistent buzzing of the doorbell. It was not yet seven o'clock in the morning. He closed his eyes again, indignant, deciding to ignore it. And then realization hit him like a tidal wave. The bed next to him was empty. Caroline was not where she belonged. She was gone.

Someone pressed the downstairs buzzer again in four long, persistent, evenly spaced bursts.

Porter flew out of bed. He decided against his robe, pulling on his clothes from yesterday instead. Whoever was now rapping firmly on the brass knocker, Porter preferred to face in wrinkled clothes rather than wrapped in the fuzzy vulnerability of pajamas.

He stopped long enough to grab his eyeglasses and run a hand through his hair. Hopefully it was the PI from Beltway Security Investigations with news of Caroline, news that could not be delivered by phone. An image came to mind of his wife far from home, badly injured or worse. The thought moved through Porter like a jolt of electricity, setting his nerves on end, as he undid the locks.

And so his heart, already primed for bad news, was hammering uncontrollably when he yanked open the door to find two uniformed police officers on his front stoop.

They watched unblinking while Porter stared, struggling to grasp the implications of their presence on his property at this unlikely hour of the morning.

A radio squawked.

Porter jumped, aware that this made him appear jittery. "Porter Moross?"

He nodded, tried to swallow past the lump in his throat and failed, which made him queasy. He told himself they couldn't hear the thumping of his heart inside his chest no matter how loud it sounded in his ears.

The man doing the talking was shorter than his partner but no less broad across the shoulders. Together they took up every square inch of space on the tiny brick stoop and, it seemed to Porter, every last molecule of oxygen in the hot, humid air.

The stocky one spoke again. "You have a wife, Caroline Hughes, who resides at this address?"

"Yes." An icy shudder began at the top of Porter's head and traveled down his spine with lightning speed. This was bad. He squeezed his eyes shut and groped for the railing with one hand. "Oh, God, no."

"Take it easy, sir, everything's okay."

Porter opened his eyes.

The stocky one frowned. "I take it your wife is not at home with you now?"

The hammering in Porter's ears turned to thunder. He blinked uncertainly, forcing his mind to grasp what was being said. They had not come with news of his wife.

The stocky one repeated his question, louder now. "Is your wife here with you?"

They were here to seek out news of his wife. "No," Porter said warily as his mind shifted gears, racing ahead now.

Lindsay Crowley.

Bitch!

He had been wrong to approach the Crowleys last night. He had hoped to prevail upon John Crowley to locate Caroline in the nationwide databank of commercial airline passengers. Porter knew Crowley and his nosy wife might come up with their own reason for Caroline's sudden disappearance. He had no control over that.

But Dr. Porter Moross knew the value of a half truth, how it could be used to ease doubts.

So he had crafted a version of the truth, one that would appeal to a man like Crowley with daughters who lived out of state. Namely, that Caroline was not well and needed to be found and brought home. Which was true. But Porter's gamble hadn't paid off. Crowley had seemed cautious but willing to help. His meddling wife had not. She didn't like Porter and never had.

He now realized he had underestimated Lindsay Crowley. She was a loose cannon who had gone to the police with her concerns. She could have said things to arouse their suspicions so they would think him capable of almost anything, Porter realized.

"She's out of town." Porter glanced down, licking his lips that had turned dry. He tasted salt. The sweat on his face prickled his skin. He took a swipe at it, willing himself to drop his hands before he scratched at the hives that were bubbling beneath his beard, making him itch.

The cops merely watched him.

The tactic was tried and true, as any mental health professional knew.

And right now it worked like a charm on Porter, a fact he was aware of but had no control over. "She's visiting her mother." His mind skipped to his mother-in-law, sallow-skinned and in the end stages of alcoholism, staring out over the muddy waters of the Gulf from her third husband's condo.

Porter realized his mistake. It would take no more than a phone call to unleash a tirade about the hurt she suffered as the result of her only daughter's longtime estrangement.

The police would have something to go on if they caught him in a lie.

"It's a surprise visit. She might not be there yet," he added, flailing about for options.

"Guess she didn't fly." The tall one spoke for the first time.

How could they know that? Porter's eyes widened and he took a step back, aware that his unease was showing.

"Sanitation turned these in last night." The tall one, smiling now, handed Porter two small booklets that were a familiar shade of royal blue.

Relief washed over Porter. "Thanks," he murmured, accepting the passports with a hand he tried to keep steady. He let out a deep breath and forced a smile.

"Sanitation found them in a trash can on Wisconsin yesterday, just up the block." The taller one motioned with his chin.

So Lindsay Crowley wasn't behind this. Porter looked down, turning the passports over in his hand, fingering their compact weight. "Thanks," he said again.

"No problem," the tall cop said. "Glad we could help."

The stocky cop was not smiling. He continued to watch Porter with a gaze that did not waiver. "Any idea how you and your wife's passports went missing?"

"Yeah." The flood of adrenaline and its aftermath was too much. Porter dug at his beard, long and hard, giving in to the urge that always plagued him in times of stress. The move bought him a precious few seconds. "Someone broke in a couple days ago. They got some of my wife's jewelry as well."

"Did you file any report with the police?" The tall one's smile faded.

Porter shook his head slowly for effect. "I know I should have, but I feel sorry for the guy. I mean, I know who it is." He let out a long, deep breath. "Our cleaning woman is in some kind of trouble. Her husband came here on a tourist visa and I know for a fact it expired. I had to let her go. They're here illegally. I'm sure they're desperate for money."

The cops exchanged glances. "You know where this guy lives?"

Porter nodded. "I should probably report him to the INS." He hated cops.

The shorter one spoke. "Look, Mr. Moross, I think you should come down to the station and file a report."

"Good idea. I should have done that right away," Porter replied thoughtfully. "I'll do it as soon as I grab a shower."

"That'll be a help to us," the shorter cop said, taking out a business card and handing it to Porter. "I'm Officer Mike Hartung."

Porter took the card, helpful now. "Thank you, Officer Hartung. Will do."

"We appreciate your time, Mr. Moross."

"No trouble, no trouble at all," Porter said. "And, by the way, it's Dr. Moross."

CHAPTER

5

WESTBOUND AMTRAK CALIFORNIA ZEPHYR

Caroline settled into a state that was neither full wakefulness nor sleep, willing herself to be lulled by the rhythm of the rails racing past beneath the train car.

She tried, unsuccessfully, not to dwell on her chance encounter with Lindsay Crowley yesterday morning, and the possibility that this information might work its way back to Porter.

It could be the death of her.

Porter would use this information to his advantage, the way he always used every shred of information to his advantage in every situation, especially when it came to Caroline.

Lindsay had spotted Caroline in CVS drug store at just after nine A.M., had seen Pippin with her, and might or might not have noticed the box of blond hair dye in Caroline's shopping basket. It was not likely Lindsay would have had a chance encounter with Porter over the last two days and, if she had, it was even less likely she would have mentioned any of this to him. Caroline was certain Lindsay disliked Porter. Still, Caroline couldn't help but think of the older woman's easy chatter with everyone she met.

That fact had made their friendship possible in the first place, despite Caroline's goal of keeping to herself once she and Porter moved to Georgetown. The tall, elegantly dressed woman was impossible to ignore, despite the fact that Caroline had learned early in her marriage that she would pay dearly for any remark or interaction of which Porter disapproved. Caroline came to dread social occasions.

So when an invitation to dinner was extended from their friendly neighbor across the street, Caroline murmured something about having other plans. The fact was she had no intention of telling Porter about it.

"You must come and meet everyone, my dear," Lindsay had said. "It's so nice to see a young family move into our neighborhood. You're adorable and I can't wait to meet your adorable husband."

The next day an invitation was dropped inside their brass mailbox. The envelope was ivory, of an expensive vellum stock.

Porter set it down in the center of the table. "What do you know about this?"

Caroline's heart sank. She picked up the envelope, turned it over, and knew by the address engraved on the back that it was the invitation to the Crowleys. "Oh, yeah," she said, trying to keep her voice light. "I think I remember."

The envelope had already been opened. Caroline removed the card that was engraved with a hot pink monogram.

Porter watched her in silence. Waiting.

The pleasure of their company was requested for supper at the home of John and Lindsay Crowley the following night.

Lindsay had scrawled a note along the bottom in a loping hand as big as Texas. "Welcome to the neighborhood. Look forward to chatting more. Can't wait to meet your DH!"

Caroline's heart raced. She took a breath and tried to sound nonchalant. "I guess I forgot to mention it. I met one of the neighbors."

"When?"

"Yesterday. I was out walking Pippin and we got to talking."

Porter removed his glasses, revealing two red spots on the bridge of his nose. He closed his eyes and rubbed them. It was something he did when he was upset. "Caroline." He sighed, not bothering to open his eyes.

Caroline searched for the right thing to say. "She seems really nice," she offered finally.

Porter's eyes widened. "Nice?" He spat the word out with a mirthless laugh. "Is that your word for everything? Nice?" He stared at her, incredulous.

Still, she said nothing. She didn't suppose he wanted her to answer that question.

Porter shook his head as though he had trouble grasping the situation he found himself in. He frowned. "Do you just walk around all day, talking to people who look like they're nice?"

This time he wanted an answer.

"No," Caroline said, trying not to sound defensive. "Not at all. That's not it at all. We just got talking, that's all. She's a sweet older lady, she lives right up the block and she was having this party and . . ." Her voice trailed off. She licked her lips and swallowed. She didn't want this to turn into something that would last all day. "She wants to meet you, Porter. She seems really ni—" Caroline stopped herself. "You'd like her."

Porter's eyes narrowed. His voice was low, his tone steely. "Then why didn't you tell me about her?"

In the end, they went to the Crowleys' dinner party. Lindsay and her husband were a good deal older than Caroline and even Porter, and Caroline hoped this fact would make Porter fit in and feel comfortable. Porter showered for the second time that day after work, then dressed with care in his usual black collarless shirt under a dark charcoal jacket. He combed his hair, then went back to check his reflection in the mirror and combed it again. He hated meeting new people.

Caroline felt sorry for him.

She had chosen her own outfit after much thought and planning. She wore a royal blue tunic, high-cut with long sleeves, over wide white palazzo pants. The clothing was new. She had stopped wearing short skirts except when they dined at home, which was their usual routine. The tank tops that had been a staple of her college wardrobe were long gone. Tonight she chose ballet flats with enclosed toes even though the summer night was warm. Porter was just half an inch taller than her five feet, seven inches, and hated when she wore heels. She pulled her hair back in a tortoiseshell clip he had bought for her on their honeymoon.

He gave her an appraising look, his gaze lingering on her hair.

"I'm wearing the clip you got me at Harrod's," she said with a smile.

He blinked. "You look like a little girl with your hair like that."

"I can wear it down," Caroline said, reaching up to remove the clip.

"Don't touch it," he said, raising his hand. "Leave it the way you want it." He gave her a once-over. "You choose the way you present yourself to the world, Caroline. And you prefer to present yourself as a little girl." He checked his watch. "Come on. We're already late."

He hated to be late. His tension was contagious. She felt his energy run through her like an electric current when she took his arm, stiff and rigid, on the short walk across the cobblestone street to the Crowleys' town-house.

Lindsay threw her arms around Caroline when they arrived. "Johnny, come and meet the new neighbors," she called. "This is the adorable young bride I told you about and this must be her husband."

A tall, distinguished man appeared, welcoming them to the neighborhood in a booming voice that left no doubt he hailed from Texas. Lindsay ushered them inside to a living room that was lavishly decorated with walls covered in what looked to be works of notable modern art. Porter stopped to examine a wall hanging, dropping out of the round of introductions.

Caroline found herself surrounded by older couples, mostly Texans, who seemed to know and like one another well. Uniformed staff passed trays of hot hors d'oeuvres. Somebody pressed a glass of white wine into her hands and she took a big gulp. She joined in the conversation as best she could, feeling like a fish out of water standing there alone.

Lindsay reappeared, steering Porter through the crowd to Caroline's side. Caroline flashed her a smile of gratitude. The only thing worse than feeling self-conscious at a party, Caroline thought, was feeling self-conscious at a party when you were the only one on your own.

Porter did not return the squeeze Caroline gave his hand, maintaining his conversation with Lindsay about her new art collection.

Caroline took a few more gulps of wine and listened, smiling and nodding occasionally. Porter seemed like he was doing okay. He enjoyed talking about art, a subject he was knowledgeable in, and as far as she could tell she hadn't said or done anything to irritate him.

"Now tell me," Lindsay said, "what brings a couple of young newlyweds like yourselves to our little neck of the woods?"

Young newlyweds. Porter had a chronic condition that had turned his hair white prematurely, making him appear even more than twelve years older than Caroline. She maintained a careful smile now, aware that Porter had stiffened at her side.

There was a bit of a pause before he replied. "I work out of the home."

"And what is it you do?" Lindsay asked.

Caroline felt her heart leap into her mouth and hang there. She took another big gulp of wine.

"I am a psychoanalyst," Porter replied.

"Oooohhh," Lindsay exclaimed, clapping her hands in glee. "A shrink!"

Caroline winced. Porter had explained to her countless times that people's issues came to the fore when confronted with a psychoanalyst. Anybody who had unresolved anger toward authority figures was likely to express it with sarcasm, he said. This irritated Porter no end, and although Caroline noticed he never confronted anybody about it, she kept this fact to herself.

There was a round of giggles as Lindsay let out another whoop. "Perfect," she trilled, laying one hand on Porter's arm. "It's nice to know we finally have a trained professional on the block."

Trained professional. It was a fortunate choice of words.

Laughter rippled through the room.

Porter smiled.

Caroline felt the lump in her throat start to dissolve.

Someone asked Porter if he carried prescriptions for Xanax.

More laughter followed, and Porter explained that he practiced the sort of therapy that involved lying on a couch three to five times a week for seven to ten years.

Someone pointed out it was the same as time served for a felony conviction, and now it was Porter's turn to laugh. He even cracked a joke.

Caroline allowed herself to relax a tiny bit as the conversation drifted, eventually returning to the subject of modern art and collecting. Porter seemed to really enjoy Lindsay's company, and if their hostess found his intense style of one-on-one conversation too much to bear, she hid it well. Porter expressed an interest in a mural at the far end of the room, and the two of them wandered off.

Caroline had downed most of her third glass of wine when she excused herself to go in search of the bathroom.

"I'll go with you," said one of Lindsay's friends, taking Caroline's arm in her own. "We can snoop around. Lindsay flew in the top man from Dallas to decorate this place."

Caroline felt better than she had since they moved to Georgetown, as if she would make friends here. She had visions of throwing dinner parties like this one and inviting all the neighbors. She would have a reason, at last, to use her wedding china. Things would work out. She followed Lindsay's friend down a narrow hallway to the rear of the house, only to discover the door to the bathroom was locked.

"Occupado," the woman said. "Let's go outside. I heard they redid the yard with tumbled stone from Milan and a koi pond."

They exited through a pair of French doors to the patio of tumbled stone, where a lone man stood smoking a cigar. His face lit up when he spotted Caroline's companion.

"Darling, hello."

They exchanged air kisses, and brief introductions were made. The man pulled the cigar from his mouth and grinned. "Where's your better half? Or excuse me, other half?"

They broke into gales of laughter. Caroline longed for the sense of ease other married couples had. She wondered when, and how, it would come for her and Porter.

The three of them chatted for a minute, until the woman spotted her own husband inside and went to fetch him.

Caroline hoped she would return with her husband before Porter chanced upon them, she and Cigar Man alone in the dark. He was old enough to be her father, but that wouldn't matter to Porter.

Oblivious, Cigar Man took another puff and watched the smoke rise. "New to D.C.? Or just Georgetown?"

Caroline explained that she and her husband had just moved in, and that she was recently graduated from the George Washington University.

"Great school. If you just graduated, the world is your oyster," he said with a smile. "Congratulations, young lady, you've got your whole future ahead of you." He offered his hand, and Caroline shook it, smiling back.

His smile faded a moment later, however, as he caught a glimpse of something behind her. Caroline heard swift footsteps approach, followed by a hand on her elbow squeezing so hard it sent a sharp pain through her arm. She forced herself not to flinch.

"So this is where you got off to while my back was turned." Porter's voice came low and tight, so close his breath stirred her hair.

She shivered.

Cigar Man's smile did a quick fade.

"I was looking for the bathroom and . . ." Caroline's voice trailed off.

"The bathroom?" Porter repeated her words slowly so they sounded stupid.

Cigar Man stopped puffing.

Caroline felt tension mount like a rising tide, engulfing them.

Porter tightened his grip on her arm.

She searched for something, anything, to say to break the tension, so this man could see past Porter's prickly side and Porter, hopefully, would realize he had not stumbled onto anything untoward.

"I got sidetracked," Caroline said, trying to sound breezy and gushing and carefree, like Lindsay Crowley and her friends. But her voice sounded weak, defensive. "I came out to look at Lindsay's gorgeous new poi pond."

"Koi." Porter arranged his lips into a tight line. "It's a koi pond."

Cigar Man chuckled and pulled the cigar from his mouth. "Poi, koi? It's just fish. Where I come from, we'd drop a line and eat 'em." He winked at Caroline, which only made things worse.

There was silence as Porter chose to say nothing and Caroline didn't dare speak.

The man popped his cigar back into his mouth and rolled it around, considering things. "You haven't done anything wrong, my dear." He shot Porter a look that was hard as steel.

"Right. Just fish." Porter's voice, flat and low, managed to be insulting.

Caroline cringed and tried not to show it.

"My wife and I were just leaving, if you'll excuse us," Porter said stiffly.

My wife. The emphasis was unmistakable. Caroline nodded farewell and turned to follow.

The man held Porter's gaze, the warmth gone from his face, and his next words came out like an order. "You have a pleasant night now, you hear?"

Porter gave a small, stiff nod.

The man turned to Caroline, his gaze softening. "I've got a daughter about your age. You remember what I said, young lady. You've got the world at your feet."

It sounded like code for something else. Caroline pictured the man's daughter, radiating confidence based on decades' worth of soccer matches and ballet recitals, secure in the knowledge that her daddy was beaming approval from a seat somewhere in the audience, even if she couldn't see his face in the crowd.

Caroline flashed the man a weak smile, ignoring the

pang she felt for the childhood she didn't get, and followed her husband to the exit. They had almost reached the front door when Lindsay Crowley spotted them.

"Leaving so soon? We were just about to serve dinner," she exclaimed. "Come along to the buffet and have something before you go. I insist." She placed a hand on Porter's arm. "I insist," she repeated, smiling.

Porter pulled his arm away as though he had been burned.

Lindsay's smile did a quick fade.

"We have to be going," he said, making no effort to keep the edge from his voice.

Something flashed in Lindsay's eyes like a light bulb. Caroline prayed she wouldn't urge them to stay. Porter could be quite rude if he felt pressured.

After a tiny pause, Lindsay patted Porter's arm. "We'll just have to have you back over when you have time to stay for supper. And you"—she turned to Caroline, giving her a quick hug and a peck on the cheek—"are adorable. You are a most very welcome addition to the neighborhood. And don't you forget it." She gave Caroline's hand a tight squeeze.

Porter already had one foot out the door as Caroline murmured her thanks. Her eyes locked with Lindsay's for a moment, and her heart sank at the concern she saw in the older woman's face. Porter had seemed to genuinely enjoy Lindsay's company, and for much of the last hour Caroline had hoped they might become friends. But now she saw that Lindsay did not care for Porter. Because of something she, Caroline, had done. Caroline followed Porter down the front steps, knowing they would never return.

CHAPTER

6

COLORADO

After a day and a half, Caroline's Amtrak train arrived in Denver.

The air was crisp, the sky an impossible blue, marked by high, puffy, racing clouds. Caroline had never been to Colorado. That was part of the attraction. She made her way through the heart of the Mile High City, marveling at its hustle and bustle against a distant backdrop of mountains that were shockingly stark, to the Greyhound station. She purchased a ticket for a local bus bound north and west. She waited to board with a group of grunge teenagers tossing a Hacky Sack. She took a seat in the back and watched, ears popping, as they left Denver's morning rush behind and wound their way up into the small towns that dotted the Rocky Mountains.

Her tongue dried out and her heart pounded as she contemplated the alien landscape rolling past the tinted windows. At first she thought it was just plain fear that had set her heart to racing, then she recognized it as altitude sickness.

Nothing had prepared her for a wilderness of this magnitude, not any photos she'd ever seen, not the atlas Porter kept in the trunk of the Saab, not even the e-mails she'd received from her college friend Tom who had passed through here once on his way to L.A. She comforted herself with the thought that Porter would never think of searching here. He'd never think she'd have the guts to move to a place so remote. She expected to see mountain lions loping along the side of the road at any moment.

The bus rumbled north, passing through ever-smaller towns carved from the rough. Finally, when the shadows had lengthened and the sun had dipped below the thick line of trees, the bus pulled off at a tiny town that dated from the great gold rush, with a miniature main street that ended at a craggy summit. Air brakes squealed as the bus shuddered to a stop in front of the town's only service station.

"Storm Pass!" the driver called. "Any takers?" This brought a round of laughter from the teens.

Caroline was already making her way to the front, heart in her mouth. "Yes, please," she called breathlessly.

"Okay, young lady." The driver opened the door and a rush of cool, crisp air rose to meet her as she stepped off. He climbed down after her, calling out a greeting to a giant bear of a man seated in a lawn chair.

"Afternoon, Gus," the driver called.

Gus lowered his *Denver Post*, raised one gnarled hand to take the pipe out of his mouth, and grinned. "Howdy do, Ray." He had white hair and spotless denim overalls.

"Can't complain," said the driver, reaching for the handle in one of the exterior panels on the bus.

"Won't do you any good if you do," Gus called, returning to his paper.

The driver turned to Caroline. "Any bags, miss?"

Caroline shook her head, ignoring the driver's quizzical look. Even the giant leaping greyhound on the side of the bus seemed to watch her.

"Thanks," she said, taking a step back. As though she had someplace she needed to be.

"Okay, little lady." The driver paused long enough to wave good-bye to the man from the service station. "See you, Gus." He pulled away, leaving Caroline in a rush of warm exhaust.

She freed Pippin from the tote.

The little dog emerged, shaking himself like an inmate getting his first taste of freedom after a term in prison. He shook, his collar jingling.

A loud hissing sound stopped him in his tracks.

Pippin growled.

A black cat, the largest Caroline had ever seen, appeared in the open doorway of the service station and glared, arching its back, baring white fangs.

Pippin yapped with fury.

"Midnight, where's your manners?" The man in the lawn chair lowered his paper again. "Don't mind her, she's not a dog person." He chuckled at his own joke.

Caroline leaned over and patted Pippin. "Neither is he. I mean, he's not a cat person."

"Well, Midnight's not likely to change her mind any time soon." The man smiled so that the wrinkles around his eyes and mouth bunched up into deep furrows. He looked like Santa Claus with brown eyes, minus the beard. He was about to go back to his paper but paused when Caroline cleared her throat.

"Um, which way to the inn?" she asked. Every mountain town had an inn, she reasoned.

He grinned again. "Same direction as everything else. 'Bout two hundred feet thataways." He motioned with one hand. "Can't miss it."

"Thanks." Caroline shivered in the lengthening shadows. A breeze carrying the scent of sage and pine worked its way through the thin fabric of her Capri pants, making her nostalgic for the Indian summer she'd left behind in Washington. The Capris, a size four, hung in loose folds from her hips. Her bare ankles protruded sharply above her Keds.

The man in the lawn chair pulled the pipe from his mouth and surveyed her thoughtfully. "They've got a decent dinner special there. Half a roast chicken with gravy and two sides. Can't go wrong with that."

"Thanks," she said, turning to go.

"Maebeth makes a good pie for dessert," Gus called after her.

"Thanks," Caroline called back, walking quickly in the direction he had indicated.

Gus Kincaid puffed his pipe and watched her go as Midnight leaped to the top of the counter and went back to sleep.

Caroline walked along the town's tiny Main Street, past a series of buildings that dated to Victorian times. Unlike Georgetown, however, these were not manicured restorations. The buildings in Storm Pass looked to be the real thing: clapboard facades fraying at the edges and frames warped by time and weather so they leaned at crazy angles. A former vaudeville theater now showed art house films, an ice cream parlor had a real old-fashioned soda fountain visible through waved-glass windows, and a scruffy tavern had a plaque boasting the oldest pressed-tin ceiling in Colorado.

At the end of the road, hard in the shadow of the granite outcropping for which Storm Pass was named, was the inn. A neatly painted sign explained the place had been in continuous operation since the 1840s, and the current building had replaced an earlier one built to serve as a rooming house for the miners who came in the original gold rush.

Darkness fell as Caroline climbed the tidy wooden steps. She liked the history of the place. She felt safe here.

Maebeth Burkle eyed the young woman across the well-worn oak check-in desk and the tiny dog panting at her feet. "We don't take pets."

The girl had just offered cash in advance for one week in a single room. She pulled her arms across her thin chest, which did nothing to banish the goose bumps on her flesh.

City girl, Maebeth thought, not dressed for the mountains. Not many tourists found their way to Storm Pass even in summer. The place wasn't like Aspen with its ballet festival and think tank. Nor had Storm Pass ever made it as a ski town, with its steep terrain of heavy pine forest. The only visitors the town drew were serious hunters and fishermen, or flatlanders who wished they were. They came in groups of five to ten, men who had hit their incentive targets selling bonds or stocks or real estate, outfitted head to toe in the latest Gore-Tex from Orvis, gear that nobody around here could afford. Their employers paid a king's ransom for the privilege of spending a few days in the wilderness with

Gus Kincaid's son, a former safety for the Kansas City Chiefs. Ken Kincaid had grown up here, and knew his way around every bend in the icy Ute River.

But the girl shivering on Maebeth's worn braided rug had not come here for fly-fishing.

People in these parts didn't tend to mind their neighbors' business, and Maebeth was no exception, but the mountain didn't take kindly to city folk. The girl would have to spend the night in someone's woodpile if Maebeth didn't let her a room. And that little scrap of a dog with the blue bow on its head couldn't hold its own with Maebeth's aging retrievers, never mind a marmot or bear.

Maebeth made a quick decision. "Okay. If he makes a mess you clean it."

A weak smile formed beneath the girl's too-large sunglasses. "Thank you."

She signed in as Alice Stevens from Joplin, Missouri.

Not likely, judging by the back East accent. Maebeth accepted the registration card and passed her an old-fashioned key, asking a question she already knew the answer to. "Do you need help with your bags?"

The girl shook her head.

"Okay then," Maebeth glanced down at the card. "Alice. Dinner will be served in the dining room. You've got the place to yourself tonight, 'cept for my husband and me. It's included in the room rate. Breakfast, too."

The girl's face brightened. "Thanks."

"Your dog might as well eat with my boys out back. Jasper and Wyoming. They're old and wouldn't hurt a fly. He's a cute little fella. What's his name?"

Alice Stevens hesitated. "Poppit."

"It suits him." Maebeth chuckled. "Not sure mine will know what to make of him but they'll behave."

"Thanks. He's my best friend."

And her only friend, by the looks of it. On impulse, Maebeth reached into a cabinet below the counter and pulled out a sweatshirt still in its plastic wrapper. On the front was a rendering of Ute Peak with the name Storm Pass stamped below it. Maebeth kept a supply in large and extra large to sell to hunters whose luggage hadn't made the transfer at Denver. She slid the sweatshirt across the worn oak counter. "We've got a weekly special on these. It comes with the room. Which, by the way, is upstairs and down the hall to your right."

"Thanks," she murmured.

"Roast chicken tonight. You take your time, Alice, I'll keep it warm till you come down."

Clutching the sweatshirt like a security blanket, Alice Stevens shouldered her tote and flicked Poppie's dainty leash.

Maebeth was certain the address and phone number were phony. No matter. Their sole guest appeared no more capable of doing harm than that scrap of a dog. And cash was cash. Later, Maebeth would remember this moment.

Caroline unpacked the tote bag, setting out Pippin's bowls and food, before donning the sweatshirt to join Maebeth and her husband, Ted, for dinner in a dining room that was papered with Victorian-era cabbage roses. A gas-inset fire flickered, throwing off welcome heat.

The food was as good as Gus Kincaid had promised. Caroline was ravenous. If the Burkles noticed how quickly she shoveled bites of roast chicken into her mouth, or the second and third helpings she took, they made no mention of it.

Nor did they ask questions about where she was from or why she was vacationing alone, a fact she was grateful for. They chatted mostly to each other about the garden and chores around the inn.

Caroline slept a deep, dreamless sleep in the narrow, wood-paneled room. She sank into the trough at the center of the aging mattress that carried the memory of countless hunters who had slept there, tired after a day spent in the cold mountain air in the company of their comrades, and felt safe.

The wind gathered sound as it passed across the branches of trees that stretched from infinity right up against the tiny window.

She had read about the sounds a forest made at night, but had never experienced it firsthand. Neither had Porter. She had chosen Colorado for precisely this reason.

CHAPTER

7

Sleep was the first element to disappear from Porter's "new normal." "New normal" was a catchall phrase he had used often during his treatment of patients who had suffered sudden loss.

Now Porter understood just how hateful the phrase was.

He gave up quickly on any attempt to sleep through the night. Insomnia, as Dr. Porter Moross well knew, was a symptom of post-traumatic stress syndrome. He knew that it compounded grief and contributed to a sense of social isolation, knew that it would pass in time. He had counseled many patients on this.

But it was different when it happened to him.

Porter stared at their wedding portrait on the nightstand next to their bed. "Why?" he asked. Caroline mocked him from the sterling frame in her silly white confection of a dress. It was a little girl's fantasy, that dress, with its puffy sleeves and yards of billowing tulle. "You think you can walk away from what we had," he whispered. "But it isn't over between us, Caroline. I won't allow that."

And so he fought back on the third night, ordering up

a girl from the escort service he had used in his bachelor days. She let herself in after midnight, entering through the street door that Porter had left unlocked, and came directly upstairs to where Porter waited with his props.

She was rail-thin like Caroline, with streaky blond hair and undertaker eyes. She glanced at his wedding photo as she shrugged off her cheap overcoat. "Wife outta town?"

Porter's hands twitched. He could knock her clear across the room before she knew what hit her. But he knew the rules. S&M was okay, but an outright beating would get him banned. Wiping his palms on his thighs, he licked his lips and eyed the place at the top of the escort's legs near the garter belt. Her flesh was starting to hang in loose folds. In five years she'd be too old to whore herself. "Yeah," he whispered hoarsely.

He locked eyes with Caroline's in the photograph when he came, straddling the prostitute from behind.

He wished he could make Caroline hurt the way he hurt.

Except he knew she was not capable of empathy.

He'd hoped for it when they met. She was young and innocent and sweet, and he'd seen she had the potential for love that was pure and loyal and true, bigger than anything Porter had experienced in his entire crappy life. At least since his mother walked out when he was six and his fledgling ego was just taking shape. He'd learned in his psych studies that he'd have been okay if she'd abandoned him one year earlier or, better yet, two years later. But that had not been the case.

The day he met Caroline Hughes, the hard black box that was Porter's heart sprang open, allowing light to shine on what was inside.

For the first time in his adult life, he felt hope that he might find redemption in the love of the girl with dark, soulful eyes and intellect to match.

But there was a problem, he surmised over time. Namely, Caroline's psyche was marbled with veins of corruption. Hiding things came naturally to her. It was Porter's studied professional opinion that he could cleanse her ego, given time, clearing the way to a true union of hearts and minds. She seemed open to it, at first, and the prognosis was good.

Just so long as she stayed the course.

But Caroline, like so many of his patients, was conflicted about her recovery. As time passed, she grew increasingly resistant to change. This tore at Porter's heart. Breaking up would only deepen both their childhood wounds, he knew, and so he redoubled his efforts to help her see.

They stayed at the world-famous Martin's Hotel in London on their honeymoon. He remembered the pleasure he took in her childlike excitement at the stock of body wash, shampoo, creams, and lotions that lined the marble counters in the giant bathroom. She tucked them away in her suitcase each night, marveling that the staff replaced them each day. She refused to let him take the wrappers off for a long time after they returned home. The hotel lobby had been crowded with foreigners, filthy businessmen who couldn't take their eyes off Porter's new wife.

Caroline reveled in their attention, swinging her hips as she walked through the lobby, giggling when she posed for a photo in front of the giant floral display.

The memory of his honeymoon brought a stab of jealousy to Porter's gut, hot and sharp as a poker. Caroline had closed her mind to him for the first time, closing him out. The memory of it even now made him wince with pain. If he'd known then that it would come to this, he would have walked away and counted himself lucky. But, as Porter knew from the patients he treated, hindsight only came on the heels of bitter experience.

That night on their honeymoon, Porter had seen for the first time just how stubborn his beautiful young bride could be. It would be their ruination, a fact he tried to explain to her over dinner in Martin's famous chophouse restaurant and later, after they made love, in the king-sized bed.

She didn't believe him. Her eyes, veiled and resentful, belied this fact despite her apology.

Porter's fist tightened now, remembering his frustration. Her lie that night caught him off guard and filled him with despair. So he taught her a lesson and put her out. Wearing only a silk negligee, she whimpered through the suite door, begging to be allowed back inside.

But Porter wanted her to see the error of her ways. He asked her a series of questions about why she craved attention from other men, and she responded like a small child, with tears and denial. She was in the hall perhaps ten minutes or fifteen at most, when a maid saw her and used her passkey to unlock the door.

"My husband is a very sound sleeper," Caroline had mumbled. "Thank you so much."

She begged Porter's forgiveness and he did forgive her, allowing her to sleep in the bed. But he didn't forget.

The phone rang early the next morning. Porter was greeted by the brisk tones of the hotel's manager.

"I do hope you've enjoyed your stay with us, Mr. Moross. We have you checking out early today and I wondered if you need assistance with your bags."

Porter scowled and looked at his watch. Barely eight o'clock. "We're not checking out. We're here five more days. And it's doctor, not mister."

"I do beg your pardon. Doctor."

There was a detectable pause between "pardon" and "doctor," as though the hotel manager had placed imaginary brackets around the word.

Porter heard laughter in the background.

"I'm terribly sorry, Doctor, for any misunderstanding. But we've got you checking out this morning. The bellman is on his way up."

There was a sharp rap on the door.

Caroline stirred in bed beside him, her eyes swollen and puffy from crying.

The rapping continued, louder now.

Porter swore.

"Please accept my apologies on behalf of the entire staff at Martin's Hotel for the confusion, but we do have you down as checking out this morning. If you'll open the door, sir, two of my hall porters are waiting to assist with your bags. I shall see you in the lobby shortly, Dr. Moross."

The phone clicked off, leaving dead silence in Porter's ear. This time there was no mistaking the note of sarcasm in the general manager's voice.

Porter scrambled to find another place to stay, settling on a filthy tourist-class hotel in Whitehall.

That day, he slapped Caroline for the first time. His hand stung but she had it coming.

She had ruined their honeymoon with her stubborn need for attention, and now she had destroyed their marriage as well.

STORM PASS, COLORADO

Caroline woke at dawn's first light, cocooned inside the lumpy double bed with Pippin nestled at her feet.

A collection of paperback novels, worn and yellow, was neatly arranged on the nightstand next to an untouched Gideon's Bible and a hurricane-style lamp that had been in fashion long ago. High up in the corner, where the paneling met the ceiling, was a network of tiny spiderwebs that most people wouldn't notice. Porter would have noticed. Caroline squeezed her eyes shut against the image and rolled over, rousing Pippin.

She rubbed the little dog's chest and kissed him on top of his head. "We're okay, Pippin," she whispered. "So far, so good." But her throat closed around the lie, and tears leaked out, hot and salty, one after another until they soaked a spot on the scratchy pillowcase.

Pippin pushed his cold nose against her, and this made her want to cry even more. But she did not. Caroline Hughes hated to cry. She was afraid that once she started, she would never stop.

She went to the bathroom and blew her nose into a wad of toilet paper, showering afterward in the vinyl stall, letting the hot spray wash away her tears. She lathered using the pink sliver of motel soap and put her Capris back on, still grimy from three days' hard travel, and her T-shirt, now stiff from air drying. She had washed it in the tiny sink last night with the bottle of traveling shampoo she had bought in CVS drug store.

The smell of coffee and frying bacon wafted through the house. Pippin raced ahead of her through the hall, where sunlight dappled the faded carpet runner and a brilliant sky showed through the windows.

"Breakfast is served," Maebeth said by way of greeting.

Caroline hesitated, her stomach rumbling so loud she was certain it would wake the retrievers, who were dozing in a corner.

"It's included in the room rate," Maebeth added.

Caroline smiled. "Good."

She ate by herself in the dining room, and when she was finished, carried her dirty dishes to the kitchen, where Maebeth was elbow deep in suds at the sink.

Maebeth looked up, surprised. "Goodness, you don't have to do that."

"I worked in a restaurant for a while, summers in college," Caroline offered.

Maebeth continued scrubbing her fry pan. "One thing about this place, we have a tough time getting help. Our kitchen man just quit. They come, they stay awhile, then leave if they get an offer at one of the big resorts."

"I could help out," Caroline said slowly. A flutter of hope, the first she'd felt in a long time, rose inside her. "I could clean rooms or do washing up."

Maebeth took her time rinsing the pan, considering things. Alice Stevens was well-spoken and had nice manners. But college kids didn't often pitch up in Storm Pass, even in summer. There was no nightlife to speak of, no fancy hotel school nearby to grant credit for changing beds at the Burkle's Inn. Besides, summer was finished. Maebeth glanced at Alice, taking in her tense eyes and hollow cheeks, and got an idea. "Season's about done so I can't use you. But I know someone who might."

Old Gus Kincaid's words came back to Maebeth. He had ambled in early this morning just as Maebeth set the coffee on.

"Sent a customer your way last night," he said, handing out treats to the dogs before helping himself to a muffin. "She make it here okay?"

Maebeth nodded. "I appreciate the business, Gus." As if there was someplace else within thirty miles, other than his son's hunting cabin.

Gus took another bite of muffin. "Nan Birmingham needs some help out at her place, I expect."

"Is that right?"

He nodded. "Filled her tank yesterday. First winter at the ranch since the Colonel died, you know. Her niece is after her to move to Florida for the winter, but you know Nan."

"Yup," said Maebeth. "Everyone knows Nan."

Gus thanked her for the muffin and left.

That had been the extent of their conversation, but it occurred to Maebeth that Gus had never dropped in for breakfast before. She made a quick decision now, one of which her husband would disapprove. "Turns out I've got a friend, an older woman, who could use a live-in housekeeper for the winter."

Alice Stevens's face lit up and she all but danced on her toes. "That sounds great."

She was pretty when she smiled, Maebeth thought. "Are you planning to stay around for a while?"

Alice Stevens's cheeks reddened and she dropped her head to stare at the checked linoleum floor. "Um, yeah."

"Okay. I'll give her a call."

Nan Birmingham stopped in later that day. Caroline liked her on sight. The woman was tiny and birdlike, energetic, with eyes the color of Colorado sky. She lived on a ranch a few miles outside of town with a feisty Jack Russell terrier named Scout.

"We don't get many visitors out where I live," Nan warned.

Caroline breathed a sigh of relief. She would be able to avoid showing her face even to the sparse population of Storm Pass. As further insurance, she kept her sunglasses in place as much as possible, along with a red St. Louis Cardinals baseball cap she had acquired and wore low over her face.

These things, she hoped, would keep her safe.

Nan Birmingham arrived at the inn bright and early the next day in an aging Buick station wagon to bring Caroline and Pippin up to the ranch.

Caroline was taken aback when Nan handed her the keys.

"You drive." Nan climbed in on the passenger side door and tossed her cane in the back with Caroline's possessions, which had grown to include a brown paper grocery bag to hold the few additional items of clothing she'd purchased at the local dry goods store.

Caroline hadn't driven a car in years. Porter didn't allow her to touch the Saab. But she was anxious to get away from the town and its tiny Main Street, so she walked around to the driver's side, climbed in, and turned the key.

Nothing happened.

She tried again, turning the key and pressing harder on the gas.

The Buick only groaned.

Caroline's heart fell.

"Finicky old boat," Nan said. "Give it a minute and try again."

Caroline waited and turned the key again. Nothing more than a clicking noise. She wanted to cry.

Nan sat watching a leaf flutter through the air.

Caroline tried once more. There was a soft whirring noise and then silence.

"Alternator," Nan said, still staring as the leaf landed on the hood. "Gus said this would happen."

Caroline closed her eyes and wished she were someplace else.

"I'll head over to Gus's garage and get him to take a look," Nan said.

Caroline knew she should offer to go but there were people about, and Nan had already grabbed her cane and set off down the sidewalk.

Caroline pulled her cap down low and pretended to nap.

Nan returned a few minutes later with Gus by her side.

He opened the hood. "Give her some gas, Alice," he called.

Caroline turned the key. There was only silence. She sighed.

Gus slammed the hood. "Well, Nan, it's like I told you last time. Looks like the alternator. But what you really need is a new car."

Nan harrumphed. "This is a good car."

Gus grinned. "But it's getting old."

"Like the rest of us."

The big man laughed. "No arguing with that. And I can fix her up again. But winter's coming, and I want you to be safe on the roads." He looked up at Ute Peak, where clouds were building as if on cue. "Colonel wouldn't forgive me if you broke down."

Nan harrumphed again.

They must have had the conversation many times. Caroline wished they would finish it now, so she could get away from here.

"I'll think about it," Nan said finally.

Gus brightened.

"In the meantime, let's try a new alternator."

Gus let out a breath. "You're the boss. I'll run you home now, ladies. And gentleman," he added, with a nod to Pippin in the backseat.

But it was his son who showed up to drive them to the ranch in his Jeep Grand Cherokee.

"Nice to meet you. I'm Ken," he said in a voice that was as deep and smooth as an easy chair. He took Caroline's hand in his, and it was by far the biggest hand Caroline had ever held.

"I'm Alice," she said, looking up into a face that gave new meaning to the term "ruggedly handsome." Large brown eyes set in a wide face with a jaw that looked as though it was chiseled from the same granite as Storm Pass.

"Welcome to town." His face, with its wide jaw and

deep-set eyes, would be intimidating if not for his smile, which was bright and warm and a perfect match for the one she'd just seen on Gus Kincaid. "It's a pleasure to meet you, Alice."

After a quick nod, Caroline was first to draw her hand away. She couldn't help but notice the warmth of him lingering where he had touched her. Flustered, she looked down to where Pippin was skittering around Ken's hiking shoes.

He shifted his weight, which set Pippin off barking at the top of his lungs.

"Hey, buddy, it's okay." Ken crouched, dangling his hand so Pippin could sniff it.

The dog gave Ken's hand one lick but backed away when Ken tried to pet him.

Ken straightened up and grinned. "Tough guy."

Ken was even bigger than his father and then some. He had the same easy way, the same slow smile, and this was now aimed at Caroline, despite the dog that raced snarling around his feet.

"Sorry," Caroline said. "Poppit, hush." She had chosen a name similar to Pippin's real name in the hope that he would obey. At the moment, it was a strategy that seemed doomed.

"Poppit," Ken repeated with a chuckle, extending his hand to pet the dog, who continued to bark. "C'mon now, Poppit."

Ken Kincaid didn't ruffle easily, Caroline decided. She smiled. "It takes him a while to warm up to people."

"Like the rest of us, I guess." He shrugged, a quick movement of massive shoulders under his polo shirt. "I happen to like dogs, Alice."

The name, chosen only because she'd never met anyone

named Alice, sounded good on his lips. She snuck a look up at him and met his glance. He was still grinning at her like he had all the time in the world. Relaxed. Carefree. And something else.

Interested.

The realization hit her like a jolt that was both powerful and unexpected. She worried that he could see behind her dark glasses into her eyes and beyond, to how she felt inside.

And the way she felt was anxious. Alert. Afraid. And, more than anything, attracted to him.

She reached down to scoop Pippin into her arms, then busied herself shepherding the dog and her few belongings into Ken's Jeep.

Nan sprang into the backseat over Caroline's protests, proving she was still spry.

Caroline climbed into the front seat, almost light-headed at what she was doing. Looking back, she liked everything about that ride, from the camp smell of the worn leather seats to the mountain's rich scent that drifted through the open windows, to the way Ken kept turning his head to smile at her and point out sights along the way.

He showed them the cutoffs to his favorite hiking trails, the middle school he had attended growing up, and the sheared-off pieces of granite left over from the last Ice Age. He and Nan did most of the talking, but Caroline understood the tour was for her benefit. He pointed out the drive that led to his place, a handsome A-frame built of hardwood logs just outside of town.

Nan bustled around after they arrived at the ranch, showing them into the front room, which was comfortably furnished and up-to-date, like the rest of the place, from what Caroline could see. Nan insisted they sit, bringing tall glasses of iced tea on a tray before disappearing into the kitchen.

Ken settled into an easy chair by the living room fireplace. "So, you wear shades inside?" His tone was teasing.

Caroline hesitated. Keeping them on now would make it seem like she had something to hide. Forcing a smile, she pulled off the glasses and cap, ruffling her short locks into waves around her face. She was aware of his gaze on her, and despite the approving look on his face, she reddened.

"Now I get to see you without the disguise."

Disguise. Caroline's stomach lurched. She looked up sharply to see if he was testing her. But the smile on his face was innocent. Not to mention the look in his eyes was one of admiration. Something she wasn't used to. "I'm sensitive to sunlight," she said finally.

He sipped his iced tea and considered this. "Guess that makes today my lucky day, getting a look at you minus the cover-up."

Flustered, Caroline took a gulp from her glass, more for something to do than because she was thirsty.

"So, how do you like Storm Pass?"

The directness of the question caught her off guard. "I wish I could stay forever," she blurted.

"No reason not to."

There were a million reasons. But Caroline wasn't about to explain them. She had learned long ago to reveal as little as possible about herself, the things she wanted and the things she wished for. Doing so only fed Porter's rage. Aware that she had just broken one of her basic rules, she felt compelled to change the subject. "Did you grow up here?"

Most people didn't notice when someone changed the subject, but Ken Kincaid wasn't like most people. He cocked his head and looked at her. "You should stay if you feel comfortable here. Storm Pass is a small town but there's always room for one more."

Caroline felt her cheeks heat up.

"And the answer to your question is, yes, I grew up here. Left for college. I went to USC on a football scholarship. I played safety." Seeing her quizzical expression, he smiled. "That's a defense position, by the way. And it's fine with me if you don't follow football. In fact, I'd kind of like it."

His words implied a shared future. The realization gave her a pleasure that tinkled inside her like music, and she smiled, flirting back. Her alma mater did not have a football team but its basketball team was top-ranked, a fact she was about to mention when an alarm bell clanged inside her mind. "I just never watched much football," she said at last.

"Never watched football?" Nan bustled back in with a plate of cookies, which she set on the coffee table. "Do you realize you're talking to one of the most famous men in Colorado?"

Caroline smiled uncertainly, but one look at Nan's face revealed she was serious.

Ken chuckled, embarrassed. "Well, maybe the most famous football player in Storm Pass. I might as well tell you now, since my father will get around to it before long."

"His father has an entire room full of his trophies. Ken's just too modest to tell you. You know, he played for the Kansas City Chiefs until season before last." Nan paused to watch Caroline's reaction.

"Oh." Caroline nodded. She recognized the team name but that was it. Her life over the last two years had not allowed for anything as normal or mundane as watching pro football on TV.

"Sit, you two," Nan ordered. "I'll get dinner started before I show Alice around." She disappeared into the kitchen.

Which left them on their own. Caroline got the definite feeling that this was what Nan had intended. She snuck a glance at Ken, who was settled against the back of the chair with his legs stretched out in front, watching Pippin race around after Nan's Jack Russell terrier, Scout.

He caught her glance and winked.

Leaving no doubt that he was happy for the time alone with her. Caroline cleared her throat, not comfortable to sit in companionable silence with him. "I can't imagine what it would be like to grow up knowing you have talent," she said truthfully.

"Everybody has a special talent," Ken said.

"Not like yours," she said.

Ken considered this, flexing the toes of his hiking shoes. "My talent is hard to explain, but I'll try." He eased forward, resting his arms on his knees and letting his feet land on the rug with a small thud.

Suddenly he was in close range, all broad shoulders and big arms. And keen eyes. "The moves were always there, a part of me, like my arms and legs. Getting drafted to play pro ball was incredible." He smiled, remembering.

"I met my wife in Kansas. Soon to be ex-wife, as it turned out." He gave a small shrug. "I got injured and had to give up the game. She wanted to be married to a football star, not a guy who used to play pro." He shrugged again and let out a long breath. "You win some and lose some, I guess."

There was silence while they both considered this. "Yeah." Caroline took a sip of her iced tea.

Ken waited, and when Caroline didn't offer any information of her own, he cleared his throat and continued. "I kicked around Kansas City for a while, then came back home to my true love."

True love. So he was with someone.

"Fishing," he said with a twinkle in his eye. "I'm happy when I'm fly-fishing, that's my big love."

It was an interesting choice of words. Living with a psychoanalyst had taught Caroline that words carried weight. She risked a look at Ken's face, and the playful twinkle in his eyes told her he had chosen those words deliberately.

She couldn't hold back a smile. "Fly-fishing?"

"Yeah," he said with a grin. "I take groups up the mountain in trout season. You ought to try it sometime."

Images of old-growth forest pressing right up against the sides of the road, with occasional glimpses of lakes that looked positively primeval, came rushing back to Caroline from her bus ride just, what, day before yesterday? "I can see why you came back," she said simply.

Ken took another sip of iced tea. "I could show you around."

His tone was casual, but the invitation was not. Caroline hadn't been on the receiving end of attention from a male in a long time, and certainly the boys she had known from GWU didn't compare to Ken Kincaid. He was a man, all grown up, and he seemed normal. Uncomplicated. Not to mention too handsome to look at. A warning flare went off in Caroline's mind. She was not free. Not by a long shot. She sipped her iced tea to stall while she considered how to decline. Spending time alone with him would mean trading confidences, personal information. But Caroline knew that a single casual remark could cost her life, and perhaps his, too. "Maybe," she said, hating herself. "Maybe sometime."

He drained his glass and stood. The room seemed to shrink around him. "Well, I've got to move along now. There's plenty of trout up there. They'll keep till you're ready." He cocked his head, his lips curved and his eyebrows raised, in a well-I-gave-it-a-try look.

"Yeah," she said, looking away. But not before she caught the warmth in his eyes, which threatened her resolve.

He took a step in her direction. "Thanks for the tea. I'll just put these in the sink." He took her glass, his fingers brushing hers in a small movement that thrilled her. Standing next to him was like standing at the base of a tall building. She didn't envy the running backs from opposing teams whose job it was to get past him with a football. But right now there was nothing imposing about him at all. In fact he seemed like nothing so much as a very large and very comfortable teddy bear. Caroline fought the sudden urge to move closer.

His gaze locked on hers, and she could swear he sensed her impulse.

Nan appeared, and the moment passed.

The sight of them standing together put a smile on Nan's face that was so wide her eyes crinkled till they were almost shut. "Leaving so soon, Ken? I made meat loaf for dinner. Join us," she said, collecting the glasses.

"Thank you kindly, Nan. I'll take a rain check." Ken looked through the picture window at the postcard view of the neighboring peaks, where clouds were piling up thick and fast. "Looks like it might turn out to be a snow check." He grinned.

"Okay, but I'll hold you to it," Nan said.

"I promise not to be the only man in Storm Pass who can resist your meat loaf, Nan. Besides," he said with a chuckle, "Gus would never let me hear the end of it."

"Well, then come back tomorrow for leftovers."

"I might just do that. I plan to check on you anyway while your car is in the shop," he said, serious now.

"Drop in any time," Nan said firmly. "Door's always open."

"Thanks," he said with a smile. But he directed his next words at Caroline. "I'll look forward to that."

Nan bustled around the kitchen after Ken left, cheerier than ever. She whipped up a steaming pot of buttermilk mashed potatoes to go with the meat loaf, and served it with garlicky creamed spinach. She watched Caroline help herself to seconds. "It's not good to be too thin," she said approvingly.

Caroline studied her plate. She was five feet, seven inches tall, and had always maintained her weight at a size six. But Porter pointed out flaws, and she began to detest the parts of her body that were weak, such as the soft flesh on her inner thighs and the backs of her arms. She learned to stop eating when he did, whether she'd had her fill or not. Ending a meal still hungry was preferable to being the only one still chewing under Porter's watchful gaze, like a cow working her cud.

"You eat slowly," he observed. "You do everything slowly, like a small child."

Desserts were always shared. Although he offered to order one after every meal whenever they dined out, Caroline learned to say no except on rare occasions.

It felt good not to have someone criticize her for every bite. She'd shrunk two dress sizes during their marriage, and it was probably more than that if she was honest. "I can't remember ever having meat loaf this good," she told Nan now.

Nan swallowed, her eyes as lively and alert as someone half her age. "Storm Pass does a body good. It's done a lot of good for Ken Kincaid."

Caroline hid her interest at the mention of Ken's name by taking another bite of creamed spinach.

"He was hurt, physically and mentally, when he came back. I guess that wife he had in Kansas liked the limelight more than she liked him."

Caroline took a bite of meat loaf, hanging on every word.

"It's her loss," said Nan. "I've known Ken since the day he was born, and there's no finer man anywhere except maybe his father. He's licked his wounds long enough. He needs to open up and share his life with somebody new. And she'll be a lucky girl. And that's the world according to me," Nan said with a laugh. She pushed back her chair and stood, waving off Caroline's offer of help. "You've had a big day. You need to soak in a hot tub and go to bed with a good book. You can get the lay of the land here and start work tomorrow."

Caroline spent the evening doing both, but nothing could quell the feelings brewing inside her. Relief that she had found a place, at least for now, and a tingle of pleasure at the thought of Ken Kincaid and his laughing brown eyes.

She lay in bed, waiting for sleep to come, listening to the wind in the trees.

Something banged, keeping time with the wind gusting outside, hard and loud.

Caroline's heart stopped. She tensed, waiting for the tinkling sounds of breaking glass, the scrape of a door being pushed.

But none came.

Her pulse slowed after a while and her muscles relaxed.

It was probably nothing more than a loose shutter.

She was not safe, she knew this with every molecule in her being. Porter would search until he found her. He was searching now.

*A*fter the paralysis of his initial shock, Porter reverted to his bachelor routine, seeing patients during the day and dining on takeout food at night. He informed the one waitress who asked that Caroline was visiting family and would return soon.

He kept himself busy with the task of putting their home in order, the new order. He purchased cartons from a do-it-yourself moving store and packed up Caroline's belongings to give to the Salvation Army. There was one exception, her cherished collection of Herend figurines handed down from her grandmother, with whom she had been especially close. These he took to a weedy lot behind a strip mall and smashed, one by one.

He ran into Lindsay Crowley at the garage as he waited for the Saab, loaded with boxes of Caroline's stuff. Lindsay had been walking by their townhouse often, waving Porter down any chance she got to ask about Caroline.

She did so now. "Don't tell me you're moving?"

Porter grimaced. The woman's voice was loud, attracting the attention of everyone within earshot. "Just some spring cleaning."

"And here it isn't even springtime," Lindsay drawled. "Isn't Caroline the lucky girl? I can't get my husband to pick up his own socks!"

The customers in line behind them laughed.

Porter stared straight ahead, ignoring the look Lindsay gave him.

"Is Caroline back?" Lindsay stared pointedly at Caroline's purse, which Porter had grabbed on his way out the door. It was balanced now on top of a moving carton, vulnerable to Lindsay's prying eyes.

His neck muscles contracted involuntarily. Porter felt his cheeks flare, aware now that everyone within earshot was awaiting his reply. "Probably tomorrow."

"Probably? You mean you're not sure? Is she driving or flying?"

It was a dig, he was certain of that. A small reminder that her husband could pull Caroline's flight records any time he wanted, if he so chose. But he hadn't. "She hasn't made up her mind."

Lindsay looked ready to say more but her Mercedes sedan wheeled into view. The attendant jumped out and held the door, waiting.

But Lindsay Crowley stayed put.

Now the attendant was watching them, too.

"How is Caroline? Is she doing any better?"

Porter held his ground. "Fine."

Lindsay didn't move.

Porter shifted his weight and swallowed.

"Well," Lindsay said finally. She dug inside her purse, jotted something on a business card, and leaned in close enough to envelop him in fruity perfume.

He wrinkled his nose.

Lindsay's voice close up was soft and lilting. But the

look in her eyes was hard enough to match Porter's own. "You tell that wife of yours she's missed. I'd be grateful if you would ask her to call me as soon as she gets back. Here's the number to my cell phone." She flipped the card with one perfectly manicured hand so that it landed on top of Caroline's purse.

Porter's only response was a quick nod. Relief washed over him when his Saab pulled into view.

He popped the trunk and laid the cartons inside, crumpling Lindsay's business card. He slammed the trunk.

The Mercedes horn blared, too loud in the confined space, making Porter jump.

He glared at Lindsay.

Lindsay Crowley leaned out her driver's side window, smiling sweetly. "You remember what I said, I need to speak with her as soon as she gets back, you hear?"

She peeled off in a squeal of tires.

The phone on Police Officer Mike Hartung's desk was on its third ring.

The woman seated across from him, outfitted head to toe in top-of-the-line Nike tennis attire, flashed him a helpful smile. "If you need to answer that, you just go right ahead. I'm not in a hurry.

"Well, not too much of a hurry," she added after a tiny pause.

Long enough, Officer Hartung guessed, to give him time to reflect on the information she had given him about herself. That she was married to the head of a powerful federal agency and lived "right around the corner" from Police Service Area 2 on Idaho Avenue, N.W. Code, meant to inform him that she dwelt in one of the priceless town homes in this part of Georgetown, an area that Officer Hartung had taken a solemn oath to protect and serve.

Hartung let the call go to voice mail. "I understand your concern, Mrs. Crowley. But in all likelihood, your neighbor is on vacation like her husband said."

The woman in the tennis skirt kept smiling but shook her head. She placed one manicured, suntanned hand on the surface of his desk.

Hartung wondered if all those diamonds got in the way of her tennis serve, and decided they did not. She was used to them.

"Ah told you," she repeated, letting her Southern accent show through. "He was carrying boxes of her things to get rid of, to put into his car, and her purse was right there on top."

Hartung shrugged. "Guy's allowed to clean his closets."

"Are you married, Officer Hartung?"

The question caught him off guard. Hartung shrugged. "Everybody's married."

Lindsay Crowley beamed as though he showed real promise. She shifted around in her little tennis skirt, and Hartung had to admit that for a woman of a certain age, she had terrific legs.

He looked away.

Lindsay Crowley leaned in close so he got a whiff of her perfume.

Something imported, he'd bet.

"I will tell you something about women's handbags, and you can check this with your wife when you return home to her this evening," Mrs. John Crowley said. "That purse was a Louis Vuitton Alma."

Straightening up, she recrossed her shapely legs, as though nothing more needed to be said.

But Officer Hartung suspected Mrs. John Crowley wasn't finished with him, not by a Texas mile.

"You see, Officer, the Alma will never go out of style. Never." Her blue eyes darkened with concern. "No woman would give her Alma away, not if she could help it."

She let her words hang in the air.

In any other city, Hartung thought, neighbors with a beef would be put through to Dispatch and that would be the end of it. But D.C. had adopted a warm and fuzzy approach, breaking its force down into PSA units so residents could get up close and personal with cops, even implementing a "ride along" program for concerned citizens. "Okay, Mrs. Crowley, here's what I can do," he said at last. "I'll take a walk over there and talk to the guy, see what I can find out."

The look on her face told him she was not feeling the love. Hartung slid one of his cards across the desk. "Here's one of my cards. There's someone here to answer your call twenty-four hours a day. Your job is to call me if you see anything suspicious or tell me as soon as his wife shows up."

Mrs. Crowley did not touch the card.

"And in the meantime," Hartung said in his best community-first tone, "I'll open a file and make an official log of your concern."

She perked up at that.

Hartung opened a file and readied his fingers on the keyboard. "Now, what is this guy's name?"

Her next words kicked Hartung's Spidey sense into full alert.

"Dr. Porter Moross."

* * *

The sixth day brought a fateful turn of events. Porter's last patient of the day departed at half past three. He donned his walking shoes in the hope that he could wear himself out enough to sleep by nightfall. He headed out and left behind the noisy hubbub of Georgetown's main streets, crossing Rock Creek on the main thoroughfare of L Street before dropping south on Twenty-seventh Street, staying clear of the western edge of the George Washington University campus.

Caroline's alma mater. A place, Porter knew, he had no business venturing.

He headed east on E Street with its monolithic office buildings.

At Seventeenth Street he reached his destination, the Corcoran Gallery of Art.

He knew he shouldn't do what he was about to do, but, like a child who picks at a scab until it bleeds afresh, he couldn't stop himself.

He climbed the steps and went inside.

The smell that was peculiar to museums, Pine-Sol mixed with preservatives, hit him as soon as he walked through the door. He had met Caroline here for the first time on a September day not unlike this one, and he realized now with a pang they had never been back since.

The Corcoran was privately funded and not a part of the Smithsonian, and so was not filled with the hordes of tourists who lined up each day to enter the National Portrait Gallery barely half a mile south. That fact alone made the place attractive to Porter, not to mention the Corcoran's permanent collection was noteworthy in its own right.

Nobody had loved the place more than Caroline, however, and it occurred to Porter now as he retraced their steps past canvases by Hopper, Cassatt, and Sargent, that he had been wrong to dismiss her taste in art as immature.

"I'm going to paint landscapes in oil," she had told him. "Open spaces."

"Landscapes don't leave much room for pure emotion," Porter had observed. His taste ran toward minimalism, works that were more likely to be found in New York's MoMA or private galleries, and he'd wound up at the Corcoran that day by default, more in search of a quiet haven from the last of the summer tourists on the Mall than anything else. He hadn't minded the Turner exhibit, and his decision to stay that day had changed the course of his entire life.

He wandered the halls now, fighting back tears, wishing he could sacrifice a limb for the chance to turn back time and try again to make Caroline happy.

But he could not.

Night was descending when he left the place at closing. He wandered the Mall aimlessly for a while as it emptied of tourists. He studied them, the parents with fanny packs and maps of the Metro corralling bickering children back to their hotels. Porter was filled with a yearning he hadn't experienced in a long time, not since his own childhood long ago.

He walked back along Constitution Avenue and up into Foggy Bottom, eerily quiet except for the stealthy horde of homeless that set up camp each night on the sidewalk grates that billowed steam from the empty buildings above.

Porter knew most of them suffered from untreated schizophrenia, and odds were one of them might act out a paranoid delusion and end his life before help arrived.

But he was too despondent to care. He wandered north and west finally onto F Street, drawn back against his better judgment directly into the heart of the jostling urban campus of the George Washington University.

Porter knew coming here would only deepen his wound, reopen it right down to its core. But that pain represented a connection to her and to another, ancient wound that would not heal. And more than anything, Porter yearned for some connection with that wound. Anything. So, powerless over his subconscious urges, like his many patients, Porter wandered the crowded streets of Foggy Bottom, alone with his ache.

"Hello. Hey, sir, hello."

Porter hunched lower into his sports jacket and kept walking.

But the caller was persistent. "Hey, mister, hello."

Porter stopped and turned. He vaguely recognized the uniformed doorman who had rushed out onto the sidewalk from the lobby of an apartment building.

The man's English was heavily accented. "Hello, sir. Where's you wife? I seen you with her sometime but no more."

Porter scowled and took a step back, signaling he was in a hurry.

The doorman paid no attention. He motioned with one hand near the ground. "And the leettle dog she no bring for me. Peepen, right?"

Porter gave a quick nod, more to shut the guy up than anything else. "Right."

"I keep treats for him, when he come to stay when missy goes." The doorman motioned with his chin, smiling, at the fortresslike building that took up the entire next block.

Porter grew very still.

"She finish her project?"

The man pronounced it *pro-jhek*. Porter became aware of a scratching sensation under his collar from the hairs on the back of his neck, which had begun to move. His wrinkled his nose at the suddenly too strong smell of exhaust from passing cars and nodded. "She did."

"That's good," the man said, still beaming. "Tell her to come say hello. Bring the doggy."

"I will." Porter did a quick about-face and headed in the direction the man had indicated.

To the GWU Gelman Library.

A bored-looking guard stopped him at the entrance.

"I forgot my ID," Porter lied.

The Gelman Library was reserved for use by undergrads.

The guard shrugged and leaned forward slightly. Interested, no doubt, by the prospect of a confrontation. "Listen man, you either come back when you find your student ID or you come into the office and fill out the necessary paperwork." The guard relaxed against the back of his chair.

No doubt he didn't get many takers on the offer to fill out paperwork.

Porter looked past him through the entry doors. He hadn't been inside the place in years. A large bank of computers took up much of the ground floor. "I, uh, just needed to get on a computer. Can I get Internet access here?"

The guard's eyes narrowed. "Whole place is wired. You can bring your own laptop. But I can't let you in without a valid student ID." The man pushed his chair back and made as if to stand, signaling this tête-à-tête had come to an end.

But Porter had learned all he needed to know. Caroline could have talked her way past this guard easily enough, especially with an ID that had only recently expired. "Thanks." Porter mumbled and left.

The walk home seemed to last an eternity, and a million possibilities presented themselves to him along the way.

A dim lamp in the foyer illuminated Porter's way past the deacon's bench in the downstairs hall. He activated the keypad, and his office door swung open. The place was silent, save for the ticking of a mahogany grandfather clock. He switched on the computer even before he turned on the brass desk lamp.

The machine whirred to life, flashing through startup screens. It held the key to his future. Anticipation made his skin tingle as though he was wearing it inside out. He scratched at the bumps that were already rising on his face. An excess of emotion always brought out Porter's old enemy.

After what seemed an eternity, his desktop screen came into view. He clicked on his Internet browser and typed in the address for the Web's most popular free e-mail account. It was the simplest, most obvious place to start.

His fingers practically shook as he attempted to sign on.

At the prompt for a username he typed "carolinemoross." He used "pippin" for a password.

The combination was rejected.

Porter tried using "porter" as password.

It was rejected.

He tried using their wedding date, then Caroline's birth date.

No luck.

He slumped in his desk chair. But the hairs along the back of his neck were still vibrating with energy, spurring him on. Porter forced himself to slow his thoughts, considering things. He tried again, with a different username.

"Carolinehughes." Her maiden name.

He entered "pippin" as password.

This time the server's response was different.

Have you forgotten your password?

Which meant the username was correct. Of course, he thought dully, she would use her maiden name as an act of defiance.

He ran through the obvious passwords and each was rejected. Her birthday, their wedding anniversary, and their street address. But none of these worked.

Porter sat back, his desk chair creaking like a rifle shot in the dim silence. He drummed his long fingers on the mouse pad, thinking.

On a hunch he crossed the room and unlocked the filing cabinet where he stored his patient records and important documents. Flipping to the P's, he located the one he wanted. The one labeled "Pippin."

He carried the folder to his desk and opened it, rifling through the papers until he came to the American Kennel Club Certificate of Registry that listed the dog's date of birth.

He swung around to the keyboard and entered the date at the password prompt. He watched, unbelieving, as the screen blinked once and a different screen took its place.

He was in.

The icon popped up for mail. The inbox contained a single saved message. The header consisted of one solitary word.

Wassup?

Porter stared. Behind the word was a voice demanding an answer. A masculine voice, Porter was certain. He double-clicked.

I know the old house routine. We live at Home Depot. Good luck. My weekend was the usual bore, the Gymboree thing with the twins, etc. Tried to make a move on Lisa after we put them to bed while she was watching TV. She shut me down. We just can't get off since the babies came. Happy Monday.

Happy Monday? From a man who was providing details about his sex life. Who was this? Without realizing it, Porter tightened his grip on the mouse until it lost contact with the pad, sending the icon careening drunkenly across the screen.

The message was less than three weeks old. It had originated from tf_activewearmodesto at a server in the Western United States. Porter and Caroline did not know anyone in Modesto.

But someone in Modesto knew them.

I know the old house routine.

The message had been sent in response to a message from Caroline. tf_activewearmodesto was familiar with the age of Caroline's—their—home. Too familiar.

tf_activewearmodesto knew how he, Porter Moross, and his wife spent their time.

The tingling in Porter's neck grew stronger and slipped down his spine, chilling him to the bone. He shuddered.

There were no other messages in the inbox. Porter clicked on "Addresses," then "Favorites."

tf_activewearmodesto was listed in "Favorites."

Tom Fielding.

Porter frowned, closed his eyes. Tom Fielding had lived on the same floor in Caroline's dorm at GWU. Tall and gangly. WASPy with reddish blond hair, blue eyes, and a smattering of acne.

That acne that would have cleared up by now.

Porter pointed his mouse at the "Sent Mail" icon and double-clicked. There were several messages, all sent to Tom.

Hi.

It was the most recent, dated earlier on the same day as Tom's "Wassup?" Caroline wrote about a movie they'd seen and the fact that he, Porter, hadn't liked it. She described their visit to Restoration Hardware in search of electrical outlet covers for the new half bath outside Porter's office.

Porter has his heart set on outlet covers that will match the period of the house. But they didn't have electrical outlets back then ☺.

Porter stared at the screen, his teeth working inside his mouth, shredding the sides of his cheeks until he tasted blood.

His wife had complained about him to another man. While Porter had scoured catalogs of upscale hardware stores so that the new half bath would blend in with the renovation of their historic home, his wife had been sending smile emoticons to a married man.

They had shared a joke at Porter's expense.

Porter felt a familiar itching along his jaw, as though each hair follicle in his beard was on fire. He raked his fingers through it and rubbed savagely, knowing this would only worsen the hives that were taking root.

He ordered the "Sent Messages" folder by date. There were half a dozen addressed to tf_activewearmodesto dating back almost two years. And these were just the e-mails Caroline had saved. To read and reread.

Porter slumped in his Eames chair, shaking his head. He closed his eyes, slipped his fingers underneath the steel rims of his glasses, and massaged the sore spot on the bridge of his nose. Then he continued reading.

He discovered a series of messages dated the week they returned from their honeymoon.

"Here's a joke," tf_activewearmodesto had written in the original e-mail, which had been copied to several other names Porter recognized as GW alum.

Caroline had e-mailed her reply only to Tom.

"I always thought you were hot," her message began.

Porter felt a slow burn start down low and deep in the pit of his stomach.

> You were not too skinny in college and judging by the photo I saw you look great now.

Slut, Porter thought. How could she do such a thing?

The heat inside Porter spread, like a fire that has been doused with gasoline.

What sort of man would ask a newly married woman if she remembered his body?

A man who was hell-bent on avoiding his own intimacy issues, that's who. And Caroline, with her unresolved conflicts about giving and receiving love, was a ready-made target for the attentions of such a man. Caroline would have been titillated by sharing secrets, too naïve to see the fissure she was opening in her own marriage. The thought of Caroline as victim was preferable to thinking of her as a willing adulteress.

But only just.

Porter continued to scroll. Later that year, Caroline had initiated another round of e-mails, asking tf_activewearmodesto how come he hadn't written. Porter's gut contracted when he read the text of yet another message that had originated with his wife.

"To my forever Valentine," she had written. There was no text. It had been intended as a simple greeting so Tom would know he hadn't been forgotten.

She had e-mailed him on the first Valentine's Day of her marriage to Porter. How hateful. His gut churned with hot jealousy as he remembered the strings he pulled to get a reservation at the hottest restaurant in town that night, how much he had paid Akua to come to the condo in Dupont Circle while they were out to sprinkle rose petals on their bed and leave his gift on the pillow, a pair of sapphire earrings from Tiffany. Porter took a slow breath and tried to calm himself.

He clicked into Caroline's "Deleted Messages" folder and found Tom's reply.

> You are as sweet as I remember from GW. Porter is
> one lucky guy. I hope he appreciates what he has.
> Gotta run, get Lisa some chocolates or something
> on the way home.

That son of a bitch. Poor, tired Lisa should know how
her husband spent his time at work.

A heavy weight descended on Porter, as though he were
a thousand feet below sea level, as he considered the implications of this e-mail. Tom Fielding felt comfortable
telling Caroline that her husband didn't appreciate her.

Which meant she had invited his criticism of her marriage.

Porter's shoulders slumped. He heard a buzzing. It
took him a moment to realize it was the sound of his
own blood pumping in his ears. "Why?" Porter moaned
softly. "Caroline, why?"

But he knew the answer. The human ego was the most
elaborate defense mechanism ever mapped by man, capable of weaving a web of deception to protect itself.
Such was the work of an undisciplined mind.

Porter clicked back to "Sent Messages." There it was.
Caroline's reply.

> P is moody as ever. Physician heal thyself!

Porter shook his head in disbelief. Could Caroline
have written this? Porter had cleaved unto his wife, revealing to her the most intimate aspects of his innermost
self, laying bare his innermost feelings. All he had asked
in return was that she do the same.

And instead she had mocked him in e-mails to this
man.

Porter scrolled through the remaining exchanges with a sinking heart.

They spoke in familiar tones, asking about each other's lives and exchanging news about people they had gone to college with. Tom confided details of his lack of sexual intimacy with his wife. He had asked Caroline about hers.

Porter hardly dared to breathe.

Caroline's response was simple.

;-) Let's not even go there.

But she had. The winking icon said it all. She even went on to tell Tom she wasn't sure she was cut out for marriage.

Porter let out a long breath and felt everything in his gut liquefy. He was glad when he reached the bottom and only one e-mail remained. He couldn't take much more.

In the end, he was very glad he had read them all.

I still think of your cross-country trip, with you and your Rocky Mountain high when I get stressed out. Somewhere over the rainbow . . .

That was it. The trail ended. The e-mail was less than two weeks old.

Your Rocky Mountain high.

The buzzing in Porter's ears grew louder. The pieces of the puzzle had been there all along. He just hadn't put them together. Beginning with Caroline's fascination with modernist American landscape artists, something Porter had written off as childish, simply one more aspect of her personality that revealed her lack of maturity. She had removed their passports as a ruse, to throw him off the trail. He'd realized the implications of that when the policemen left that morning, seen of course that Caroline had not traveled overseas, although she would have been wise to do so.

But of course she'd had no interest in Europe.

She'd gone West.

Porter saw that now. She'd sought refuge in a small town, something of a size that would have presented a manageable counterpoint to the chaos that was raging inside her.

Another thought followed quickly, snaking through him and laying waste to everything in its wake. What if she had arranged to meet Tom Fielding?

Porter checked his watch. Not yet ten P.M.

Early enough to find someone in his office on the West Coast if he was working late, if he wanted to avoid going home.

Porter directed his browser to Google and within seconds located the phone number and address of a sportswear manufacturer in Modesto. He dialed, expecting to get an after-hours voice mail greeting.

He was shocked when a woman answered on the second ring. "Hello?" As an afterthought, she stated the name of the company.

Porter tightened his grip on the receiver. "Uh, hello," he said, his mind racing. "I, ah, didn't expect anybody to be there at this hour."

"We're officially closed."

"I was trying to get in touch with Tom Fielding. Voice mail's fine," Porter said, trying to sound bright.

"He's here. I'm his wife."

So it was a family business. Which meant, according to California law regarding community property, Tom Fielding was in no position to file for divorce.

There was another pause. "Can I help you?"

Her voice had acquired an edge. As though she was practiced in snooping.

No wonder. Porter cleared his throat, grasping wildly. When he spoke, he forced his words out fast so they tumbled free and easy. "Well, uh, actually I haven't met him. One of my, uh, sales guys must have met him at some point. My guy just came back from a trade show just, what? This past week in Vegas."

"My husband wasn't in Las Vegas this past week."

My husband.

Mrs. Tom Fielding's tone was sharper now, so each syllable dug in and hung on. She was losing patience.

"Hold on a sec, lemme see. I got chicken scratch here." Porter gave a smooth, throaty chuckle. "I can barely read this guy's handwriting. Hey, maybe I was supposed to look your husband up next week in Phoenix. I've got a kind of a mini-trade show thing there." He let it hang in the air like a question, hardly daring to breathe.

"Sorry." Mrs. Tom Fielding allowed the irritation to show in her voice. "Tom's in the office all month. I can put you through to leave a message but it's after hours so he won't pick up. Do you want his voice mail?"

Relief flooded through Porter. He felt a loosening in his shoulders and the buzzing in his ears dimmed. Caroline still belonged to him. She had not yet acted out her fantasy of betrayal. Which meant there was still hope. He smiled, giddy, even though she could not see him through the receiver. "That'd be great."

"No problem."

Porter waited until he heard the click that indicated she was transferring the call. Then he hung up.

He turned his attention back to the computer screen, pointed the mouse back to Caroline's inbox, and stared.

Wassup?

He fingered the mouse, reviewing his options. What he was about to do was risky, he knew, and yet it was his best option. And most likely the only one that remained.

Taking a deep breath, he clicked on the button marked reply.

Hey handsome. Just checking in. Hope to get out of Dodge, maybe see some leaves turn. Road trip!! What was the name of that place in the Rockies? Chat soon ☺ C.

Porter hit send and waited.

He'd bet anything that prick in Modesto would keep his wife and twins waiting until he'd replied to Caroline.

STORM PASS, COLORADO

Caroline awoke to a room bathed in soft amber light. Mornings came suddenly here, more than eight thousand feet above sea level. Stretching luxuriously, she pushed the patchwork quilt aside and slid out of bed.

With a whine of protest, Pippin jumped off and followed her down the hall, his toenails clicking on the polished wood floor. Caroline surveyed herself in the bathroom mirror while she brushed her teeth. She was no longer startled by the face that looked back. She had grown used to her short blond hair. But the biggest change was her eyes. They no longer looked haunted.

There were scrabbling noises on the floor behind her. Nan's dog, Scout, had come to greet them in his usual way. He rubbed himself, catlike, against Caroline's legs and then tackled Pippin. Pippin was the smaller and more docile of the two, and no match for Scout.

"Morning, boys," Caroline said. "Break it up or take it outside." She nudged the wiry Jack Russell terrier off Pippin with her foot, and reached for a plush bath towel from its hook on the back of the bathroom door. She shook the towel at them to break it up and they scurried ahead of her down the back staircase.

The sun was just rising next to the massive peak to the southeast, sending rays of warm pinkish light into the large kitchen. The pasture behind the house was becoming visible through the wall of windows, and the pine forest beyond the split-rail fence. A fieldstone fireplace, big enough to stand in, lined the interior wall. A long oak table and an assortment of antique chairs took up the center of the room. Large stone tiles lined the floor, giving the place the feel of a genuine frontier homestead.

But it was an illusion. The ranch house had been maintained in top condition and fully renovated, right down to the professional-grade appliances. Nan's late husband, Colonel Charles Birmingham, had been a gourmet cook, among other things.

Caroline busied herself with the imported espresso machine now, measuring out French roasted beans and grinding them with the flip of a button before setting the dial to brew.

The dogs raced around her feet, excited the day had begun. They tripped over themselves on the way to the door. Caroline collected a fleece parka, shoved her bare feet into moccasins, and opened the back door. The dogs raced past, out onto the grass that was rimed with frost.

The air was sweet and sharp, carrying the first hint of autumn. Caroline saw steam when she exhaled, following the dogs along the path across the pasture and into the woods. The aspens had already dropped most of their leaves. Austrian pines stood shoulder to shoulder with mature cedars. Birds chattered above, including the family of blue jays that lived at the back of the pasture.

The dogs raced along ahead of her, barking at birds and everything else, until the path opened out onto a small clearing. The unmistakable scent of sulfur gained strength as Caroline approached a small, rocky pool. Heavy mist rose from the surface, which bubbled like stew underneath.

She climbed onto a large, flat boulder at the water's edge, took off her clothes, and slipped in.

The dogs darted around the rocks at the edge of the pool as Caroline swam a few strokes through water that was warm like a bath in some places, roiling like a hot tub in others. When she reached the middle, she flipped onto her back and did a survival float, watching steam rise from her stomach.

The entire experience was incredible.

Caroline had never imagined a place such as this. She knew she had less to fear in the wilderness than she'd had in the life she'd left behind. Big animals, she learned, took great care to keep themselves hidden. Nan reassured Caroline she could spend years on the mountain without seeing one in daylight.

Nan had inherited the ranch from her husband, whose family had settled here four generations ago, making them the oldest Anglo family in Storm Pass, Colorado. None of which amounted to a hill of beans in these parts, Nan pointed out. The site had been selected for its proximity to this hot sulfur pool, considered by the indigenous Ute people to have mystical properties. Miners and ranchers settled the area next, followed decades later by a smattering of tourists who soon discovered the healing properties of the bubbling springs.

Nan's swimming days were behind her, but she told Caroline she still made the short hike in summer. The

Utes believed breathing the mineral-laden air could push evil spirits away. Caroline drifted now, taking in deep lungs full of air and holding them. She exhaled each as fully as she could, imagining she was pushing out all remnants of her marriage to Porter.

When she was too breathless to continue, she paddled to the edge and toweled off, showering the dogs with droplets from her hair.

She dressed quickly and headed back, her skin tingling and alive with energy. The forest had come to life around her, bright with the light of morning, the air so still she could almost hear the beating of her heart. The breezes that were a constant at this altitude would not pick up until later in the day.

Emerging into the pasture where the last of the tall summer grasses still stood, yellowed and dry now, she spotted Nan in her teak rocker on the porch, nestled under a wool blanket. Her long hair, the color of brushed steel, flowed down her shoulders, not yet coiled into her usual braid.

Nan smiled as Caroline approached. "Mornin', Alice."

Caroline smiled back, pausing at the bottom of the steps. "Good morning. Looks like another beautiful day."

The older woman nodded in agreement. "This is my favorite time of year. Things will start to change in another week or two. October is a tricky month. That's when storms start to brew up in the mountains."

Caroline followed Nan's gaze to the jagged peaks visible above the tree line.

"Cold air comes down from the north and collects here below the pass. This time of year it collides with the warm air from farther south. Most every afternoon in fall, the gods put on quite a show," Nan explained.

Caroline contemplated the peaks. She had never experienced anything like the constant breezes that were a part of everyday life this high up. She shivered now to imagine what the coming weeks might bring.

Nan chuckled. "We'll make a mountain girl out of you yet. If you make it through a winter here, you'll be a native."

It was the most obvious reference yet to Caroline's sudden appearance in Storm Pass, and she chose to ignore it. She climbed the steps and rested at the top, winded. The locals were right, she decided. Altitude sickness was a small price to pay for living here.

Nan seemed to read her mind. "This high up, we're close to God, as the Colonel used to say."

Caroline considered this. "He must have been a special person."

Nan's smile deepened. "He was. I was lucky to have him."

"You were lucky to have each other. A lot of people don't have that." It was more than Caroline meant to say, and she looked back out over the pasture to avoid Nan's gaze.

Nan made no comment.

Caroline was growing to appreciate the Western custom of talking less, listening more.

"We both loved this place the best in all the world," Nan said reflectively. "I have no intention of leaving. My niece wants me to spend the winter with her in Florida." Nan grimaced. "She sent me a round-trip airline ticket, even one for Scout. But I told her I can manage just fine."

"I don't doubt that," Caroline said with a smile.

"I might go for a short visit. You could stay here and look after things." Nan caught the round-eyed look on her employee's face as she surveyed the big house and surrounding land. "It'd be good for you to have some time on your own."

The young woman nodded, thoughtful. "I guess."

There was no mistaking the lightening of her expression. "You'll have it easy," Nan said with a smile. "I'll bring Scout with me."

At the mention of his name, Scout trotted over with Pippin close behind.

Pulling liver treats from her pocket, Caroline began their morning ritual. She directed Pippin to sit, lie down, and shake, rewarding him with a treat. Scout was not as easy, but Caroline worked patiently with the stubborn Jack Russell, repeating the commands until the little white dog gave in at last.

Nan watched her new employee work with the dogs, her face relaxed and animated for the first time since they'd met. Alice was young, beautiful, and in a heap of trouble. Nan had seen her share of trouble in seventy-seven years of life, enough to know this girl had plenty. Which was why Nan had offered her a job on the spot at Maebeth's. Nan had taken an instant liking to Alice, and it was good to have company. The ranch was too quiet since the Colonel died last spring.

Caroline cupped a treat near Scout's mouth and tapped his paw with her free hand. "Shake," she ordered.

They had been practicing with little result.

"Scout, shake," Caroline repeated the command.

The little dog finally lifted his paw the barest centimeter off the ground before snatching his treat greedily.

"He's learning." Caroline beamed.

Nan laughed. "Are you training him or is he training you?"

A smile lit Caroline's face. "It takes time. You just have to keep at it every day. An animal can be trained to do just about anything."

"Relax, Caroline, relax."

She would never forget the heat of his breath on the back of her neck as he repeated the words that would become for her a dark mantra. Soft and beseeching at first, increasingly strident as his own sense of urgency grew. Each time pushed her farther down a path that turned and twisted on its way into a realm she dared remember only with pain and fear. But something else lived there, something too dark to acknowledge.

Caroline gave away more of herself each time, despair seeping inside her like drops of ice-cold rain.

"Relax."

She learned to tell Porter the words he wanted to hear, all the time focusing on her mantra from long ago, burned in the brain of that little girl who got used up and left alone.

"Relax."

Adult Caroline closed her eyes and opened herself to Porter so he wouldn't tear open the old wounds. But on the inside she bled.

Porter's breathing turned ragged, his voice hoarse with excitement. "Say it."

She lay facedown, screwed her eyes closed, and whispered in the dark. "I want this."

Looking back, Caroline wondered when her life with Porter had spiraled so far out of control. It hadn't started out that way. She'd met him on a crisp fall afternoon that was full of possibilities. She had walked the short distance from her dorm across Foggy Bottom along E Street past the historic Octagon House to the Corcoran Gallery of Art. She preferred this area, rich in history and relatively quiet, to the Mall that was always jammed with tourists.

There were few people about in mid-afternoon, with the semester young enough that Caroline could afford a couple of hours off to admire the Corcoran's private art collection instead of locking herself away to study it in the school library.

The Corcoran was the first stop on a worldwide tour of select works by J. M. William Turner, the English painter of romantic landscapes.

With a thrill of anticipation, Caroline crossed Constitution Avenue, entered, and waited in a short line to check her coat, noting with satisfaction the place wasn't completely jammed yet. She passed up the audio tour kit. She had already researched the featured works.

Caroline Hughes was twenty years old, midway through her senior year studying art history at the Columbian College of Arts and Sciences at the George Washington University.

The exhibit was overwhelming. She stopped to rest in front of a particular favorite, *Arundel Castle*.

She pondered the mural, her printed guide forgotten, until the lights and colors danced before her eyes, and the room receded from her consciousness in the presence of such exquisite beauty.

So she was shocked to hear her private thoughts spoken by a soft male voice. "He uses light to draw us closer, always closer to the center. Pure genius."

Caroline found herself nodding in agreement even before she turned to look. The man sitting beside her was older than she by a number of years, she estimated. Well dressed in what looked to be a black Armani suit jacket over black sweater over black designer jeans, and black ankle boots of fine leather. The overall effect was distinguished, she decided. His hair was long and wavy, prematurely white, as was his close-cropped beard. His skin was white as porcelain.

His eyes were fixed on the canvas, oblivious to Caroline's gaze. When he spoke again, his voice was hushed, his tone refined. Reverent. "He uses light and shadow to invite us in, steering us always to the center. The mark of a master."

Intrigued, Caroline turned back to the painting. Indeed, the colors were deeper in the center of the canvas. "The artist wants us to find our own way," she offered, feeling a little like she had just been called on during a school lecture.

The man nodded. "He draws us in and presents us with his truth." He turned, revealing the palest blue eyes she had ever seen, beneath lashes that were startling and pure white, as were his brows. He wore round steel glasses like John Lennon. All of which had the effect of intensifying his gaze.

"Few people appreciate the subtle power of Turner," he said.

Caroline might have pointed out that plenty of people appreciated Turner, enough to have an entire wing named after him at London's Tate Gallery, but already she sensed the man beside her was too sincere, too sensitive, to tolerate undergrad sarcasm. She searched instead for something intelligent to say, something to convince him she shared his appreciation for life's subtleties. "Turner wasn't very popular in England during his lifetime," she said finally. "Critics didn't take him seriously."

The man smiled and nodded again, taking in the printed guide and backpack on her lap. "They underestimated him."

Something about the expression on his face told Caroline the man in black knew all too well the pain of not being appreciated. She nodded. "Nobody had ever used light in this way."

"True," the man murmured. "But that wasn't the reason." He turned back to the painting, lost in his own thoughts. "It was his style, his use of space. It gives the landscape the feeling of floating, not being anchored. Almost as though he wasn't certain he wanted to be present in the work himself. It poses a challenge to the viewer. Upsetting for most people."

Caroline was anxious to show him she was not Most People. "You have to work to know Turner."

She was rewarded with a smile that revealed two tiny rows of perfectly spaced teeth.

"Most people don't get Turner," he said sadly. "Even at the Tate, few people take the time to understand him."

The Tate Gallery was located on the banks of the River Thames in London, a fact he hadn't felt the need to explain. Caroline was flattered. She liked the long pauses he took, considering things she said before opening his mouth to reply, giving weight to each word they uttered. As though Caroline's contribution to the conversation held deep meaning. She felt listened to, not just simply heard. They chatted, quickly discovering a shared love for the visual arts. He had traveled to Florence many times. He was a Freudian psychoanalyst with a medical degree from an Ivy League school.

He invited her to dinner Saturday night at a French restaurant she had heard of but never dreamed of dining in.

Caroline skipped pizza and beer in the rathskeller that night, dressed with care in a twin set and borrowed pearls, and headed out in pumps for her first date with an older man.

A security alert had all but shut the city down. Caroline arrived at the restaurant twenty-five minutes late.

Porter Moross was seated at the bar, dressed head to toe again in black, nursing a whiskey on ice. He did not smile when she rushed in, breathless and apologetic.

"Sorry I'm late. They shut down the whole block around the Old Executive Office Building. It took forever."

Porter took another sip without looking at her, and Caroline wondered whether he had heard.

"Porter?"

He set the glass down, hurt etched around the corners of his mouth. "I was about to leave."

"Leave?" Caroline was caught off guard and laid a hand on his arm. "Look, I'm really sorry. I couldn't help it."

His arm was stiff, unyielding.

She drew her hand away.

His voice was tight. "If you had taken a cab, you would have gotten here in time. I assumed you had changed your mind and decided not to come."

Caroline felt her cheeks color. Her budget didn't allow for cabs, a fact she was too embarrassed to admit. "I'm so sorry," she said, putting her hand back and squeezing his arm a little.

She felt his arm muscles tighten inside his sports jacket. Somewhere deep inside, her mind registered the fact that Porter Moross was a complicated man. But at the moment, she was too preoccupied to notice. At the moment, she was concerned with wiping the sad look off his face. She threw her arms around him in the sort of casual hug she'd bestow on a roommate. "I'm usually never late. I'm so sorry." She shrugged, helpless now that she'd said all she could.

He was visibly moved by the hug, and it occurred to Caroline that Porter Moross was in need of simple physical affection. This fact was captivating to her. Caroline Hughes collected wounded people in much the same way that some people collected stray animals.

"Okay," Porter said after a long pause. "I accept your apology. Our table is ready. I'll tell the maitre d' that you've arrived."

He took her coat and motioned her to sit. "Shall I order you a glass of wine?"

Caroline slid onto the tall, smooth bar stool and nodded as he signaled the bartender before excusing himself to check her coat.

Something none of the boys from GW would have done.

Porter's steady gaze on her at dinner, combined with the way he leaned forward to listen when she spoke, made Caroline feel for the first time in her life like she was at the center of someone's universe. Porter did everything with a careful deliberation that, she decided, was the hallmark of a genius.

Porter asked the waiter to explain each of the main selections in detail. Then he asked if the waiter would choose their entrees.

"Excuse me?" The waiter spoke with a heavy French accent.

Porter repeated his request.

Frowning, the waiter shifted his weight onto one leg. "I don't know what you and the young lady would like to eat. You should order what you think she would like." He shrugged.

Porter was undeterred. "But I have asked for your help. I want you to suggest something."

It was somewhat odd. Caroline felt her spirits flag and her cheeks redden, even as she carefully arranged her features into a smooth, reassuring smile. Porter was, after all, only trying to ensure that they would have the best possible dining experience.

The waiter glanced around the crowded dining room, letting his impatience show on his face. "They are all good, sir."

Porter said nothing.

The waiter sighed.

Porter glared.

Caroline squirmed in her seat, searching for some way to end the standoff. She wound up blurting out a request for the only dish whose name she could remember.

She had no idea until the sweetbreads arrived that they were brains.

And so that night over dinner in Washington's best restaurant, frequented by senators and heads of state, known the world over for its menu that featured the meat of rare and endangered species, Caroline adopted her mission in life. It was one that had its roots planted long ago with the little girl on the bed. Caroline would dedicate her life to doing whatever was required to please Porter.

Porter stared at the computer screen glowing grayish green in the darkened office, throwing bits of dust on the keyboard into bas-relief. His office at this late hour was silent as a grave.

He should turn the computer off. It could be hours or days before he got a response from tf_activewear-modesto. Perhaps longer.

But Porter's gut told him otherwise.

And so he sat, waiting. Each time the second hand on his watch swept past twelve, he aimed his mouse at the refresh button and clicked.

He was rewarded before many minutes had passed.

"Wassup? Re: Re:" popped into Caroline's inbox.

Hardly daring to believe his eyes, Porter double-clicked on the header. He was in.

> Storm Pass. Great little town near Durango. Denver has more flights tho and drive up is awesome. Good hiking but weather is iffy now. I want a pic of you soaking in a hot spring. . . Yummy! :-). Gotta run, duty beckons.

Porter stared at the screen.

Yummy!

The flirtation between tf_activewearmodesto and Porter's wife had progressed, edging ever closer to the line between fantasy and reality. Left to their own devices, that line would be crossed because both of them wanted it.

That realization filled Porter with sorrow. Caroline had failed him. Because somehow he had failed her.

As he reached for the phone, Porter uttered a silent wish that he would get to Caroline in time, before she found some other way to act out her fantasies of betrayal.

He listened carefully to the after-hours message from Beltway Security Investigations, directing callers with business of an urgent nature to a beeper for immediate callback. Porter dialed the number, making note of it for future reference in his leather-bound folio.

He busied himself waiting for a callback by printing out hard copies of Caroline's e-mail correspondence with Tom Fielding. These he ordered by date and stapled. He reached for a FedEx mailer at first but thought better of it. The end result would be further enhanced, he realized, if the recipient had no way to trace the origins of the package. This realization made Porter smile.

He slid the packet into a plain manila envelope and applied postage stamps in an amount he judged to be double what was required. Using his customary neat handwriting, he carefully wrote out the name and address of the sportswear firm in Modesto. When he was done he reviewed his efforts carefully. The devil, Dr. Porter Moross knew, lay in the details. Satisfied the address was perfectly legible, he sealed the envelope and wrote across the bottom in large block letters: FOR THE PERSONAL ATTENTION OF MRS. TOM FIELDING.

He stowed the envelope in his leather portfolio, ready to drop in any mailbox at such time that he judged to be to his best advantage.

The callback from Beltway Security Investigations was prompt, as promised, and within minutes Porter had contracted for surveillance in Storm Pass, Colorado, to be dispatched from Denver within twenty-four hours.

Porter hung up. Mixed in with everything else, he felt a small measure of satisfaction. He had regained some control. His limbo had ended.

The hunt for his wife had begun.

Two thousand, eight hundred miles away, Tom Fielding hit the send button and sat staring at his computer screen. Something wasn't right. Caroline Hughes knew the name of the town Storm Pass, for one thing. He had told her the story many times about some locals who had turned him on to peyote while soaking in a hot springs there, in what he and his friends had jokingly referred to as Tom's spiritual awakening, his "Rocky Mountain High."

Tom Fielding was not an airy-fairy kind of guy. Which was why the weird vibe he was getting right now caught him off guard, and creeped him out enough to make him turn a deaf ear to repeated buzzing of his office intercom.

Over the last year and a half, his e-mails with Caroline had gotten more intense. They had even toyed with the idea of meeting up in Storm Pass, if Tom could sell his wife on the idea he had business prospects there. Yeah, right.

If Caroline Hughes needed a break and wanted to head out West, why wouldn't she check with Tom first to see if he could get away and meet her? And why, for the love of God, would she plan a trip with that asshole husband of hers?

Almost all of their communication since Caroline's marriage had been via e-mail, but she made sure Tom always knew her latest cell phone number. He lifted his desk blotter now to where he kept it hidden on a sticky note.

"You coming?" His wife stood in his office doorway, arms akimbo. "I've been buzzing you for, like, the last ten minutes."

Tom dropped the blotter. "Just finishing up."

Lisa's eyes narrowed.

He knew that look. "Sorry," he muttered, powering off the computer and switching off the desk lamp. He stood. "Let's go."

She threw him a look, and Tom knew that look. Even though she was justified, she had no way of knowing she was justified, and this fact irritated Tom Fielding. So he picked a fight. "You wanna go, so let's go. I was ready fifteen minutes ago but you weren't."

Lisa glared but did not take the bait. She shrugged. "So, let's go."

This was so out of character for her that it had the effect of amping up the volume on Tom's weird vibe. He had never given much thought to ESP, but the hairs on the back of his neck were telling him loud and clear that Caroline Hughes was in trouble.

He wanted to call her but Lisa was hanging back, waiting for him to walk out first, and so he did, but not before he noticed Lisa took one last hard look at the blotter on top of his desk. It had been sitting there, undisturbed, since his father-in-law promoted him and he moved into this office.

"We're late," Lisa said. "The sitter will be pissed."

Tom Fielding made a mental note to hide that sticky note somewhere else first thing tomorrow.

CHAPTER
12

The day turned out sharp and clear, the coldest since Caroline's arrival in Storm Pass almost a week ago. High, puffy clouds skittered across the sky and around the peak like distant gray smoke. Wind gusted off the mountain. The dogs were inside, preferring to nap where the sun warmed the oak floorboards.

Caroline tracked the source of the banging she'd heard in the night to an overgrown branch from an Austrian pine near the garage.

Nan gave a knowing smile when Caroline told her she planned to trim the tree. "It took me a long time to get used to the noises this place makes at night. There's nothing here to harm you, nothing to worry about."

Caroline considered this in silence.

"If it's bothering you I'll have one of the ranch hands come out and trim it." Onions and peppers sizzled in a cast-iron skillet. Nan was cooking a batch of sirloin chili, her first of the season. The secret to good chili was to let it sit for several hours, she explained, giving the contents a stir.

"If it's all the same to you, I'll trim the tree myself. I don't want you to bother any of the men," Caroline

said. The truth was she'd be embarrassed to have any of
the ranch hands come. The branch was small and didn't
really make much noise. Just enough to make Caroline
wonder what the sound would be if someone attempted
to break in through the back door.

"But Federico usually takes care of these things. I'll
call him now." Nan set her spoon down and reached for
the portable phone. One look at Caroline's face stopped
her. "Well, if you want to, suit yourself. There's a saw
and some gloves in the garage."

"Great."

"The rest of the day is yours, though. Take a hike."
With a soft chuckle to indicate her suggestion was serious, Nan turned her attention back to the cloves of fresh
garlic waiting to be peeled and chopped.

Caroline found the gloves where Nan said they'd be,
hanging from a peg among an orderly collection of tools
on the wall at the back of the four-car garage. The work-
bench was shipshape except for a thin film of dust.

The gloves were meant for a hand much larger than
Caroline's, but she managed. The branch causing the
problem was crossed with another. Caroline had read
once in a gardening book that the lower of two crossed
branches should be pruned back at its base. She'd had to
satisfy her interest in gardening with books. Porter did
not want to live in a house with a yard in the suburbs.

The memory brought an ache so strong she placed a
hand on her stomach, remembering the old hurt. She'd
wanted, expected, to bear Porter's children. She had
imagined playing with them in a sun-drenched yard,
maybe Falls Church or even Bethesda, making an event
out of Porter's return from the city each night.

A shadow had crossed Porter's face when she raised

the possibility of a house in the suburbs, and Caroline realized too late she had said something wrong.

"The suburbs? Tell me something, Caroline. Where are the bookstores? Where are the museums? Where is the culture? Can you tell me that?"

Caroline stared at him, feeling her heart sink. She didn't know her way around any of the towns outside the Beltway. In fact, she hadn't ventured much beyond the reach of the Metro during her four years on a scholarship at GW. She shrugged. "I don't know."

The dark look on his face intensified, as tension mounted inside.

It was a look Caroline was beginning to recognize. Most of the time their life together was what she had always wanted. Porter was attentive and loving, in bed and out. He always took time to compliment her when she dressed nice, always made sure to walk ahead to open doors for her, and cooked a roast with all the trimmings every Sunday. He was always leaving small gifts for her to find around the house, just to please her and, he said, to make his princess smile. Caroline learned they were happiest in private, when they were on their own with nobody else around.

But sometimes, even when they were alone, Porter's temper rose up out of nowhere. As now. A shiver of fear rippled through her. She tensed. "You're right," she said quickly, hoping to head things off. "We don't need to live in the suburbs."

Porter blew air from his nostrils and gave a quick shake of his head. "Correct. The suburbs are a place for men with too little money and not enough brains. And do you know what their wives do out there all day, Caroline?"

He leaned in close to her so she could see each individual white lash around his eyes, close to the vein that was throbbing bluish gray under the thin skin of his forehead.

She swallowed and tried not to let him see her wince. She felt her shoulders hunch up around her neck and drew her arms in close.

He noticed.

She read it in the flicker of his eyes.

Her heart sank. They were slipping down again into a vortex. No matter how she tried, once it started there was nothing she could do. They were sucked down, down, down. No matter how their arguments began or how she tried to stop them, once that spiral began there was no pulling out. It always ended the same.

Caroline's mind raced. If she could find the right thing to say or do, maybe this time would be different. "No," she whispered. "I have no idea what wives do."

His lips tightened, and he shook his head as though he was weary of her and sighed. "They cheat on their husbands." His lips curled around the word "cheat" and he watched, gauging her reaction.

She shook her head, stalling while she reached for the right words. So much would depend on how she answered. "That's terrible."

"Terrible?" He leaned in close, his nostrils flaring. "You say it's terrible? Yes, Caroline, a wife who cheats on her husband commits a terrible crime. On so many levels, it is a violation."

He was so close she felt his breath on her face. A faint ringing sounded in her ears. The room began to spin slowly around them. It was their downward spiral. Their dance.

She closed her eyes now in an attempt to block out the memory of what followed, events that were typical of their routine of betrayal and punishment.

Things didn't start out that way. The change had come gradually, an inch at a time, so that at first she wasn't aware of how much her life was changing. She moved into Porter's apartment after they were married while they looked for a bigger place. She was lonely, lonelier than she had ever been in her life. Her school friends had graduated and gone off in search of jobs at art galleries in New York, Miami, and even London. Caroline was alone with her new husband.

Many days, she met Porter for lunch. She got to know the waiters at the small café near his office, and soon realized Porter was more relaxed when they were seated at a table served by the café's sole female waitress. Caroline learned to ask to sit in the woman's section, pretending to be especially fond of her, even bringing her a small bouquet of flowers one time.

At night, they stayed in. They didn't entertain. Their wedding china sat in boxes, unused.

By July, they found a house. It was a historic townhouse on an immaculate street in the heart of Georgetown, in a row of homes dating from Colonial times. Porter designed an office on the ground floor for his psychotherapy practice. The upper floor would house their residence.

Caroline was giddy at the prospect of living with her brand-new husband on a street of million-dollar homes while her college chums were crammed into group rentals in places like Astoria and Adams Morgan.

Porter rose each day at six-thirty, showered, and brewed coffee while Caroline slept. He collected his

Washington Post from the front stoop and skimmed it in his office before returning to wake Caroline at eight.

He would stand soundlessly in the doorway until she woke. At first she wouldn't stir until he took a seat on the edge of their bed, but as time passed she learned to waken when he stood in the door. The idea that she sensed his presence in her sleep pleased him. She yawned and stretched, knowing he enjoyed watching her while her defenses were down. "You're like a teenager," he would tease. These were the happy times.

He would ask what she had planned for the day. At night, over dinner, he would ask about her comings and goings. If she forgot something, he would point it out.

"Smile at me when you pass my office window," he told her. "Not a big smile. Just a small one that only I can see." They practiced until she got it right.

Gradually, she stayed inside more and more often except to walk her dog, the one vestige of her single life that she refused to surrender. She had inherited Pippin from one of her suitemates, and never quite believed Porter's claim that he was allergic to animals. Pippin came to represent Caroline's only diversion; she spent most of her time with Porter. They did the major grocery shopping at a Safeway on weekends together, and if she needed something during the week Caroline did without or waited until Porter could accompany her. Finally, they agreed that two walks per day for Pippin was enough. Twenty minutes was enough, unless she explained it ahead of time. Too late, Caroline realized the folly of living above her husband's workplace. The townhouse in Georgetown had become her prison.

Those days were gone and best forgotten, Caroline told herself. She would never let it happen again. Never.

Tightening her grip on the wood saw, she clenched her teeth and attacked the Austrian pine as though she could set right her part in the wrongs that had been committed back in that townhouse.

The saw bit deeper into the wood, releasing a fresh pine scent with each pass. Caroline worked the tool until she was breathless and sweat stung her eyes. She was rewarded for her efforts when at last the branch dropped to the ground with a satisfying thud. She grunted with satisfaction.

A car door slammed close by and she jumped. She wheeled around and heard Pippin and Scout inside the house, barking.

She saw a familiar Jeep.

Ken Kincaid stopped and flashed her a peace sign. "Hold your fire. I mean no harm."

She realized she was brandishing the saw like a weapon.

He grinned.

She lowered the saw, feeling her cheeks redden. "Sorry. I didn't hear you pull up."

"Don't mention it," Ken said easily. "I should know better than to interrupt someone working in the yard." After a moment he added, "Especially a woman with a saw in her hand."

"I decided the tree needed a trim."

"Nice job," Ken said, eyeing the trunk's fresh cut. "Like a pro. I got some at my place that need pruning, if you're interested."

She was. Embarrassed, she swallowed and looked away.

"That was a joke there, Alice. Not a very good one, I might add."

She looked at him, all happy grin and big white teeth and plaid shirt. She couldn't help but smile back.

"I came to ask a favor. If you're done cuttin' down trees, that is."

She couldn't imagine what favor he might ask of her. "Sure."

"Will you come into town with me to pick up my other car? I need to lend it to Nan. Gus is laid up and can't finish the repairs on the Buick today."

Caroline thought of big Gus and his kind face. She frowned. "I hope everything's okay."

"It's just his arthritis acting up. He'll bounce back in a day or two. He always does," Ken said lightly. But there were small lines of worry around his eyes.

"Sure," Caroline said. "And thanks for lending your car." It was a generous offer, the sort of thing nobody would offer to do in a big city or the hardscrabble exurb in Baltimore where she'd grown up. Or maybe they did all the time, but she didn't know it because she and Porter didn't have any friends.

Inside, Nan was ready with a covered pot to go. "Put this on the stove and let it simmer for an hour or two before you serve it to Gus."

Ken lifted the cover and sniffed. "Mmmmm. Gus is going to be one happy man." He winked at Caroline. "Nan makes the best chili in the county. Probably the world."

"I don't know about that," Nan said with a laugh. "But it'll tide Gus over for tonight. And there's plenty more where that came from. You tell Gus I said not to lollygag in bed too long. I want him to fix my old boat."

Caroline donned her jacket, hat, and sunglasses and followed Ken out to the Jeep.

He held the passenger door and waited till she was settled inside before closing it.

The small act made Caroline feel as though they were out on a date. Which, she reminded herself, was not the case. But a small thrill came over her like sunshine on the cool mountain breeze. It felt good just to sit next to him with the windows rolled down as they drove along the county road.

Ken steered with his left hand and looked at her often, his smile bigger than ever beneath his aviator shades. At one point, he slowed the car to a stop and leaned over, pointing up into the tops of the trees.

"We're in luck," he said in a low voice, shifting so close on the seat beside her that she could feel the muscles in his broad back. His scent filled her nostrils.

She breathed deep.

"Look there." His voice dropped to a whisper, low and close and way too intimate, until she practically squirmed in her seat. But what she saw next made her forget her discomfort.

"Look." He pointed straight up. "An American bald eagle."

Caroline ducked her head through the open window. There, some fifty feet up, atop a towering pine, was a big messy nest. Peering over the edge was the largest bird she'd ever seen.

Ken pulled binoculars from the glove compartment and pressed them into Caroline's hands.

She focused on an enormous brown bird with a crown of snow white and a mighty yellow beak. It moved its head, and she glimpsed the fierce expression she had seen only in textbooks.

"Ooh," she murmured. The bird was noble, just as

she had imagined. But nothing had prepared her for the real thing, and the thrill that swept over her now.

She looked at Ken, and he smiled like he was a teacher and she was his star pupil. "No matter how many times I see her, she takes my breath away."

Caroline ducked her head out the window for another look. Without the aid of the powerful field glasses, she would have mistaken it for a hawk, if she had bothered to notice the bird at all. "Wow," she breathed.

Ken leaned lower on the seat, looking up through the windshield.

She thought how easy he was with his body, how free of tension he was, how relaxed. As though he didn't have a care in the world. He didn't. Most people didn't. There were people who went about their day, not explaining anything to anyone and not worried about anything. Caroline marveled at the thought. She didn't realize she was holding her breath until Ken straightened up.

"You can usually find her here," he said. "That's her nest. If you check back in spring, she'll have her little ones with her." He replaced the binoculars in the glove compartment, which overflowed with Audubon Society guides, trail maps, and a large knife inside a worn leather holster. It was a comfortable clutter, filled with items required by a man who spent a great deal of time outdoors.

"Sorry about the mess," Ken said, pushing the jumble to the back of the compartment so he could snap it shut.

Caroline found the clutter reassuring, a sign of messy sanity.

He put the Jeep back into gear. "I know this is her

home, and I know I'll probably see her every time I drive down this road. But it still knocks me out every time." He smiled. "Birds are smarter than you think. They build their nests near the road, which you might not expect, but it works out. They don't have to worry about hikers. Most people drive right by and don't ever look up. So she can raise her young in peace."

Caroline was intrigued. "Hide in plain sight."

Nodding, Ken turned and gave her a look of approval. "Alice Stevens, you've just named the basic rule of survival. Hide in plain sight."

Slowly Caroline had withdrawn from life. She tried to draw as little attention to herself as possible. She didn't want to provide Porter with ammunition when he fell into one of his black moods.

Looking back, she couldn't pinpoint when her goals had shrunk so small.

She had dressed with care for her second date with Porter, making sure she was early. She waited in the lobby to save him the long walk from the elevator to her dorm room and the round of introductions that, she feared, would be awkward.

She perched on the edge of the worn lobby couch for a time before standing to pace, checking the clock on the wall again and again to be certain she was prompt.

His cab arrived exactly at the appointed time. He wore a black coat of pure cashmere, with a white scarf of silk knotted loosely at his throat. Despite the light snow, he got out to greet her properly. "You're on time," he said approvingly, taking her hand in his gloved one, brushing her cheek with his lips.

Caroline quivered with nervous excitement.

They were off to see his friend's art show at a gallery that was crowded, and well beyond the reach of the Metro. Caroline was younger than most of the patrons, and noticed with smug satisfaction she appeared to be the only college student in attendance. She took many small gulps of white wine from her plastic stemmed glass, content to let Porter lead her through each room. Once, she caught her reflection in a mirror, ghostly and pale, a fact she attributed to poor lighting rather than nerves.

They wound slowly through the gallery. He stopped and asked her what she thought about each and every painting. It was flattering, at first. She had dedicated the last three years of her life to studying art, after all, laying the foundation for her life as a fine artist. She hoped one day to see her own paintings for sale in a gallery such as this. Not in a big city, but maybe in a small town with wide-open spaces where she could clear her mind and paint what she saw.

Porter introduced her to a well-dressed, older woman. Another psychoanalyst. The three chatted briefly before leaving.

In the cab, Porter informed the driver there would be two stops. First stop would be Caroline's dorm in Foggy Bottom.

"That was fun," Caroline said.

Porter stared out the window, wordless.

Caroline wondered if he had heard. "I like going to art shows. And it was fun meeting one of your friends."

"She is a professional colleague, not a friend." His tone was ice.

Caroline sat, aware that she was witnessing one of Porter's mood changes, which happened lightning-quick. She was annoyed, and was about to tell him so, but the mournfulness in his tone stopped her before she said anything.

"I'm so embarrassed, I just don't know what to do."

There was no doubting his sincerity as Caroline pondered his delicate profile, confused and embarrassed herself.

The cab crept along Massachusetts Avenue, thick with Saturday night traffic. People walked in groups, the sound of their laughter drifting through the window.

Inside, the cab was silent and cold like a bank just before closing. A knot formed in Caroline's stomach, twisting tighter and tighter as it gathered all the promise the night had held. She suspected she knew the answer to the question she was about to ask, but she asked it anyway. "You're embarrassed?"

His lips tightened, moving his pale beard ever so slightly. He turned to her at last and blinked. "Do you hear yourself speak?"

"What?" The knot in her stomach twisted a few more turns.

"I mean, do you have any sense of the way you sound?"

In her mind, she reviewed everything she had said, everyone they had spoken with. She toyed with the idea of telling him she hadn't talked to any French waiters, but she was already learning never to make light of Porter's hurt feelings. "Do you mean your friend?"

He stared at her, his pale eyes wide. "She's not my friend. She is a psychoanalyst who trained with me. Which means every nuance, every word you use, carries meaning for her. What you said tonight revealed to her your basic personality trait. Dishonesty."

"Huh?"

The glance he gave her was accusing. "You used the word 'switch.' Not once. Twice. To describe the artist's use of colors."

Caroline frowned, not following.

Porter shook his head, as though he realized he was speaking to an idiot. "It's a loaded word, Caroline. Words have meanings on many different levels. And that word . . ." His voice trailed off. He shook his head and stared out the window.

She had hurt him. The whole thing seemed silly to her, but she could see it mattered to him. Something about him, this serious yet sincere man dressed in black, mattered to her for reasons she could not understand. She pictured him dressing to come out tonight, choosing the white scarf with care, knotting it just so at his throat, making himself ready for his date. So that he would appear attractive to her. And she had ruined it for him without meaning to. He'd told her about the tough breaks he'd had in life, and she wanted more than anything not to add to Porter's list of emotional injuries.

Caroline placed one hand gently on his arm, which was stiff. "Listen, I didn't mean to embarrass you. I was so excited to come tonight, to meet a friend of yours and get to know you better. That's all." She drew in a deep breath and tried to swallow around the lump in her throat.

Her words seemed to soften something inside him, and this made her happy.

She felt a tremor in his arm, his chest.

He leaned forward, pulled off his glove, and took a swipe at his eyes.

Caroline realized with shock he was crying. Mortified,

she looked away. Then leaned across the seat, closing the distance between them. "Porter, it's okay," she murmured, trying to comfort him. "I'm sorry. I didn't mean anything by it. I want to meet your friends. Really."

He looked at her, his pale eyes filled with remorse. He swallowed. "It's me," he said gently, gesturing at his white hair. "I have trouble when I'm around groups of people. I get nervous."

Caroline threw her arms around him. This man who seemed so powerful and sophisticated one minute was so vulnerable. He was like a rare and exotic bird. He needed her. She needed to prove to him that she cared little for the color of a person's hair. "Hey, Porter, don't worry about it." She smiled. "We all get nervous. Dating is hard."

He looked in her eyes. She saw a frightened boy inside him, anxious to be loved. Her heart melted. She smiled and kissed him on the lips.

His mouth was warm. He gathered her close and parted her lips with his tongue. He thrust it quickly inside her mouth, hard and probing and insistent, in and out.

Exotic.

Excitement hissed through Caroline with the speed and intensity of a downed electric wire. She had never kissed anyone this old. He was thirty-two.

They kissed until the driver pulled up outside her dorm. Porter murmured that he wished she could spend the night with him, just holding him, nothing more.

They went to his place.

Later in the dark, in his bed, she marveled at his body, lean and muscled and sinewy. Every hair on it from head to toe was white.

Not gray, he explained, but lacking pigment due to a rare genetic disorder that made him look older than he was. The onset had come at puberty years after his mother had left, but her fault, he explained, just the same.

Unsure what would be the right thing to say, Caroline settled for stroking his hair, which was the shade and consistency of dried straw.

"Do you know what it was like to go through high school with a head full of white hair? I got beat up every week." Tears thickened his voice.

Caroline was moved beyond words by this admission. She wanted to prove to him that her feelings were more than skin-deep, that her sincerity matched his own. And so she did, using her lips, her hands, and her arms to prove herself worthy of him.

"Don't ever leave me, Caroline," he whispered, over and over. "Don't ever hurt me with another man. Promise me."

And so she promised him with her caresses. She came to believe on that night that she could heal the terrible scars from his past, make Porter whole and secure simply by loving him.

It felt good to be needed.

When they were done, he lay beside her. "Why didn't you tell me?"

Thrilled that her unique gift hadn't gone unnoticed, Caroline smiled in the darkness. "Because it was my decision. I wanted to make you happy."

"Oh, Caroline," he breathed, rolling over to face her. He took her in his arms and covered her long brown hair in soft kisses. "Such a rare and beautiful princess. What a treasure you've given me."

In that dim room with the steam heat hissing softly through the radiators and the traffic sounds rising up from Dupont Circle, Porter Moross was sweet and happy and easy to please. The way Caroline imagined he had been as a boy. Before the world turned sad for him, before his mother left and his own body turned against him. She could restore him to that safe, warm place simply by loving him. And the act of loving Porter would transform Caroline as well, setting her free forever from her past as a damaged little girl with a dark secret, into a grown-up with a whole new life.

The next day she received a FedEx package at her dorm from a Japanese company she had never heard of with an address on Fifth Avenue in New York City. It contained a small rectangular box made of chocolate-covered velvet. Inside was a strand of pearls that gleamed like steel.

The note was simple.

So my princess will never have to wear borrowed pearls again.

P.

They were married five months later.

WASHINGTON, D.C.

*H*ow was work?" Lindsay Crowley stood in the doorway of their master bedroom suite.

A question that meant, John Crowley knew, his wife wanted to tell him something interesting about her day. "Good." He had already removed his seersucker suit jacket and loosened his tie in the limo. Now he undid the buttons on his dress shirt in preparation for the shower he was about to take, his second of the day.

D.C. in summer was not all that different from Houston. "How was yours?"

"Interesting, in an odd way." His wife, cool and crisp in a Lily Pulitzer shift, took his sweaty clothes from him. She told him about her visit to the local police. "I don't think that young man appreciates the information I gave him. Something's wrong, John." Lindsay jutted her chin in the direction of Moross's house across the street, but her tone left no doubt she was disappointed in the police response as well.

"I mean, I fail to see how sending a squad car over is going to help that girl, wherever she is, if he's already giving away her things." Lindsay wrapped John's sweaty suit into a ball and tossed it into the dry-cleaning bin.

If the cop who took his wife's complaint today thought he'd settled things with Lindsay, either he was a very poor judge of people or else the guy had never been married. John Crowley surveyed his wife, whipping things into place before his work clothes could muss the designer silk bedspread and matching dust ruffle. "Do you want me to make a few calls tomorrow?" John waited for Lindsay's answer.

There was no point in playing possum with a woman when you were standing in your undershorts, sweaty and wanting a shower.

Lindsay smiled. "Oh, John, that would be such a help."

"You got it." John checked his watch. The Astros were hosting the Mets in Houston tonight. He had just enough time to shower and get settled in front of the TV with a cold beer before the opening pitch.

"You'll let me know what you find out, won't you?"

"You bet."

"Wherever that little gal went, I hope she gets there safe and sound," Lindsay said.

John nodded in agreement.

Lindsay gave him a quick peck on the lips. "Dinner will be ready in ten minutes, how's that sound?"

"Good." John headed for the shower.

"I'll leave your Astros shirt on the bed," she called after him.

STORM PASS, COLORADO

Nan Birmingham adjusted the back burner and gave the chili one more stir before heading through the living room to answer the doorbell.

"Shush, boys," she called to the dogs, though it did no good. They raced ahead, barking and snarling, as someone pressed the bell again. The chimes rang out, little used and over loud in the stillness of the afternoon. The dogs went wild, and no wonder. It was rare for anyone besides Federico or one of his sons to come to the main house without calling first, and when they did come they always came around back.

The dogs took turns launching themselves at the storm door once Nan pulled open the main one, which was made of solid oak.

Figures, she thought, a traveling salesman.

He smiled. "Good afternoon, ma'am."

Nan gave a short nod in response and attempted to sweep the dogs back with a mild kick. It did no good.

"I see you have your friends with you today," he remarked, speaking extra loud to make himself heard through the glass.

Nan nodded.

"I don't want to take up too much of your time, ma'am. May I ask, do you currently have a cable connection for your modem?"

Frowning, she shook her head. They didn't get many solicitors out here where the houses were miles apart.

Scout, fangs bared, jumped high in the air, over and over again. Poppit kept on barking.

"I thought not," the man replied smoothly. "I'm from ClearSky Cable with a limited-time offer today."

"No thanks," Nan said, preparing to close the oak door.

The salesman spoke faster now, moving closer to the storm door so that Nan's thoughts turned to the antique shotgun hanging above the mantel. The gun was loaded.

"I can get you six months free on your TV and waive the signup for a high-speed Internet hookup," he said hopefully.

Nan shook her head. "I don't go on the Internet." The chili could do with another stir by now, and the gas probably needed lowering.

The salesman motioned with his clipboard, took another step closer to the door, where the dogs continued to bray, leaving wet sprays of slobber on the glass. "Say, you're a cute little fella," he said, dropping to one knee and tapping on the glass.

Nan stared. He must be daft.

He pulled a treat from his pocket and tapped it against the glass.

Poppit, the smarter of the two, stopped barking once he caught sight of the treat and dropped to his haunches.

Confused, Scout cocked his head.

Both dogs, thankfully, quieted down.

"Well, that's something," Nan breathed.

The man looked up with a quick smile. "May I?" He pulled the storm door open without waiting for an answer and tossed the treat inside.

Scout pounced on it at once.

"Don't worry, there's more where that came from." The man pulled a handful of treats from his pocket and tossed one to Poppit. "They're great little dogs you got there." The man propped the door open with his knee, careful not to let the dogs escape, and fed them more treats.

"Thanks," Nan replied, watching as Poppit gently nibbled from the salesman's hand.

Scout, on the other hand, snapped his jaws closed so fast around the treat he nearly bit the man's fingers.

Poppit approached the salesman and sat, waiting.

The man ruffled the soft fur behind Poppit's ears. "This one has got nice manners."

"He sure does." Nan glanced at Scout who stood, panting, just out of the man's reach.

The white dog yipped, demanding another treat.

The salesman complied. "There you go, fella."

Reassured now that the man had abandoned his efforts to sell her cable, Nan loosened up a bit. "That one's the only one belongs to me, I'm afraid," Nan said with a smile. "Can't take credit for the other."

"Well, they're both great little dogs. What kind are they?"

"The white one's a Jack Russell and the other is a Yorkshire terrier, I believe."

The salesman had been studying the dogs. He straightened up now. "You get 'em both at the same time?"

"No, the Yorkie is—" Nan stopped herself. That chili needed lowering. "He is a good dog. Sorry I won't be doing business with you today."

The man considered this, gave a pleasant smile. "Well, I'll just say that even if you don't want it for yourself, that Internet connection sure will come in handy for keeping in touch with the grandkids, or for when your grown children come to visit." He glanced at Poppit, and Nan understood the implicit question about the little dog and the grown son or daughter who might be visiting.

Nan was country in her heart, enough to have opened her door to a strange man in the middle of the day. But she was also a Westerner, and a woman who lived alone far from the nearest town. She didn't take the bait. "Sorry," she said, pulling the handle on the storm door and clicking the lock into place.

He nodded, still smiling. "No problem. You change your mind, you just give us a call. Thanks again for your time, ma'am, and have a pleasant day."

"Will do." Nan closed the oak door and hurried back to the chili that was, as she suspected, close to burning.

Steering with one hand, the PI jotted two words on his clipboard with the other as his blue minivan bounced down Nan Birmingham's drive.

Yorkshire terrier.

He had been told to watch for a small dog. He couldn't remember what breed it was, but that would be easy to check later in his file. The old lady hadn't wanted to give anything up, no more than the innkeeper in town. But he'd gotten enough. And he'd been at this business long enough to know that all it took was a little bit to get the job done.

He smiled and turned onto the county road.

This assignment was turning out to be a piece of cake.

From the eagle's nest it was a short distance to Ken's place. A drive of crushed stone led through a pasture to an A-frame house of rough-hewn logs set well back from the road. The scent of sagebrush was everywhere. The front porch held an old-fashioned wood swing and a container garden with the season's last small clusters of cherry tomatoes staked and secured with twine.

Ken followed Caroline's gaze. "I have a proper vegetable garden out back in summer, but these are all that's left now."

Caroline's eyebrows lifted. "You cook?"

He laughed. "I give it the ol' college try. I do okay, if I do say so. Beats taking my chances with Gus."

"You could always rely on Nan," Caroline pointed out. "She'd never let you starve."

"Nan Birmingham's got a heart of gold," Ken agreed. "She adopted my father and me after my mother died. When I moved home again from Kansas City a few years ago, I discovered she's a really good listener. It really helps."

He was giving her a subtle suggestion, and one that Caroline knew she could not take. Aware of his gaze on her, she pretended to study the neighboring peaks and hoped he wouldn't ask how she came to be here.

She was grateful when he patted one of the cushions on the porch swing. "Have a seat. If you've got a minute, I'll get you a glass of sun tea before we head back."

Caroline hesitated. It was best not to linger. Her strategy for survival did not include spending time with a man who was so handsome she couldn't think straight.

But it was too late. Ken had already disappeared, returning moments later with two glasses of ice. He filled them with amber liquid from a jug that was propped against the railing. Pressing a drink into Caroline's hand, he raised his glass. "I propose a toast. To nothing in particular." Grinning, he clinked her glass with his. "Make yourself at home, Alice. You're in my favorite place to watch the world go by. I'll be back in a minute." He went inside again, the screen door slamming behind.

Which gave Caroline no choice but to do as he had said. She settled back against the cushions and realized immediately he was right. The view was fantastic.

Cardinals and starlings darted across the meadow, hawks wheeled on air currents high in the sky. Above it all was majestic Ute Pass. She removed her sunglasses to get a better look at the colors, raised one foot to the porch rail, and let her head lean against the back cushion. It felt good. Her Cardinals cap tumbled off her head. She shook out her short locks and closed her eyes.

She loved this place. She could paint it. But she had vowed to live on the run rather than risk discovery by Porter.

"Told you it's the best seat in the house." Ken reappeared with a tray of chips and guacamole. He stopped short in mock surprise as a slow, easy smile took hold of his jaw. "Wow. Your hat's off."

Flustered, Caroline sat upright.

"Um, take it easy there, Alice, I didn't mean anything by that." His tone was sincere but he didn't allow the moment to linger, a fact she appreciated. He set the tray down on a small table and pulled it close, lowering himself firmly onto the seat beside her.

She was aware of how the swing shifted under his weight.

He held the bowl of chips out. "Dig in. I made the guac myself."

She dipped a chip and popped it into her mouth. It was delicious, tangy with a hint of heat. "Very good." She chased it with a sip of tea, which was sweet and cold.

"Glad you like it. I grew the cilantro myself. And the tea is a secret Kincaid family recipe that's been handed down for generations." He knit his brows together in a mock serious expression. "A couple of tea bags and some water with honey and lemon thrown in at the end." He laughed, reminding her again of his father. "Here's to you, Alice." Ken took a deep swig and looked around. "I'm a country boy at heart."

"I can see why," Caroline said, sneaking a glance at his face.

He seemed relaxed, at peace, taking it all in. "Takes my breath away," he said, shifting his gaze to her.

The flirtation was too much. Caroline took another sip of iced tea, mostly for something to do. Ken Kincaid seemed to say whatever was on his mind, plain and simple. What would it be like, she wondered, to have a man like him for a partner in life, to go through all her days and nights with a man like him at her side? There were people, she thought, who did not walk through life on eggshells. The realization of how much she had traded away by pledging her life to Porter filled her with regret. She drew in a long breath and looked out over the meadow.

Shifting his gaze to some point in the distance, Ken gave the swing a push with one foot. "I don't rush things. It's just not the Western way, I guess. Life is good." He raised his glass in another toast and sipped, his Adam's apple bobbing above the fleece collar of his jacket.

Caroline didn't trust her voice, so she nodded. She was experiencing none of the nervous energy she had felt when she first met Porter. She felt no need to smooth Ken's feelings or find three different ways of saying something to make him understand she meant no insult. In fact, she felt no pressure to do anything. So she sat, listening to Ken tell her in his gentle, deep voice some of the facts of his life. And this broke through the protective shell Caroline had built during her life with Porter, revealing something of the person who had been locked up inside.

"I would have given anything to grow up in a place like this," she said at last, gazing up at the peak. "I read that book *Heidi,* you know? It was a really old book with woodcut illustrations, and I still remember one that showed Heidi in her little bed at night, all tucked away with her long braids underneath a pretty quilt, looking up at the mountaintop and the stars that were right outside her window." Caroline's mind flashed back to an image of her bedroom overlooking the grime-filled streets of Baltimore, how she wrapped her pillow tight around her ears at night to block out the sounds inside the tiny apartment, praying to God to make her sleep through till morning no matter what. "I don't know why, I just always remembered that picture," she said, aware that Ken had turned to look at her.

There was a pause, during which time he let the rocker slow and turned his gaze back to the vista that lay before them. "I guess I would have always thought about that book, too, Alice. If I was you."

She was not at all sure whether he was making fun of her so she looked at him, and to her surprise he was smiling. Not a big sarcastic smile and not a sympathetic smile and not even a knowing, tell-me-more smile like Porter would have done to draw her out. Just sweet, making a little joke. His smile made her aware of how sad she was, and somehow made some of it go away so she smiled back. "Yeah. I know it sounds weird, but I feel like I stepped inside the pages of that book."

Ken's smile deepened into laughter. "Well, I guess you did." He reached one arm lazily across the back of the porch swing so it rested behind her shoulders. His fingers brushed the top of her arm, and this made Caroline giddy. "You want me to yodel?"

Caroline burst into laughter at that, and the feel of it inside her throat was like an old friend. She hadn't laughed in a long time and it felt good. "You don't yodel. Um, do you?"

This set Ken off and he laughed some more. "Nope," he said at last. "Sorry to ruin your childhood dream."

Something about the way he said this, like he truly wanted to apologize for her ruined childhood even though he knew nothing about it, combined with the look in his eyes that was like warm brown velvet, broke away even more of Caroline's shell. Tears sprang to her eyes. Mortified, she squeezed them shut.

"It's okay there, Alice," Ken said in that voice of his that managed to be deep and low and soft all at the same time. He used his foot to set the swing into gentle motion again. "Come to think of it, I could always learn to yodel."

Caroline opened one eye and smiled despite the tear that had snuck out. She swiped at it.

"You could, too, you know." Ken was smiling at her again. Making no mention of her tears, a fact she appreciated.

Porter would have asked a probing question.

"We could learn together, maybe open the Rocky Mountain School of Yodeling."

Caroline giggled. "We could," she blurted even though she knew this was a dangerous game. Building a future, even a pretend one, was not something she could afford. But the look in his eyes and the smile on his face were as dizzying as the air at this altitude. "Alice and Ken's School of Rocky Mountain Yodeling." She laughed harder.

"That'd work," he said happily.

She felt his fingers move so that his hand was cupping the top of her arm, and now his face was inches from hers, near enough that breathing in filled her lungs with Ken's scent, piney and clean and strong. She swallowed.

Ken's smile was gone, his jaw working on something else now, but she saw the look in his eyes hadn't changed or lost any of its warmth. A girl could get lost forever in those eyes, she thought, and never bother to try to find her way out. He angled his face toward hers, and she knew those lips would carry the faint taste of sweet tea.

It was too much. Caroline moved away, sitting up straighter on the swing so it tipped forward and froze in place. "Sorry," she said, not looking at him. She could not allow this to build into any kind of friendship. "I probably need to get back. Thanks for the tea."

Ken swung his feet down to the porch boards. "Any time, Alice," he said easily. "Now you know the way here. The welcome mat's always out."

"Thanks," she murmured.

Rising, he steadied the swing as she rose. "Yodeling practice daily at four," he said.

"I'll remember that." She smiled but did not have the nerve to meet his eyes.

"Come on, I'll give you a quick tour before you go. You don't need those inside," he teased as Caroline fingered her shades and cap.

She followed him into a large, airy room, bright with diffused light from a skylight set high in the timbered ceiling.

Her attention was drawn at once to a large oil painting that hung above a stone mantel.

Caroline gasped. "That's an O'Keeffe."

Ken nodded.

"*Shell on Red*," she said, her eyes widening.

He arched a brow. "Most people know an O'Keeffe when they see one, but you're the first person who knew which painting it was."

Caroline was too preoccupied to acknowledge the compliment, or the question behind it. She walked closer to get a better look. "It's one of her early still lifes."

High-altitude sunlight played across the canvas, deepening the yellows, pinks, and deep reds, drawing out their sharp contrast to the ivory background. This was the way Georgia O'Keeffe had intended her work to be viewed, Caroline was certain. In natural light inside a home like this, not locked away in a museum.

The painting all but pulsed with sensual energy that radiated throughout the house. Caroline gave Ken a searching look. "How did you get it?"

"I got it at an auction. I fell in love with it and had someone bid on it. And here it is."

"She dreamed of the Faraway," Caroline said, studying the canvas.

"Yeah," Ken said softly. "She found it out this way, in the west Texas plains and northern New Mexico."

"She believed the ultimate reality of an object could be expressed in art," Caroline said. Memories of her studies came flooding back. "She studied Buddhism." She gestured to the painting. "You can see it here in the bold colors and strokes. She captured it, the spirit of the shell. O'Keeffe had a wilderness inside."

Ken nodded, watching Caroline.

Aware that she had revealed more of herself than she had intended, Caroline looked down, twirling her sunglasses in one hand, ignoring his gaze. "I've done a bit of reading about her," she said at last.

"Right," Ken said.

He wasn't buying it. But he was not the type to pry.

He walked to one of the floor-to-ceiling bookshelves that lined both sides of the fireplace, withdrew a large book about Georgia O'Keeffe, and carried it over. He stood, flipping through pages, leaning close so his shoulder and arm almost touched Caroline's. "Here's the part about her time out West," he said. "She grew up on a farm in Wisconsin. When she visited this part of the world, it changed her life." He closed the book and handed it to Caroline. "I'd like you to have this."

The act of generosity moved her. Standing close to him, she could well imagine he was a force to be reckoned with on the playing field.

At that moment he shifted his stance by perhaps a centimeter, no more, angling his body closer to hers, and this made it difficult for her to catch her breath. She felt less sure of her stance on the tightly woven Navajo rug at their feet. Summoning all her courage, she risked a glance at Ken's face and saw the soft expression in his brown eyes, the muscles working in his jaw.

The air between them turned into a vacuum so that she had a sudden urge to close the small space that separated them. "I want to paint like her," she blurted, because telling him something about herself was the next best thing to doing what she really wanted, to lose herself in his kiss.

Ken took his time before making any reply. "Well then, I think that's what you should do, Alice." His eyebrows lifted a notch as he watched her, and something about this small act opened a space inside her that had been cooped up inside the shell, and suddenly following her dreams seemed like the most logical thing to do with her life.

Caroline could only nod, marveling at the shift that was taking place inside her. She forced herself to take a step back, holding the book to her chest as though it could shield her from revealing any more of her own Faraway. "Thanks," she said, her voice not as strong as she had intended. "I really need to go."

Sensing her ambivalence, Ken moved away. "No problem." He cleared his throat. "We probably need to get you on the road."

She took a quick look around. The furnishings were of good quality, generously sized to hold Ken's large frame. There was a leather couch draped with quilts in bright Southwestern colors, several oversized easy chairs, each with its own ottoman, and a sleeping alcove set high above.

The living area opened onto a kitchen outfitted with stainless appliances. A large oak table lined with massive chairs sported bright blue checked place mats. In the center was a glass bowl filled with small river rocks.

Despite the fact that everything was supersized to fit Ken's frame, the overall effect was cozy. Not in a fussy way. Completely masculine.

"You have a wonderful home," Caroline said.

He nodded. "Thanks. I knew what I wanted when I came back here to live. I'd always had my eye on this piece of land. So I bought it and bunked with Gus while I had this place built." He looked around. "It's mostly everything I wanted."

Except that he lived here alone. The words popped into Caroline's mind so clearly she could have sworn he'd said them out loud. The look he gave her left no doubt as to what was missing from his life, she realized with a pang. She bit her lips against making any reply.

"Anyhow, that's the tour. Most of it anyway." He led the way through a side door from the kitchen to the garage.

Moments later Caroline found herself behind the wheel of a candy apple red Porsche 988. The engine purred, vibrating up through the leather bucket seats so it caressed her like a living thing.

Ken explained the gears and various gauges but it was hard to concentrate on anything but the fact that they were reclining together, side by side, their hands touching over the gearshift. He grinned ear to ear. "This car's a holdover from my time with the Chiefs. These days, I prefer the Jeep."

"I've never driven a car like this," Caroline admitted, worried.

"You'll be fine. This car practically drives itself."

She gave him a doubtful look.

He laughed and gave her shoulder a quick squeeze.

Her skin tingled inside her blouse where he touched her.

"You'll do just fine," he said. "A little road trip will do you good."

He slid from the passenger seat and smiled through the open window.

Caroline wasn't at all sure of the truth of this statement but now was no time to argue. She pulled her Cardinals cap low over her face, donned her shades, and shifted into gear. The car shot out of the garage like a cougar sprinting after prey.

"You got it," Ken called, giving a whoop of triumph.

Caroline had no chance to respond because she was busy shifting into second as the car leaped down the drive with all the grace of a living animal.

Ken Kincaid watched his Porsche inch down the driveway with Alice Stevens behind the wheel. He couldn't stop smiling. Once upon a time, that Porsche had been his prized possession. Now it only had value for him because it came in handy as a spare for Alice.

Buying it had been Suzie's idea, even though Ken did love driving it. Thinking of her now was odd, mostly because of how different this day was from those early days when he'd first begun dating Suzie. Odder still was the fact that Ken felt no pain at the thought of her.

He'd been unsure of himself with Suzie from day one, Ken realized now, despite the fact that he was a rising star at the time they first met.

Alice Stevens couldn't be more different. She was smart, not just educated but smart, and she had a very sweet way about her. She was beautiful, not in a flashy way, but beautiful from the inside out.

Alice Stevens would age well.

That realization hit Ken Kincaid head-on with the force of an opposing tackle. Even after he had been dating Suzie for a while, long enough to bring her home to meet Gus (she had sneezed constantly, allergic to cats), he didn't remember ever wondering what she'd be like at forty, fifty, or seventy.

Alice would keep painting what she saw with those sweet brown eyes, he just knew it in his heart.

Once Caroline maneuvered the Porsche out onto the county road, she relaxed enough to become aware of the breeze in her hair and the warmth of the sun on her skin. After a while, she felt bold enough to loosen her grip on the wheel and flip on the stereo. She was rewarded with Xydeco music from Mardi Gras. This was how it felt to be in Ken's world. Carefree. Young. Happy.

She didn't realize she was smiling until her jaw began to ache.

Nan came out and waved when she pulled in at the ranch. "That's quite a machine."

Caroline turned off the ignition and stood, her legs still vibrating from the engine. "I've never been in that kind of a car."

"That's quite a loaner for my old boat. I've never seen anyone drive it but Ken in the two years since he's been back. Not even his father."

Caroline couldn't hide a proud smile. Ken had granted a special privilege to her and her alone. Her heart did a small flip-flop as she cradled the art book close to her chest.

That night in bed, she paged through it cover to cover while outside a wind roared down off the mountain. From her window with the curtains pulled back, Caroline could see the treetops pitch and sway in a crazy dance. She heard a soft rumble from low inside the house as the boiler kicked on, and later, the eerie yip-yipping of coyotes.

Pippin whined.

Caroline hushed the dog and burrowed deep under the covers. Nan was right about October here in the Rockies.

The change had begun.

CHAPTER

14

MODESTO, CALIFORNIA

Tom Fielding took a sip of his double latte. Still hot even after the fifteen-minute drive from Starbucks. The office was dead quiet, which was also good. In stark contrast to the morning routine inside the Fielding ranch house, where Lisa would be putting on makeup and giving the twins breakfast before the sitter arrived.

Lisa was pissed when Tom told her he needed to head in early for a conference call with a client on the East Coast.

He fingered the sticky note with Caroline's cell phone number. He had about twenty minutes before the offices of ActiveWear Modesto came alive for the day.

Tom reached for the phone, ready to call Caroline twice, and both times he changed his mind. He pulled up his deleted mail files and scowled.

There it was, Caroline's message to him.

Hey handsome. Just checking in. Hope to get out of Dodge, maybe see some leaves turn. Road trip!!

What was the name of that place in the Rockies?
Chat soon ☺ C.

It wasn't right. Tom Fielding drummed his fingers on
the desk. He could call her. They had always kept each
other's cell phone numbers, just in case. Calling, they
knew, would cross a line. Lately, they had inched closer
to that line.

Lisa regularly checked Tom's cell phone records as
part of her job as bookkeeper in the family firm. She
also went through his car and desk on a regular basis,
searching for a spare cell phone from Costco with pay-
as-you-go minutes. She assumed he was not aware of
her snooping, and Tom let it go at that.

No, he didn't dare place a call to Caroline's cell phone.
If Lisa was hip to checking cell phone records, it was a
sure bet that Porter Moross was checking Caroline's call
records and then some.

Moross was a freak. They'd all seen it the very first
night Caroline brought him to a kegger up on the roof
of Mitchell Hall. Tom Fielding had the hots for Caroline
Hughes back then. Everyone knew it and just assumed
they'd wind up together. But Caroline was really shy, so
Tom decided to play it slow out of respect for her. He
had regretted it ever since. They all mocked the medical
resident she'd brought with her that night looking like a
circus sideshow. As Moross stalked his skinny ass out of
the party that night, Tom caught a glimpse of something
else that was much worse: a flash in Moross's intense
blue eyes of pure rage.

"Just let him go," Tom said, reaching for Caroline's
hand as she hurried past.

"You don't understand, he's just really shy," she'd

said, brushing Tom's hand off so she could catch Porter at the elevators.

And that, as Tom's roommate Kent used to say, was the situation in microcosm.

Thinking back on it even now made Tom Fielding shake his head. He stared at Caroline's e-mail. The more he thought about it, the more certain he was that she didn't write that e-mail. Porter Moross had written it. Which meant things in the Moross household had gone from bad to worse.

Tom drummed his fingers harder, faster. Considering things. Caroline wasn't happy and hadn't been for a long time. Hell, who could be with an asshole like that?

What if she'd finally left him? Where would she go? She had a mother and stepfather, once upon a time. They had shown up at commencement so drunk the old man was thrown out for heckling. Poor Caroline. She wouldn't have gone there.

Tom scrolled opened his "Sent Mail" folder and reviewed his reply:

> Storm Pass. Great little town near Durango. Denver has more flights tho and drive up is awesome. Good hiking but weather is iffy now. I want a pic of you soaking in a hot spring . . . Yummy! :-). Gotta run, duty beckons.

Tom Fielding groaned aloud. Because if what he suspected was true, he had just steered Moross in exactly the right direction.

"What's wrong?" Tom's wife appeared in the doorway.

Tom nearly jumped out of his seat. How come his wife

didn't make noise like normal people when she walked down a hall? "I didn't hear you come in."

She shrugged, pissed off, the way he knew she would be. "I just got here. What's up?"

"Ah, it's nothing, no big deal." He fingered the mouse, frowning, and studied his computer screen. "I can straighten it out with an e-mail."

"Hey C," he wrote. "Are u ok? Call me on my cell. Urgent." Lisa was still watching from the doorway but Tom didn't care. He typed in his cell phone number, even though Caroline already had it. He requested notification of when the message was opened by the addressee, and hit send. That should call Moross's bluff.

Asshole.

Tom checked his watch. He'd give it a day or two, just to be sure, even though Caroline usually wrote back on the same day. And then he'd figure out what to do next.

WASHINGTON, D.C.

Everything changed for Porter Moross after the discovery of his wife's e-mail correspondence with Tom Fielding. His emotions made the transition from panic at being abandoned by his wife, into something else. Something far less stable. Far more dangerous.

Porter tried to be patient, awaiting confirmation of her whereabouts from Beltway Security Investigations and their freelance agent in Colorado.

Deep inside him a tectonic shift was taking place, as he shed the mantle of pleasant civility he had adopted long ago. In its place was something else, emotion that ran deeper and truer to Porter's core. Anger, the kind that simmered at a constant steady burn, ready to erupt on a moment's notice, all the while roiling and building into something that had the heat and predictability of molten lava.

The fact was, Porter Moross had developed the propensity at a young age for rage that could scorch everything in its path, leaving behind a landscape of ruin.

Which was fine with him. He had taught himself early on that anger was preferable to the helpless despair of hurt.

STORM PASS, COLORADO

The next day brought cooler air from Canada down across the continental spine that was the Rocky Mountains. Nights turned cold, and the tall grass in the pasture crunched underfoot when Caroline went for her morning swim.

Nan Birmingham observed a change in her young employee. Alice's face had opened up some and the tight lines around her mouth had relaxed. Once, Nan overheard Alice humming. Nan was grateful the young woman was finding relief from her troubles, which led her to make a request of Alice she wouldn't have dreamed of making even yesterday. She asked Alice to take her to Storm Pass for the town's annual Heritage Day Festival.

She was surprised and pleased when Alice agreed.

Caroline had vowed to avoid town at all cost but she was feeling bolder, buoyed by her attraction to Ken, and she knew Nan would be unable to attend without her. Caroline owed a lot to her new employer.

Despite the chill the day was brilliant and bright. They piled lawn chairs, lemonade, and sandwiches in the tiny backseat of the Porsche and drove down after breakfast.

A white bedsheet was draped high across two telephone poles on Main Street, proclaiming the town's motto in hand-painted letters: "Storm Pass, A Great Place to Rest Yer . . . !"

Caroline parked in the grassy lot next to Kincaid's Garage. The bright red car attracted some looks, and she wondered uneasily if coming here had been wise. She unloaded quickly and they headed for the sidewalk in front of the service station door, open wide to the room inside that served the dual purpose of office and den for the proprietor.

Gus Kincaid ambled out to greet them, his steps slow and labored.

Caroline glimpsed a walker inside, which she noticed he was not using. It was easy to imagine Gus had been a lady-killer in his day.

"Mornin', ladies," he said, tipping his baseball cap.

"Mornin', Gus," Nan said.

Gus's big cat leaped up to the counter and hissed.

This set off a frenzy of barking from Pippin and Scout, who strained at their leashes.

"Where are your manners, Midnight?" Gus said in a voice that was gruff and soothing at the same time.

The cat sank down on her haunches and glared.

Gus reached inside a jar, pulled out a large biscuit, and broke it in two before bending slowly to give each dog a half. He took a long time to straighten up.

"How are you feeling?" Nan asked.

"Comin' along," he replied.

"And where's your son today?"

It was as much of a direct question as anyone in Storm Pass ever asked. Caroline shifted the lawn chairs against one hip and waited to hear the answer.

"He's around. Just back from the pass." Gus motioned north with his chin. "Had a Denver group overnight for some angling."

"It's late days for trout fishing," Nan remarked.

"Just about the end of the season," Gus agreed. "Good day for a parade, though. Let me give you a hand with those chairs."

"No need," Caroline protested, while Nan waved him off with the cane she used in town.

Gus looked none too steady on his feet.

Not wanting to cause him any embarrassment, Caroline hurried to the curb to prop open the lawn chairs, already regretting her decision to come. The narrow main street was packed with locals, and she knew there were bound to be out-of-towners as well. All it would take was one person, one chance overheard remark, for someone to put the pieces together. But it was too late now.

A clash of cymbals and the beating of a drum signaled the start of the parade.

First came the children and pets, mostly dogs, a good number of cats, a monkey, and a crateful of rabbits. Next were historic cars, or just really old cars, or even any car at all. Bikers followed, revving their engines and setting the dogs into a frenzy. Next came the marching band from Storm Pass's single tiny school. And finally people on foot passing out fliers on a variety of subjects, everything from La Leche League (pro), to nuclear weapons (anti), to rBGH-enhanced dairy milk (definitely anti).

"There you have it," Nan said when the last peaceable demonstrator had passed. "Storm Pass on parade."

Caroline was grateful it was over. She folded the chairs, gathered their belongings, and turned to go.

A Harley-Davidson revved nearby and backfired, startling her so she lost her hold on the lawn chairs and they clattered to the ground, sending the dogs straining at the ends of their leashes.

She tried to rescue the chairs but got tangled up, losing her hat and sunglasses in the process. Leaving her exposed. She bent over, making a mad grab for them.

And sensed the presence of a large man at her side, close enough to gain a whiff of his scent that was woodsy and clean like the pine trees lining the town.

There was no mistaking that scent.

Ken Kincaid's arm brushed hers as he reached down and scooped everything up in one motion. "I've got you covered," he said, straightening up.

Caroline stood. In the afternoon sun, he looked like the golden boy he was. Colorado's gift to the NFL. "Hi."

He reached out and gave her shoulder a squeeze. "How are you today, Alice?"

"Okay." Lie. If she had said she was doing great, it would have been closer to the truth. But that would only move things further along in a direction she could not afford to go.

Her response did nothing to dim the wattage of the smile Ken was shining her way. "Just okay? What can we do to change that to great?"

He leaned in close, and the nearness of him melted something inside her.

Ken Kincaid was like a big, happy puppy. Disarming and sweet, he would win her heart and make her forget she could never give him a proper home. Caroline looked away.

"How about an ice cream soda? We got a real old-fashioned soda fountain here, just across the street."

The offer would have been corny coming from anyone but him, anywhere but here. As it was, her insides swelled with happiness and turned as light as a sunbeam. She felt like she was inside a movie set about a happy life in a small town.

Ken was smiling down at her while she tried to figure out how to turn him down without hurting his feelings, which seemed, thankfully, pretty hard to do, and while they were standing this way the sound of nearby laughter made Caroline freeze.

A group of teens had stopped to watch. One of the boys cleared his throat. "Hi, Ken."

Ken turned and waved. "Hey, guys. You came out to watch the parade?"

There was a round of nodding heads and hellos.

"It was a good one. I'll see you all at practice." He turned back to Caroline. "I coach the high school team."

There were people like this, Caroline thought, people whose lives were peaceful and ordinary and what Porter would call boring.

Ken handed over her sunglasses and hat. "Personally, I think you look better without these."

"Thanks." Caroline couldn't remember what it was like to be on the receiving end of attention from a man.

She mumbled something about taking a rain check, aware the kids were still watching. They were interested in Ken, not her. But that didn't change the fact that a small crowd had gathered with her at its center. She was standing next to a celebrity, the hometown hero who had made it big playing safety for the Kansas City Chiefs.

Caroline had broken her first rule of survival, to draw as little attention to herself as possible. She jammed the hat and sunglasses back into place with hands that shook.

She was too jittery to notice the man who had come to a standstill across the street. He stood close to a family eating ice cream cones in the shade of a pin oak. In his hand, at waist height, was a small digital camera aimed directly at Caroline.

She drove back to the ranch a short while later, her mind whirling with images of her day in town.

Little did she know, those same images were at this very moment being broken down into a million tiny pieces of data before hurtling through cables for reassembly two thousand miles away.

*B*ingo.

Porter stared at the letters on the tiny display screen of his cell phone. He had programmed his computer to place a call automatically if it received an urgent message from Beltway Security Investigations.

And it had.

The implications made his blood dam up and stop flowing. He traced a finger across the screen of his cell phone as a tingle of excitement tripped up his spine, raising the tiny hairs along its length.

The chase had begun.

He pushed his chair back from the table, his takeout lunch of steamed vegetables and chicken forgotten, and raced down the stairs. He activated the keypad and the lock clicked open. His office was silent on a Sunday, save for the ticking of a mahogany grandfather clock and the hum of his computer, which he always kept on.

He scratched at the bumps that were beginning to rise on his face. An excess of emotion already.

The mailbox contained a single message, flagged in red, from Beltway.

Every nerve ending in Porter's body froze as he double-clicked.

What he saw next sickened him.

"Oh, Caroline," he whispered. "Oh, Caroline, no."

A digital photograph filled the screen, larger than he could bear. Caroline with short hair, bleached a freakish shade of yellow, standing someplace in the mountains, a place Porter had never been. Storm Pass. A place she had never been, as far as he knew. This fact alone sent pain like a dagger working its way deep into his heart. His sense of injury increased the longer he studied the photograph. She looked different. Her face was rounder somehow, the cheeks fuller beneath a ridiculous base-ball cap and sunglasses that were too big. There was no mistaking the curve of her lips, or the roundness of her hips inside a tight pair of jeans. She had deliberately altered her appearance.

Porter tapped his fingers on the desk, considering this, as the implication settled over him like a heavy weight. She had done this to herself to hide from just one person, him. The only person in the world who would give his life for her.

Tears stung Porter's eyes.

What he saw next stopped Porter's tears in their tracks, however. As he scrolled down, his grief turned to rage.

The next image showed Caroline laughing up into the face of a strange man. Her mouth open, her lips full. Inviting. Sensual.

A flame of hot jealousy tore through Porter, searing his loins and curdling the food in his stomach.

Whore.

He stared at the photo, barely aware of the switch it tripped inside his brain, turning his sorrow to rage. The wetness of her lips. The way she leaned in close to the man. The contours of her breasts, easy to make out, in a tight jersey knit shirt. But it was the expression on her face that fueled Porter's rage. She was laughing. Laughing out loud so the sound echoed here in his office, cold and still as a funeral parlor.

He had known it would come to this.

The tiny measure of triumph he felt disappeared as he studied the man beside Caroline. Large body, athletic build. Broad jaw with wide lips and big white teeth. Sunlight played on rich, dark hair. The sort of man who would draw Caroline to him like a moth to a porch light. The man leaned over Caroline, dwarfing her body with his. His hand rested on her arm in a gesture of proprietorship. His mouth hung open, hungry, so Porter could almost hear his booming laugh.

First step in the classic mating dance.

Whore!

Jealousy snaked through Porter, spreading heat in his loins, turning him hard. He felt himself stiffen and grow until the fabric of his trousers strained in his lap. He stared at the screen, studying the look on Caroline's face. Her mouth open, her lips shining, wet.

Porter's fingers slid from the mouse. He unzipped his trousers, his breath coming like a ragged bellows as the heat inside mounted. Keeping his gaze on the screen, his fingers warmed to their task with each stroke.

He climaxed quickly.

Slumping back in his chair he waited for his breathing to steady. He felt sick, disgusted. He grabbed a handful of tissues from the box on his desk, one of several placed strategically around the office, and mopped at his trousers and skin.

On the screen, Caroline continued to laugh in silent mockery.

Cold now and spent, Porter shuddered as he scrolled through the remainder of the e-mail.

He found another photo of his wife, her mouth now open in a round O, reaching to take a pair of sunglasses and bright red baseball cap from the man. Her disguise was in place in the next, but the heart shape of the chin, the delicate lips and teeth were unmistakable.

Porter ran a finger along the lines of her jaw. A wave of grief washed over him for the life he'd hoped for, planned for. Now it was lost forever.

That realization filled him with mourning as he contemplated the garish woman that had taken his wife's place. The clownish hair, the hat, the sunglasses, all part of a twisted lie told for his benefit. So that he, Porter, would never find her. The knowledge hollowed him with grief. He would have given his life for her. His fingers slid slowly off the screen, leaving tracks of moisture like tears.

He scrolled down. In the next photo Caroline was seated in a lawn chair next to an old woman. Nan Birmingham, her new employer, according to the accompanying memo.

A heavy sigh escaped him now. He had dreaded this since she left, vanishing like a ghost into the shimmering heat just eight days ago, taking with her everything that mattered, everything that gave his life meaning. That day had changed everything. Now they were deep into autumn, the season of change that led to death.

Porter typed a brief message to Beltway Security authorizing preparation of a full dossier.

When the message was sent, he went back and reread

the memo accompanying the photos. Caroline was using the name Alice Stevens. She lived with Nan Birmingham on a ranch several miles outside the town called Storm Pass. The laughing man in the photo was Ken Kincaid, former safety for the Kansas City Chiefs. The fact pricked at something in Porter's memory. He remembered reading about the guy in the paper a few years back. His career had been cut short by an injury. His wife left him for one of his teammates. Porter shrugged. Son of a bitch got what he deserved.

Porter closed the file, switched off the computer, and sat in the still office.

He had no choice now. This was all her doing. "Damn it, Caroline," he said, his voice strange and loud in the empty room. Tears sprang to his eyes, and he dug at them with the backs of his knuckles. Inside his mouth his teeth began to work, shredding the inside of his cheeks until he tasted blood.

"Why, Caroline?" he whispered. "Why?"

But he knew the answer. She had been destined for this. He had known it from the day they'd met. Known it and ignored it, allowing himself to be lulled, drawn in by her sensual youth, fooled by her keen intellect into thinking she could heal the wounds of her childhood and become the soul mate he had yearned for. He had tried and tried to make her see the dark corruption that was seeded inside her, poised and waiting to unfurl when it would render a permanent shadow on her mind like a poisonous cloud.

But it was no use. His beloved bride had closed her mind against him. She, who had married a man who would trade his soul to save her, a man who had devoted his entire life to the intricacies of the human mind.

The one man in ten million, perhaps, who could understand her flaws and even, perhaps, one day cure them. Caroline's resistance to Porter and his love was ironic, a tragedy in the classic Greek tradition.

His gaze fell on the couch where so many patients had lain, spewing the intimate details of their private pain. And now he, Dr. Porter Moross, was experiencing a pain equal to the one he had suffered once long ago. It was the inevitable conclusion of their life together, his and Caroline's, sealed by fate when she walked away.

The way his mother had.

He went to the couch and laid himself down, resting his head on the cushion where his patients rested theirs.

There and then he surrendered to his pain, fresh and sharp as the first night without his mommy all those years ago. Pulling his knees to his chest, he wrapped his arms around them in an effort to stop the shivering that wracked his body. But he was not able to stop the sobs that rose up inside him. He was not crying for himself, for the pain he had endured and would continue to endure. He was crying tears of sorrow for her.

For Caroline. For the price she would pay for ruining Porter's life, for the steps he would have to take to rectify her mistake.

CHAPTER
16

Nan took a sip of coffee. "Weather's turning."

The morning after the parade was bright and clear in Storm Pass. But Nan was right. Something had changed. The angle of the sun had shifted, the air had a sharp scent.

More than that, something had changed inside Caroline. Her sense of safety was fading. She was jittery after her careless mistake in town yesterday. She tried to lose herself in work, installing storm windows under Nan's direction. The physical activity helped lessen Caroline's anxiety.

They were about to tackle Caroline's bedroom at the back of the house when the sound of an approaching car set her nerves on edge once more.

Caroline froze, unable to hide a sharp intake of breath.

A knock on the door sent the dogs into a snarling fit.

"I'll get it." Nan said. "I'm sure it's Federico or one of his men with news from the stables."

Caroline stayed where she was, rooted to the spot, dismayed at the feelings that were flooding through her. Fear. Anxiety. The tapes were playing once more in her mind, telling her she would never be safe. And all because she had been stupid enough to spend the day in town yesterday, and clumsy enough to lose her dark glasses and hat on Main Street.

"Stupid, stupid, stupid," she whispered miserably. She did a quick inventory of her belongings and cash reserve, which had dwindled on the trip out here and more after she'd bought some new clothes, but still amounted to several thousand dollars. Three thousand, one hundred forty, to be precise. She could leave on five minutes' notice if she had to.

The dogs stopped barking, and she heard Nan's voice, calm and welcoming.

Next came the rumble, low and deep, of a familiar male voice.

Ken Kincaid.

Then came footsteps on the front stairs, heavy but fast. She had just enough time to check her reflection in the mirror that hung over the Jenny Lind bureau before he appeared in the doorway.

She whirled around to face him.

"Hey, Alice." His voice was low and sweet, the way she remembered. He wore Levi's, hiking shoes, and a green plaid shirt. "Relief crew's here."

"Hey." Caroline jammed her hands into the pockets of her jeans, suddenly conscious of her messy hair and the smudge of dirt she hoped she'd wiped clean from her cheek.

He gave the room a swift glance, taking in the bed and its pretty chenille spread. "I didn't mean to barge in. Nan said there's a window up here giving you trouble."

That was not true.

Caroline looked down at the storm window she was balancing against one knee.

"Let me get that." He took the storm window from her and crossed the room to throw open the back window. The window slid smoothly into place. He repeated the process on the remaining windows before turning to her with a look of satisfaction on his face. "That should do it," he said, leaning over to smooth a wrinkle his knee had left on the spread.

"Thanks," Caroline said.

"No problem. If it happens again, all you need is some silicone oil. Or, better yet, call me." He stood, his posture easy and relaxed, and grinned.

Caroline found it impossible not to smile back.

"You've got a great view of the peak," he observed.

She nodded.

"It's a good sight to see when you wake up in the morning."

Caroline thought of how cozy it was to lie here, watching the peak come into view by moonlight. That first night her worries had kept her up, her stomach in knots, her heart pounding at every sound. She woke each morning to find a bit more of her tension had drained away during the night. "It's beautiful by moonlight, too." She regretted the words as soon as she spoke them. Her basic rule was to reveal nothing about herself. But Ken Kincaid made her forget that rule. He was so easy to talk to, so laid-back, that she just couldn't help herself.

He skipped the opportunity to make an obvious pass at her, a fact for which she was grateful. "We'll make a mountain girl out of you yet. You'll have to change your name to Elly May," he teased.

Caroline's eyes widened in alarm. Had he guessed Alice was a made-up name? "I don't feel like an Elly May," she said cautiously.

He laughed. "Give it a winter up here and we'll be calling you Elly May. 'A rose by any other name would still smell as sweet,' you know." He continued to check out the view, looking up at Ute Peak. "Stick around for all four seasons and you'll know how special this place is."

She could tell by the look on his face he meant it. "I bet you missed the mountains when you were away."

"Pretty much. I guess it's in my blood."

Her mind jumped. She wondered if there was a place that would ever be inside her blood but she didn't know the answer to that. All she knew was that her time in Storm Pass had given her a taste of freedom from the prison Porter had built with her help. That was over now. But she knew the prison cell remained, ready and waiting for her return. Caroline became aware of Ken's eyes on her. Curious. Thoughtful. Judging? The possibility unnerved her. She cleared her throat, shifting her weight as her glance drifted involuntarily to her bed. "Well, thanks for helping out." Coloring, she looked away.

He gave a quick nod but stayed put. "Any time, Alice."

They heard footsteps on the stairs and Nan appeared in the doorway.

Not a moment too soon, Caroline thought.

Nan saw the windows and gave an approving nod. "Good work. They're up. How's Gus?" She directed this last at Ken.

"He's doing okay, Nan, thanks for asking."

"Glad to hear it. Have you come to join us for lunch?"

He cleared his throat. "Actually, I came by to see if I could take Alice fishing. If she's not too busy, that is."

They both looked at Caroline.

"That's a fine idea," Nan said quickly. "We're about done here for today."

Caroline shifted her weight. The prospect of an afternoon with Ken made something flutter inside her like a butterfly preparing for flight. And yet it was a risk she could not, dared not take. Looking down, she traced a pattern in the wool rug at their feet, studying it as though a good excuse might be written there.

Nan spoke up. "Alice needs to get to know the area before winter sets in. My niece is pestering me again to fly down to Florida for a visit. I might just do it. Me and Scout." She looked down at the little dog waiting at her feet. "Won't be gone long. Alice could keep an eye on the place."

Caroline nodded. She couldn't hold back a twinge of excitement at the thought of having this big, beautiful place all to herself for a week with time on her own to paint or hike or read or do anything she wanted.

"That's a great idea," Ken said. "I'd just be a phone call away."

Caroline couldn't hold back a smile, even though in her heart she knew it was best for all of them if she kept her distance from Ken. Starting now.

But Nan's next words silenced the protest Caroline planned to make about the fishing trip. "Besides, I could use an afternoon on my own. And I wouldn't turn down fresh trout."

"You've got a deal, Mrs. Birmingham," Ken said. "We'll bring you back plenty of fish. That's a guarantee."

Ignoring the look of hesitation on Caroline's face, Nan smiled. "Good. It's settled. I'll pack a lunch."

Ken waved her off. "No need. I've got us covered." He looked at Caroline and winked. "I was betting you'd say yes."

Caroline was at a loss for words. The fluttery feeling in her chest got bigger at the prospect of spending time with him, or maybe it was due to the warning bell clanging in her head. Not to mention she was suddenly aware of how sweaty she was from wrestling all morning with the storm windows. "I, ah, am not much of a fisher," she said finally.

Nan chuckled. "Don't you worry about that, Alice. You're headed out with the highest rated wilderness guide in the state of Colorado. Bring me back some trout and have fun." She led the way downstairs.

Caroline swallowed. Nan made it sound as though they were going on a date. But one look at Ken's face, lit from inside with a big, relaxed smile, was enough to push Caroline's misgivings aside at least for the moment. "Well," she said slowly, "I suppose I'm ready for my fishing lesson."

Ken nodded happily. "I guess you are, Alice. Come on, I'll show you the prettiest place in the world."

Porter Moross woke up shivering. His office was eerie, unfamiliar viewed from this angle, where he lay on the therapy couch. Too quiet at this hour, late on a Sunday afternoon. His gaze drifted and he saw this as his patients did. Except the wing chair was empty. There was no mommy figure to provide comfort.

His heart ached with the old, childhood ache and he rose stiffly, feeling hung over, and walked to the window. The street outside was bleak, deserted at this hour. His breath left a small circle of fog on the pane.

A change had come. Autumn, harbinger of the season of death.

Porter checked his watch. Barely four. He had many things to attend to.

He took one last look around the office, his heart heavy with sadness. This place had been his and his alone. This was where he had spent his days, confident in the one aspect of his life where he excelled. Dr. Porter Moross, nationally renowned psychoanalyst. People sought him out for his expertise. They had read his quotes in the *New York Times* or the *Washington Post*, or simply heard him mentioned by word of mouth. It astounded

Porter how little his patients actually knew about him, about what he did and what sort of results they could expect, when they came to him. His patients were accustomed to seeking out and demanding the best. They led lives of privilege and power. Here, they were reduced to children, clamoring for Porter's attention.

And now it was over. This space, like the home above, had been profaned.

He went upstairs to shower and change, donning clothes that were identical to the ones he'd slept in. Black mock turtleneck, black sport jacket over black jeans, and black loafers. He brewed coffee, not bothering to wipe up the loose grounds that spilled on the granite countertop. Cleanliness didn't matter any longer. The place already had an abandoned feel, like a college dorm the day after final exams.

He returned to his office and settled in his desk chair, not allowing himself to mourn the fact that it would be for the last time. He set about his tasks with the precision that had placed him at the top of his graduating class.

He scanned his BlackBerry until he found the contact information for a fellow psychoanalyst he'd met last year at an annual Freud conference in Miami, a man who practiced in the elite suburb of Bethesda, Maryland. Porter dialed the after-hours emergency number that was printed on the card.

The man answered on the first ring, his tone cordial and measured. He remembered Porter and said the usual pleasantries, asking about Porter's family and whether he was headed to Miami for their annual conference next week. All the while trying not to show he was taken aback when Porter revealed the nature of his call.

"Aaahh, yes," he said, "I can take on new patients. Shall we set up a meeting to review?"

What he meant was he wanted to know why Porter was clearing his roster. Porter explained there wasn't time due to a family emergency.

The man offered regret for Porter's family emergency.

Behind the expression of sympathy was a question, and it was one Porter chose to ignore. "I will provide my patients with referrals to you at once."

The referrals were priceless, and they both knew it.

In the end, the man agreed to treat Porter's patients, but not before he made one more attempt to pry into Porter's business. "Dr. Moross?" His voice transformed from colleague to caregiver, oozing with professional concern. "Is everything okay? I mean, if there is anything you'd like to discuss, I could even see you this afternoon."

It was the line used for reeling people back from the ledge. Porter was the superior psychotherapist of the two and they both knew it, a fact he was tempted to point out. He closed his eyes instead, against the pain of countless tiny pinpricks digging at the insides of his lids. Porter's skin condition worsened at times of stress. "I've got things under control. Thank you for asking."

There was a pause. "I see."

Which meant, of course, that he did not see. But Porter had, after all, just handed him a portfolio that young residents would bid ten years' salary to get. Porter pushed his glasses aside and knuckled his eyes, which only intensified the ache.

"I do appreciate your confidence in me," the man said. "Please call if I can ever return the favor in any way."

His voice held a question.

Porter pictured him now, stocky and balding, with his ordinary face. "Will do." As though they both didn't know they would never speak again.

Porter hung up and drew a line through the first item on his to-do list. He looked at the framed photo of Caroline on his desk. Happy, laughing, young. His grip tightened until the tip of the pencil snapped, shattering the surface of his desk with jagged lead shards.

He called patients while his long, thin fingers raced across the keyboard, shifting funds in his accounts, canceling his newspaper subscription, and checking e-mail once more, both his and Caroline's.

He found the latest message from Tom Fielding, flagged urgent. Reading it made him double check the postage on the envelope containing Fielding's e-mail correspondence with Porter's wife. That asshole. Porter hit delete.

Finally, he signed on to MapQuest and ordered driving directions from Washington, D.C., to Storm Pass, Colorado.

STORM PASS, COLORADO

Ken drove through town and then out past his house before heading north up into the state wilderness area. The road climbed higher in a series of switchbacks carved against the side of the mountain.

Caroline's ears popped with each hairpin turn. She was grateful for Ken's skilled driving, because the higher they climbed, the smaller the guardrail looked. The landscape changed as the air thinned, turning cooler. Once, they rounded a turn and saw what looked to be a dozen white tails bobbing as a herd of elk bolted into the brush.

They stopped at a scenic overlook. A series of neighboring peaks rippled up from the earth's mantle. Ken explained the Rockies had been formed by a violent collision of tectonic plates during the last Ice Age.

Caroline traded her fleece jacket for the down parka Ken offered. They had gained two thousand feet in elevation and the air was fifteen degrees cooler here. He handed her a wool stocking cap, watching with interest as she pulled off her baseball cap and shook out her hair. "It's a day for rare sightings. First a herd of wild elk and now Alice Stevens without her St. Louis Cardinals cap," he teased.

Caroline ran a hand through her hair. The breeze felt good on her scalp, like everything else about this day so far.

They drove higher to the end of the county road. A rustic wooden sign warned they were leaving the area of regular patrol by Colorado authorities, and entering a private wilderness area. All visitors were urged to sign in on a yellowing loose-leaf pad that sat beneath a battered plastic cover inside a wooden shelter. Caroline shivered, mindful of local pueblo lands that were strictly off-limits to day-trippers.

She cast a sideways glance at Ken as he shifted the Jeep's engine into overdrive and turned onto a bumpy dirt track. "Is it okay for us to be here?"

Ken nodded, steering onto a jutted track through a sparse forest of spindly pines, the only trees that grew at this altitude. "It's mine," he said with a shy smile. He shrugged. "It feels silly saying that about this." He motioned with one hand at the grandeur surrounding them. "The indigenous people who lived here first don't believe you can own a place, and I agree. But, according to the state of Colorado, everything from the county road on out belongs to me."

It took a moment for his meaning to sink in. "It's hard to believe this all belongs to one person."

"All that time on the playing field in Kansas City paid off, I guess," he said with a rueful smile. "I always loved it here. And now at least it will never be developed."

"Why don't you live up here?"

"Well, for one thing I don't think the neighbors would like it." He grinned, pointing up to where two large hawks wheeled high above. "Plus, I like my creature comforts, running water and electricity. The place in town is fine. I come up here and stay for a few days whenever I need some one-on-one time with God."

She had never heard a man speak this way, and it was touching. Ken was a success by any measure, strong and in control. And yet he spoke plainly of God. Something, she realized, Porter Moross with his post-doctorate education would never humble himself to do.

She was unsure what to say, and settled on thanking him for bringing her.

"My pleasure," he said with another smile. "It's the best place I know to come and clear the cobwebs from my head. I've been coming up here to do that since I was a kid. The door's always open, Alice. If you ever want to come here and rest your mind, the place is yours for as long as you want."

Because there were a lot of things in her mind that needed sorting out. He didn't say so, but Caroline sensed that was what he was thinking.

"You might even catch a fish or two while you're at it," he teased.

They drove past other grass tracks, little used by the look of them, and finally turned down one that would have been easy to miss except for a fallen log that was piled with rocks in the shape of a pyramid. This was a cairn, Ken explained, used by hikers to mark a trail-head.

The trees thinned out even more, and Caroline sensed they were about to enter an open space.

The Jeep bounced out onto a mesa.

Facing them was a vista unlike anything she had ever imagined. Straight ahead was a lake whose crystalline waters mirrored the sky above. Tiny waves lapped at a muddy shore, littered with boulders taller than Ken. Mounds of tall grass dipped and swayed in the breeze that was constant at this altitude. She traced a trickling sound to a granite cliff beyond the far shore, where a steady flow of rocks bounced onto a valley floor. She half expected to see a woolly mammoth lumber into view. The place was positively primeval.

She blinked, trying to take it all in. She had only seen views like this on calendars or travel posters. She let out a long, low breath. "Wow."

Ken spoke in a hushed voice. "It's my favorite place in this world."

The setting demanded reverence. Caroline pulled her glasses off and tried to take it all in.

Ken got out and came around to the passenger side. "Come on, I'll give you the tour."

She stepped out into another world. The earth beneath her feet felt supercharged, practically bouncing under her weight with energy stored up from the birth of the mountain that, Ken explained, had been a relatively recent event in the earth's history. The air was crisp, flavored with the scent of pine needles from the trees that seemed to start here and stretch into eternity. The slamming of the car door was out of place here, leaving Caroline to wonder how many animals were startled, watching their movements from hidden lairs. She inched the zipper high on her down parka and thrust her hands in the pockets, grateful for the wool mittens stashed inside.

After a few steps she lost her breath as the landscape tilted dizzily.

Ken placed a steadying arm around her waist. "Easy, Alice. Take a few deep breaths, slow and steady."

For one giddy moment his face swam out of focus. Up close, he was more handsome than he was from several feet away. She allowed herself to lean on him, marveling at the feel of his arm and shoulder that were so formidable compared with Porter. She was helpless to do anything else until the dizzy spell passed. But the fluttery feeling inside her remained.

"It's the altitude," Ken explained, keeping his arm tight around her middle. "Just take it slow. Take deep breaths in through your nose, out through your mouth."

Caroline did as she was told. She wasn't in any position to argue, not with her heart hammering like it was trying to jump right out from inside her chest.

"Some people feel it more than others. It has nothing to do with physical fitness. Just take it easy till you get acclimated. I've got plenty of bottled water inside. That'll help."

Caroline nodded, yielding to the fact that her skull felt like it might bounce off her shoulders. She was glad for the warmth of Ken's hand around hers as she took a few steps, very aware that she was intruding on a vast wilderness that could easily swallow her up without a trace.

Ken steered her to a small cabin tucked just inside the tree line.

The place was tidy, built of hardwood logs with a small porch in front and a single great room inside. A pair of skylights in the ceiling provided natural light. Several stands of bunk beds sported striped wool blankets in a sleeping alcove. Brightly colored Navajo rugs covered the broad oak plank floor. A large black iron stove stood in the center of the room with a pipe leading up to the ceiling. A corner of the room served as a spotless kitchenette, from which Ken now produced two bottles of spring water.

"Cheers," he said, clinking his bottle against Caroline's. "Here's to the patron saint of trout."

Caroline giggled, and couldn't help but notice the way his gaze lingered on her face when she smiled. She took a long swig and looked around. The room was completely masculine and cozy at the same time.

"Have a seat while I get our gear," Ken said.

She settled onto a Scandinavian-style settee with leather cushions. It had a comfortable feel, and a small ottoman that had seen its share of booted feet.

"I don't get many female visitors up here," Ken said, rummaging through a large closet that had been built into a corner of the room. He came out with a pair of polypropylene waders, long johns, and an oiled jacket. "These should fit," he said, sizing her up.

They looked to be a perfect fit, and Caroline wondered who had worn them originally, his ex-wife or a girlfriend?

Ken must have read her mind. "Most of my clients are men, but every now and then I get some women. Last summer, I hosted an all-female editorial board," he said, naming a popular women's lifestyle magazine.

The explanation cheered Caroline more than she wanted to admit, a fact that made her blush. "Did they have a good time?"

Ken whooped. "Did they ever! They're already booked for next year. Got myself a lifetime subscription to the magazine, too. Gus likes the recipes."

Caroline giggled again, holding the waders at arm's length. "Where is the, ummm . . ."

"Brace yourself, Alice," he said with a twinkle in his eye. "This is where the 'roughing it' part comes in."

He led her through the back door to an outhouse in the woods. "I promise it's better than you think. In fact, I've got an outdoor shower you'd love."

She pictured herself in golden sunshine standing naked under a stream of sparkling water. The thought undammed something deep inside her and she felt it flow through her veins like sweet lava. She felt the heat in her cheeks and knew she must be blushing, and this only broadened Ken's smile.

"I'll be out front when you're ready."

He was poring over the contents of a large tackle box in the back of the Jeep when Caroline shuffled across the grass, unused to walking in rubber overalls. He gave a low whistle like she was a contestant in a beauty pageant.

Despite feeling like some sort of sea monster, Caroline laughed. "Next up, talent contest."

"I predict you'll do well with a lure," he said. Two fishing rods were propped against the open hatchback. "There's no better way to spend a day than this, in my opinion."

Caroline was worried there might be live worms involved, but a short time later she agreed with him. They were standing up to their thighs in the clearest water she had ever seen, watching thick brown trout dart along the bottom.

Ken was a towering presence at her side, positioning her hands on the rod while he taught her how to cast off. His strength flowed through his shoulders as he flicked the reel, sending the lure flying in a great arc before landing with a splash.

He stopped, his face close to hers.

She hardly dared to breathe and when she did she got a lung full of his clean scent. His arms brushed hers when he positioned her rod, one forearm steady and firm against the small of her back. Once he had the reel in place, he moved his arm away, and she felt his hand travel slowly across her waders.

The world stopped. There was no mistaking the reason now for the thumping inside her chest. She drew in a breath.

Ken felt it, too. His eyes met hers. She got a flash of what it would be like to be with him, watching him take his time with her the way he did everything. She had only ever been with Porter in bed in her adult life, and Porter's touch was something she had grown to dread. So the desire that sprang up inside Caroline now caught her off guard.

Ken stood close enough that she need only signal him.

He swallowed, his Adam's apple bobbing above his open collar, and brought his face down close to hers.

She felt his breath on her cheek as the lids dropped low on his eyes, dark with want.

He took a breath in and looked in her eyes. Waiting.

Caroline's stomach went soft inside like warm oatmeal. She licked her lips, her breath turning shallow. She was off balance, as though the lake bottom beneath her feet was lurching in another clash of tectonic plates. She reached a hand out to steady herself.

He took it and pulled her to him.

His chest felt like a wall of solid granite. One that

was warm and yielding. He gathered her to him until the only thing between them was her forearm sliding up around his neck like it had taken on a life of its own.

She wanted him.

He lowered his face to hers and brushed her lips with his.

She closed her eyes. She felt his breath on her face, his warm solid feel against her from her feet all the way through her body, and this awakened a yearning in her that took away her balance and left her knees soft. It was so easy to yield to him, and she did. The lake bed stopped its careening then, and she lifted her lips to his.

They kissed, slow and soft but long enough to fill Caroline's mouth with his. She was surprised by the depth of her emotions, and how good it felt.

After a moment he drew back and gauged her response with eyes that were soft now, dark and frank. "I think you're special."

She breathed in, feeling shaky, and looked away. "I . . ." she began. "It's just . . ." Her voice trailed off to a whisper and she was surprised to feel hot tears sting her eyes, burning her throat.

Ken straightened up, but not before planting a soft kiss on the top of her cap. He gave her shoulder a quick squeeze. "Don't explain. You don't owe anybody anything." Keeping one hand firmly on her elbow to steady her, he sorted out the fishing rods while Caroline dug a tissue from the pocket of her jeans.

He busied himself winding the lines while she dabbed at her eyes and tried to calm herself. He did not, Caroline noticed, stare at her and root around in her mind until he found the cause for her tears.

After a time, she risked a glance up at him. He was whistling something snappy while he tended to the lures.

He met her gaze and winked. "The thing I like about trout fishing," he said, "is the fact that they don't just swim up to the hook and ask to get caught. You have to be patient, wait till the time is right."

Relief washed over her. He wasn't going to press her for any explanations. Her breathing slowed to normal and she regained her footing.

"Okay now?" he said, studying the surface of the lake as though that was all that mattered.

But his jaw was working.

"Yeah."

He cast off, sending his lure wheeling through the air in a perfect arc. "It doesn't matter how long it takes, because even if they won't bite you get to spend time here." He looked at the sky, then back to his line as he reeled in, slow and steady and deliberate, taking his time.

The way he did everything, Caroline thought.

He gave her a quick glance and smiled. "Life is beautiful, Alice Stevens."

Caroline nodded. She didn't dare tell him what she really thought. That the way he wore life like a loose garment melted her heart and made her brave, like she could try again to have a normal relationship. She drew in another deep breath, fighting the urge to tell him everything. Ken Kincaid was as gentle and sweet inside as he was rugged on the outside. But Caroline didn't dare allow herself to get close to him, or let any man view the pollution of her past. To do so now would only put Ken's happiness in jeopardy.

She was overcome with sorrow for the doors that had slammed shut for her on the day long ago that she had chosen Porter.

Ken reeled in his line. "Don't think they're biting for me today. Let's see how you do, Alice." He positioned her rod expertly in her hands and raised it in alignment with her right shoulder. "Okay, cast off like I showed you."

He watched Caroline's line whirl through the air and splash into the lake. "Excellent!"

She reeled it in, slow and steady, dragging the lure across the surface.

"You're a natural."

They repeated the process until gradually any tension Caroline had felt disappeared, and for a while at least, she was able to forget her problems. She beamed.

"When you least expect it, there's a fish out there with your name on it that's ready to be caught. The thing to remember about trout, Alice, is they are not dumb," Ken said, focusing on the lines. "They won't get caught by just anybody. Trout are smarter than people give them credit for."

His words echoed in her mind late that night as she watched clouds scuttle past the moon from her bed, thinking about her life, the things she had done and the things she still wanted to do, find a small town and someday open an art gallery there and maybe even sell her own paintings. She also could not help but replay over and over the way Ken had looked at her today, the way his arms had felt around her, and the way she had felt when he kissed her.

Porter started driving west the next day. He pulled over at a truck stop in Missouri to gas up. Inside the restrooms he splashed cold water on his face, which burned and itched with fatigue. He'd slept fitfully the night before, his last in the townhouse.

He bought a small pizza and a giant slush drink flavored with cola, and used it to wash down a handful of antihistamines.

The clerk with the bright red apron behind the counter took Porter's money and said something.

Porter looked up from his wallet and frowned.

The young man flashed a wide smile. "I said, here's your change and have a nice drive."

Startled, Porter mumbled thanks. He gathered his purchases and walked away as the young man called after him.

"Hey, mister, you get a free package of chips with that."

Porter kept walking. He found Midwesterners annoying.

He ate the soggy pizza as the miles rolled. He took Interstate 70, following the line he had highlighted in yellow on his atlas. A small tube of lip balm rolled in the console between the seats. He opened it and saw smudges of coral lipstick on top. Caroline's favorite color. He rubbed it across his mouth, erasing her imprint, and this small act gave him a feeling of satisfaction.

He spent the night in a motel at the edge of St. Louis. It was one of those places where you pulled the car right up to the room, like he had stayed in one time with his parents when he was very young. He remembered lying in one bed, cranky and carsick following a day in the backseat of their Ford LTD station wagon. His parents shared the other, watching muted images flicker from the TV screen while his father checked the sports scores. There were no more vacations after his mother left.

Motels made Porter mournful.

Porter parked the Saab outside the battered steel door and cinder-block walls of the St. Louis Sojourner Inn. Exhausted from his day on the road, his arms vibrated from the feel of the road beneath the wheels. But he was on schedule.

He opened the door to a tiny room that stank of cigarettes. The bored girl at the front desk had promised him a nonsmoking room. He propped the door open to air the place out, shivering in the chill night air.

The Saab was hanging low with a heavy load. The trunk was packed full. There was a printout of the file from Beltway Security Investigations containing the full dossier on Storm Pass and the people his wife was associating with. Shopping bags, full to bursting, with items purchased at the wilderness outfitter in the upscale pedestrian mall on M Street's Potomac Canal. His valise, heavy with the weight of a Smith & Wesson .38 caliber semiautomatic pistol. A length of sturdy rope, should the need arise, and a gleaming red container of kerosene. A roll of heavy plastic sheeting and some blankets. Sterile syringes with rubber tubing and a small glass bottle containing Pavulon, a drug with which Dr. Porter Moross had more than a passing acquaintance.

Everything he needed for his fishing trip.

CHAPTER

20

Caroline fell into bed exhausted but happy after her afternoon up on the mountaintop with Ken. She slept fitfully, dreaming vivid dreams as her mind explored the perils and possibilities that awaited her in the days and weeks to come . . .

The first wave of flights touched down at Atlanta's Hartsfield-Jackson International Airport, bringing the day's first group of transfer passengers. Most were traveling north or south along the eastern corridor of the United States. Uniformed staff checked boarding passes at the entrance to the first-class lounge, ushering premium-class passengers inside, away from the hustle and bustle of the terminal, so they could help themselves to complimentary cocktails, juice, snacks, and gourmet coffee. At this hour the lounge was filled mostly with businessmen working on laptops and talking on cell phones.

And one elderly woman in a wheelchair. On the woman's lap was an FAA-approved Sherpa bag for the carriage of live animals. A small dog pushed its nose through the steel grid in the container door.

"Hello. Welcome to the Red Carpet Club," said the

passenger services agent. "I hope we can make you com-
fortable today." She smiled at the elderly passenger.

The old lady smiled back and handed over her board-
ing pass and ticket.

The dog·snarled, working its sharp fangs around the
steel grid opening.

"Good morning, Mrs. Nan Birmingham," the agent
said, entering something into her computer. "You are
connecting from Denver to Naples, Florida, is that
right?"

The old lady nodded.

Inside the container, the dog growled.

"And your dog," the agent said.

"He hates to fly," the elderly woman explained.

"We sure are glad you chose Delta," the agent said
brightly.

The dog snarled.

The passenger services agent walked out from behind
the desk and leaned over to greet her first-class special
assist.

Which sent the dog into another round of frenzied
yapping.

The agent's smile lost some of its sparkle. All airline
employees hated pets, at least when they flew. "Let's find
a quiet spot where you and the doggy will be comfort-
able." She steered the old lady and her wheelchair to the
farthest corner of the big lounge, settling her with hot
tea and a package of sugar cookies. She winced when
the woman requested cheese, a bottle of water, and a
bowl for the dog.

"It's time for his tranquilizer," Nan said.

A series of low growls emitted from the cage.

The agent frowned. "I'm afraid all dogs must be kept

inside their traveling container at all times inside the airport. For their safety as well as that of your fellow passengers."

"It'll help him sleep," Nan explained. "It's a long trip from Denver. Which is why I paid for first class."

That settled it. The passenger services agent looked around. The only person nearby was a guy in a black suit, traveling on a group fare to a conference in Miami, hunched over his Sony Vaio laptop like it contained the Da Vinci code. He didn't look up.

"Okay," the agent replied. "But remember, I told you we don't allow it. If you open the door to his cage while my back is turned, that's another story."

First-class passenger Birmingham gave a happy smile.

"Please don't let him off the leash." The passenger services agent took one last look at the tiny fangs that were working the cage door before heading to the kitchenette for some mini cheese packages, which she loaded onto a china plate. She chose two bottles of mineral water, one sparkling and one still, a glass, and a small bowl. She placed them all on a tray with some napkins and deposited them on the table in front of her wheelchair passenger.

The old lady beamed.

The passenger services agent bent down, close enough to the cage to set the animal growling again, and whispered, "Please, Mrs. Birmingham, please don't let him off his leash."

Nan smiled and waved her off. "Not to worry." She searched her purse for the medication the vet had prescribed. The little terrier didn't behave well on planes. He didn't behave well off planes, for that matter. Scout had been the Colonel's dog.

"*Wretched animal. Take your pill,*" *Nan grumbled,
stuffing one of the pills inside a wad of cheese. She set
the cage on the floor, opened it, and quickly clipped his
leash to his collar.*

*Scout nosed out and gobbled the morsel. He sniffed
the carpet for crumbs, straining at the end of his
leash.*

"*No exploring,*" *Nan said quietly.* "*Sit.*"

The dog pulled harder and whined.

*The man at the table glanced up from his laptop and
frowned.*

Scout tugged at his leash.

Nan tugged back. "*Hush,*" *she whispered.*

Scout whined, louder this time.

*Nan sighed. She reached for another mini cheese
packet.*

Scout sat on his haunches and barked.

*Frowning, Nan broke off a piece of cheese and tossed
it to him.*

*Scout gobbled it and backed away, ears erect. He gave
a low whine.*

Nan took another piece of cheese and held it out.
"*Sit.*"

The dog inched closer and sat.

"*Good dog,*" *Nan said, the way her new housekeeper
had shown her.* "*Now shake.*"

Scout did not move.

Nan repeated the command. "*Shake.*"

Scout licked his chops.

"*Shake,*" *Nan said again, louder.*

*The man in black released an audible sigh, closed his
laptop noisily, and stood.*

Scout eyed the cheese and yapped once.

*Nan scowled and shook the cheese near Scout's mouth.
"Shake," she commanded.*

Scout did not move.

"Stubborn dog," Nan muttered.

*The man in black collected his belongings, his face
twisted in a grimace.*

Nan tried one last time. "Shake."

*Scout rushed at Nan's hand and nuzzled it, looking
for the cheese.*

The man began to walk away.

Exasperated, Nan opened her hand.

Scout gobbled the cheese.

"It always works with Pippin," she muttered.

The man stopped and stood, stock-still.

*Nan unwrapped one more piece of cheese and tossed it
to the dog. "Might as well," she said, "We've got a long
way to go."*

*The man did an about-face and surveyed Nan through
steel-rimmed spectacles. He walked over and smiled.
"That's a good-looking dog you've got there," he said . . .*

Caroline woke from her dream with a pounding
heart, her breath shallow and ragged. It was only a
dream. A nightmare, something about Porter. She
couldn't remember the details, only that it was something long and complicated and twisted. Her mouth
was dry and had the taste of wet slate that, she had
learned long ago, accompanied panic.

She tried to calm herself with knowledge she had acquired from Porter. Nightmares, she knew, were usually the acting out of conflict, in this case guilt from
kissing Ken. Which, in turn, was an externalization of
guilt from that other, older stain that was stamped on
her soul forever.

And yet Caroline's gut had a different interpretation.

She would never be safe if she stayed in one place too long.

Going back to sleep was impossible now. She rose and went to the window. The night was crystal clear, the yard silvery with light from a brilliant orange moon that hung low in the sky. The harvest moon, Ken had told her, explaining that every full moon had a name.

She watched as a ghostly shape unfolded itself from a branch, taking flight across the night sky on giant black wings. The creature wheeled across the pasture like a phantom and was gone. An owl on the hunt.

Her grandmother had believed in omens.

A shiver passed through Caroline, wracking her all the way to her core. A familiar claustrophobia took hold of her chest, sending tendrils of despair up into her throat so that breathing became difficult. She could not escape the past. Not really.

She spent the hours until dawn in a restless state that was neither sleep nor wakefulness, rising at dawn to let herself out.

The dogs scampered past her into the yard. Snow had fallen on Ute Peak overnight, dusting it with white so it looked like a confectioner's dessert. The air was clear and shimmering with frost.

Lack of sleep left her edgy, nervous. She loved the pinkish light of dawn when the day was new, but today was different. The sky didn't seem bright enough, leaving the forest in shadow. Small sounds made her jump. She decided too late she would have felt safer in bed.

Great billows of steam rose from the pond.

She stripped, anxious for the soothing effect she felt in the bubbling water, and waded through the shallows until she was knee-deep. She sank down, turned onto her back, and floated, drifting toward center. The shoreline receded, and all that remained was the steamy wet cloud hanging just above her head, masking all sound except the splashing of her own limbs in the dark water.

It was a lonely sound.

Pieces of the nightmare drifted back, slowly at first. Porter. He was hunting her like she was some sort of animal. Her pulse quickened at the thought of him focused on one single powerful objective. Finding her. Her pulse quickened as the night terror returned.

She was not safe. Not here, not anywhere.

She forced herself to draw deep breaths, reminded herself of where she was, that she was awake now. But it was no use. Unease took root at the base of her spine and spread, like spiders racing across bare skin. She shuddered, telling herself the dream was induced by her own guilt and meant nothing.

But guilt was a powerful emotion.

More snatches of the nightmare popped into her mind, crowding in faster and faster until they fit together and told one terrible truth like pieces of a puzzle.

Porter was good at solving puzzles.

Panic set in. She imagined unseen hands pulling her down into murky depths. She began to flail, her limbs jerky and uncoordinated, rudderless in the dark water. She was gripped by a terror that, she realized, had taken hold of her in her sleep. It grew in ferocity now, gripping her, filling her mouth with the taste of slate, panic.

She screamed, and the sound hung in the air above her head as she scrambled for the shallows, splashing loudly. The sound, she was sure, would alert the unseen phantoms that would reach up to pull her down.

The pond, usually so inviting, had turned on her.

She gasped for air and took in water instead. She rotated her limbs, splashing wildly, and felt herself sinking down into that vortex.

The message of her nightmare hit home. Porter would find her. And once he did, she would not have many hours left to live.

Caroline screamed again.

Her feet touched bottom. She scrambled on all fours to the edge, bracing to be grabbed from behind at any moment.

As though Porter had already arrived.

She nearly jumped out of her skin when Pippin and Scout appeared in the mist at the water's edge. She barely toweled off, pulling on her clothes with hands that shook.

She ran back through the woods, gripped by the fear that she was pursued by phantoms. She recalled that the ancient people who had settled here believed the waters held powerful magic. If the mountain didn't accept a person, it would turn its power against him.

Caroline knew the time had come to leave Storm Pass.

CHAPTER
21

Tom Fielding had spent a restless night, wedged onto an ever smaller area of their queen-sized mattress by a cranky febrile twin. Sometime around dawn, he gave up and went to the couch in the den.

But still, he could not sleep.

He had received a notification message in his inbox indicating his e-mail to Caroline had been opened and read, but no phone call. Not even a reply to his e-mail.

This bothered Tom, but he didn't feel any real sense of urgency about it until he was lying there in the darkness just before dawn, trying to stay warm beneath a small SpongeBob blanket that smelled of milk.

That's when the truth struck Tom Fielding, in that awful way of truth.

Caroline Hughes was in danger. He knew it then with such certainty he wondered why he hadn't seen it before.

The two hours that followed were the slowest of Tom

Fielding's life, but he found himself at last in his office with the door closed so he could talk on the phone without interruption.

He entered the number he had Googled on the Web, hoping he wouldn't come across sounding like a nut.

A woman answered on the second ring, her voice robotic with efficiency. "Washington, D.C., Police Service Area 2. What is the nature of your call?"

Tom took in a breath. "I, ah, I am very concerned for the safety of one of your residents."

DENVER, COLORADO

Porter Moross watched a look of pure elation wash over the car salesman's face. The guy tried hard not to show it. He was in his late forties, with a thickening middle and ruddy patches of skin around his nose and mouth. A drinker who fought for every sale. And those, Porter suspected, would come fewer and further between with each passing year.

The salesman swallowed and licked his lips, tilting his head closer to make sure he'd heard Porter right. "You'll take it?"

"Yes," Porter said with no hint of a smile. He kept his features neutral, enjoying the salesman's nervous attentiveness. The man had offered Porter a shitty deal, and now he couldn't believe Porter was taking it. Porter kept his steely blue eyes locked on the man's face, certain the guy was probably creaming in his pants right now.

"We have on-site financing with a bank here in

Denver," the salesman began, his eyes darting around the showroom floor.

In search, no doubt, of another salesman he could do a mental high five with, to celebrate selling the biggest gas-guzzling SUV ever to roll off a Detroit assembly line. Porter cut him off. "I have cash."

The man swallowed again, his bushy eyebrows yanking up into his forehead. "Okay. Okay, then. I'll just get the paperwork going, Mr. Moross."

"Doctor."

"Doctor. Dr. Moross."

There was, Porter thought, nothing like cash to improve someone's attention to detail. Especially for the specimen of shallow humanity who even now was pounding his keyboard as fast as his meaty fingers would go, no doubt trying to calculate whether he'd get laid tonight if he blew some of his commission on dinner with his wife at the local chain steakhouse.

"There we go," the salesman said, reverting to his smooth, professional bullshit voice. He pressed one last key, and a nearby printer whirred to life. He busied himself with things on his desk, opening and closing drawers with an air of importance like he had just unlocked the genetic code for cancer. But not too busy, Porter noticed, to check out the ass on one of his coworkers when she walked by. The salesman collected the papers from the printer and brought them back to his desk, bouncing them several times on the Formica. He raced through the contents, tapping at places for Porter's signature with an expensive gold-plated pen.

"This signifies your agreement to sell us the Saab at the price we agreed on." He watched Porter sign, keeping his voice bland as though what he had just witnessed wasn't the best thing since Guinness started bottling ale for export.

"This is your agreement to the terms of purchase for the Yukon, including the discount for your trade-in." He tapped the paper again with his pen and waited for Porter's signature. "So, Dr. Moross, once we, ah, finish up, I can get you temporary plates and get you on your way. Once we receive payment," he sat, eyes narrowed, waiting.

A deal wasn't a deal until money changed hands. The basic fact of every salesman's life. This was the moment when the guy sweated bullets, because the pendulum would take one last swing in favor of the customer he had just spent hours or even days greasing. The time when the guy's thoughts were no doubt running through the list of repairs needed on the crappy tract house he shared with the wife, smiling in a dated wedding gown from the frame behind his desk.

Porter sat for several moments longer than the salesman would have liked, enjoying the stillness that settled around them. He watched as the guy fumbled for a tissue, pretending to wipe his nose.

"Allergies," the salesman mumbled.

But Porter saw him mop at beads of sweat that had clustered along his upper lip.

Porter hated the salesman. Not because the man had just ripped him off, deepening the fissure of corruption that ran through his personality. Not because the guy would never scratch below the surface of his stupid life to understand the reasons he'd never make district sales manager for southern Colorado, or why, after a few beers, he was compelled to stop at the local whore-house on his way home. No, the reason Porter hated the guy was that it didn't matter in the end. Because the man across the desk, who had been sneaking sideways glances for the last hour at Porter's too white skin and albino hair, had achieved everything he had bargained for in life.

Whereas he, Porter Moross, had not.

To his credit, the salesman said nothing. Only waited.

Porter opened his portfolio, black leather hand-crafted in Milan. It contained a mixture of old and new, including keys to the townhouse in Georgetown as well as those few items he needed now, such as a heavy manila envelope he had obtained from Riggs National Bank in Washington, D.C., and his gleaming .38 semiautomatic.

Porter undid the purple string outside the envelope now and withdrew a thick stack of hundred-dollar bills, counting them out with his slender fingers.

Across the desk, the salesman shifted in his seat and mopped once more at his lip.

WASHINGTON, D.C.

From his office window, John Crowley could see historic Blair House, official guest residence for visiting dignitaries and heads of state, located just across Pennsylvania Avenue. The view did not quite make up for the tiny office he was squeezed into, at the end of a twisting hallway that led through the rabbit warren that comprised the Old Executive Office Building.

What the place lacked in comfort, it made up for in prestige.

So when he called the DA for the Capitol district, his call was put through immediately.

The young woman was guarded. Relations between the feds and local lawmakers were not known for warmth. Which was fair enough, John Crowley reasoned, and in keeping with the way the nation's founders had intended things to be. He kept his request simple. "I am calling to ask a favor if you feel it is appropriate for you to do."

"Of course," came the guarded reply. "I'll be happy to help if I can."

"My wife is quite concerned about the well-being of a neighbor of ours, a young woman who appears to have gone missing," he explained. "She has voiced her concerns and filed a report with our local police—"

The DA didn't wait for him to finish. "What area?"

"PSA 2." Georgetown, the crown jewel of the D.C. tax base. Crowley chose his next words carefully. "My wife was assured that they would send someone over to look into it, but the husband seems to have left town. We are quite concerned."

He waited. The DA could either move this to the top of her inbox or not. It was her call.

There was the sound of a breath being released on the other end of the phone. "Let me look into this, Mr. Crowley, okay? I'll take some information from you and see what I can find out."

"Thank you." Crowley waited while the DA took down Caroline Hughes's name and address. Then she asked for the name of the person they both knew was the real reason behind Crowley's call, the one whose actions perhaps would render his home and property liable to search and seizure by D.C. law enforcement under terms of a warrant that would be issued if there was probable cause.

"And the husband's name?" The DA's tone was professional and still guarded.

"Porter Moross," John Crowley replied. "Allow me to spell that for you."

CHAPTER

22

STORM PASS, COLORADO

Caroline spent the early part of the day working at a feverish pace, readying the ranch for her departure. Coming to a small town in the off-season had been a mistake, she realized. "Hide in plain sight," Ken had explained. And so her next move would be to seek anonymity among the crowds of a large city.

She would leave Colorado soon, and she needed to be ready.

She topped off containers of rock salt from a giant bag at the back of the garage, stowing them near the back patio and front. As though by keeping Nan's steps free from the ice to come she could thaw the chill in her own heart. She drove herself in the Porsche to a warehouse-style store, loading up on supplies Nan would need.

"Are we expecting an army?" Nan watched, eyebrows raised, as Caroline lugged boxes into the kitchen.

"Just wanted to make sure you don't run out."

Nan frowned. The way Alice talked, it sounded like she had no plans to eat any of the five-pound bag of basmati rice, wash her clothes using the jumbo box of laundry detergent, or feed Poppit from the twenty-five-pound bag of dog food. Nan Birmingham was not the fretful sort, but she was worried. Alice hadn't smiled at all today. In fact, she had reverted to the girl she had been when Nan first laid eyes on her. Nervous. Distant. Silent. Nan resolved to bring it up at dinner tonight.

A problem shared was a problem halved, was what the Colonel always said.

With that plan in mind, she stayed out of Alice's way, leaving the young woman to go about her business like a whirling dervish.

Caroline washed all the bedding including dust ruffles and winter quilts, dusted, vacuumed the place including lampshades and down between the couch cushions, and even changed the light bulb that had burned out years ago in the crawl space below the house.

By the middle of the afternoon, Caroline's lower back ached.

Still, she cleaned. Every pass of the mop across the oak floors bought time for Nan to locate a new house-keeper, she told herself. But something else drove her. It came to her when she was on her knees under the kitchen sink, scrubbing the far reaches of the cabinet before replacing its contents in size order, smallest in front and largest in back.

Her life with Porter had been governed by a series of rituals and rules. Looking back, she realized she had no idea how far they had strayed from normalcy.

No bathmats or kitchen sponges were allowed. Porter had majored in microbiology, a fact he credited with his fear of germs. Caroline was not allowed to pet Pippin without washing her hands immediately using anti-bacterial soap. Nor could she speak to the dog. Porter believed the transference of emotion would weaken their marriage.

Once, she had left a blob of toothpaste lying in the sink. As punishment, Porter hid the toothpaste for an entire week, wrinkling his nose in disgust whenever she opened her mouth to speak.

Caroline learned to do everything his way, in an attempt to avoid the vortex that always lurked, ready to suck them down. But she made mistakes.

One night in bed, he noticed a spiderweb where the plastered walls met the low timbered ceiling. A workman had told her there was no way to rid a two-hundred-year-old house of spiders.

"Damn it, Caroline. It's your job to check Akua's work," Porter said, his face draining of all color. The cleaning lady had come that day for her twice-weekly visit. "Why did you allow this?"

It was midnight. Caroline was tired. "Porter, I didn't notice. I'll get rid of it in the morning as soon as I wake up."

He grew still, and she knew she'd made a serious mistake. He pursed his lips and rolled out of bed, reaching down for the box he kept underneath.

Caroline sprang from her side of the bed. "I'll clean it now."

But it was too late.

"This isn't about your filthy housekeeping, Caroline, and you know it," he said without looking up.

"Porter, I'm sorry," she began.

He waved off her protest, directing her to remove her nightgown, and she did.

He took his time, studying the contents of the box while she waited, shivering.

Caroline's stomach twisted when she saw his choice. "No," she moaned softly. "Porter, please. I'll clean the cobweb. I'm sorry. It won't happen again."

His blue eyes glittering with excitement, he flicked the horse's tail he had chosen so each long strand of hair swirled like original sin. He motioned at the floor. "Get down."

Arguing would only make him angry. She dropped to her hands and knees, doggy-style.

He stepped out of his briefs, keeping his grip on the horse's tail. He fondled his penis, now erect, with his other hand.

Closing her eyes, she pleaded. "No, Porter, no."

He kicked her once in her side.

The bruise on her ribs would take weeks to fade.

"Tell me," he ordered.

She drew in a breath, searching for words that would convey progress, authenticity, and sincerity. Not that, after more than a minute or two, it would matter.

He moved behind her now. "Do you see what I have?"

This was part of it, what he wanted. Caroline turned her head.

The horse's tail was bunched in a tight knot at its base, which consisted of a black rubber shaft that was knotted at intervals with round knobs of increasing size.

He shook it again. "Do you know why I chose this?"

"Because I'm stubborn," Caroline whispered.

"Yes." He reached into the box again and withdrew a leather riding crop, snapping it so it whistled through the air and landed near the tips of Caroline's fingers.

She tried not to jump. That would just make it worse.

He tucked the riding crop under one arm and stood over her, fondling himself with his free hand. "You like to live in filth, Caroline. Tell me why."

"Because of what happened to me," she whispered.

"And what was that?"

She shook her head. "Porter, please, don't do this to me."

"I'm trying to help you even though you are probably beyond help. Tell me what you did."

"I let my stepfather touch me . . ." She stumbled over the words.

"Touch you?" Porter snapped the crop again, and this time it landed on her fingers. "How?"

They had been over this many times. She knew what he wanted to hear. "I let him fuck me," she whispered.

Porter began jerking his penis, licked his lips with excitement. His voice was hoarse. "Where did you let him fuck you?"

"In my ass."

"How many times?"

"I don't know, maybe ten times."

Porter bent over her and she felt his breath, ragged and hot on her back as he worked the tail into place. "Why did you do that, Caroline, tell me."

"Because I liked it," she said, willing herself to be still, forcing her mind to go to the empty place she had built so long ago. "I wanted it because I was born a filthy whore."

Later that night on the cold tiles of the bathroom floor, Caroline plotted her escape. One week later, she was gone.

CHAPTER

23

Porter was not prepared for the pleasure he derived from driving the SUV. He had denounced them as the transport of choice for the uncouth, but he quickly discovered the Yukon had its benefits. He enjoyed making cars scatter in front of him on the highway, signaling fast to change lanes when they glimpsed the Yukon barreling down on them in their rearview mirror.

The last leg of the journey passed quickly.

The weak light of late afternoon worked its way inside the high, narrow windows of the shower room inside the Pueblo, Colorado, truck stop. Porter had the place to himself. He snipped off his beard as his whiskers fell in tight, colorless coils into the chipped basin. He lathered his face and cut long, even swaths with a razor. He rinsed and got his first good look at his face since college days. He was patting it dry when the door opened.

A trucker walked in, acknowledging Porter with a short nod. Porter watched in the mirror as the man's eyes widened in surprise, mixed with something else. Revulsion.

Porter's skin was ghost white, dotted with purple splotches like overripe fruit. Pustules along his jaw bled where he had cut them with the razor. He had grown used to curious stares that lasted long enough for most people to figure out that the dense, colorless beard adorned the face of a young man, not an old one. Now it was gone, revealing the pocked skin beneath that announced his weakness to the world.

Porter Moross hated his face.

He took a bottle of Caroline's makeup from his leather portfolio, poured some into his palms, and rubbed it into his cheeks. The makeup did nothing to disguise the weak lines of his chin, but the lesions were less purple. He surveyed the results in the mirror and decided he was no longer recognizable at forty feet.

He did not want to be identifiable until someone was at close range.

He gathered his things to go.

A door slammed and the trucker emerged from the shower area. He chose a sink at the far end and prepared to shave.

The man was large, dressed in a flannel shirt, dungarees, and scuffed work boots.

The sort of man Porter had always found intimidating. He lingered now, patting the top of his leather portfolio, feeling the comforting bulge of the pistol inside. Its presence made him bold.

Porter stared at the trucker.

The man pretended not to notice, whistling while he shaved.

But Porter could see he was nervous.

The man nicked himself and swore. He put his razor down and reached for a paper towel, careful to avoid Porter's stare in observance of the etiquette that was the rule in bathrooms between heterosexual men. When the

trucker had finished patting himself dry, he could avoid
Porter no longer, and his gaze traveled to Porter's face.

Their eyes locked.

The man's eyes widened with revulsion and he looked
away. He cleared his throat and ran a hand through his
hair before dabbing at a fresh cut on his chin.

Porter continued to stare, licking his lips loudly and
smirking, watching in satisfaction as the big man at the
sink hunched over to avoid the confrontation.

Porter walked out, stopping at the door long enough
to give a short laugh. "Who's afraid now? Just tell me,
who's afraid now?" He kicked the door so hard it hit the
wall and bounced. In the parking lot after, he eyed an
eighteen-wheeler that was idling, debating whether to
shoot out all its tires. He decided against it. Apprehension for vandalism now would keep him from his larger
objective. Still, the encounter in the restroom buoyed
his spirits.

After a career spent coaching people about taming
their inner demons, Dr. Porter Moross had discovered
just how good it felt to let one's inner demons run wild.

After a late lunch of huevos rancheros, Caroline made
one final trip into town to stock up on fresh eggs and
dairy at the local co-op so Nan wouldn't have to shop
for the next week, at least. Early tomorrow morning
she would go to the community college the next town
over. There, she could gain Internet access to research
bus schedules and connections to her next destination:
Seattle, Washington.

Clouds were rolling in when she left the co-op late in
the afternoon. She drove back to Storm Pass with the
windows down so she could draw in deep breaths of

the mountain air, wishing she could stamp the memory of the place inside her. The wind had picked up, tossing piñons and brush. As though the mountain itself was in torment. A large bird soared overhead, and Caroline leaned over the dash, wondering if it was a bald eagle.

A vehicle up ahead brought her attention back to earth. A white SUV was coming toward her, too fast, in the oncoming lane.

Caroline braked and signaled to turn right.

The SUV was almost abreast of the Porsche when the driver apparently decided to make the turn as well. He jammed on his brakes and banked hard to his left, cutting Caroline off in the Porsche.

The Yukon made the turn but just barely, bouncing across Caroline's lane before careening off onto the shoulder of the road to Storm Pass.

Caroline took evasive action, jamming on the brakes and steering the Porsche hard to her right. The sports car clamped down hard and tight, screeching to a halt just short of the Yukon's massive rear bumper.

Porter pulled off the highway late in the day at the exit for Storm Pass. Darkness was already settling in the heavy forest that pressed up to the edges of the road, and he marveled that his timid mouse of a wife had found her way here, far beyond the bounds of any community she had ever known. All on the basis of an e-mail from some pimply-faced kid she had known from the GW dorms.

The scheming bitch.

Porter tightened his grip on the wheel. It had been two long days of hard driving. And now he was here. He would see her soon. His heart raced as he reviewed his plan to get her alone, talk to her, convince her to come home. They would work things out. They both needed to change. He glanced down at the leather portfolio on the passenger seat. He hoped she wouldn't require convincing to get into the car and come with him, but the .38 was there if she did.

His mind turned to his other plan, the one that had sprung to mind the night he sat in his office contemplating photos of her with the man. Kincaid. Porter was prepared for that, too.

The SUV bounced across a dip in the road. A large, wet dollop of bird shit hit the windshield from a great height, startling Porter. He cursed and fumbled for the windshield spray. The wipers came on first, smearing the mess across the windshield in a broad, blue path.

He cursed Caroline for leading him here, to this asswipe of a place.

He almost missed the turnoff but spotted it at the last minute, thanks to a bright red sports car coming toward him with its turn signal flashing. Porter yanked his wheels hard to the left and made the turn just in time, gravel crunching beneath the Yukon's giant tires. He hit the brakes hard, stopping so fast his seat belt cinched tight across his chest. The leather portfolio tumbled to the floor.

The red Porsche car screeched to a stop behind him. He glanced in the side mirror long enough to make out a young woman in a baseball cap behind the wheel. A young woman who had witnessed Porter's mistake.

His shoulders hunched down with embarrassment. Until he remembered his SUV was so big he could drive right over her and her lousy Porsche without even scratching his bumper.

The polite thing would be to get out and apologize. But he didn't. He stomped the gas instead so the Yukon roared to life, leaving the Porsche and its driver fading in his rearview mirror. Porter laughed out loud. A woman like that had no business behind the wheel of a sports car anyway. He never once allowed Caroline to drive the Saab.

There was, indeed, a freedom in allowing one's demons to roam free. They didn't teach you that at Yale.

Caroline sat in the driver's seat, shaking. She had narrowly avoided the SUV's rear bumper. She had come so close to impact, in fact, that the Porsche's nose had come to a rest underneath it. One more inch and the two cars would have collided.

Luckily, there were no other cars on the road.

She'd learned in her short time here that people helped each other. It was the only way to survive. The wilderness around them was unforgiving. Shifting the Porsche into reverse, she edged it back a car length before parking it. She undid her seat belt.

Before she could leave the car, however, the Yukon lurched to life in front of her. She glimpsed a pale, thin man behind the wheel as the SUV bounced back down onto the pavement and roared off.

Eyes wide with surprise, Caroline recalled Nan's words of caution about the perils of sharing roads up here with SUVs. "City folk with more money than sense," she'd said. With a shake of her head, Caroline put the Porsche in gear and headed into town, keeping a generous distance between herself and the Yukon. He turned onto Main Street, no doubt headed for the inn. A tourist.

She caught herself. She was beginning to think like a native.

WASHINGTON, D.C.

Officer Mike Hartung felt a yawn coming on. His shift had ended an hour ago and he was knee-deep in paperwork.

The appearance of his commanding officer stifled the yawn.

"Incoming." The CO deposited a writ on Hartung's desk. "Hot off the presses."

Hartung stopped what he was doing at once and picked up the document. The CO did not usually hand-deliver search warrants. Hartung saw what it was and let out a low whistle. Judges did not usually issue warrants the same day as a prosecutor established probable cause.

Not unless they were in a big hurry.

His boss watched him. "Ring any bells?"

Hartung grinned. "Like Big Ben at midnight." It was good to see the wheels of justice turn so fast. Hartung had just typed up the request for the warrant yesterday to search the domicile of Dr. Porter Moross. He had thrown in, for good measure, a request to extend the warrant to Moross's vehicle and any off-premises storage facilities they might discover. Hartung had added that based on the neighbor lady's story about the handbag. That, and the fact that Porter Moross came across like a complete bastard.

Officer Mike Hartung believed in hunches.

The call that had been logged on the night shift from

a concerned friend in California had only added to Hartung's hunch.

His CO stood, jangling change in his pockets. "You've been to the Moross residence and met the suspect on that one occasion, right?"

Hartung nodded. "Right. We returned their passports to him." A vision popped into Hartung's mind of Porter Moross with his purple junkie pockmarks and beady little eyes, darting and watching and twitching and nervous.

Scared.

"Something's not right." Hartung had done his homework.

The CO gave a quick nod. "So the guy took off?"

"Oh, he took off. Shut down his business, stopped the mail, fired his cleaning lady, and even ratted out her husband to the INS."

"Nice guy."

"A real prince."

The commander rubbed the stubble on his chin, considering things. "What do the next of kin have to say?"

"Not many of those. Wife's got a mother in Florida who gets a Christmas card about every other year and that's it."

"And him? Everybody's got a mother."

"That's the thing," Hartung said, the muscles folding in tight along his jaw. "She was living out in the Midwest with some guy for a long time. About six years ago there was a fire in their place, a bad one. Guy died. Momma ain't been seen since."

"Bad luck."

"I thought so."

The commanding officer squeezed his eyes shut and rolled his head from side to side on his massive neck. When he opened them again, the look Hartung saw in them left no doubt his boss had a bad feeling about this one, too. "And the neighbor lady is—"

Hartung finished the sentence for him. "Wife of John Crowley."

The CO scowled. "BFF of you-know-who."

"Yeah." Hartung thought of Lindsay Crowley in her tidy little Nike tennis dress and tried not to wince. He wished he had acted faster to respond to the concerns of the wife of a man who had been personally chosen for his job by the president.

Really he did.

Lucky for him, the CO was not one to cry over spilled milk. So long as Hartung didn't spill too much. "Let's move on this. We got an audience now."

"Yes, sir."

STORM PASS, COLORADO

Porter swung the SUV onto Storm Pass's tiny Main Street. He recognized the tidy white sign for Kincaid's Garage from photographs in the Beltway Security dossier. Gus Kincaid was inside. Father of Ken Kincaid.

Porter peered at the doorway, half expecting to see Caroline standing there. But she was not. No matter. He would be reunited with her soon enough.

There wasn't much to Main Street, just a few run-down clapboard buildings, a bank, and a tiny post office. He pulled over in front of the post office. It was time to cross off one more item on his to-do list.

Porter pulled out his manila envelope and dropped it in the mail chute, first stop on its way to Modesto, California. He allowed himself to envision Lisa Fielding waving the envelope and its contents in her husband's face. Porter hoped Tom Fielding would have the presence of mind to note the postmark: Storm Pass.

It was a nice touch, Porter thought.

He got back in the SUV and made for the giant stone

crag at the end of Main Street, rising into the sky like a big phallic symbol.

Caroline had been drawn to this place for reasons she would never admit, Porter reflected sourly.

He reached his destination where the street dead-ended. Pools of yellow light spilled out onto the yard in front of a Victorian rooming house. A wooden sign on a wrought-iron post proclaimed "Rooms to Let."

Porter followed the grass drive around back and parked near the only other vehicle, an aging Ford pickup truck.

Two massive black Labrador retrievers ambled over to greet him when he entered. One of the dogs thrust his thick snout into Porter's crotch.

Porter kneed the animal, hard. "Get off," he muttered. Porter hated dogs.

"Jasper!" A graying woman appeared and pulled the dog away by its massive shoulders. "Come on, old man, back to your bed." She surveyed Porter head to toe with a practiced look. A frown appeared on her forehead. "Sorry," she said through pursed lips.

She'd seen him knee the dog. Too bad, Porter thought. If she was in the hospitality business, she should know that paying guests didn't want to be slobbered on by big, smelly animals. "It's okay," Porter lied. "I like dogs." He watched the woman's eyes widen as she registered his pale face and white hair.

She shooed the dogs through a doorway. "Stay there," she ordered. Brushing her hands on the back of worn corduroy slacks, she turned back to him. "How can I help you?"

Her voice had the same smooth quality as the used car salesman, cold like new plastic and just as sincere.

She had him pegged, Porter figured, for a weekend warrior from Denver or maybe even Chicago, here in search of trout before the nights turned cold enough to drive them deep into the lake bed till spring. She looked like the type who liked to be right. Too bad she was wrong this time. The thought made him smile. "I'd like a room."

Her eyes narrowed. She was about to tell him they had no vacancy. He forced himself to smile wider, speaking in the flattest Midwestern accent he could muster, before she had a chance to turn him away. "And if you got a map that tells where the trout are biting, I'll buy it off you."

She paused, considering this. Considering him.

Porter thought of the deserted parking lot out back.

"It's late in the season for trout," she said, putting one arm on her hip. Her gaze never wavered from Porter's face.

He shifted his weight to one hip and pushed the opposite leg out in front, scratching his head lazily with one hand in his best I'm-okay-and-so-are-you mode. "That's where Ken Kincaid comes in. I hear he's the best guide around."

She lightened up at the mention of Kincaid's name, as he figured she would. "You're booked with him?"

Porter took a chance. "Yeah," he lied. "I was supposed to come up last month, originally, then things got kind of crazy at work. Lucky for me he agreed to squeeze me in."

That seemed to settle things in the innkeeper's mind. "Okay," she said finally, walking around behind an oak check-in desk. "How long will you be with us?"

The look on her face told him the less time, the better. Grumpy old bitch, Porter thought. "Just a night or two."

She slid the registration form his way and watched him fill it out, entering the name and address of the man who had sold him the Yukon.

Her gaze lingered on the form, long enough for him to wonder if she was going to ask for identification.

She disliked him enough to do it, so Porter cut her off before she got the chance. "Yeah, I spent a lot of Sundays watching Ken hold up the Chiefs' defensive line. I can't wait to meet him in person."

"He's a fine man. You won't be disappointed." She didn't bother to look up, as though she'd had this conversation a hundred times.

Porter heaved a small sigh of relief as the moment passed.

She filed the registration form and withdrew an old-fashioned skeleton key from a hook on the wall and handed it to him. "We've got a good room for you at the top of the house, facing front so you can see all the action on our Main Street."

She smiled at her own joke, the first she'd cracked since he walked through the door.

A man, obviously her husband, appeared in the doorway. "Maebeth, are you about ready? Dinner's on." Seeing Porter, he stopped himself. "Oh, hello." His gaze lingered on Porter's face a moment longer than necessary. He looked away.

"I'll be right there." Maebeth turned to Porter, her tone brisk. "Continental breakfast starts at seven and goes till half past eight. It's included in the rate. If there's anything I can help you with, just let me know. Enjoy your stay." She came out from behind the desk, signaling her business with him was finished.

Porter didn't budge. "There is one thing. Can you recommend a good restaurant for dinner?" He had purchased coffee and a sweet roll at the truck stop near Durango, but that had been hours ago.

The man opened his mouth to speak but his wife shot him a look. "Sure," she said. "Head back out to the county road and take a right. There's a pretty good diner about seven miles along. If you see signs that you've entered the Pueblo reservation, you'll know you've gone too far."

Porter's stomach rumbled. He wasn't in the mood to spend any more time behind the wheel of the Yukon again tonight, but an idea came to him. An idea that brightened the prospect of a nighttime drive through a wilderness area. "Thanks," he said.

Maebeth Burkle smiled but her eyes held no warmth. "Don't mention it." She watched him go, gathering her cardigan more tightly around her. Something was not right about Jim Bell. His hiking gear, for one, so new it still smelled of a high-end department store. His soft hands with nails that gleamed under a coat of clear polish, for another. And his sickly complexion. And now he'd gone out for the evening without bothering to check the room first, something even corporate execs on expense accounts did. That fact didn't sit well with Maebeth.

"So?" Her husband shot her an amused look. After thirty-six years of marriage, they didn't require many words to communicate.

She shrugged. "I don't know." She wasn't the type to

talk about weird vibes or bad karma, like half the young people who moved up here these days to eke out a living and homeschool their kids. She shook her head.

Her husband chuckled. "Looks like he rubbed you the wrong way. That diner is the last place you'd want to eat. And you gave him the worst room in the house."

Together they watched the headlights of the Yukon swing past the front parlor.

A thought sprang unbidden to Maebeth's mind, startling her with its ferocity. And the thought was this. That Storm Pass and everyone in it would be better off if Jim Bell from Denver got lost out there tonight and never came back.

Caroline spotted two familiar cars in Nan's drive, and two familiar figures climbing out of them.

Nan's old Buick had returned, parked alongside Ken's Jeep.

The Kincaid men waved.

She felt a funny little pang at seeing Ken.

He flashed a smile her way. "You look right at home behind the wheel there, Alice."

Caroline smiled.

"You can keep it as long as you like," he said, lifting a brow.

Gus let out a laugh. "Now, there's an offer you don't get every day. I've been waiting for a test drive since the day he bought that thing."

Caroline held out the keys, embarrassed. "Thanks. It's a beautiful car but more than I can handle, I'm afraid."

Ken took the keys, allowing his fingers to brush hers, and she felt their warmth. "Car looks like it's still in one piece," he observed. "Don't sell yourself short."

"I had a pretty close call out on the county road just now," she admitted.

Concern knit his brows together. "Are you okay?"

"A little shaken but that's all," she replied. "I saw a big bird in the sky, close to that eagle's nest. I looked up to get a better look and all of a sudden there was a big white Yukon heading straight for me." Caroline felt her face color.

"No harm done," Ken said. "Just so long as you're okay. And if you were busy checking out our eagle, I'd say you're going native. It's a good sign." He grinned.

Gus chuckled. "Next thing, you'll be taking the day off work to go fishin'."

"I should have been paying more attention," Caroline said with a frown. "The other driver didn't signal, and he turned so fast I almost hit him. I got out to help but he took off," she said with a shrug.

"Tourist, most likely, up from Denver," Gus grumbled. "Probably one of your clients, Ken."

They both laughed.

"I don't have anyone booked again till spring. Season's about over," Ken said with a glance at the Porsche. "She handles well, doesn't she?"

"Like a dream," Caroline agreed.

"Good," Ken said. "I'm glad you liked it. You know, a car like that is easier to handle than a regular car. You just have to make the engine work for you. Downshift on the curves, stay wide to the outside on switchbacks. That car can handle a lot more than you'd think."

The look on his face implied he believed she could, as well.

Caroline knew he was being kind. She looked at Gus and changed the subject. "How are you feeling, Gus?"

The older man dipped his head in a small bow, but it was clear the movement cost him effort. "Just fine, thanks for asking. Any better and I'd be twins."

Ken rolled his eyes but the concern on his face was evident.

"I finished up the repairs on Nan's car this afternoon," Gus said. "Good as new. Like me."

The back door opened and Nan stepped out.

The dogs raced barking down the steps and ran in circles around the Kincaid men.

Caroline noticed a stiffness in Gus's movements when he reached down to pet the dogs.

"That's quite a welcoming committee," he said in a gruff voice.

Caroline shushed them and tried to make them stop jumping.

Ken patted Scout, who was heaving himself at Ken's shins. "I can't figure you guys out. You always act like you're going to take a bite out of my leg, but you never do." He laughed when Pippin crouched at his feet before rolling onto his stomach to be patted.

"It's a terrier thing," Caroline ventured.

"I guess so."

Scout followed suit.

"Good to see you up and around, Gus," Nan called, wiping her hands on her apron. "Glad you could make it for dinner."

Caroline took the news in silence, noting Nan had failed to inform her there would be guests for dinner. No doubt she had figured Caroline would have begged off if she had known. Nan was right about that.

"Thanks for having us," Gus said, making for the porch steps. "I don't like to be late when Nan's cooking."

"Don't worry, you're here in plenty of time. It's good to have the old boat back," Nan said with a glance at the Buick.

"She'll be all right for a while. Right as rain," Gus said, grabbing the railing. "I still think you ought to get something new, with four-wheel drive, before winter sets in. Won't be long now." He looked up at the pass, where the first snow of the season shone soft and white in the fading rays of daylight.

Caroline shivered.

Nan harrumphed. "That car will do just fine for another winter, you'll see." She turned her attention to Caroline. "Welcome back. Alice hasn't sat down all day. She whipped through this house like a white tornado."

"Sounds like you need one of Nan's famous dinners," Ken said.

"I, for one, will not lollygag any longer." Gus pulled himself up the steps, gripping the handrail so tight his knuckles were white.

Ken hung back, keeping a watchful eye on his father.

Ready, Caroline thought, to spring into action if he was needed.

"Ken's the one who's going to do all the work tonight. Nobody broils trout better," Nan said.

"I brought my special seasonings," Ken said, motioning to a small jar he carried in one hand. "And some chocolates for dessert from that place you like in Durango."

"My favorite," Nan exclaimed.

From the top of the porch steps, Gus let out a loud guffaw.

"Watch out, Mrs. Birmingham, my son is setting you up."

Arms akimbo, Nan shot Ken a mock glare. "Is that right?"

"Uh-oh, my cover is blown," Ken said, casually placing a hand on the small of Caroline's back as they walked up the steps.

It was a small gesture but significant, an act of proprietorship, one that staked hope for the future. But right now it just made Caroline sad.

"Told you Nan would see straight through a bribe," Gus teased.

Ken positioned himself near Caroline, close enough for her to breathe in his piney scent, sense his solid presence.

He stood close so they were almost touching, and she got a brief flash of a parallel universe where things were normal, where she and Ken were like any young couple having dinner with their parents. Except they weren't. Caroline's heart ached with sorrow for the ordinary life she had wished for and never could have.

Ken's voice was rich, resonant at close range. "Nobody's meaner at poker than Nan Birmingham. Hide your money, Alice."

Caroline thought of her tiny nest egg, folded neatly inside a handkerchief in the nightstand drawer in her room at the back of the house. Ready to go on a moment's notice.

"Nonsense," Nan retorted. "And don't scare Alice. Don't you worry, my dear, it's only penny ante."

"I've got you covered, Alice. Thank you for allowing me to escort you to dinner." Ken smiled down at her, trailing his hand lightly across her back.

She couldn't help but feel that something passed between them in that moment and she wished she could hold it forever, separate from all the hours and minutes and days of her life, and keep it close to her heart always. The crisp night breeze and its scent of wild earth flowing down off the summit and across the meadow, even the clouds piling up in the darkening sky, and more than anything the way Ken looked at her.

"I wouldn't want it any other way," she said truthfully.

He felt the same way, she realized. He tightened his hold on her, and his smile, which she wouldn't have thought could get any wider, did. "The pleasure's mine," he said in a husky voice.

But Caroline knew this place and the people in it were beyond her reach. "Mine, too." She meant it. "You know, I'm always going to remember this." She wanted to say more, but her voice caught in her throat.

"You don't have to remember it, Alice, we'll just have a lot more nights like it." He gave her a searching look, and the desire inside her to tell him everything was so strong she felt it pulling on her like gravity.

It took everything she had to tell him one more lie. "Yeah."

They went inside, and Caroline couldn't have felt any better if she were being escorted across a red carpet for the Kennedy Center Honors.

Nan had set the table with freshly ironed linens, a bouquet of mums, and a plate of fresh-baked corn muffins.

Looking back, the night was probably the best in Caroline's life. She had been lonely so long she had forgotten what it was like to spend an evening joking and playing cards with friends. She let her guard down, relaxing long enough to let happiness bubble up inside her, warming her from her toes all the way up to the top of her head. She was one of the crowd, her heart light from good food and company. This night, it was okay just to be herself, with nobody to watch her, analyzing her every word, passing judgment.

She was wrong about that.

CHAPTER

26

Porter settled on the blue plate special. Half a chicken and two sides. The chicken was stringy, heated in a microwave, with limp green beans from a can and lumpy mashed potatoes.

The waitress had stared when he asked if she could recommend the chef's special dish. She cracked her gum and glared, her gaze lingering on the bumps and scabs along Porter's chin. "Specialty? Of the house?"

Porter leaned across the Formica table, which was chipped and worn, repeating his request and enunciating each syllable. Like he was talking to an idiot. Which was in fact the case.

The waitress turned to the low window behind the counter, where a man with a shaved head leaned out, listening, propped on arms thick with blue prison tattoos.

She cracked her gum again.

The cook eyed Porter and sucked his teeth.

The waitress shrugged. "We got a lotta food here. That's your personal choice."

The cook squinted to get a better look at Porter.

Porter wondered if the place got held up often and

decided it did. The creep in the kitchen looked more like a bouncer than a cook. Christ, Porter hated the West. "I'll have the blue plate special," he said through tightened lips.

All business now, the waitress jotted something on her pad, rattling off beverages.

He settled on a Coke, grimacing when she yelled his order across the room. As though the goon in the kitchen hadn't already picked up on every word.

Porter ate fast, ignoring the snickering that was most certainly directed at him, the sole customer. He paid the bill and left a nickel on the table as a dare to the goon to follow him outside.

Porter had granted his demons free rein.

A light snow was falling. He attempted to use his new Swiss Army knife to slash the tires on a beat-up Honda Civic, the only other car in the parking lot. It was harder than it looked, and in the end he settled on using the tip to siphon out all the air from the nozzle. He did a second one as well, for good measure.

When he was finished he popped the Yukon's hatch and dug out the items he would need. Night-vision goggles, a small flashlight, and a map, even though he had already memorized the route to the Birmingham place. His heart pounded. He was about to see his young wife again.

The road was dark as ink and he was not used to this. He rounded a turn and saw a pair of yellow eyes gleaming in his path. The headlights picked up the ghostly outlines of a large body and antlers. He slowed but didn't brake hard, not wanting to risk another skid on a dumb animal that would barely dent the Yukon's massive front grille.

The thing disappeared at the last second in a flash of hindquarters and white tail.

Porter hated the outdoors. Except for a couple of day trips to Bear Mountain State Park, he had little experience with it.

He slowed near the Birmingham place, pulling into the scrub brush as high as he could so the Yukon could not be spotted easily by anyone driving past. But he hadn't seen another car since the diner. He got out, and millions of tiny snowflakes whirled around him. The night was filled with sound. Wind raced through trees as though the forest was alive. A branch snapped close by and Porter jumped, crying out before he could stop himself. He grabbed the driver's side door and tore it open, ready to leap inside to safety. But there was nothing. Porter was alone, his ears filled with the clanging of the door alarm and the racing of his heart.

He tore the keys from the ignition, and they felt sticky in his hands despite the temperature, which had dropped below freezing. He reached for the .38, slipped the safety off, and stood, trying to get used to the forest that snapped, moaned, and moved all around him.

He was alone.

He donned his Gore-Tex camouflage jumpsuit, not bothering to remove the price tags, topping it off with a black knit cap. Stuffing the .38 in his pocket, he strapped on the night-vision goggles. The forest took on another guise then, an eerie, shadowless world of gray and black, like the televised images he'd watched during the Persian Gulf invasion. Porter's palms were sweating and he wiped them on his thighs. Despite the goggles and the gun, he was afraid. He wrapped one hand around the .38 in his pocket, telling himself he had the advantage over anything or anyone that might cross his path tonight.

He made his way up the long grassy drive, staying in one of the wheel ruts. It wouldn't take long for the snow to cover his tracks. Nor would he be seen or heard on the moonless, dark night.

His fear turned to anticipation when he glimpsed the house with its broad bay window in front. He slowed his pace when he got near, and what he saw made him come to a complete stop.

Inside were four figures around a table. One of them was Porter's wife.

He felt as though he had been punched in the stomach, something he remembered well from adolescence, but this was much worse. He felt his gut collapse around the force of some unseen fist that, he knew, had wedged in deep.

Inside Nan Birmingham's house, Caroline threw back her head and laughed.

His wife was laughing.

She was happy. Apart from him. Her corruption was complete.

The realization pitched Porter into a despair so thick his limbs felt like lead weights. His skin tingled up and down the length of his arms and legs, the result, he knew, of the amygdala inside his brain redirecting blood from his outer extremities to his gut in the classic fight-or-flight response. The sounds of the forest lessened around him, and this, he dimly noted, was another classic symptom of the fight-or-flight directive inside his brain.

He gasped for breath. His goggles fogged. He wrenched them off and dug at his eyes, which burned as though they had been splattered with acid. The effect, he knew, of adrenaline mixed with cortisol, the stress hormone. Porter grabbed for his binoculars, the one item he hadn't purchased especially for this trip. He'd bought them years ago to use at the opera, when all he could afford on his intern's salary were cheap seats all the way at the back. Caroline had never needed binoculars to see the stage, he thought bitterly. By the time they were married he could easily afford season passes for the best seats in the house at the Kennedy Center for Performing Arts. Not that Caroline appreciated opera.

Porter brought the binoculars into focus, recoiling from what he saw. Caroline's face was that of a stranger, lips stretched wide in a carnal smile that was an open invitation to the man seated at her side.

Kincaid touched Caroline's arm in a gesture that spoke of ownership, and she smiled at him.

Ken Kincaid.

Inside Porter, all hope died.

He let the binoculars drop so they bounced on the end of the strap around his neck. "No, no, no," he moaned, blinking back tears of despair. The wind gusted, tearing his breath away. He fell to his knees, realizing his worst fears had been confirmed. He pounded the ground with his fists.

She was lost to him.

A sob tore loose from his throat. His face burned and itched and swelled like someone had put a torch to it. Porter tore at his skin, not even bothering to remove his wool gloves, rubbing with all his might until the tiny sores on his chin opened, trickling blood. He rubbed and rubbed savagely until he could stand it no longer, dropping his face down into the snow to seek some relief while sobs tore through him and snot mingled with his tears and pus and dripped onto the frozen ground.

After a time Porter raised his head. His grief, for the moment, was spent. What moved in to take its place was a cold, hard rage. He rose slowly to his feet, raising the binoculars once more, taking his time now.

There was Kincaid. He was a big man, probably the biggest Porter had ever seen up close. His posture was relaxed and confident. As Porter watched, Kincaid raised his glass and took a long swallow. Kincaid never once took his eyes off Porter's wife.

The old woman was there, looking at the playing cards in her hand. Nan Birmingham. An old man sat next to her, leaning heavily against the back of his chair.

The old man said something.

This made Caroline laugh again. But she did not look at the old man. She looked only at Kincaid.

Porter let out a groan of despair. Caroline didn't play cards. She had agreed with Porter that it was a waste of time. Porter had played poker during the night shift when he interned at Bellevue, just to get in good with the orderlies. Rumor had it the old wing was haunted. The real danger at Bellevue was the patients, brought in against their will to the world's most infamous asylum since London's Bedlam Hospital. Bellevue was also the best classroom for the study of abnormal behavior, and Porter had been proud to win an internship.

Two months before he arrived, one of the residents had been knifed to death by a patient. Word was out that the orderlies had to be handled with care, or a radio call for help on the graveyard shift might go unanswered. So Porter played poker and let them win.

The sight of his wife now playing cards was an affront to him. He fingered the trigger of the gun in his pocket. He could shoot them all right now and end the mockery. He ran his tongue across his chapped lips, considering the satisfaction this act would bring.

But one single opportunity remained to regain the life he had lost, to get his wife back, to make her see the truth at last. He needed to put his hurt feelings aside and stick to his original plan. Dr. Porter Moross knew that the hallmark of a mature mind was the ability to delay gratification.

He moved closer, until he was near enough to hear muted sounds from inside the house.

Caroline was speaking.

The others smiled.

Jealousy tore through him. Porter was on the outside looking in, as always. He had blamed this on his skin condition. But that was a lie, and he knew it. The fact was, Porter Moross had been born a mean son of a bitch and he stayed that way. Seven years at Ivy League universities and an internship most doctors would give their right arm for had never changed that basic fact of his personality. Acknowledgment of this simple fact now made Porter laugh. Once he started, he could not stop. He laughed until tears flowed. He doubled over and eventually collapsed onto one knee.

Inside, the dogs heard it.

"What was that?" Caroline's case of jitters had returned.

Pippin stood at the front door and barked once.

Caroline looked out the window, the cards in her hand momentarily forgotten. "What was that?"

"Eh?" Gus continued to contemplate his hand.

"Just the wind," Nan murmured, not lifting her gaze from her cards.

Pippin whined uncertainly. He sniffed around the edges of the front door, ears pricked, tail wagging. Finally he sat, head cocked.

Scout growled.

Goose bumps rose along Caroline's arms. She peered out the window at the darkness beyond, but all she saw was her own ghostly reflection in the pane, frowning back at her. "I thought I heard something."

Ken set his cards down. "Me, too."

Gus blew a breath out through his nose. "Coyotes. You need to keep the dogs inside come nightfall, 'specially when it's cold."

As if to prove Gus's point, Pippin scratched at the door.

Caroline nodded, but was not convinced. She shivered. She wished the drapes were closed. But they hung open, held in place with braided loops that hadn't been used in years. She couldn't get used to bare windows at night, and had asked Nan about it when she first arrived.

Nan had laughed, observing she owned all the land within sight. "Nothing out there but deer."

Caroline had accepted this, but her urban instincts were never at ease. They shifted into high gear now, making it impossible to focus on Texas hold 'em.

"If it was a coyote we'd have heard," Nan said firmly. "It's just deer, maybe elk."

Caroline caught the look that passed between Nan and Ken, and realized her situation had been discussed.

Nan set her cards facedown and spoke in a soothing tone. "Before you know it, you'll be more at home here than any place you've ever been."

There was no chance of that. Caroline reached for her iced tea in an effort to hide the tears that suddenly misted her eyes.

The dogs refused to shush.

Ken pushed his chair back. "I'll go out and take a look."

"Guess that's the end of that hand. Three jacks. Best I've had all night," Gus grumbled, tossing his cards on the table.

Ken grinned. "You didn't think we'd let you win, did you?" He took his jacket from a peg near the door.

Caroline was gripped with fear that was as familiar and old as a pair of worn bedroom slippers. "You shouldn't go out there."

"Oh, Alice, you needn't worry," Nan began, reaching out a hand to calm her.

Ken looked at Caroline and grinned. "Not much out there but snow and trees and probably a raccoon or a marmot trying to raid the trash. I'll take a quick look and make sure the lids are on tight." He gave her a glance that was meant to be reassuring, but did nothing to quell her apprehension.

She shivered.

Pippin was making sounds that were not in his repertoire, a series of excited yips mixed with high-pitched whining.

Terriers were born hunters.

"I'm going with you," Caroline announced.

Ken shrugged, halfway into his jacket. "Okay. I'll get a flashlight."

Nan pushed her chair back. "I've got one in the utility closet."

Ken waved her off. "Don't bother. I've got one in the Jeep."

"A pot and a soup ladle would do you more good," Gus remarked. "The noise will scare off the coyotes."

Caroline knew they were trying to reassure her. But nothing could slow her quickening pulse or banish the sense she had of danger.

The dogs felt it, too. Scout's hackles were up and he continued to bark at the door. But it was Pippin who turned Caroline's mouth dry and set her heart pounding. The Yorkie simply stood facing the door, ears erect, cocking his head one way and then the other. He turned to Caroline and barked once.

Pleading to go out.

She slipped into her parka and zipped with hands that shook so badly she missed it on the first try. She told herself for the millionth time there was no way Porter could have traced her here, two thousand miles from their home. No way, no way, no way.

Ken took her hand. "Ready to meet Wile E. Coyote?"

Nan chuckled. "He'll be clear across the county line before you get off the steps. If there is one out there, that is."

"That's true," Ken agreed. "Come on, I'll show you how pretty this place is at night."

Caroline nodded. But every instinct she had told her the dogs were right. Something was out there. Not coyotes or a marmot or even a bear. Something worse.

Ken reached for the door.

Caroline wondered if he had ever been scared on the football field, if he had ever pondered the sight of those opposing players gunning for him like a fleet of Mack trucks. She knew something of the discipline that was required to train a mind, and it occurred to her now that Ken must know a lot about living with fear, or in spite of fear. She managed a smile. "Let's go see."

"Probably best to keep the dogs inside," Gus called.

Showing, Caroline thought, he felt it, too.

Ken nodded but it was too late. He had opened the door, propping his foot up to bar the way, but Pippin shot through like a miniature rocket.

"Crap," Ken muttered. "Sorry."

Scout tore after him.

"Poppit! Scout!" Caroline was too late.

The animals had already disappeared into the cold, swirling darkness.

Caroline stepped out onto the porch and called again.

Nan flipped the floodlights on, illuminating the area immediately surrounding the house and garage. Fine flakes of snow whirled through the air in every direction as the wind shifted first one way and then another.

Caroline clung to Ken's hand as though her life depended on it.

The dogs were gone.

Ken stepped down off the porch, not seeming to mind the wind and snow. He took a few steps onto the snow-covered grass and stood.

Caroline was trembling so hard her teeth clattered. She snapped her mouth shut and tried to focus on the man at her side. His size was reassuring.

Ken looked around lazily, beginning with the sky. "Up behind those clouds is a full moon, the harvest moon.

Too bad you can't see it right now, because Colorado is about the only place I know where you can see your shadow in the middle of a snowstorm." He smiled down at her, waiting to see if she shared his pleasure in this fact.

Caroline winced. His voice was loud enough to be heard by anyone standing just inside the nearby tree line. This was crazy thinking, she told herself. Porter had told her she was crazy enough times that she came to believe it, especially now. She nodded at Ken and tried to force a smile because she didn't dare speak.

As though her silence might keep them safe.

Ken walked farther from the house, into the large meadow that was Nan's front yard.

Caroline followed, afraid to stay alone, aware they were leaving the safety of the floodlit zone.

"I'm going to get my flashlight."

Ken made for the Jeep and noticed Caroline wasn't loosening her grip on his hand. "We can both go," he said with a grin.

"Where do you think the dogs went?" Caroline asked in a voice that was not much more than a whisper.

He responded in a tone that was normal, conversational. "They're just fine or we'd hear it. I imagine they found the spot where the marmot was and probably Poppit's lifting his leg to mark it right now." He gave her fingers a reassuring squeeze. "Trust me, it was just a marmot or a possum and it's long gone. You and I are making enough noise out here to scare it clear off the mountain. If animals stood their ground, I'd need to find a safer way to earn a living." He laughed.

She wanted to believe him. She loosened her grip.

What they heard next proved him wrong.

Pitiful wailing.

Ken sprinted into the woods in the direction of the cries.

Caroline raced after him.

In their haste, neither of them noticed the place where the snow was tamped down just a few feet outside the living room window.

Moving shadows on the snow caught Porter's attention. He sniffed, raised his head, and saw to his alarm that Ken Kincaid was making for the front door.

The big man's chest was wide open like a perfect bull's-eye.

It would be a clean shot.

But the commotion that would ensue would prevent Porter from having the conversation he so desperately wanted to have with Caroline. His wife.

She was donning a jacket. In another second or two, they would step outside.

The door opened and Porter heard shrill barking.

He made a dash for the woods.

The binoculars, hanging forgotten around his neck, thumped his chest as he gained the tree line. He fumbled for his night-vision goggles, slipping them on over his tear-streaked face, running as fast as he ever had.

The dogs were on his trail. But Porter had a decent lead, enough to get him well inside the forest that began at the side of the house.

Dropping to a crouch, he loped through the low brush and zigzagged around trees. His steps sounded like thunder to his own ears, so when he heard the storm door slam he dropped to his knees behind a fallen tree and waited, struggling to catch his breath. His heart was pounding so hard he was sure it would burst through his ribs. He counted the beats, wondering if he was going to have a heart attack. His tongue stuck to the roof of his mouth. He fingered the trigger of the .38 and waited.

The dogs came for him. The white one, the old lady's dog, arrived first. It skidded to a stop in front of him, just out of reach and stood, barking its head off. Porter toyed with the idea of shooting the animal. But the gunshot would give him away.

Porter picked up a rock and took aim. The dog flinched and skittered away. Dogs were cowards.

Pippin posed a different sort of threat.

The Yorkie barreled straight at Porter, panting with excitement, his tail wagging so hard his entire body shook.

Porter grabbed for the only thing within reach, a small branch from the log. He drew his arm back.

Pippin yipped happily and edged closer, ready to play.

"Pippin," Porter whispered. "Go home!"

Too late he realized his mistake. The Yorkie closed in, wagging his tail in circles. Ready to play.

Porter drew his arm back once more.

Pippin barked once, waiting for Porter to toss the stick.

Porter pursed his lips in fury. He should have killed the dog when the idea first came to him. He had been tempted to drop the leash many times on Georgetown's busy streets. Caroline must have sensed it, because she insisted on walking the dog herself.

And now the dumb animal would be Porter's undoing.

Porter scrabbled around in the snow until he came up with a heavy rock.

Pippin's tongue hung out and he yapped again.

Porter lowered his face to the dog's eye level and hissed in another attempt to scare him away.

Pippin cocked his head and barked.

There were sounds of branches cracking as Kincaid closed in, calling the dog by name. The sound cracked the air like a sonic boom.

"Pippin!" Caroline screeched from the yard.

Rising from his crouch, Porter took aim and threw the rock.

He knew it hit home when the dog howled in pain. Porter took off, racing deeper into the forest behind the house.

He heard a crashing sound as Kincaid burst into the woods behind him.

Scout raced across the yard to Caroline and Ken, barking excitedly.

Which meant the dog crying in pain somewhere in the woods was Pippin.

Caroline screamed his name.

Ken was gone, at a run into the woods. "It's okay," he shouted from a short distance away. "I've got him."

A sob tore at Caroline's throat as she took off in the direction of his voice, her fear of the night momentarily forgotten.

Pippin stopped yelping.

"He seems okay," Ken called. "We're in here, near the garage."

Caroline followed the sound of Ken's voice, her fears momentarily pushed aside.

She got near enough to see Ken cradling the dog. He handed Pippin to her when she got close.

She scooped him up and held him tight.

The dog wriggled with happiness, poked his nose at her face, and gave a delicate sniff.

"He's okay, definitely no other animals around," Ken said. "Something spooked him, that's all."

Looking around at the woods that were alive with wind and snow, Caroline could understand how the dog became spooked. They stood near the remains of a fallen tree, a trunk that was maybe ten feet long and at its widest, more than a foot high.

Big enough to hide behind.

The wind died and the air turned still, and in that brief moment she smelled it. A prickling sensation rose on the back of her neck and spread quickly up into her scalp and down her spine like wildfire. Caroline would know that smell anywhere, the unmistakable combination of medicinal cream Porter applied to the hives on his face, mixed with the sweet Ralph Lauren cologne he used to cover it.

He was here.

Every single hair on her body stood up straight as her nerve endings jangled.

Telling her to run.

Caroline felt her breath freeze in her lungs.

The trees around her were moving now with another gust of wind. The forest spun around her like a crazy Tilt-A-Whirl.

She heard a low sound, a kind of keening, and didn't realize until she saw the look on Ken's face that it was coming from her.

He had been staring at a spot on the ground behind the log. Turning now, he frowned and reached out to her. "Steady, Alice, just take it easy."

She was already backing away. He had no idea the danger they were in. But there was no time to explain. She broke into a run, praying they could make it to the house in time. She risked just two words of warning. "Hurry! Run!"

"Alice, it's okay," he called, loping after her. "Whatever it is, it's gone. Nothing here will hurt you."

But Caroline knew better. She clutched Pippin tight and bounced forward on feet that had turned to rubber. She tripped once, grabbing a branch before she went down. She righted herself, her breath coming in ragged gasps, and kept going.

Ken caught up easily. She got a brief glimpse of his face in the darkness at her side, registered his look of concern, and realized dimly that he had come to some sort of understanding in that moment, not of the danger they were in but that she was mentally unbalanced. It didn't matter. She ran, bracing herself every step of the way for the flash of light, the sharp popping sound, the tearing of flesh. She thought of the handgun Porter had once shown her, acquired during his residency on Manhattan's Lower East Side.

"It's okay." Ken grabbed her hand in the open grassy area in front of the house.

The motion detector switched on, flooding the area with light.

Turning them into easy targets.

"Hurry," Caroline urged, racing for the porch. She took the steps two at a time.

She tore open the storm door and raced in, slamming the front door shut behind them as soon as Ken made it in behind her. She was grateful to feel the lock click into place, more grateful still that the door was constructed of solid oak. Her legs gave out then and she collapsed against a wall, sliding down into a crouch on the floor. Exhausted and spent.

"Good heavens." Nan rose from the table, her brows knit tight together with concern. "Are you hurt?"

Unable to speak, Caroline shook her head and kept a tight grip on the dog in her lap.

Porter was out there. He had come for her.

Gus cleared his throat. "Don't tell me the little guy tangled with a coyote?"

"No," Ken said in a tight voice. He reached down and smoothed Caroline's hair.

She didn't move.

"Didn't think so," Gus replied. "Wouldn't have been anything left of him if he had."

Nan shot Gus a look.

Caroline said nothing.

Scout, who was already inside, came over to sniff Pippin, who squirmed free of Caroline's lap and shook himself.

Caroline drew her knees up to her chest and wrapped her arms around them in an attempt to stop shaking. It was no use.

Pippin took a few steps onto the rug. He was limping.

Ken dropped to his knees and pulled the dog close. "It's okay, little fella." He ran his hands across Pippin's body, starting at his ears and working his way down and back.

The dog yelped when Ken reached his midsection.

Ken made soothing noises, gently parting Pippin's fur until he found the sore spot. "Looks irritated right here, a little red and swollen, like something bit him. But I don't see any teeth marks. That's good news." He flashed Caroline a smile that was meant to cheer her.

But she knew better. There were no teeth marks because Pippin hadn't been bitten. He'd been hit, she thought miserably.

Porter hated animals.

"He'll be just fine," Ken pronounced. "This area right here on the side of his stomach looks a little irritated, but nothing serious or he'd let us know."

"See how he does by morning," Gus said helpfully. "Vet opens at nine."

"He looks right as rain," Nan said soothingly.

Caroline was aware on some level that their perception of her had shifted.

They chatted and watched the dogs as though Pippin was their only concern, but Caroline was aware that each of the three snuck glances in her direction. Measuring her. In an instant she had ceased to be their equal. She had been a stranger who was timid and shy and perhaps odd. But tonight she had shifted into someone who was worse than odd, she imagined, someone unbalanced and curled in a fetal position on Nan's living room floor.

"Dog probably got caught on a log or something," Gus was saying.

Ken lowered himself onto the floor near Caroline. "Could be."

But he had taken a good look at that log, a good look at the red mark on Pippin's side. Caroline was grateful when, after a moment, he stood once more and bolted the extra lock on the oak door.

The drapes, she noticed, had been pulled shut for once as well. As though Nan, too, had misgivings about who or what had been out there.

The dogs went to sit on a cushion near the fire and eventually quieted down.

Caroline couldn't stop shaking.

"Well," Nan said, as though everything was settled. "This calls for hot tea all around." She went to the kitchen.

Caroline could think of nothing but the long row of bare windows in that room. She wanted to warn Nan but didn't dare. She realized, miserably, there was nothing she could say or do to convince any of them. These people had never known terror, never feared for their lives. They would not understand. They would think she was crazy. Besides, Porter wasn't interested in Nan.

He had come for Caroline.

Now that he had found her, nothing would stop him.

Caroline became aware that Gus was watching her with a frown on his face.

She rose before he could say anything and took a seat on one end of the couch. She lowered herself gingerly, every nerve ending still on high alert, as though the cushions were booby-trapped and might explode.

Her old familiar way of life had returned.

The tea was lemony and minty with a generous dollop of organic honey. She took small sips and tried not to gag.

Ken didn't drink his tea. He walked through the house, checking locks on doors and windows, closing blinds, and pulling curtains shut.

The dogs dozed. Nan put more logs on the fire and traded stories with Gus about days gone by. She passed around chocolates from the gold-foiled box Ken had brought.

Caroline did not contribute to the conversation. She sat on the end of the couch with her knees pulled up in front, measuring her odds.

She couldn't leave tonight, much as she wanted to, not

without stealing Nan's car. And she wouldn't get far on foot. No, she would leave tomorrow at the first chance she got. Greyhound only stopped in Storm Pass once a week in winter, but she could pick up a connection in Durango and leave Nan's car there with a note in it. The sooner she left this place, the safer everyone would be. She didn't dare think of all the things that could go wrong with her plan.

The hot tea and the soothing rumble of voices, combined with exhaustion, set Caroline's mind adrift and made her drowsy. She felt her eyes flutter closed and felt comforted at last, like a little girl whose parents allowed her to stay up past her bedtime. She felt her head nod, and before she realized it she had dozed off.

A burst of cold air woke her. She sat up in time to see Ken close the oak door and bolt it.

The logs on the fire had burned lower, meaning she had slept for fifteen minutes, perhaps longer. The room was quiet.

She heard the rumble of a car driving off.

Nan stood at the foot of the stairs, one arm on the rail, speaking to Ken in a low voice. "Call your father in twenty minutes to check that he makes it home okay."

Ken smiled at her. "Old Gus in my Porsche? I should check the casinos in Vegas."

Nan nodded. "You have a point there."

Caroline blinked and yawned. Someone had wrapped a caftan around her shoulders.

They both looked her way.

"Someone's awake," Nan said.

"I must have dozed off." Caroline rubbed her eyes. The teacups had been cleared, and two fresh glasses of ice water were in their place.

She took a deep sip. The cold water felt good on the back of her throat.

"It's been a long day. I'm heading up to bed," Nan said, climbing the stairs. "Ken has volunteered to bunk on the couch, even though I told him we're just fine on our own."

There was a pile of sheets, blankets, and a pillow on the rocker. Caroline opened her mouth to protest, but Ken was already settling into the easy chair.

Nan called instructions over her shoulder. "If you open the front door to go out, you have twelve seconds to press the buttons on the keypad. Code's taped to the wall." With that, she wished them good night.

A light on the keypad shone a steady red, armed and ready.

Nan had told Caroline the first day she never bothered with it.

Caroline looked at Ken. "You don't need to stay," she began. But she knew he wouldn't leave.

"Don't worry about it," Ken said with a shrug. He misinterpreted the shiver that passed through Caroline, making her gather the caftan more closely around her shoulders. "You're safe with me, Alice, I mean it." His tone was soothing.

"It would be better if you weren't here," Caroline said simply. Porter was insanely jealous, but Ken couldn't know that. No, she decided, he was staying to keep an eye on her. They didn't trust her alone with Nan.

Ken smiled casually. "And leave you to rely on these killer dogs for protection? Not a chance, even if you are here with Nan Birmingham, who I wouldn't mess with. I think the Colonel rubbed off on her." His gaze traveled to the mantel, where the Colonel's shotgun hung.

So he, too, suspected someone had been out there tonight.

Caroline shivered.

Ken watched her with a steady gaze. "Gus and I took a walk outside while you slept. Everything seems okay. Whatever it was, it's long gone." He stretched back in his chair. "Nobody would be crazy enough to hang around here on a cold, snowy night anyways."

Almost nobody. She wished she could warn Ken. But how could she? Who would believe her?

Ken leaned forward, and she saw sympathy in his expression. "Don't freak out, Alice. You're among friends. You're safe now. I won't let anything happen to you. I promise." He smiled like that settled everything.

He thought, she mused, that she had mundane problems with an ex, perhaps a boyfriend or a husband who turned moody after downing too many beers. How could she begin to explain to Ken that she was married to a man who believed he would curl up and die without her? Or that Porter's psychic wound really was deep enough to open wide and swallow all three of them whole? "Thanks," was all she said.

Ken pulled off his hiking boots, swinging his stockinged feet onto the oak coffee table as she imagined the Colonel had done countless times. He leaned back like he had all the time in the world, watching her. There was no pity in his eyes. Only questions.

It occurred to Caroline that Ken Kincaid was rooted firmly in reality. When he spoke his voice was soft, but he did not bother with pleasantries. "Do you want to tell me about it?"

His directness caught Caroline off guard. Her eyes widened in surprise. But she said nothing.

He waited.

"Sorry," she said at last, trying to retreat into some kind of formality that sounded silly, and she knew it.

He didn't blink. "Look, I'm divorced, too. Whatever it is, I've probably heard it before."

She didn't know what to say.

He reached his arms high over his head so his sleeves rode up, revealing powerful forearms.

He was strong. He could protect her. But she knew as soon as the thought flitted through her mind that it wasn't true.

He twined his fingers behind his head. His gaze did not waver.

She shook her head and closed her eyes. She could not afford to have this conversation. "I doubt that," she said at last.

A log sputtered in the fireplace. She weighed telling him the truth, allowing him to comfort her, allowing herself to believe him when he told her he could help. Except she knew better.

"C'mon, Alice, nothing's that bad."

She looked away from the fire and finally met his gaze. Still, she said nothing.

He let his hands drop to his lap. "I think I have a pretty good idea of what the problem is, and I'm pretty sure I can help. You're not in this alone. Unless you want to be."

His words tore at her heart. Tears sprang to her eyes and she closed them again, burying her face in her hands.

He was beside her on the couch in an instant, gathering her in his arms and whispering the name he knew for her. "Alice, I can help you. Just talk to me, tell me about it. I can take care of you and little Pippin, too."

He used the dog's real name. He knew. Or thought he did.

Ken's lips brushed her hair, her cheeks, her neck, and Caroline breathed in the scent of him, woodsy and clean and *strong*. She wanted more than anything to relax into his chest and let him gather her close until his arms were wrapped tight around her.

His voice turned husky and he whispered her name again.

She kept her eyes closed because it was easier that way and she felt his lips on her face, soft like a butterfly's wings, whispering across her forehead and her cheeks until they found their way to her mouth.

He closed his mouth on hers, covering her lips with his, and they were hard now.

She gave herself up to him for one crazy moment, filling her mouth with the taste of his as she allowed herself to relax into him.

He ended the kiss as slowly as he had begun and said her name again, soft and deep. He planted a quick kiss in the middle of her forehead, and this was somehow even sweeter to her and choked her with tears.

He shushed her gently. "Listen to me, Alice. You're too pretty and too special to be this scared. I'm not going to let anything bad happen to you. I'm not going to let anyone hurt you. Got that?"

She nodded, filled with self-loathing. If he knew the truth, he wouldn't say such kind words. "I'm sorry," she said, shaking her head.

Releasing her, he looked down at his hands in his lap. "I've made mistakes, Alice, we all have. I'm just a guy who's good at sports. And I like to catch fish." He gave a small chuckle. "Those are the only two things I know much about."

She couldn't hold back a protest. "You're just being humble. You're as smart as any doctor and the kindest, handsomest man I've ever met. You're a good person. I can tell." She blurted the words out before she could stop herself.

He looked at her thoughtfully. "I've reached a point in my life where I know what I want, and I've learned a few things along the way. One of them is you can tell the most about a person when they're under pressure. What I've seen of you, Alice, tells me you're a good person, too. Maybe you made some mistakes, but whatever is going on right now with you, you don't deserve this."

"This" being the fact that she had turned up here with no suitcase and no car and no history, slightly less than two weeks ago.

His words were matter-of-fact, but they unleashed a torrent of emotion inside her. "Don't," she whispered, hunching forward in an effort to hide the sobs that were boiling up inside her.

He stroked her hair, not in a coming-on way but in an effort to soothe her. Her head felt warm where his hand touched it.

He cleared his throat. "Look, I'll tell you something else and then I'll shut up. Whatever this thing is you're struggling with, you need to put it behind you. If you tell somebody about it, you can put it to rest. And if you want that somebody to be me, I'm here for you. Deal?"

Caroline nodded, hating herself for everything she had done and what she was about to do. But she couldn't trust Ken, couldn't bear to see the change in his eyes if he knew the truth. And besides, she didn't dare.

Porter was close, ready to pounce. She knew that now for a fact.

Without waiting for an answer, Ken stood. "It's late. We should both get some sleep. I'll be right here if you need me."

She nodded and stood, hoping he would remember what she was about to say. "I've never met anyone like you, Ken. You're a really special person." Her voice trailed off and she looked up, hoping he understood she meant every word.

Another man might have seized the compliment as an invitation, but Ken only nodded.

She climbed the stairs with Pippin at her heels, donned her nightgown in the dark room, and walked to the window, parting the curtains for one last time to look out on the place she had grown to love.

The night was moonless. It took her eyes a while to adjust to the gloom. Gradually, familiar shapes took form as Caroline tried to etch the scene forever in her mind.

Something flickered in the line of trees. A branch snapped into place, releasing a small cloud of snow into the air like smoke.

As though something had fled. She stared hard at the tree line, watching for another sudden movement.

But she saw only darkness.

A cold fear took root low and deep inside her, claiming Caroline's insides like cancer. She climbed into bed, curled into a ball, and screwed her eyes shut tight.

But she could block out neither her memories nor the danger.

Ken woke early and let himself out. The air had a wintry tang and he breathed deep. He loved winter in Colorado as much as he loved spring, summer, and fall. Ken Kincaid was a mountain man.

He checked Nan's yard, front and back, in the first light of the new day. His breath formed small puffs of steam. Old injuries cried out in a dozen places on his body after the night spent on Nan's couch. He would have slept better in a bed. Alice's bed. With his arms wrapped tight around Alice. Her face filled his mind, her intelligent eyes, the delicate line of her cheeks, the way she smiled.

Ken smiled. He was smitten.

He walked the length of the long drive, surveying the freshly fallen snow that was crisscrossed with the tracks of small animals. He found no sign of an intruder.

But someone had been here. Ken frowned, his mind on full alert. He'd learned as a small child to trust his gut, following its lead even before his brain had time to catch up. As his body matured, he acquired a strength and speed that surprised him, but he never questioned his gift. He discovered his instincts could guide him where his intellect could not.

Someone had been out here last night. When Ken tracked Pippin's cries, he smelled fear hanging in the air like a fog. Fear had a scent all its own, and once you identified it you never forgot. Cops could smell it. So could prison guards and animals. Playing ball, Ken got so he could pick up the scent on the pads and uniforms of men on the line. He learned to tell who was on their game and who wasn't. Guys with hangovers. Guys who had argued with their wives, guys who hadn't slept. Guys on the opposing team who got an eyeful of Ken Kincaid and had second thoughts about playing that day.

All Ken would have needed was a few seconds in the woods to close his eyes and breathe, and his feet would have led him where he needed to go. But Pippin howled and Alice panicked. She was scared enough to lie about it later. That fact bolstered Ken's resolve to put an end to this entire situation.

Alice Stevens was in love with him and Ken knew it. As sure as he knew he had fallen for her. It was not just his ego talking. Girls had started throwing themselves at Ken in junior high. He'd had more than his share. But that lifestyle played itself out, leaving him cold. He'd hoped his marriage would end all that. Then he'd torn the ligaments in his thigh, and discovered during his long rehab that his wife had fallen in love with the man on the line, not the man.

He spent some time thinking, and figured out that the flash, glamour, and glitz of his old life had served as bait for women who required a steady diet of the stuff. Heck, it had left Ken feeling like the catch of the day.

He had come back to Storm Pass to heal. It was a

quiet life, but he'd been happy. Until Alice showed up with her soulful eyes, and Ken's gut told him life could get much bigger.

The fresh layer of powder yielded no clues but he was satisfied, at least, that whomever or whatever had been out here last night was gone. He started up the Jeep and headed down Nan's drive, aware of a lightening in his heart like an old lost friend. He was falling in love with Alice and she loved him back. Something in her past needed settling, no doubt about that. Some asshole of an ex with a jealous streak. That was common. She'd tell Ken eventually, and together they would resolve the situation.

The guy would come to his senses and move on after he realized Ken was on the scene to stay.

Problem solved.

Ken and Alice would ride off into the sunset. Happily ever after.

Ken Kincaid, despite some setbacks in his life, retained the confidence of a winner.

He'd go up to his cabin today, close it up for winter, then head back out to Nan's place after lunch and take Alice out to dinner.

He whistled snatches of a happy tune on the drive into town. He passed Gus's place. The Porsche was parked out back. No lights on. His father was still asleep. Too early to wake him up and demand a cup of coffee. Which was too bad, because Ken could have used the company. He wanted to talk to somebody, work Alice's name into a conversation, just to hear himself say it out loud. There'd be time for that later.

He drove to his place to prepare for the ride up to the cabin. They'd have good times up there next spring. She had liked it. In fact, she looked pretty darned cute in hip waders.

The memory of it made Ken happy as he tuned the radio to the all-news AM station in Durango. He needed a weather report.

CHAPTER

30

Maebeth Burkle looked out her kitchen window and frowned. What she saw there made her lose count of her coffee scoops. The white Yukon was parked out back, wheels caked in mud with bits of fallen leaves stuck to the sides. As though her odd guest had gone four-wheeling last night after dinner. During the first snow of the season. After his long drive from Denver. Odd.

Not that it was any of her business. She went back to measuring coffee, and had to start over again. "Darn," she muttered. She put the pot on and glanced at the clock. Almost seven.

The timer went off. She slipped on a pair of well-used mitts and opened the oven to check on her muffins. Carrot raisin, her husband's favorite. Except they didn't look quite baked enough in the center. She pulled off a mitt and leaned in to check.

It was then that she felt something brush the back of her legs. She turned.

A man stood there. Jim Bell, their lone guest. Too close for comfort.

With a cry of surprise, Maebeth jumped. The muffin tray slipped from her grasp and clattered to the floor.

Jim Bell did not move.

Maebeth took a step back, straight into the oven door. She reached out a hand to steady herself. Her fingers landed on the hot steel. She snatched her hand away with a shriek of pain but it was too late. Searing pain shot up her arm. She raced to the sink for cold water.

Jim Bell did not move. He stayed where he was, a strange glittering look in his eyes as he watched Maebeth flex her fingers under the running water.

"Honey, you okay?" Ted barreled through the swinging door, his face lathered in shaving cream. The dogs ran in after him and made a beeline for the muffins that were scattered on the linoleum.

All three did a double take at the sight of Jim Bell, standing stock-still, dressed head to toe in camouflage browns with a wool cap pulled down low over his face. The cap couldn't hide the ravaged look of him. His skin was ten shades paler than yesterday, if that was possible, with purplish bumps on his cheeks. They were oozing in places. Most disturbing of all was his expression. Or rather, lack thereof. His eyes were hollow, glittering cold and hard behind his steel-rimmed glasses like pale blue chips painted on a robot's face.

Ted looked from his wife to Jim Bell and back, drawing himself up to his full height. "What the hell happened?"

Closing her eyes against the searing pain that pulsed the length of her arm, Maebeth took a deep breath. "I dropped the muffins and burned my hand on the oven door." She looked at Jim Bell.

Their guest said nothing.

It made Maebeth's hand throb even worse.

One of the dogs let out a low growl from the back

of his throat. The retriever braced, facing Jim Bell, and lowered his head. Hackles rose on the back of the dog's neck, and he growled louder.

Ted Burkle walked to the oven, closed the door, turned it off, and faced Bell. He had three inches on their guest.

Ted looked comical with his face covered in shaving cream, and Maebeth would have laughed if her hand wasn't throbbing enough to take her breath away.

Her husband frowned. "You okay?"

She nodded weakly.

Ted turned to Jim Bell. When he spoke, his voice was low, carrying an edge she didn't recognize. "Sorry, no breakfast today."

Jim Bell blinked. Maebeth had seen a look like that on someone's face just once before. She'd come upon the scene of an accident before paramedics had arrived. It was obvious the ambulance would be of no use to the driver, who was already dead. The man's teenage daughter knelt beside him, holding his hand. She never took her eyes off him and never spoke a word, as though she was bracing herself for the tidal wave of grief that was about to descend upon her. Maebeth had never seen anyone in shock before, but she recognized it that day and knew she was seeing it again now.

She wanted to help, at least settle their guest down with hot coffee, but didn't dare remove her hand from the running water.

Her husband took a step closer to Bell, invading the man's personal space.

Licking lips that were caked with white spittle, Jim Bell made an effort to focus. "That's okay," he said in a low, dull voice. "I left my room key on the counter."

He gave a quick glance at Maebeth's hand. "You should see a doctor."

"Why don't you take a seat in the dining room? We'll bring you coffee and cereal before you go," Maebeth began.

But Bell was already going.

Maebeth gave her husband a questioning look to see if he would go after Bell, maybe try to help him.

But Ted only shook his head.

The response was out of character for the man who had been awarded the Mid-State Innkeeper Golden Key for Hospitality three years running.

"Let it go, Mae," he said now, stepping to the sink for a closer look. The skin hung in flaps from her hand. "He's right about one thing. Let's get that looked at right away."

The Yukon rumbled to life and pulled past the windows.

Maebeth remembered Jim Bell said he had booked a fishing trip today. "I need to reach Ken Kincaid." She turned off the faucet and winced in pain. She turned it back on again. "On second thought, bring me the portable phone."

His face set with worry, her husband brought her the phone, careful to step around the dogs who were wolfing down muffin crumbs.

Maebeth dialed Ken's number. No answer. She left a message, then hung up and dialed again for good measure. Still no answer. She hung up, disappointed. She wanted more than anything to hear Ken's voice.

"Ken's not answering his phone," she said while Ted prepared an ice pack. "I think we should stop by his place on the way to the hospital."

"It's out of the way," her husband replied. "We'll swing by on the way home."

That would be too late, a fact Maebeth would have pointed out if the pain in her hand weren't so intense. She vomited. Her hand had taken on the color and consistency of raw hamburger meat. She spent the ride holding her head between her legs, telling herself over and over that Ken could take care of himself.

Gus Kincaid slept later than usual, till almost eight. He rose carefully from his bed, grateful he could stand despite the stiffness in his joints. He reviewed the events of last night as he dressed. Nan and Alice were all right, so no problem there. Ken had stayed the night with them. But Gus was anxious to tell his son what he had seen on the way home.

A white SUV parked in the bushes, at the head of an old logging trail that ran alongside the Birmingham ranch.

Gus glanced at the clock. Not quite half past. Plenty late enough, if you thought about it, to call Nan's place. She was probably up and about. Most folks in the country were early risers. But he didn't want to alarm her.

Nope, he'd discuss it with Ken first. Probably nothing. Gus reached into a cabinet to pull out the coffee can when a snippet of conversation from last night came back to him. Alice told them she'd almost collided with a white Yukon out on the county road yesterday. Most likely, some darned tourist from out of town. Which got Gus to thinking.

He put the coffee away and grabbed his jacket. Gus felt snow in his bones when he bent to scratch the cat behind her ears.

"Watch over the place, Midnight."

The cat yawned and went back to sleep.

The temperature outside had dropped dramatically since yesterday. More snow was on the way. Early in the season but there you had it.

Gus walked along Main Street, taking his time due to the stiffness in his bones. If he was lucky, he'd reach the inn while Maebeth's muffins were still warm.

Ken showered and changed at his place. He never shaved when he went to the cabin, just like he had never shaved on game days. He'd do that later, before he saw Alice again.

He grinned at his reflection in the mirror.

Draining the last of his coffee, he packed the items he'd need. Extra batteries for the flashlight, his short-wave radio, his toolbox. He'd swing past his father's place once more to check on him before heading up to the cabin.

Ken gathered his stuff and headed out. The sky was gray. The wind had picked up, pushing a few tiny snow-flakes through the air. It was cold. The forecast called for light snow. Which meant there could be significant accumulations up on the mountain.

The Jeep had new tires and shocks. There was plenty of water and canned goods stocked in the cabin. Not that he'd need it. He planned to come back in time to take Alice to dinner.

He slammed the hatch and heard a small sound close by. He turned, and found himself face-to-face with a sight that put his instincts on high alert.

Caroline waited until she heard Ken's Jeep drive off then slid out of bed. Her plan was to leave for Durango as quickly as possible, taking her chances there until the next Greyhound passed through. There was no time to make plans now. Last night proved it.

She took a quick shower and checked herself in the mirror.

The bruises were fading but not gone.

She heard movement in the kitchen and knew Nan was awake.

She gathered her things into a neat pile. A few items of clothing, toiletries, a brush for Pippin, and her savings. Enough to tide her over until she found another job. Her gaze fell on the picture book Ken had given her. She packed it in the knapsack as a reminder that life could be wonderful.

Just not for her.

She carried her things down the front stairs and left them near the front door where Nan wouldn't notice.

The smell of frying bacon greeted her. Nan hummed a cheery tune at the stove. " 'Mornin', Alice."

The older woman's eyes looked bluer than usual today.

"Good morning, Nan."

"Coffee's on," Nan lifted the splash cover on a cast-iron skillet to give the bacon a stir.

The dogs crowded around Nan's feet.

Caroline couldn't leave until breakfast was done. She poured herself a cup of coffee.

A timer went off and she nearly jumped out of her skin.

"My spoon bread is done. I'll start the eggs in a minute."

Caroline gave her a quizzical look as Nan bustled over to the oven. Nan didn't eat much in the morning, not to mention the fact that it was the one meal Caroline usually prepared.

"I figured we'd have company for breakfast," Nan said.

By which she meant Ken. Caroline shrugged. "I heard him leave a while ago. He told me last night he'd check on you, ah, on us, later."

"Ah, well, we'll save some for him," Nan said, draining the bacon. "He's a lovely man. I've known him since he was born." She cracked brown eggs into a bowl and whisked in milk and fresh-cut chives. "No matter what sort of situation you might find yourself in, Ken Kincaid is a good man to know. There's nobody better."

Their eyes met.

Nan looked happy. Caroline decided Nan knew of Ken's attraction to her, and approved. If Nan knew the truth about Caroline's past, however, she wouldn't look so happy. Caroline studied the remains of her coffee. "He's a good person."

Fortunately, Nan was like most folks in Storm Pass, considering a subject finished after a sentence or two.

She spooned great heaping piles of eggs onto Caroline's plate, along with thick-sliced bacon, fresh fruit, and slices of warm bread topped with butter. She fussed over Caroline like a mother hen, pouring glasses of fresh-squeezed orange juice like it was champagne for a celebration.

Seeing Nan like this only sharpened the pain in Caroline's heart for the hurt she was about to cause by running off. She wasn't hungry but did her best. It could be days before she had a hot meal. "This is the best breakfast I've ever had."

Across the table, Nan beamed.

CHAPTER

32

The man on Ken's driveway had empty eyes and the drunken look of a fighter who'd taken too many punches. Any similarity with a prizefighter ended there, however. The man was thin, with ghost white skin dotted with pockmarks and an intensity that rolled off him in waves.

Ken took in the red-rimmed eyes and the leather bag he was clutching to his chest like a kid with a security blanket. A white Yukon was parked at the end of the drive. Ken did some quick calculations. One, he could take this guy blindfolded with one hand tied behind his back. Two, there was a razor-sharp bowie knife in the Jeep glove compartment. Three, there was a shotgun gathering dust inside the house. While Ken pondered why he was cataloguing ways to hurt the guy, the man cleared his throat to speak.

"I, ah, wanted to go fishing." He licked his lips and flashed a nervous smile. "That's all. I heard you're the man to see." He let his head drop with a pleading glance that reminded Ken of the way a small dog will roll on its belly in the presence of a bigger one.

Something in Ken's gut tightened. "How'd you get here?" His voice came out colder than he'd intended.

The stranger winced like he'd been stung. He looked in the direction of the Yukon, which was parked well out of earshot.

Ken remembered Alice's story about her close brush with an SUV yesterday.

"I parked down near the road. I didn't want to intrude, seeing as how busy you are and all." The man shoved his thin hands into the pockets of his fatigues, which were still crisp like they'd never been washed. He kicked at a clod of dirt with the toe of one barely worn boot, shifting his weight. "I promised my boy we'd come here all summer, then I got stuck at work, then he got real sick and my ex wouldn't let me bring him."

The man stared at his feet.

Ken watched, frowning, as the man's thin shoulders hunched. He waited wordlessly while the guy cleared his throat and looked up at him again through steel-rimmed glasses.

"He worships you, you know? You're Ken Kincaid. He's got posters of the Chiefs all over his room, and I promised him I'd come here, bring him back some fish we caught together, and . . ." The man's voice trailed off.

Ken suspected then that he understood what he was seeing. The wild look, the nervousness, the dry mouth. The strange little man in front of him was acting like any groupie outside the Chiefs' locker room after a game. "Look, I'm sorry, but the weather up on the mountain is unpredictable this time of year. I'm not taking any more fishing clients up till next spring."

The man's nostrils flared like a bull as he pushed a

breath out his nose. A flash of something crossed the guy's face as his lips worked themselves into a thin white line.

Disappointment?

But the man pulled his fishing cap, the overpriced variety that was designed to block out UVA rays, down low over his face so it was impossible to tell. He shook his head slowly and spread his bony hands in disbelief. "I don't know what I'm going to tell him. He's been in the hospital awhile this time, and he can finally eat again. His favorite meal in the world is fried fish sticks, and—" His voice broke.

Ken swallowed. He pictured the guy's son watching every pro game from every sport on TV, dreaming he'd make himself into more of a man than his loser of an old man. "I'll tell you what," he began.

The man brightened.

"I've got some old publicity photos inside, and a football or two. I'll sign one with your son's name." A football with Ken's autograph could still fetch a decent price on eBay. If the guy was after money, this should be the end of it.

The man's face fell. His lower lip quivered, and his pale blue eyes glinted. He blinked a few times and shrugged. "Don't get me wrong, he'd love that."

Ken drew in a breath, considering. He was headed up to the cabin anyway. He could bring the man along, send him back to Denver or wherever with enough frozen fillets to feed his son for a month. Something made him hold back. Whether it was the fact that the guy had showed up unannounced or that his face was oozing like a skid row junkie, Ken swallowed the impulse to invite him along.

As though he could read Ken's thoughts, the man glanced at the gear inside the Jeep. "I didn't mean to interrupt anything. It looks like you were about to head off for the weekend. Probably got your girl waiting on you somewheres." He gave a small smile, revealing rows of tiny white teeth set in bright red gums.

His folksy manner of speaking didn't match his expensive gear. Ken wasn't overly curious as a rule, but he kept thinking of Alice and her near-miss yesterday. "Where are you from?"

He extended his hand. "Oh, pardon my manners. I'm Jim Bell. I live just south of Denver."

The guy's hand was soft to the touch, and Ken released it as quickly as possible.

Jim Bell licked his lips and wrung his hands before rubbing his chin, which was already raw. He kept his leather purse tucked firmly under one arm and cast another glance at the Jeep. "I guess you need to be going. Someone's waiting on you."

"She's not waiting on me." The words were out before Ken remembered his old rule for dealing with fans. Never give them any personal information. But he was out of practice. And he felt sorry for this guy, who had managed to sweet-talk just one woman in his entire life. And she'd thrown him out, despite the sick kid. Poor guy. "I was headed up on my own."

Jim Bell perked up, his voice high with wonder. "So, you're headed up to your cabin right now?"

The guy's hair wasn't really gray, it was a dingy shade of white. Which made him younger than Ken had thought, probably near his own age. Spooky. Ken nodded.

Jim Bell watched Ken intently. "Oh," he breathed. "My son would just not believe this."

Ken pictured the kid, bald from chemo treatments or worse, a patchwork of clumps the color of old straw like his dad. Ken wanted a big family. Boys or girls, it didn't matter. In the end, that had been the deal breaker with his ex-wife. And in the last few years, he had come to accept the possibility it might not happen. Until Alice. The thought of her softened him. He shoved his hands in his jeans pockets. "How old is your son?"

A big smile spread across Jim Bell's pale features, as though he sensed an invisible tide had changed direction. "Seven." His voice broke.

Ken glanced up at Ute Peak, which was disappearing behind a telltale gray mist. "Okay, Jim, I can bring you up to my fishing camp."

The man's smile deepened.

He didn't have the look of someone who smiled as a rule. "I have to warn you, though, I was headed up there mainly to shut the place down for winter. There's a storm brewing. We might get some fishing in, and we might not. We may just turn around and be back by late afternoon."

Jim nodded, triumphant. "That's fine." He reached into his hip pocket. "I'm happy to pay you anything at all for this."

Ken waved him off. "No charge, Jim. You save the money for your son."

The man protested, which struck Ken as funny. He would have pegged the guy as the type who had never bought a round in a bar in his life.

"Please," Jim Bell said in his intense way. "Money's no problem. Really. This means the world to me. You have no idea."

Fans were the same no matter what their age. "No,

I won't take your money, Mr. Bell. Anyhow," he said with a chuckle, "I can't promise you'll catch any fish up there today. This isn't going to be your typical fishing expedition."

Jim Bell's eyes narrowed behind his steel-framed glasses. He spoke slowly, measuring each word. "You know, I think you're right."

Caroline stashed her stuff in Nan's Buick and ducked back inside to finish clearing the breakfast dishes. She loaded the dishwasher and ran it although it was not even half full, emptied the garbage, and tried to take care of as many things as she could for the woman who had helped her when she'd needed it most.

And then it was time to go.

"I'm taking Poppit to the groomer," she announced.

Nan looked up from her needlepoint. Outside, Ute Peak was already hidden behind a white curtain of snow. "You picked quite a day," Nan said. "Come back early, Alice. You're about to discover why they call it Storm Pass."

Caroline forced a smile, not trusting her voice to speak. Her plan was to drive to Durango and catch the next Greyhound to Denver, whenever that might be. She would map out her next move from there, leaving the keys tucked under one wheel of the Buick and a note in the glove box. She would call later to say where the car could be found. She took one last look at Nan, her brilliant blue eyes set in her lined face, snug and sound in her cherished home, surrounded by a lifetime of happy memories. "I'll be careful," Caroline promised.

Nan smiled and went back to her needlepoint. "Enjoy your outing, Alice."

Caroline tried to press the scene into her mind so she would remember it forever.

They made decent time up to the entrance of the state wilderness area. The roads were slick. The temperature had dropped eight degrees since they left Ken's place, and the snow fell thicker the higher they climbed.

Ken kept the Yukon headlights in his rearview mirror. Jim Bell was not a mountain driver. That was evident after the first couple of switchbacks. He took the turns too fast and jammed on the brakes midway, like someone used to flat roads at sea level. The SUV had dealer plates, fresh off the lot. No matter. That Yukon could pretty much drive itself at slow speed. Ken kept the Jeep in low gear and took the turns extra slow, hoping Jim Bell was paying attention.

Unless this storm blew past quickly, they'd stay at the cabin just long enough to turn off the gas and drain kerosene from the portable heater before heading back down. Ken had some rainbow trout fillets stored in his freezer that the guy could take home to his son.

In the second car, Porter drummed his fingers across the dash, his heart racing faster and faster. His mouth was dry inside like a piece of cotton. He took a swig from the Coke left over from yesterday, swishing the flat syrup inside his mouth before swallowing.

Things were going his way.

One side of the road was edged by a narrow band of loose rock and a wall of granite. The other had a guardrail and a sheer drop to eternity. The goddamned snow kept falling. Porter shifted into overdrive. He kept one eye on the Jeep and one eye on the guardrail. He could take Kincaid out now, make it look like an accident. But chances were the Yukon would fly off the mountain after the Jeep. And that would spoil his plan.

Kincaid at close range was exactly what Porter expected. Tall, dark, and handsome. Right out of an ad for men's sportswear with a suntanned face and big white teeth. Porter knew guys like Ken Kincaid always got exactly what they wanted. Except this time he had gone after Porter's wife.

Caroline would have fallen for him right away, Porter could see that. Swooning in her slut mode for the guy's easy smile and big hands. Tall guys always got laid without even trying. Kincaid, with his pro-football career and A-frame house on the side of a mountain, screamed cock. No doubt, Caroline didn't understand the true nature of her motivation.

The thought of his wife raised bile at the back of Porter's throat. If she could just see this for what it was, if she would only open her eyes and look at the truth. He'd tried so many times to get her into sessions with a Freudian analyst. Hell, most people could never afford what he had offered. Three times a week for nine years, maybe as little as seven. And she could have achieved what most people were too limited even to dream of. A detailed map of the inner workings of her own mind.

In the beginning she laughed, insisting she didn't need therapy to love someone. Her soft lower lip would drop into a pout when they argued, and she would tell him he couldn't expect to win just because he was a shrink.

She had little respect for his vocation.

Eventually, something shifted in her. Porter sensed it as soon as it came to pass. Her eyes shuttered against him and he knew he had lost her, as completely as he had lost his mother that day long ago when she walked out. Caroline had been corrupted by the violation she had suffered as a child by the simple fact that she had liked it. Unless and until he could make her admit this, she was doomed to act out her corruption again and again.

Porter balled his fist and pounded the wheel, groaning aloud. One chance remained. Perhaps she would gain insight into her own moral corruption after she witnessed the damage she had caused.

That's why Kincaid needed to die.

Convincing Kincaid to bring him up here had been easy. Porter had learned at a young age how to read people's faces to get them to do what he wanted. It was his primary survival skill.

Porter's strategy didn't work with downtrodden types like the gum-cracking waitress and her tattooed boyfriend. People like that could smell a con, since they were often cons themselves.

He'd watched Kincaid size him up. Kincaid had taken care not to show aversion to the boils on Porter's face, or his albino-like skin and colorless hair.

Surprisingly, Kincaid hadn't looked away, locking in on Porter instead with an unflinching gaze. Athletes had the capacity to shut out everything and focus.

He knew Kincaid wouldn't want to take him to the cabin. Kincaid had no good reason for doing it.

So Porter chose his moment and played his trump card.

Kincaid had leaned his weight on one hip, considering Jim Bell's sickly son.

Porter had fidgeted shamelessly, running through the catalog of body language indicating low self-esteem, knowing that a lack of physical control would be a sign to Kincaid of ultimate weakness. Which in turn would make him feel superior. Guilt would follow, which in turn would motivate him to make a decision he would later regret.

Pippin perched on the passenger seat of the Buick, ears pricked, happy to be out. The car slogged through the snow until it lost traction and fishtailed. Caroline hit the brakes, worsening the skid. They slid to a stop in the middle of the road. She sat, hands shaking, working up the nerve to try again. No wonder Nan called it the old boat.

The pavement gleamed wet. Tiny snowflakes flashed past the headlights. She prayed Greyhound would be running on schedule.

She passed the turnoff for Storm Pass but didn't take it, heading straight out to the county road. She glimpsed Kincaid's Garage, with Gus's pickup parked outside. The inside bays, she knew, provided shelter in winter for Ken's red Porsche.

She bid a silent good-bye and tightened her grip on the wheel, which did nothing to quiet the quaking of her body. She wasn't used to driving in snow. At this rate, she would be lucky to make it to the Greyhound stop in one piece.

She pressed her foot on the accelerator. The Buick responded slowly, sliding into another skid. This time Caroline kept on the gas, slow and steady, steering into it until the car righted itself.

There was, Caroline thought, a method to winter driving.

WASHINGTON, D.C.

Officer Mike Hartung loved his job, he really did. Like now, where the last of the morning rush was wheeling past him in Eckington, a neighborhood that was most definitely not listed on D.C. tourist maps.

He had grabbed a few hours' sleep at home last night before heading back to Georgetown just before dawn to see what the night crew uncovered. They had done their jobs thoroughly. By the time Hartung's takeout coffee had cooled, there was little they didn't know about the habits and lifestyle of Dr. Porter Moross; his wife, Caroline Hughes; and their dog, Pippin.

The dog, for example, was a purebred.

The wife had a cache of things hidden up in the attic crawlspace. E-mails and cards from an old beau, along with some Milky Way bars and an unopened bag of cherry Twizzlers.

The collection of DVDs, pills, and syringes would have been enough to convince anyone that Dr. Porter Moross was a straight-up freak. And that was not taking into account the contents of the Sterlite container Moross kept under their bed.

A hush fell over the room when one of the officers pulled out a horse's tail and riding crop.

"Thank God for latex," he said, referring to the gloves they all wore when handling evidence.

There was a snicker or two. One guy shook his head and left the room. Everyone else just kept working.

They hit pay dirt in the office, after the computer had been hauled off to have its hard drive analyzed and the safe had been cracked.

They hit the mother lode inside Moross's locked files, in the form of an old-fashioned check ledger where Moross had kept backup entries in his tiny, precise hand-writing of every dime he spent. Control freak, Hartung thought. The contents of the ledger would be reviewed by a forensic accountant if the wife didn't turn up safe and sound pretty soon, but Hartung never forgot something he had first heard as a rookie.

In the end, money is what brought down Al Capone.

He figured it was worth a minute or two to check out the latest entries. One jumped right off the page. Two years' payment in advance to a U-Store facility across town.

Judging by the location, Moross wasn't using it to store the leftover antiques that wouldn't fit in this place.

Officer Mike Hartung looked up from the ledger and motioned for his partner to take a look. "We got something here. I got a good feeling." Hartung grinned. He loved his job. He really did.

And here he was, loving his job and loving life, loving the look on the face of the sleazebag proprietor of a self-storage facility inside a gray slab of a building that could have passed for a Third Reich bunker but for the gang graffiti on its walls.

The proprietor was falling over himself to be helpful, despite the fact he didn't know guests were coming. The goons posted outside had disappeared when the first squad car pulled up.

"No problem, no problem," the man said, waving away Hartung's warrant. "Come right in, come right in." Despite the morning coolness and a breeze that promised autumn at last, the proprietor was sweating like a pig. In fact, he looked ready to wet his pants. "Please," he said, "look around, whatever you need."

It was amazing, Hartung thought, what the sight of six cops armed with bolt cutters and semiautomatic AR–15 assault rifles could do.

He waited while the proprietor went through his files. "Here it is, a five-by-ten walk-in on the top floor. That's a corner unit, our very best, our very best," the proprietor said, slicing one hand through the air with a proud little flourish.

As though, Hartung thought, the biggest selling point of this place was you could stash your assault rifle for safekeeping when it was not in use.

The proprietor handed over the passkey and Hartung signaled his crew. Two men headed back outside to take up positions at the exits. Two ran up the rear stairwell, leaving Hartung and his partner to take the front.

The proprietor looked ready to throw up.

Hartung leaned in close, keeping his voice as hard and cold as the steel entrance door. "Nobody comes in, nobody leaves. I'll let you know when we're finished."

The man's head was bouncing like a bobble-head doll in a van with bad shocks. "No problem, sir, no problem at all." He backed away from the counter, and this time Hartung was positive he smelled urine on the guy's pants.

Hartung turned away to follow his partner, who was already taking the concrete stairs two at a time.

The forest was awash in shifting, swirling snowflakes. The Jeep bounced onto the turn for the grass track. The Yukon followed close behind, its lumbering shape indistinct against the white snow. The Yukon could handle the rutted track easily, Ken decided. Jim Bell, however, was another story.

The guy was off balance. That fact, combined with the dealer plates, prompted Ken to formulate a Plan B. They would leave Bell's car here and retrieve it tomorrow. The least he could do was make sure the guy didn't wreck his new car on the way back down.

Ken took the track slow and steady. Snow changed the landscape, masking familiar landmarks. But Colorado weather was apt to change. The wind at this altitude could clear the clouds at any moment, leaving a sunny afternoon for trout fishing. Maybe.

The sky lightened as the track opened onto the mesa. Ken pulled the Jeep up close to the cabin. The lake was choppy and dull, the color of the shale that lined its shores. Clouds hung low. The only sound was wind.

Ken took it all in. If the Rockies were close to heaven on earth, this place was its cathedral.

The Yukon rumbled to a stop behind him and Bell climbed out, clutching his leather briefcase.

Bell was, Ken thought, every inch the businessman who goes on vacation and spends his time in search of wireless access.

Bell zipped his parka as high as it would go. "Does it always snow like this?"

Ken grinned. "Sometimes." Bell seemed even more jittery after the drive. Ken already regretted his decision to bring him. The snow was really coming down. He did a quick inventory. The first aid kit was inside. The shortwave radio was in the Jeep. His cell phone would be of no use here.

The first rule of wilderness survival was to avoid dangerous situations, and Ken knew he'd broken it.

One look at Bell's face told him he couldn't afford to narrow his margin of error any further.

Bell removed his glasses to rub at his eyes.

He looked like he hadn't slept in days.

"So, this is what you like?" Bell said.

"Yeah."

Bell hunched deeper into his jacket. When he spoke, his voice had a dreamy quality, soft and weak. "This is the edge of everything. One small move and you've crossed over. It's perfect." He laughed at some private joke.

Ken did not join in. He'd expected Bell to make the usual comments about the beauty of the landscape, or ask what sort of animals lived here or, like the group of commercial Realtors he'd hosted back in June, ask how much he'd paid. Ken ignored the remark and set to work. The sooner they got out of here, the better.

Bell chuckled, and the sound had a brittle quality. "What I meant was, I've never seen anything like this."

Balancing his gear in one hand, Ken slammed the trunk shut. He eyed Bell's expensive parka and leather gloves. They were smooth dress gloves, not suitable for outdoor use. The getup was as conspicuous as Bell's lowland style of driving. Ken's eyes narrowed. "Come on inside. You can wait in the cabin while I do a few things." He did not add the fact that they'd be departing again within minutes.

Bell followed, still clutching the leather briefcase. The silence inside was eerie.

Ken filled two large glasses with spring water from a container and handed one to Bell. "Take a seat and drink this. It's important to keep your fluids up at this altitude."

Bell pulled off his ski cap and raked one thin hand across his scalp. The gesture had the look of a ritual that was compulsive. Bell caught Ken watching. "I lost every bit of pigmentation in my hair and skin when I was fourteen."

Ken shrugged. Bringing Bell up here had been a mistake. The man was unbalanced. "Sit down," he said again. "I'm going to turn off the propane at the tanks outside, take care of a few things, then we'll head back. This weather's no good for fishing."

Bell's mouth twisted, his eyes glinting in a sudden flash of anger. He opened his mouth to speak but changed his mind and snapped it shut. He rubbed his jaw and looked away. "Please," he said in a pleading tone. "Can you just show me around? My son will want to hear all about it and I . . ." Bell's voice faltered. "I'm not feeling well."

The man's simple acknowledgment of his own fragile mental state softened Ken. The drive had taken its toll.

Bell's eyes were shot through with red, and had dark hollows underneath. Putting something in his stomach might settle him. "Have a seat," Ken repeated.

Bell sat at last, keeping his briefcase on his lap. He took a tiny sip, then wiped his upper lip on his sleeve.

It was out of character for a man with manicured nails. "You okay?" Ken asked.

Blinking rapidly, Bell nodded.

The man's face had regained a tiny bit of color.

Ken drained his own glass, keeping an eye on Bell. By the look of it, the guy hadn't eaten in days.

He was toying nervously with the leather bag in his lap, his pale blue eyes flickering with something Ken had learned to recognize at an early age.

Resentment.

Bell tried to hide it, out of politeness, perhaps, and averted his gaze.

Ken sat, crossing one ankle over his knee, keeping his posture relaxed. But he never let Bell out of his line of sight. He wondered if the guy was addicted to drugs. One look at his pocked face told Ken it was a distinct possibility. His goal was to calm Bell enough to get him back to Storm Pass and from there, get him some help. When Ken spoke, he kept his tone steady and firm. "Does your son enjoy all sports, or just football?"

The room was silent as Bell considered this. "Just football."

Ken nodded. "He lives with his mother?"

"My wife? I suppose I should say, the woman who was my wife." Bell gave a short laugh that held no merriment. "She was something. Smart. Fun to be with. Beautiful. You would have liked her." Bell looked at

Ken, his eyes narrowing as a small smile curved his thin lips. "She's your type. Definitely."

Ken became aware that the hairs on the back of his neck were rising. He uncrossed his leg and crossed the other again, disliking the intensity in Bell's gaze.

"But I suppose I shouldn't say that, knowing as little about you as I do. Being a big football star and all, any woman would be your type, I'd imagine." Bell leaned forward, warming to the subject.

If he wanted to, Ken could lift Bell off the couch with one hand and choke the air from his lungs. Ken pushed away the impulse that had risen, unbidden, to his mind. He stood. "Drink the rest of your water. I'll get you something to eat." There were PowerBars in one of the cabinets. He got one now and set it down in front of Bell with a napkin.

Bell stared out the window, light glinting off his glasses.

"You need to eat," Ken said.

Bell roused himself from his reverie, tore the wrapper from the PowerBar, broke off a small piece, and chewed it.

Ken glanced outside. Snow continued to fall, thick and fast.

Bell sipped his water and swallowed with difficulty. "I get overwhelmed. She left me. I tried to make it work. Tried to make her see. And now she's with someone else." He shook his head as his face twisted with sorrow.

Ken was well acquainted with the kind of pain Bell described, but it was clear the guy was at his wit's end. The saddest fact was that he seemed to know it in his lucid moments. Like now.

"I never wanted it to end," he continued. "And then one day she was gone. Not even a good-bye note. All I really want is to bring her home again."

Ken flashed back to the first weeks after Suzie moved out. He ate in restaurants every night. He slept on the couch with the TV on, so if he woke he wouldn't hear the silence. He finally rented a suite at the Fairmont at Country Club Plaza, one of the best hotels in Kansas.

Ken knew better than to share his own story, however. Bell had more problems than the fact that his wife had walked out on him. "It's rough, I know. But you need to stay strong, Jim. You'll get through this. You are getting through it. Think of your son. He needs you now more than ever."

Bell stared at Ken. "Yeah. But I wish things could be different. You've got to believe that, Ken."

The intensity in Bell's gaze was unsettling.

"Things will work out."

Bell smiled. "Yes, Ken, they will. It was her call all along. She's the one holding all the cards. She knows that, and now she has to deal with the mess she's made." His voice broke. His face crumpled, and he covered it with his hands.

Wherever Mrs. Jim Bell was, Ken hoped she was happy. She had earned it.

Maebeth Burkle leaned against the flimsy white pillow and drifted off to sleep. The throbbing in her hand had lessened, thanks to the morphine and antibiotic drip in her arm.

Her husband conferred in quiet tones with the surgeon about the skin graft operation that was scheduled for later that afternoon. Hopefully, there would be no permanent nerve damage.

After checking on his wife, Ted Burkle went off in search of a pay phone. He needed to call Gus Kincaid and ask him to look after the dogs.

Ted dialed Gus's number and got the answering machine. He kept his message brief. "Maebeth will be fine, back to her old self in no time," he concluded. "Say, give Ken a call and tell him we need to speak with him about Jim Bell." He paused, at a loss for words. "Though I guess with the snow, he'll probably cancel."

Gus's answering machine clicked and reset itself on the kitchen counter. The sound disturbed the empty stillness of the place, waking Midnight. The black cat flicked her tail and went back to sleep.

* * *

The front door to the inn was still locked from overnight. Gus went around back and let himself in through the kitchen, which was always open. The Burkles' pickup was gone.

Gus stepped inside and looked around. A muffin tray lay on the floor, licked clean.

Jasper and Wyoming ambled over, tails wagging, planting themselves at his feet.

"Okay, boys, you know what's coming," Gus took liver treats from his pocket and fed them each in turn.

The dogs waggled and grunted happily.

"Where's the missus?" Gus asked.

The dogs licked their jowls and watched him.

Gus picked up the muffin tray and set it on the counter before heading into the dining room. The table was set for a breakfast that had not been touched.

The place was quiet.

The dogs followed him to the front parlor. Gus stood, jangling the change in his pockets. His glance fell on the leather guest book and he opened it, fumbling for his reading glasses. He flipped through the heavy book till he came to the last entry, dated yesterday. Jim Bell from Denver, Colorado. Under the "Comments" section, Jim Bell had written, "Came for the trout."

"Hmmph," Gus said. It was late for trout. Even a city type should know better than to waste his time coming up here this time of year. Ken would have told him that. In fact, Ken was just saying yesterday he didn't have any clients booked till next spring.

Gus frowned. The only sound in the place was Jasper grooming his front paws.

Where was everybody?

Gus hoped this man Bell wasn't fool enough to head into the wilderness on his own. It made no sense, but Gus Kincaid had seen a lot of things in seventy-eight years that left him scratching his head. He did so now.

He walked around the desk and pulled out Maebeth's registration file. The cards were in chronological order from the beginning of the year. He flipped to the back and studied the last card. The same hand, this time using tiny block letters, perfectly aligned, listed Jim Bell's Denver address and phone number.

The section marked vehicle registration had been written in Maebeth's familiar, looping hand in blue ink. Jim Bell's car had dealer plates. But it was the make of the car that caught Gus's eye. White GMC Yukon.

Gus frowned. He glanced at his watch. Quarter to nine.

He reached for the phone and dialed the home number listed on the registration card.

A male voice answered on the second ring. "Good morning. Mile High GMC, Denver's best. Jim Bell speaking."

he Buick was losing speed. The old car slowed whenever Caroline eased up on the gas. She pressed down harder each time, trying to keep her speed up. She was only one mile from Storm Pass, not even as far as the turnoff to Ken's place, when the car died.

She steered onto the shoulder where snow was piling up. There was silence. The green ALT light flashed when she tried the ignition. She stared, shaking her head in disbelief. It was as though the car, the weather, the place itself were all conspiring against her plans.

Pippin whined.

She switched off the lights, flipped on the hazards, and waited before trying again. Nothing. Not even clicking.

"Oh, no," she muttered, dropping her head against the seat. She closed her eyes and massaged her temples, trying to think.

Pippin jumped into her lap, sniffing at her face. The Greyhound would pass through in less than an hour.

She tried the engine a few more times before giving up. She released the hood, donned her wool cap, and got out, squinting her eyes against the driving snow. She opened the latch and looked underneath at lots of metal parts and hoses, coated with road grime. She was wondering what to do when she heard a powerful rumble.

She saw a pair of headlights, low to the ground, come into view as the candy apple red Porsche pulled up.

Relief flooded through her as the driver's side door swung open and Gus Kincaid stuck his head out.

"Top o' the morning," he called. "Need a hand?"

"Yes, please." Caroline hurried over and offered her hand as he worked to pull himself out of the low racing coupe.

Gus waved her off with a chuckle. "Thanks, young lady, but I'm afraid I'd take you right down with me. Give me a minute. I can manage." He hoisted himself to the edge of the leather seat and gathered his weight under him before pushing himself upright. He let out a mighty breath of air and smiled, embarrassed. "My son's the only one who can drive that thing."

Caroline nodded, wondering why Gus was out in a storm. She didn't ask because she didn't want to be questioned in return. Besides, she had no right. She was about to disappear from their lives forever.

Gus was already poking around under the hood. "Take a seat inside and start 'er up when I tell you," he said.

Caroline climbed back in and gave it gas at Gus's signal.

Again, there was no response.

Gus slammed the hood shut. "Generator's gone."

Caroline's heart sank in frustration. She had no idea what a generator did, but she wished it hadn't picked this day to stop working.

"Time for a new car, I think," Gus said, surveying Caroline's overflowing tote bag and backpack that took up most of the passenger seat. He picked up one of her hands in his and squeezed it. "Where you headed, Alice?"

The feel of his hand combined with his frank gaze was disarming. Caroline choked up.

Gus waited, keeping a grip on her hand.

"I need a ride to the groomer," she said finally in a low voice.

"I can manage that," he said kindly.

He did not point out it was a terrible day to drive halfway across the county, a fact she was grateful for. "Thanks," she whispered.

He collected her bags and waited while she scooped Pippin into her arms and climbed out.

He chatted about nothing, his tone soothing, as she got settled inside the Porsche. Nan told her he'd lost his wife at a young age and had raised their infant son alone. And now that son had grown into a man as strong and kind as his father. Caroline forced herself to hold back the tears that were pulsing behind her eyes. Tears she dared not shed.

Gus shifted into second and pulled out. "This car isn't meant for driving in snow but she'll take the road in second gear."

Within seconds Caroline saw that he was right.

"I can probably manage to get your errands done and get you back to Nan's in one piece. I'll have hell to pay if I don't." He winked.

She managed a weak smile.

He slowed at the turnoff to Ken's place. "I just need to make a quick stop here first."

Caroline's heart did a flip-flop. Time was tight, not to mention the last thing she wanted was to see Ken. But she had no choice. Gus's detour might cost her a seat on the Greyhound bus, a fact he couldn't possibly know. Or did he?

"I want to trade cars and use his Jeep. 'Cause this thing isn't worth a darn in the ice and snow, if you ask me." Gus harrumphed. "Might as well drop by while we're in the neighborhood."

Ken's place was empty. The drive had fresh tire tracks in the snow. The Jeep was gone.

"That's strange," Gus said.

A feeling of dread settled over Caroline. They went in, leaving Ken's spare keys dangling in the door.

She had been here just once before, but a wave of emotion hit her as soon as she stepped inside. A woodsy scent filled her nostrils. Ken's scent. She looked around, expecting to see him come around a corner any second to greet them.

But the place was silent as a tomb.

On the counter, his answering machine blinked with several new messages.

Ken kept a close watch on Bell, every muscle in his body primed and ready to pounce. Ken could take him out in three seconds. But he'd bust the coffee table in the process.

Bell was weeping softly.

Ken wished he could help. He'd taken in strays as a kid, once even getting Gus to drive clear across the county for an eyedropper from the twenty-four-hour pharmacy so they could nurse a baby blue jay. But Bell's strange fits of emotion were alarming. His moods shifted too fast, for one thing. Ken had seen his share of rage on the field, some of it fueled by steroids, but there had been less of it as he rose through the ranks. Men who made pro had mastered their emotions, even in a sport known for its punishing physical contact.

Which meant that Jim Bell's top-of-the-line SUV and state-of-the-art gear didn't match up to the seesaw of emotion he displayed.

A lot of things about him weren't right.

Porter ripped off his steel-rimmed glasses and dug at his eyes with his knuckles. He snuck a glance at Kincaid, and didn't like what he saw. Kincaid was watchful.

Wary. Time was running out, Porter knew. Things were no longer going as well as he had hoped. He needed to choose his moment soon, or his opportunity would pass.

Watching Bell, Ken recalled how frightened Alice had been last night. She was convinced there had been something in the woods. Not something. Someone. A man she might be fleeing from. It was hard to believe Alice's ex could be the man sniffling on Ken's couch right now. The idea was repugnant to Ken. And yet, once it presented itself, it quickly took root in his mind.

Watching Kincaid, Porter saw Ken's eyes harden in a look that had made many an opposing halfback brace himself for the worst. Porter flinched. He stopped crying and blew his nose. "Okay," he said, shifting gears. "Okay."

Ken stood, drawing himself up to his full height, which was considerable. Squaring his shoulders, he centered his weight on the balls of his feet in the classic fight stance. "I'm going to go outside for a minute, and you're going to wait right here, Jim."

Porter took another sip of water with hands that shook. "Shall I, shall I, ah . . . ?"

"Wait here. I'm going to turn off the propane tanks, then we'll head down."

Porter gave a vigorous nod, not meeting Ken's gaze.

Satisfied that Bell was settled for the moment, Ken stepped out the back door into the swirling storm.

Snow came at him from all directions. Several inches lay on the ground and more was coming. He could feel it.

He drew the cold air deep into his lungs and held it before expelling it fully through his lips in an attempt to rid himself of anxiety. He wanted to get out of here as quickly as possible.

Ken could just make out the surface of the lake, dark as slate. He was glad for a few minutes alone. His high spirits of the morning were all but forgotten.

He headed for the twin tanks along the rear wall of the cabin and reached for the first valve. It screwed shut easily. Not so the second valve, located back at the base. Ken knelt on the cold ground, his fingers pushing at the safety clamp. It refused to budge. Ken pushed harder.

The clamp still refused to yield.

"Damn," he muttered. He had tools in the Jeep, but retrieving them now would add precious minutes to the task. And he wanted to get out of here as quickly as possible.

Bracing himself, he closed his hand around the clamp once more and pushed with all his strength.

The clamp had begun to give way when he felt a prick on his leg like a bee sting.

He gasped in surprise and rocked back onto his heels. He caught movement from the corner of his eye and swung around, to find himself staring into the barrel of a gun.

WASHINGTON, D.C.

The key worked and the lock sprang open. The police officers announced their presence, kicked the door open, and burst into the storage room, taking up positions the way they had drilled.

There was no one inside.

What they saw, however, was enough to stop all four cops dead in their tracks.

Inside was an altar of sorts.

Hartung was the first to break the silence. "Bullshit."

"Amen," someone said.

He fumbled behind him for the wall switch. The dim light of the overhead bulb only served to heighten the sense Hartung had that he had stumbled onto the set of a Hitchcock movie.

Officer Mike Hartung hated scary movies.

The room was spotless. In its center was a gleaming steel barrel, the kind used for hazardous waste, draped in ivory lace. On top was a single snowy white candle in a holder. Next to it was a pack of matches and a framed photograph of a young woman, and in her lap sat a little boy.

The woman could have been any young mother wearing a silk blouse with shoulder pads and Boy George spiky bangs, which made Hartung guess the photo had been taken sometime in the late 1980s.

But there was no mistaking the identity of the little boy with thick brown hair and pale blue eyes, peering anxiously into the camera.

Next to the barrel was a daybed with pillows.

It was a match for the one in Moross's office. A therapy couch.

If the whole setup wasn't spooky enough to begin with, this realization alone would have been enough to kick up Hartung's Spidey sense. But Spidey was already in high gear.

Next to the therapy couch was a straight-backed chair, extra matches, and a big box of candles.

Spares.

Hartung was the first to move. Donning latex gloves, he swiped a finger across the base of the candle. "No dust."

The rim of the daybed was just as clean.

Which meant it got frequent use.

They collected the items atop the barrel and sealed them inside evidence bags, after photographing the scene.

"Well, here goes." Hartung's partner began working the rim of the barrel with a crowbar, with an assist from a couple of officers who held the container steady. The room was quiet as a tomb while he worked.

When the lid finally popped, Hartung was very glad he hadn't stopped for bagels.

The musky odor of decay worked its way out through countless layers of industrial-gauge plastic sheeting.

There were audible groans as the officers donned masks and kept cutting away layers.

Hartung fished in his pocket for the Kleenex he always carried to homicide scenes, and pressed it against his mask.

It did nothing to blot out the stench, but it gave him something to do besides ponder the grisly contents of the container.

When the last of the plastic sheeting had been worked open, the officers stepped back.

"Jesus Christ," someone muttered.

The room fell silent out of respect for what they had found.

Gus hit the play button on Ken's answering machine, offering no apology for listening to his son's private messages. He didn't have to. The worry lines on his face said it all.

Maebeth's voice, sounding worn and frayed. "Ken, it's Maebeth. Call us before you head up to camp today. We need to speak with you before you leave."

Not her usual, cheery self.

The dread inside Caroline morphed into a suspicion that was too ugly to think about. But Maebeth's next words confirmed Caroline's worst fear.

"I doubt you'll take your client up there in this weather, but call us." The call ended abruptly.

The machine whirred and reset itself.

But Ken had taken his new client up to the cabin, against his better judgment and his common sense. Caroline was certain of it.

His client would have persuaded him.

Because this client knew all there was to know about manipulation.

Suddenly, she couldn't catch her breath. The room tilted around her. She swallowed and looked at Gus.

Gus was staring at the machine. He met Caroline's gaze and winked, trying to reassure her that everything was okay.

Except they both knew it wasn't.

"Just a second here," he said, clearing his throat. "Maybe Ken's left a message for me." He dialed his own number and entered a code.

There was one new message, from Ted Burkle at the county hospital. Something about Maebeth burning her hand.

But Ted's final words added weight to the heavy feeling that was pressing down on Gus's chest. Something about Jim Bell, the guest who had arrived yesterday. He drove a white Yukon.

Gus hung up and chose his next words carefully. Alice was fragile on her best days and her face had turned white as snow, her eyes wild and unfocused, the pupils already constricted to the size of tiny dots.

She was staring out the window up to where the pass would be visible on a clear day. When she spoke her voice was dull and faint. "He's up there."

There was no use pretending. Gus nodded.

Alice swallowed hard with trembling lips.

Gus Kincaid wasn't the type to get worked up over things. Nor was he one to mince words. He recalled the conversation he'd had a short while ago with the real Jim Bell, the car dealer who had answered the phone in Denver. Gus looked at Alice now, his gaze steady and direct. "Does the name Porter Moross mean anything to you?"

She recoiled as though she'd been punched. "No," she whispered, squeezing her eyes shut, grabbing for the counter to steady herself.

Gus reached out to calm her. "Take it easy, Alice. Ken can take care of himself."

Her eyes sprang open in alarm. She sprinted to the door and grabbed Ken's spare keys.

Gus moved to stop her. "Alice, now . . ." he began.

But she was halfway out, with Pippin racing past her. "Call the police and tell them to come right away. He's got a gun."

"Alice, hold on. If you know this man . . ." Gus kept his voice steady in spite of the alarm he felt.

The terror in her voice made itself heard as she ran into the storm. "Porter Moross is my husband."

The Porsche rumbled to life as Gus dialed the sheriff. There were just two in all three hundred square miles of Sky County. With any luck, one of them would be close by.

Ken stared at the handgun. His mind struggled to make sense of it while his body coiled instinctively into a protective crouch. Even more puzzling than the gun in Bell's right hand was the syringe he clutched in his left.

Ken felt pins and needles in his leg.

Bell sneered, his voice calm and steady, his accent sharply East Coast now. "Get up. Or I'll kill you right here."

One look at Bell's eyes, glittering and hard like broken glass, was enough to convince Ken. Bell was Alice's ex, Ken was certain of it.

Ken stood, or rather, attempted to. His legs were heavy, wobbling under him like rubber. Walking required all his concentration. He shook his head in disbelief. "Jim, you don't need to do this . . ."

Bell let the syringe drop to the ground and backed up, never loosening his grip or his aim. "But I do, Ken. It's time for the truth, time for everybody to get honest. With themselves. And with me. I'll even go first." His lips curled into a mirthless smile. "My real name is Porter Moross. I am a doctor in Washington, D.C."

Ken felt a wild thumping in his heart. His face flushed with heat despite the cold wind whipping around them.

Moross surveyed him coolly. "The dose is kicking in, I see. Move inside while you can."

Ken fought for every breath, feeling his heart pound slow and heavy inside his ribs. Walking had become a task that required all his concentration.

"They use this for lethal injections. To kill people who've done bad things," Moross said with a short laugh. "And you've done some bad things, Kincaid, haven't you?" Moross looked at Ken through eyes narrowed to tiny slits, his lips pulled back into a smile as false as that of a wax figure.

Ken saw the madness in Moross's face. He judged his odds of tackling Moross head-on, despite the heavy-gauge pistol in Moross's hand. But Ken knew his timing wasn't what it had been, his bad knee was no longer trustworthy. And his legs were turning to lead. Inside the cabin was a loaded shotgun at the back of the wardrobe near Ken's bed. A box of shells was stowed on the shelf above it. That was his best option at the moment. Ken took in a deep, ragged breath.

Moross watched him with interest. "Another man would have collapsed by now. You'll have use of your legs for another minute or so. Walk while you still can." He motioned with the gun and stepped back, careful to stay out of Ken's reach.

There was no choice but to do as Moross ordered. Ken shuffled ahead of him with uncertain steps, bracing himself at every moment for an explosion in his spine. He made it to the cabin and almost as far as the couch before his legs gave way. He managed to get his arms under him to break his fall, using the last of his strength to prop himself against the side of the couch. He had lost all feeling in his hips. He lay back, his breathing labored and heavy.

Moross watched, his eyes glittering with satisfaction. "It's awful to be helpless, isn't it? I could cut you with a knife right now and guess what? You'd still feel pain." He laughed, revealing tiny rows of teeth.

Ken thought of Alice with this man, and his mind recoiled in horror. He focused on the gun inside the wardrobe. Twenty paces away. He could drag himself to it while he still had the use of his arms. He flexed his fingers. They still worked.

"But why am I wasting words on you?" Moross said, smiling. "You're just a dumb jock."

Moross appeared more relaxed, in control now. But his hands remained wrapped around the pistol, his finger on the trigger. "And I am a doctor. Not just any doctor, Ken. A special kind of doctor. Not that you give a shit."

Anger flashed like lightning across Moross's face again.

Ken wondered if Moross would shoot. He looked down, closed his eyes.

But Moross kept talking. "Actually, this is your one and only, last chance to have the best therapy session of your life." He chuckled. "People come from far and wide to consult with me, Kincaid, just like they used to come to see you play. I was a star," he said, his voice dropping. "We have a lot in common, if you think about it." His eyes narrowed. "Even more so if you count my wife."

Moross's knuckles were white where he gripped the pistol. His voice shook with rage. He licked his lips.

"We're going to do a quick review of your life, Ken, and bring you to a deeper understanding of how it all fits together." Here he paused. "And how your actions have impacted my life. How about that?" Moross's voice dropped another notch, unsteady with emotion.

Ken stood still. A heavy weight was working its way up through his abdomen and chest, squeezing the air from his lungs and causing his heart to thump like a jackrabbit. Breathing now required all his strength. His arms felt numb and he had probably lost the use of his hands, but he couldn't be certain. He didn't want to risk flexing his fingers while Moross watched, even though the man was now gazing up at the ceiling with a lunatic stare.

Ken swallowed. He could feel movement only at the back of his throat, nothing below that. Claustrophobia gripped him. He'd felt this way once before, after he took a bad hit in the chest on the field. He'd lain there while the medics worked on him, unable to feel his legs. The stadium fell silent as Ken was carried off. Luckily, he'd recovered. That time. Ken fought the unease that rose inside him now. Panic was the enemy. To clear his mind, he summoned his strength to speak. "Why?" His voice sounded thin and weak to his own ears.

"Good question." Moross smiled. "You show promise as a psychotherapy patient. I mean that as a compliment, you know."

Moross was enjoying this. But the smile faded from his face. "You already know the answer to that, if you think about it. The answers are always there. Beginning with this one." He leaned forward to be sure Ken was paying attention. "You stole my wife." Moross licked his lips, fighting to keep his voice steady. "You've probably done it before, lots of times. But this time you picked the wrong woman. You chose my wife."

Ken saw the jealous rage in Moross's eyes. It was a flash of humanity that gave him hope he might reason with the man, make him see the truth. Mainly, that his wife was afraid of him and couldn't live with him right now. But the moment passed.

Moross's voice dropped to a whisper that was barely audible. "She left me. And you took her. My wife. Caroline."

CHAPTER 40

Snow continued to fall from a sky that had turned a cruel shade of slate.

Caroline jumped into the Porsche, her fingers shaking so badly she nearly dropped the keys.

The engine caught on the second try and the car roared to life.

An inch or two of snow was already on the ground, with more falling at a steady pace.

It would be much deeper up on the mountain.

Ken was there. Fighting for his life. And it was all her fault.

Her palms were so wet she had trouble keeping them on the wheel.

Gus yelled after her. "Alice, this isn't safe! Come back!"

The rest of his words were lost as the Porsche took off. The rear wheels caught unevenly and spun, rotating the car in a slow quarter circle.

Gus tried to tell her something else but the working of the machine was the only sound Caroline heard.

The tires gained traction at last, propelling her down the drive.

Porter had tracked her down. Just as he promised.

Panic mounted inside her, constricting her chest and filling her ears with a buzzing that crowded out everything else. Her mind flashed to the cabin in the woods, miles away from help along a wilderness track, and the way Porter's eyes turned flat and dead when he was sucked down into the vortex, their vortex, his and Caroline's.

But this time someone else was being sucked down into it with them.

Despite the wind buffeting the Porsche Caroline felt she was going to suffocate.

She clung to the wheel, praying she could get there in time. Treetops did a wild dance in the wind, which was gusting all around. She needed all her concentration just to keep the sports car in check.

The drive was wet and slick, causing the Porsche to jerk to one side. Caroline tightened her grip and steered it back to center. The tires slid, and they careened onto the snow-covered grass while Caroline jerked the wheel again back to center. Pippin did a crazy dance on the leather seat beside her, his nails scrabbling to find a hold.

The end of the drive came upon her too soon. She jammed on the brakes, which sent the Porsche sailing out onto the blacktop, spinning in a slow circle across both lanes.

When the car finally came to a stop, straddling the double yellow lines, Pippin propped his front legs against the dash and let out a small cry as though he, too, was desperate to see what lay ahead.

Caroline clutched the wheel so tight her fingers hurt, lifted her foot from the brake, and eased up on the clutch. The car leaped forward again. She spun the wheel northbound and gave it some gas, shifting directly into second on the slick pavement. This time the car held steady and picked up controlled speed, tires singing in the snow. Eventually, she risked shifting into third. Every second counted.

Leaning forward, she peered through the windshield, at a landscape that was alien to her, like the inside of a paperweight globe that's been shaken. Leaves whirled through the air, mixing with snow on gusts of wind that shook the car as if the mountain itself was heaving in the throes of death. She flipped on the headlights and wipers, watching snowflakes careen past the windshield like a million tiny ghosts. Her heart pounded so loud the car was filled with the sound of it.

Her life was coming to an end, she thought dully. Today was her last one on this earth. Porter had told her many times she could never leave him, and Caroline knew she would never go back with him. But her relationship with Porter no longer mattered. All that mattered now was saving Ken. "Please, God," she whispered, driving as fast as she dared. She had long ago lost any faith in a loving God, but she said the Lord's Prayer now. It was the only one she could remember. She downshifted at the turnoff to the mountain road.

Her headlights flashed on a "Caution, Falling Rock Zone!" sign. Just beyond was another, warning motorists and hikers to avoid the area during periods of heavy rain or snow, due to limited access by law enforcement authorities.

Fear settled in the depths of her stomach with its cold, familiar weight. She tightened her grip on the wheel with fingers that were already numb, and braced herself for the first switchback.

Speed frightened her. She lifted her foot from the accelerator so the car slowed. The quieting of the engine gave her some reassurance. But the lack of acceleration caused the wheels to lose traction. The Porsche drifted into the switchback and spun out so Caroline felt like she was trapped inside an amusement park ride, the kind she had hated as a kid. Trees tilted crazily, and the granite side of the mountain flew at them close, too close. The Porsche skidded, slamming into the guardrail with a terrible sound of metal on metal. The car heaved at impact, and stalled.

After that everything was silent.

Caroline sat, gripping the wheel, afraid to move.

Pippin had somehow landed on the floor. He shook himself now and hopped back up on the seat.

Together they surveyed their surroundings. The car had taken impact on its side, and the guardrail had held. If it hadn't, they'd be goners by now.

The Porsche sat, nose out, half on and half off the pavement.

The inside of Caroline's mouth was so dry her tongue stuck to her teeth when she tried to swallow.

The next switchback was on the cliff side.

There was no time to waste. She pushed the clutch in and turned the key, praying the car would still run.

The engine whirred back to life. She shifted into second and eased up on the gas. The wheels spun, but the car remained where it was. She pressed the gas harder. The wheels spun in place, whining louder as the car vibrated with effort.

Pippin yelped.

Caroline applied the brakes. She looked around helplessly, wondering what to do. Then something she had read once came back to her. She shifted into reverse and gave it a tiny bit of gas. The car moved an inch. Quickly she shifted back to second. The car rocked forward and got stuck again. She shifted back into reverse and gained another inch. Dropping back to second, faster now, she eased up slowly on the clutch until the car shot free, back up onto the road.

The wheels caught the pavement and the Porsche zoomed down the road. Directly into the next curve.

Caroline fought the impulse to brake as Ken's words came back to her, *Make the engine work for you. Steer to the outside of the switchbacks*, he'd said.

Fighting every instinct she had, Caroline aimed the car at the guardrail on the outer edge of the curve. She pressed down, slow and steady, on the gas and dropped down into first as they entered the switchback. The engine whined but the car slowed, gripping the road. It took the turn. She let out the breath she'd been holding and allowed herself a grunt of triumph. Depressing the clutch and shifting back up to second, allowing the coupe to pick up speed on the straightaway. She wiggled her fingers to get her blood flowing through them again.

The clock on the dashboard showed it was eleven A.M.

Ken had been safe and sound on Nan's couch four hours ago.

He had been alone with Porter for at least two hours.

The light grew dimmer the higher she climbed, even as the trees thinned out. By the time she neared the turnoff for the cabin, the forest was lit by an eerie twilight from the storm. At times, she could make out fresh tire tracks and she followed them, praying they would lead her to the right place.

She almost missed the turnoff. The headlights flashed on a snow-covered mound at the side of the road and she recognized it just in time, braking hard to make the turn. She remembered with a pang how Ken had explained it was a cairn, like the ones used in Stone Age times by Celts to mark their graves.

She recognized the metal taste in her mouth as fear. She was shaking so hard that her spine rocked against the seat, making it difficult to keep her foot in contact with the gas pedal.

She drove the Porsche as hard as she dared, careening along the dirt track, feeling out of control. She felt a tickle inside her shirt and realized it was icy perspiration. The snow was deeper up here, and it required all her concentration just to guide the Porsche from one skid into another.

Pippin bounced across the seat with each twist. The car finally swung off the track altogether, sinking into the soft snow at the side. The engine bucked once, then stalled. The sudden silence was eerie and terrifying. Caroline turned the key again and the engine started up, but it was no use. The wheels spun crazily when she tried to rock the car out. "Please," she moaned softly. But the car just sank deeper into the rut she had created.

She tried to remember how far she'd driven with Ken, and gauge how much distance she'd covered just now. All she could recall, however, was the way the sunshine had played across Ken's face as he rested one arm on the open window, pointing out sights to her, sharing with her the beauty he saw in the wilderness.

But that sun-drenched scene was gone, hidden today beneath a drifting, swirling gloom.

Caroline donned her gloves and left the keys dangling in the ignition. They were no longer of any use to her.

The air inside the Porsche was cold and still. Using clothes from her backpack, she crafted a nest for Pippin on the front seat, praying someone would find him soon. She scooped him up and kissed him good-bye before pulling the wool cap low on her face and zipping her parka as high as it would go.

She stepped out into the storm.

A branch snapped close by like a rifle shot.

Caroline jumped. She whirled around, expecting to see Porter standing there, waiting for her. But there was nothing. Only the wind and the trees, stretching into a gray eternity.

Pippin jumped out of the car.

"Pippin, no!" Caroline called. But it was too late. The dog scrambled off to investigate the snapping sound.

"Pippin," Caroline called. "Come back!"

But he was gone.

"Good-bye, my friend," she whispered. But the wind tore the words from her lips.

She started walking.

The woods were alive with swirling snow and moving branches that gave off a sound like moaning. But she was not afraid of the forest. She was beyond that. With the minutes of her life that were still allotted to her, she needed to rescue Ken. She tried to comfort herself with the thought that by now, at least, he knew whom he was dealing with. Perhaps he could fight back in time to save himself. She fought to shut out the images crowding her mind, images of Ken injured or worse . . .

After what seemed like forever but probably was no more than a mile, she saw an opening in the trees overhead and knew she was entering the mesa. Heart pounding and out of breath, she left the track and kept inside the tree line.

She pieced together a plan as best she could with her panicked mind. She would gain entry to the cabin and offer herself to Porter in exchange for Ken's life. She had no doubt that Porter was vengeful enough to kill Ken in order to punish her. But if she found the right words perhaps she could persuade Porter to spare him. It was a slim chance but it was her only option.

She crept forward until the cabin came into view, and sought cover behind a tree.

Ken's Jeep was parked in front of the cabin, ten feet from the door. A white Yukon was parked behind it.

The windows of the cabin showed light inside. There was no sign of movement.

The woods seemed empty.

She thought of the Smith & Wesson pistol Porter had kept, oiled and ready to use, and wondered what her next move should be. There was a hunting knife in the Jeep's glove compartment. Caroline remembered how Ken had used it to gut the trout, the way the blade had glinted in the afternoon sun.

There were high-powered binoculars in there, too.

She remembered the tangle of stuff in the Jeep's trunk, and wondered if there might be a gun. It didn't seem likely. Only a fool would store a gun in with a heap of camping gear.

And Ken Kincaid was nobody's fool.

The thought of Ken spurred her on and she inched closer to the edge of the tree line closest to the cabin's front door.

At that moment the door swung open and a figure

appeared, a familiar contour even through the dim light of the storm, from his narrow shoulders to his precisely measured gait. His right hand hung stiff at his side, weighted with the unmistakable form of a gun. Caroline recognized him instantly. She would know him even in death, her husband.

Dr. Porter Moross.

CHAPTER
41

Caroline. Her real name. The sound of it was a melody in Ken's ears, like the pealing of church bells on Sunday morning, or birds singing to greet the first light of dawn. Soaring. Elegant. Beautiful. Like her laughter or the expression on her face when she gazed up at the sky over Colorado. Impossible blue, she'd called it.

Caroline.

Just hearing her true name brought Ken joy.

He tried to shake his head, so he could tell Moross how wrong he was. Ken hadn't stolen his wife. Nobody could steal Caroline. She was not some possession that could be taken. Nobody was. Caroline simply was Caroline. The name filled his mind like music. She just was, like the Aspen trees blazing with color in autumn, or the fields yellow with sunflowers in summer, or the snow that was falling thick and fast right now.

But Ken could no longer move his head. He shifted his gaze to Moross, took in the flat look in his eyes, the tight hold he kept on his pistol.

Moross continued to stare down at Ken, his gaze unmoving and blank, like a shark. "Nobody's innocent,

Kincaid. Not you. Certainly not her," Moross said, his voice a monotone, devoid of all emotion.

He dropped into an easy chair. "By now you've lost the ability to move, though you can see and hear everything around you. And you can still feel pain." He chewed his lip and paused, long enough for Ken to realize Moross's descent into madness was complete.

"We'll get to that in a moment," Porter continued. "But this issue of paralysis. It must be especially hard for you." He considered Ken with genuine curiosity.

Ken watched the gun.

"There's a certain poignancy to it. Irony, really." He gave a small shrug. "But that's just a matter of interest, a side note about the drug. Not that they'll be able to trace it. By the time I get through with you, there won't be enough left for a proper autopsy." Porter turned his gaze to the Franklin stove. "It's a shame, the way accidents happen even with the most experienced outdoorsman, even with a big he-man such as yourself." His voice was thick now with sarcasm, and he laughed. "Caroline will take it hard."

It required all of Ken's strength to focus on his breathing. He closed his eyes. Nobody knew he was up here. Even if they did, the sheriff wouldn't reach him anytime soon.

Forcing himself to stay calm, Ken ordered his thoughts based on a lifetime of rigid training. He was in the place he loved best, and he thanked his Creator for that. He filled his mind with images of other things that had touched him in this life. The lake on top of the mesa reflecting crystalline sky on a summer's day, the scent of sage on a breeze. His father's eyes, steady and strong. His mother's face in the only memory he had of her,

squeezing water from a rubber frog he'd had for his
bath. She laughed, and the sound flowed like silk. Caroline whispering his name, Ken.

Shoes scraped the floor.

Ken opened his eyes.

Moross stood. He let out a sad-sounding sigh and
shook his head. "Such a waste. I never wanted it to
come to this. But she's a stubborn girl. More trouble
than she's worth, as you'll soon agree. If only she had
listened. I begged her to get help. But she is corrupt
inside. She won't admit that, no matter how much I try
to help."

Ken focused on Moross's new hiking shoes as he
paced the room.

"If anybody could have turned her around, it would
have been me. Should have been me. She was just an ig-
norant girl when I met her. I married her and gave her a
home, the first real home she'd ever known. I lived with
her and worked on her for two years, and she blinded
herself to the truth." Moross's voice rose, tinged with
hysteria, on the final words.

Poor Caroline. The sunglasses, the baseball cap,
the way she kept her head down. Ken recoiled at the
thought of what she must have endured at the hands
of the deranged man who paced his cabin. Ken realized
now the risk she had taken in speaking to him, coming
with him to his house that day. Not to mention the
courage she'd shown by coming to Storm Pass to try to
make a new life. He felt a rush of admiration for her.
He was grateful for the joy these thoughts brought to
him now, during what could well be the final moments
of his life.

Moross walked to the cabin's door.

The ache in Ken's head was growing worse. Pressure was building behind his eyes.

Moross stopped with one hand on the knob. "I am one of the greatest and most respected psychoanalysts in the entire world, you know." His voice shook. "It's an art. And nobody appreciates it. Do you even know what I'm talking about?"

Ken kept his eyes on Moross's feet. Moross could have the satisfaction of killing him but that was all. He wouldn't get the satisfaction of believing his twisted tirades had been heard. That was simply not going to happen. Not while Ken had a heartbeat or a breath remaining. Gus had taught his son to seek out the good in people, but Ken was also gifted with the ability to see things as they actually were. And right now, Ken knew he was in the presence of pure evil.

He braced himself for a bullet.

Instead, Moross opened the door.

Gray light spilled into the cabin with a gust of cold air, fresh and clean on Ken's face.

"You'll know soon enough, Kincaid. Death brings perfect understanding, if you believe Carl Jung. We'll all be liberated. You first, of course." With a laugh like broken glass, Moross stepped out into the storm.

Seeing Porter again was like watching a corpse rise from his casket and walk. It was wrong, wrong, all wrong. Caroline's world had turned upside down. She swayed, flailed, and her hand found a tree for support. She screwed her eyes shut and held fast, praying Porter would somehow be gone when she opened them.

But he was still there.

She shrank back, willing herself to become invisible.

Porter looked around.

Fear tripped up and down her spine, cutting her resolve like razor blades. She wondered if he could see her, smell her, sense her presence so close to him. He had told her they were soul mates.

He had tracked her here.

She drew her breath in and held it.

Keeping a tight hold on his gun, he walked to the Yukon, opened the rear hatch, and pulled out a large red tin. On the side was an image of yellow flame. Caroline's insides gave a sickening lurch.

There was no mistaking Porter's intent. He was going to burn the cabin down.

The contents of her stomach heaved up to the back

of her throat and she choked it down rather than risk making a sound. Porter's cruel streak had caught Caroline off guard on many occasions, but somehow she never thought he was capable of cold-blooded murder.

But he was.

Unless she could find a way to stop him.

Porter hoisted the can and lugged it inside.

Caroline was shaking so hard now her knees barely held her weight. She considered her options. She could tackle him from behind. Not likely. She looked around for a rock, something heavy to smash his skull. But she saw only snow. Her panicked mind could not come up with anything else.

The opportunity passed.

Porter stopped on the porch, set the kerosene tin down, and steadied the gun in his right hand before reaching for the door handle with his left.

Which meant Ken was alive.

Porter took one more look around before nudging the door open with his foot. He collected the tin and disappeared inside.

Which meant, for a few seconds, his back was to her.

Caroline sprinted for the Jeep, crouching low to the ground, too frightened even to risk looking up to see if she'd been spotted.

She clambered inside, expecting a shot to ring out at any moment.

But there was nothing, just the hammering of her heart and the dome light shining like neon in the gloom.

She eased the door shut and crouched, breathless and shaking, on the floor of the car.

She screwed up her courage and checked the passenger side window, bracing herself to see Porter's face, mottled red with rage, looming over her like some horror movie.

But there was nothing, just gray sky.

She reached for the glove compartment with fingers that trembled so hard they couldn't manage the latch at first. But she got the compartment open on the second try, fumbling around inside until her fingers closed around the worn leather sheath of the bowie knife. She unsheathed the knife and tested the blade. The edge was razor sharp.

Caroline had never held a hunting knife.

She tucked it carefully inside her jacket pocket. She did a quick search of the remaining contents, but found nothing else that would help.

She crouched, wondering what her next move should be.

Porter chose it for her.

CHAPTER 43

Moross reentered the cabin, lugging a five-gallon tin of kerosene, which he set down next to the Franklin stove.

The liquid made a sloshing sound.

He still carried a gun in his right hand.

Ken had once been on a plane that nearly crashed. His then-wife had spent months planning a vacation to New Zealand. It was the trip that was supposed to save their marriage and impress all their friends. They had spent the day hiking the Milford Track down to the sound at the rugged tip of the South Island, literally the edge of the earth. A private plane would carry them back out. The winds picked up as the day wore on, turning the sky an ominous shade of green with flashes of white lightning. The bush pilot decided to take off, assuring them they'd be aloft before the storm settled in.

The pilot was mistaken. The tiny plane shook during takeoff, fighting for every foot of altitude, and then got caught in a burst of wind shear. The fuselage bucked like a twig, its single engine screaming. Ken's wife clung to him as the pilot fought to keep the plane's nose up.

But the plane plummeted, sinking tail-first back toward earth.

Ken's wife screamed.

Ken prepared to meet his Maker.

And then, miraculously, the pilot regained control. The plane leveled out and resumed its climb.

It was as close to death as Ken had come. Until now. He surveyed the kerosene tin, calculating his odds.

Most likely he'd succumb to smoke not flames.

Moross hummed something tuneless and low. "Wood," he muttered. "We need wood." He headed back outside.

*P*orter reappeared on the porch.

Caroline prayed he couldn't see her in her hiding place on the driver's side of the Jeep.

But he didn't glance her way, striding purposefully across the porch and around to the back of the cabin.

She remembered a woodpile there, perhaps fifteen feet from the cabin's rear wall.

It was her best chance. Porter would require a minute, give or take a few seconds, to fill his arms.

She scrambled across the small clearing and up the stone steps, certain she would collide with Porter coming around the corner of the porch.

She didn't.

She opened the door and stepped inside, easing it shut behind her. Her eyes needed a moment to adjust to the dim yellow light from a single lantern that lit the room. Everything was quiet and still. Too still. Her throat yawned open wide with mind-numbing terror.

Ken was on the floor, propped against the side of the couch with his eyes closed, his head hanging on his neck at an angle that was crazy.

Time stood still. Caroline felt her heart climb into her throat. If she had arrived too late, nothing mattered.

She called his name softly in the gloom, a plea to heaven above. "Ken."

His eyes fluttered open.

She had never been so relieved in her life.

*K*en was paralyzed.

Caroline remembered times Porter had held her down, delivering a pinprick to her buttocks or legs, followed by shadowy memories of pain and nightmare images. She'd regain consciousness hours later, heart pounding, mouth dry, bruised and bleeding in places she was afraid to touch.

"My God," she whispered, horror mounting inside.

Ken winked.

Her soul fluttered with joy.

Her elation turned to despair, however, at the sound of footsteps, slow and measured, on the porch.

Her knees were shaking so bad she nearly collapsed.

Ken rolled his eyes at the wardrobe. He looked back at her and blinked.

Porter was close to the door, his footsteps heavy and deliberate.

Caroline raced to the wardrobe. She stepped inside and managed to shut the door behind her, but just barely, before Porter entered the cabin. In the dark, she waited for him to hear the pounding that was the sound of her heart hammering inside her chest. He would trace it to the wardrobe and kill her.

But he did not. She heard him instead walk to the center of the room with unhurried steps before dropping the logs onto the floor, one at a time.

Her insides quaked with a terror so large it edged all the air from her lungs. She pressed herself against clothing that hung behind her in the darkness, seeking comfort in the scent of Ken's aftershave that smelled of cedar and pine and the scratchy feel of wool on her skin. She held herself stock-still, and tried to listen.

Porter's steps made a menacing sound on the floorboards. She flinched at the sudden screech of metal as he yanked open the door to the Franklin stove. And then his voice, falsetto with cheer. "There's nothing like a roaring fire on a snowy day."

Logs hit the inside of the stove, landing with a thudding sound one by one, like nails hammering shut the lid on a coffin.

Realization hit Caroline in the gut, bringing a fresh wave of panic that liquefied her insides with sickening speed. She pressed her fingers to her mouth and held them there, gagging back the vomit that was rising again at the back of her throat.

Porter moved through the cabin now, spattering liquid as he went. "Kincaid, I'll just bet you were a Boy Scout."

He was enjoying this.

Caroline searched with her hands in the darkness, grasping for something, anything. And then her hands found something useful.

A smooth piece of metal, long and slim. Its purpose was unmistakable.

She traced its cold perfection from the twin holes at the top to the trigger, her fingers slick with sweat and shaking with adrenaline. She hoped it was loaded.

The splashing stopped, and the sharp scent of kerosene penetrated the wardrobe.

"Well, Kincaid, this is how you'll be remembered," Porter said, setting the can down with an empty clanging sound. "A famous football player who died a senseless, ordinary death. A stupid hunting accident." Porter laughed.

Caroline's fingers fumbled desperately to find a home inside the trigger mechanism. She picked up the gun, surprised at how bottom-heavy it was, and pulled it to her chest. She knew her only chance was to surprise him. She gathered her courage to open the wardrobe door but it would not come. She tried to mouth a prayer but her lips stuck together, and this only magnified her fear. She reached for the closet door handle, closed her fingers around it, and willed herself to turn it.

But a sound from outside the cabin stopped her.

Tiny nails scratching at the outer door.

Caroline's heart sank.

She heard a yip, followed by more scratching.

Then the stillness exploded with another sound, one she knew well.

"Caroline!" Porter bellowed.

A moan rose in her throat. "No," she whispered in the darkness.

Porter walked to the cabin door and yanked it open.

Pippin rushed in with a burst of wind, toenails clicking on the wood floor. He made a quick tour of the perimeter of the room, before heading straight for the closet where Caroline hid.

"Caroline!" Porter stamped his foot. "Come out of that closet or I'll blow Kincaid's head off!"

She was trembling so hard she was afraid to move, afraid the small act of propping the shotgun inside the wardrobe would be too much for her. But it wasn't, and she managed to accomplish this without setting off the gun.

"Come out now!" Porter slammed the cabin door so hard the walls shook. He moved into the center of the room.

Caroline stepped out and faced her husband.

He'd changed. The beard was gone. In its place was sickly white skin pocked through with purple lesions. His cheeks were hollow, and there were deep lines around his mouth, which seemed thinner. But the real change was Porter's eyes, rimmed with red and recessed deeper beneath colorless brows.

His gaze was focused now with glittering intensity on Caroline.

So was the gun in his hand.

Caroline held tight to the closet handle. She tried to swallow and couldn't. Fear had robbed her even of the ability to do that. Porter had sworn he would find her, and he had. She watched him look her up and down with those eyes, glittering like shards of broken glass.

She braced herself.

"Here we are. Reunited at last, the loving wife and her husband." Porter's mouth twisted into a cruel smile.

Pippin sniffed the air uncertainly as though he, too, did not know what to expect.

Caroline was silent.

"Speak to me, devoted wife." Porter's voice was low,

laced with sarcasm. He kept the pistol trained on her face.

She looked down, trying to think.

"Now, Caroline," Porter said, his tone chiding. "You can't avoid the issues any longer. This time we have to talk." His lips formed tight around each syllable.

His sarcasm, she knew, could change in a moment into rage.

"Look at me," he ordered.

She steadied herself, certain he would read the revulsion in her eyes. It was all that remained of her feelings for him.

"I'll wait," he said in a voice that was stripped of all humanity.

She raised her eyes to meet his gaze at last. Desperation made her voice small. "Porter, I know you're hurt and it's my fault."

"Hurt? And it's all your fault?" His voice climbed to falsetto, mocking her. "Hurt?" He paused.

Caroline tried not to wince.

When he spoke again his voice had dropped low, into the doomsday range. "Why don't you tell me more?"

He was falling, working his way down deeper into the vortex that would claim them once and for all.

Unless she could figure out a way to stop him, something she had never been able to do. A wilderness opened inside her, squeezing all feeling from her chest and face, leaving her numb. Like a stooge bettor in a shell game that was rigged, Caroline knew she was bound to lose. She felt the cabin around her drain of all energy as the vortex swirled around them, sucking them down. Except for one point that was dead center.

The loaded gun in Porter's hand.

Caroline struggled to stay calm. Her voice came out thin and reedy. "Porter, this is about us, you and me. Nobody else. Let's settle it alone. We need to go away from here." She tried not to sound pleading. "Let's leave, just the two of us."

Something in his face gave way, and for a moment she held out hope that she had accessed the sanity in him. She glimpsed the old Porter, the one who had whispered his secrets and dreams to her in that dimly lit room high above Dupont Circle so long ago.

His face crumpled. "I wish I could trust you."

"Porter, you can. You really can." She was lying. Lying and pleading with him. If he sensed it, or felt manipulated in any way, the sane Porter would disappear.

Caroline swallowed hard, willing her voice to hold steady as she uttered words she knew were untrue. "I want us to go back to the way we were."

The corners of Porter's mouth turned down and his eyes cinched shut with pain. "I wish we could, too, Caroline," he whispered. "I wish for that, too."

She moved, raising her hands as if to comfort him. She fought the urge to step closer, for that would take her farther away from the wardrobe and the shotgun inside.

Porter sensed her movement. He tightened his grip on the gun and tensed, his eyes springing open.

Caroline's heart sank.

Porter stared.

Measuring her, she knew, trying to decide whether she was telling the truth.

A tear slid down his face. "If you want to work things out, why did you run away?"

His voice rose higher, turning plaintive. Childlike. It

was the tone of a little boy who'd watched his mother put on her makeup and dress with care on that fateful day, pleading to go along in the car. Promising to behave. She'd promised to bring him a present when she came back, a surprise. But she never did.

Caroline swallowed. So much depended on her answer. She settled on the half truth, the three-quarters truth. "I've tried to be a good wife to you, Porter. I wanted that more than anything. You have to believe me. But I failed. I needed space to think things through."

Porter moaned.

"I'm sorry," she whispered. Before the words left her mouth she realized it had been the wrong thing to say.

"Sorry?" His voice was soft, laced with sorrow, and his eyes closed around his tears. "What's the use of sorry? You never should have done that to me."

"I didn't mean to hurt you." Too late, Caroline realized these were the wrong words.

Porter's eyes sprang open. "Liar!" His lips curled around the last word.

The Porter she knew was gone again, dancing dangerously close to the edge of the vortex that spun around them gathering energy. In seconds, he would tumble into it. Tightening her grip on the wardrobe handle, Caroline willed her mind to shift course away from the vortex. She forced herself to consider new options, reaching for the right words, the magic ones that might save her now. "I know I was not honest with you, Porter," she began. "But I want to start now. There's just so much I want to tell you."

He stared, unblinking.

The room was quiet. Caroline's words dropped into the void that had formed around them. She forced herself to go on, facing the man who had picked over her private wounds, tearing them open again and again so the scars would not heal. "I guess I never thought anyone would love me if they knew the things that had happened to me as a child, what my part in it was." She looked down, again reaching for three-quarters of the truth.

"I loved you, Caroline." Porter's voice, barely a whisper, shook with emotion.

"I know that, Porter." This, at least, was a complete truth. "And I loved you, too."

He moaned again. "I never wanted it to come to this. I want you to know that."

"It doesn't have to, Porter," she said quickly. "We can still go, just walk away from here. Just you and I."

He shook his head swiftly, as if to clear it.

"Porter, please." She was pleading and it was the wrong thing, she saw that in an instant.

His lips tightened. He sniffed once and blinked. When he opened his eyes again she saw that it was too late.

Porter was gone. He had slipped away.

"You don't care about us, Caroline. You're just trying to save him. Kincaid." His voice hardened on Ken's name.

The room started to spin again as the vortex gathered energy. Caroline calculated her odds. Reaching inside for the gun would require four seconds. Propping it into position would require at least three more. She shook her head. "Porter, please, let's just talk."

"Talk?" Porter's voice rose to a screech.

Pippin pricked up his ears.

"All I do is talk." Porter's eyes glittered again. "Talk, talk, talk."

Pippin let out a low growl.

Porter licked his lips, excited now. "I'm the only man that ever loved you. I'm the only man that ever could. Nobody will ever accept you the way you are. You're damaged." He spat the words out. "You know that."

Caroline nodded, like a student signaling that she has memorized her lesson.

"Nobody else could ever understand you. Nobody else would even want to. You're not worth it. Do you see that?"

"Yes," she whispered. But she saw in his eyes it was no use, there was nothing she could say now to change things. He was beyond compassion.

Porter shook his head in disgust. "I don't think you do. I'm sick of your lies." He redoubled his grip on the .38, his voice dropping as he motioned at Ken with his chin. "I could shoot him right now."

Caroline forced herself to be still so he wouldn't see her flinch.

"And the sad thing is, that's all you care about. Isn't it?" Porter waited, his lips working in fury.

The room turned deadly still. Caroline searched desperately for words, the right words, the ones that could turn this around and save their lives, hers and Ken's. But nothing came.

Porter flicked his hand so the gun moved.

Caroline jumped.

He gave a cruel little smile. "Answer me, wife. He's all you care about, isn't he?"

Pippin growled.

Caroline's mind raced. Anything she said now would tip Porter over the edge. She could tell by his eyes, flat and cold with rage.

"Talk!" Porter shrieked, flicking the gun once more.

Caroline jumped.

There was no way to appease him. There never had been, not since that day in the museum when they first met. She had aged a thousand years since then. He had been choking the life out of her, inch by inch, beginning on that day.

She risked a glance in Ken's direction. She could see only his legs stretched out on the floor in front of him, motionless and still. She pondered the millions of moments, known only to him, that made up the sum total of his life. Moments of pain and passion, love and glory, loss and joy that belonged to him. In a moment or two, it would all be finished, released into eternity and fading like a whisper on the mountain wind.

Grief came to her then, and something else she had never known for even one day of her life with Porter.

Acceptance. It was finally done and spent, this dark love they had shared. It was finished, and the vortex had won.

Game over.

Caroline had nothing to lose now.

Oddly, this gave her strength. She straightened to her full height. She was almost as tall as Porter, a fact she had been careful to cover up with ballet flats. "I thought I loved you once, Porter. But no matter how much I tried, it wasn't enough."

His eyes widened with shock.

"My love wasn't good enough," she continued. "Nobody's love was ever enough for you. Not your father's. Not mine. Not even your mother's, if you think about it."

"Don't you tell me about my mother!" Porter pointed

at her with a finger that trembled as his voice rose to a hysterical screech. "Your problem"—he spat the words out—"is that you are corrupt. You were born that way. You liked what was done to you. You won't admit it, and you refuse to grow up."

His screeching sounded to her ears like a record that was worn and scratched. Caroline shook her head. "No, Porter. I did not choose the things that were done to me. But I chose you, and I don't want you in my life anymore."

His eyelids fluttered up into their sockets, showing white. "No! You can't leave me. I won't let you leave me again!"

Terror made Caroline drift, watching these changes in Porter as though they were flickering across a screen at a movie, and she was safe in the last row. It was a sensation left over from her childhood, and it served her well now.

"I'm sorry," she said quietly. "But all you've done is destroy my love for you. It's the one truth you couldn't analyze."

Caroline vowed she would not slide down into the vortex with him again. Never again. Not even if she paid for it with her life.

Porter's lips curled back. His voice shook with rage. "I have dedicated my life to uncovering truths about people, the truths they won't face."

Caroline shook her head. "You won't face your own truth, Porter. You torture anyone who tries to get close to you. You made my life hell."

"Your life was never going to amount to much anyway." Porter's face twisted with rage.

Caroline had once considered him sophisticated,

exotic. "Porter, it's over. I don't love you anymore. I did once but you pushed me away. And now I never will."

Porter's features collapsed. "No!"

Caroline saw beyond his anger to something else. Despair. She shook her head.

His voice turned pleading. "You can't leave me. I can't let that happen." Porter motioned at Ken with his chin. "You can't leave me for another man. I'll kill him first." Porter swung the pistol to Ken.

Caroline thought of the shotgun in the wardrobe, the knife in her pocket. Two options. The knife was closer. Her fingers moved.

It was a small motion, but Porter caught it. His voice was low and cruel in the tone he used with his riding crop. "What are you hiding?"

Caroline forced herself to stand still. She tried to swallow.

Porter's eyes narrowed. "Show me."

He'd told her countless times he knew when she was hiding something, that deceit flowed from her core. There was nothing left now but to tell the truth. She pulled the knife from her pocket.

Porter looked from her face to the blade in her hand and back again, shaking his head. His voice was no more than a weak croak. "You would use that? To hurt me?"

Caroline said nothing.

Porter's face twisted as a sound worked its way up from deep inside him, a terrible high-pitched howl such as an animal would make in distress.

And the animal in the room responded.

Pippin sprang at Porter, sinking his sharp tiny fangs into Porter's leg.

Porter grunted in surprise and knocked the dog off. In doing so, he lowered his gun for a precious few seconds.

Which was all the time Caroline required. She reached for the wardrobe door and grabbed for what lay inside, careful not to turn her back on Porter.

Everything after that happened in slow motion.

She fumbled for the gun, pulled it out by its neck and swung the stock up to her chest. Her fingers closed around the trigger.

Porter stared, his mouth dropping open.

Caroline saw inside to the rows of silver fillings in his teeth, and thought idly how upset he must be to let his mouth hang slack like this, considering how fastidious he always was with his appearance.

He snapped his mouth shut, swallowed once before swinging his pistol back around to Caroline.

But he was too late.

The barrel of the shotgun was already where she needed it to be.

Their eyes met, long enough for Caroline to regret her part in this, bringing them here to this moment in time. She hesitated, dropping the barrel a millimeter and no more, so it was aimed at his legs and not at his heart.

Porter's eyes glinted like shards of ice. He aimed his pistol at her head.

But Caroline had the advantage. She squeezed her trigger first.

The room exploded with a crack of thunder and a flash of red, followed immediately by the pistol shot.

Pippin howled.

The kick from the shotgun knocked Caroline off her feet. She landed on her back and felt the bullet from

Porter's gun whiz past her ear. She rolled, still clutching the shotgun, and scrambled onto her knees to take aim again.

But there was no need. Porter lay sprawled on the floor, his face deathly white as a horrible dark liquid spilled from his gut.

The .38 skittered to rest on the floor nearby.

Porter groaned. He turned his head and spotted the gun when Caroline did.

Quick as lightning, he reached out to make a grab for it.

"No!" Caroline screamed, lunging forward.

Porter's fingers closed around the pistol.

Caroline leaped forward and slammed the butt of the shotgun down on his hand.

It connected with the sickening crunch of bones breaking.

Porter howled in pain and released his grip on the .38. His fingers dangled uselessly. "Please give me another chance," he moaned.

Their eyes met; his were wet with sorrow.

"Porter, I'll get help for you," she whispered.

For one moment she imagined that salvation might be theirs.

Porter blinked, gathering his broken hand to him like a bird with a crushed wing.

Then his good hand shot out and locked on her leg in a vise grip.

It knocked Caroline off balance.

"Bitch," Porter hissed.

Pippin circled, barking furiously.

She went down hard, landing on her elbow. Pain shot up through her arm. She kicked his hand with her leg and swung the butt of the shotgun down onto him with all her strength, despite the stabbing pain in her arm.

The blow hit home with a sickening thud, landing in the soft tissue of Porter's belly that was already seeping blood.

Porter fell back into the puddle of crimson. "Don't destroy us," he begged.

Pippin stopped barking at last and sat, watching.

"It's too late, Porter," she said, kicking the pistol out of his reach. Still clutching the shotgun, she raced to Ken's side.

Ken was deathly still.

She set the shotgun down and shook him by the shoulders, calling his name.

His eyelids flickered.

Thank God. She grabbed him and pulled with all her might. He didn't budge. She tried again, straining with effort. His head bobbed lifelessly against her knees as sobs of despair rose in her throat.

A small sound caught her attention.

She whirled around.

Porter had struck a match. He held it close to his face so its light danced near his eyes.

She saw only madness there.

"Come back to me, Mommy," he pleaded.

"Porter, no!" Caroline raised her hand to stop him.

But it was too late.

"I wanted you to stay with me," he said.

"No, Porter," she screamed. "Don't do it!"

But it was too late.

He dropped the match. A thin flame raced along the wet trail of kerosene with an audible whoosh.

Porter's face was waxy and white, his breathing labored. He clutched his stomach with hands balled into fists and licked colorless lips. His hatred had imploded, curling his body into a fetal position. "Help me, Mommy! Don't leave me!"

The flames were already leaping up walls and climbing furniture.

The cabin was no longer quiet. Now it was filled with the sound of a hot, choking wind.

Caroline crawled to Ken's legs since they were nearest the door and grabbed them.

A shooting pain, hot like a knife, tore through Caroline's arm.

Panic gave her strength.

She pulled at Ken's legs with all her might.

Her hands slipped off and she fell back onto the floor.

Ken stayed where he was.

The flames were starting to give off heat.

Porter moaned, begging to be rescued.

Caroline scrambled to a crouch. She grabbed Ken's ankles and tried again.

The smoke was not as dense here near the floor, but still thick enough to sting her eyes and fill her nostrils, making it difficult to breathe. She squeezed her eyes shut and pulled, grunting aloud with effort.

Just when she thought her back would break, Ken's body began to yield, just a tiny bit and then a tiny bit more. She crept backward, dragging Ken across the floor like a dead weight.

Flames licked the floorboards like snakes on a mission from hell. In an instant, she knew, the rugs would catch, blocking her exit.

She dug her heels in and pulled, willing Ken's body to move with every fiber of her being.

They inched along this way through smoke and bits of ash that were whipping through the cabin. Ken's arms were splayed helplessly out at his sides.

His eyes were closed, and this only added to the wild terror Caroline felt.

The back of her throat burned with scalding air. She could no longer see the stove in the center of the room, or even the couch. She fumbled behind her, giddy with relief to feel the door at her back. She reached behind her and pulled it open.

A blast of cold air rushed in. Caroline had never felt anything so good in her life and she drew it deep into her lungs in great, greedy gulps.

Ken blinked.

But the wind fed the flames, whipping them into a leaping frenzy.

Caroline was choking, gasping for air. Ken was coughing, too, a weak sputtering sound that, she feared, would stop at any moment.

She heard more coughing from deep inside the wall of heat and smoke and knew that Porter was choking, too.

She pulled Ken free of the door, groaning with the effort. She bounced him down the steps, his skull hitting each one like a dead weight.

But she couldn't do anything about that now.

She managed to get them both free of the small wooden porch before collapsing on the snow in a spasm of coughing.

Flames shot out the door behind them.

They needed to get farther away.

She reached for Ken's legs once more, inching along the ground until they were far enough, at last, to escape the heat and breathe cold air. Caroline's arm felt like it had been ripped clear of its socket.

She left Ken on the ground and ran back to save Porter.

But she was too late.

The cabin erupted in a bright orange ball of flame.

The ground shook.

The impact shattered windows and knocked Caroline off her feet.

She landed in the cold, clean snow. She lay there safe in the arms of the mountain, watching helplessly as the cabin turned into a fireball.

Bits of debris floated through the air like feathers.

After a minute or two, she willed herself to move. She crawled on all fours to Ken, who was lying where she had left him, pale and terribly still.

Sobs rose in her throat. She heard moaning and realized it was coming from inside her. She knelt and pressed one ear to his chest, praying to hear his heart beat.

She did.

She screamed his name.

He moaned.

She crouched, cradling his head in her lap, and gave in to the sobs that rose inside her. Through her tears, she called the name over and over of the one friend she loved so much. "Pippin."

A siren wailed in the distance.

"Pippin." The effort of speech, mixed with her hot tears, brought on a choking fit. Tears streamed down Caroline's face, not just from the smoke but tears of anguish for the dog, for Ken, for Porter, for all of them.

The sirens got louder.

Which masked the other sound at first.

Then it grew louder. Caroline held her breath, listening intently, praying she would hear it again.

And then she did.

Barking.

Pippin raced around the corner of the flaming cabin, yipping for all he was worth.

He made a beeline for Caroline.

*T*he storm passed, turning the town into a shimmering landscape that winked blue and silver beneath a moonlit sky.

The view from the second-floor window of Sky County Medical Center was of a world transformed, of calm after a storm. Or so it seemed to Caroline from her seat in the visitor's chair near Ken's hospital bed.

The last several hours had passed in a blur. She got her arm tended to and tried to explain events that defied explanation to the county sheriffs who videotaped her statement. She answered questions as best she could. Such as, did she set out to kill her husband up on the mountain?

No.

Was Ken Kincaid involved in any plan to kill her husband?

No.

Had she expressed the desire to Ken Kincaid or to anyone else at any time that she wished her husband dead?

No.

And, most shocking of all, did she know anything

about the human remains inside of a storage locker held by her husband in Eckington, a neighborhood in Washington, D.C., she had heard of but never visited?

Other questions were not asked. The kind that made her duck her head in shame and stare down at her hiking shoes, covered in gray ash. Such as, why had she married Porter in the first place? How could she have loved him? These questions were left unspoken, but she saw them in the sidelong glances of the EMTs who rushed them down the mountain in the county's all-terrain SUV, siren blaring and lights flashing, and again on the face of the Sky County sheriff who videotaped her statement with an unwavering stare.

At the hospital, they gave her hot coffee and a blanket while she relayed for the camera the bizarre facts of her marriage to Porter, and the events that had taken place at the cabin.

The law enforcement officials treated her fairly, faces impassive as they asked questions and recorded her answers. Reciting the plain truth, saying these things out loud, made Caroline realize how complete had been her descent into a life of utter madness.

She responded in a voice she barely recognized, flat and matter-of-fact. It was time for the truth to come out. She saw the curiosity in their eyes, mixed with revulsion, and hung her head in shame. But she forced herself to go on. Her days of telling lies were over.

The interview ended, and she was allowed to see Nan and Gus.

Nan threw her arms around Caroline. "You put this thing behind you now and move on."

Any reservations Caroline had about seeing Ken's father melted away when she faced him.

Gus grabbed her in a bear hug.

Overwhelmed with regret, Caroline couldn't say anything at first. She had stayed with Porter for reasons she didn't fully understand, telling herself that at least they weren't hurting anybody but themselves. Seeing Ken's father now made her realize that, too, was a lie.

Gus placed his hands on both her shoulders and looked straight into her eyes.

She saw no resentment in his gaze. Only concern.

"You've been through a lot, young lady. You saved my son's life. He's going to be fine."

She shook her head in protest. "It's all my fault."

Gus gave her shoulders a squeeze. "What happened up there was someone else's doing, and that's over and done with now. The important thing is you're okay and so is my son." Gus's voice broke, and he steeled himself before continuing. "Now you put this behind you."

His words were spoken so matter-of-factly that Caroline couldn't argue. "I've got a lot of work to do on myself," she admitted.

Gus said nothing, just patted her once more.

That had been an hour ago. Nan and Gus had decided to visit Maebeth Burkle down the hall, with Gus grumbling that half of Storm Pass was out of commission today. The nurse promised to fetch them at the first sign that Ken was awake.

A small sound indicated this was happening right now.

Ken groaned and rolled his head from side to side. His eyes sprang open. He smiled at Caroline. "Hey."

His voice was barely more than a hoarse croak, but the sound of it melted away some of the terror she'd experienced this day. She smiled. "Hey, yourself."

He cleared his throat and grimaced.

Caroline handed him a glass of ice water with a straw and held it while he took a few small sips.

A look of cheer came over his face as he realized he was able to move, to swallow. He raised one arm, the one without the IV tube, and flexed his fingers. He looked at her and smiled. "Caroline."

The sound of her name on his lips made her blush despite everything.

"Suits you better than Alice," he said.

Caroline pressed a hand to her mouth to try to stop the tears that welled up inside her.

"Sshhh." He tried to lift his head from the pillow but couldn't.

She frowned. "How do you feel?"

"Like a bad hangover." He grinned. "Better with you here."

"They said you're going to be fine. Thank God." Caroline's shoulders shook as a great sob heaved inside her.

Ken frowned. "Don't worry."

A nurse walked in.

"You're awake," the nurse observed.

Ken grinned. "I am."

"A lot of people have been waiting for this." The nurse pressed a button on the intercom and paged the doctor on call, stat. She got busy next taking Ken's blood pressure and pulse. "Your vitals look good, Mr. Kincaid. How are you feeling?"

"Like elephants sat on my head."

The nurse chuckled as she entered her readings. "We've got you on a mix of fluids that will help. The doctor should be along in a minute." She looked at him. "I promised your dad I would call as soon as you opened your eyes. And the sheriff, who's waiting to take your statement. I'll make those calls, but first tell me if you need anything."

"No. I'm all set." Ken's eyes were on Caroline. "Thanks."

"My pleasure, Mr. Kincaid." The nurse turned to Caroline. "And how about you? Everything okay?"

Caroline nodded. She sat with one hand over her new cast.

"How about some juice and a turkey sandwich?"

Despite everything, Caroline's stomach rumbled. She hadn't eaten since breakfast this morning at Nan's, and that seemed a lifetime ago.

"Okay, thank you."

From the bed, Ken protested. "How 'bout me?"

The nurse smiled. "Not till the doc gives you the all-clear. But I'll see if I can bring you some more crushed ice."

"You're on," Ken said.

She turned to Caroline. "I left you an overnight kit in the bathroom."

Caroline nodded again, aware that her clothes reeked of smoke. She had cried so much over the last several hours, she was afraid to look in the mirror.

The nurse lowered her voice. "There are a couple of news crews outside. We'll get you out through the ambulance bay when you're ready to go."

"Thanks," Caroline replied.

The doctor came in next. He was young with a scrubbed face and cheerful eyes. He gave Ken's hand a vigorous shake. "You look a heckuva lot more like your picture in *Sports Illustrated* than you did when they brought you in. I used to watch you play on Monday night football. It's a pleasure to meet you, Mr. Kincaid."

"Pleasure's mine," Ken said hoarsely. "Thanks for fixing me up."

"No problem." The doctor flipped through Ken's chart, studying the printout of Ken's vital signs. "Wow," he said, glancing up. "Your vitals are pretty good, considering you nearly died today. I heard professional athletes have a lower pulse rate at rest than the rest of us. And now I know it's true."

Ken watched him. "Just what, exactly, have I been through?"

The doctor pulled up a chair. "For starters, you were administered a honkin' big dose of Pavulon."

Ken frowned.

Caroline felt her stomach lurch.

"That's the designer name. Technically, it's called pancuronium bromide. It's a muscle relaxant that's mixed with other drugs during surgery to induce a state of general anesthesia. It brings on paralysis," the doctor said cheerfully. "Works like a charm, no?"

"Yeah," Ken replied, still frowning. "But I could see and hear things." He looked at Caroline.

"That's because you didn't get the other drugs mixed in," the doctor explained.

Caroline dropped her gaze to the linoleum floor, thinking of what Ken had witnessed inside the cabin.

The doctor continued. "Things would have seemed fuzzy and out of focus, like a VCR tape that came off track."

Ken nodded. "Everything seemed far away."

"Yup," the doctor said. "Classic presentation of pure

Pavulon. Lately it's gotten some play on the news. It's being abused on college campuses and in bars."

Caroline's mind spun with images she'd tried to bury. She remembered lying in bed, wanting Porter to stop but unable to protect herself. The first time it happened they hadn't even been married. She'd woken the next day, cringing when memories came tumbling back, hating herself for what had happened, chalking it up to too many glasses of red wine. She shuddered now.

The doctor closed his chart. "The good news is Pavulon doesn't have any lasting side effects. The bad news is you were given a dose strong enough to knock out two men." He gave Ken a sober look. "You are one strong individual, Mr. Kincaid. Thanks to your athletic training and sheer size, you have nothing to worry about. Other than a wicked hangover."

Ken winced. "You can say that again."

"Some of that aching head is the result of your companion bouncing you down those steps."

Companion. The word hung in the air as they both turned to look at her. Her life, Caroline knew, defied easy description. She risked a glance at Ken.

He winked.

The doctor continued to watch her. "And you are stronger than you look."

For the first time in her life, Caroline knew that statement was true. She nodded.

"She doesn't know her own strength," Ken said.

"You saved his life," the doctor said simply.

Caroline could think of nothing to say, considering the fact she felt responsible for putting Ken's life at risk in the first place.

"Guess that means I owe you," Ken teased.

"Now, that's dangerous talk," the doctor said with a chuckle. "You won't catch me talking that way to my wife."

Wife. As though she, Caroline, was capable of a relationship that was normal. She felt her cheeks flame.

Ken laughed.

"On that note, I'll leave you." The doctor stood. "We'll keep you here tonight for observation. You look ready for some real food, so I'll write the orders. But I can't vouch for the cooking, okay?" He smiled.

"Sounds good."

"And as for Xena, the Warrior Princess . . ." The doctor turned to Caroline. "You're good to go. But you've been through a lot. You take it easy, okay?"

Caroline nodded. "Thank you."

"I'm off to my rounds. I'll check back a couple times during the night. Can't wait to tell my son I met Ken Kincaid."

Ken flexed his fingers again. "The pleasure's all mine. Bring your son in. I'd like to meet him."

"That'd make his year," the doctor replied. "As for now, I'll tell the sheriff you're awake and ready to give a statement. I've held him off as long as I can."

With that, he left.

Caroline looked at Ken, suddenly shy at finding herself alone with the man she had nearly died with.

Ken patted the bed. "Hey, come on over so I can talk to you."

She stepped to the side of the bed and stood, too emotional to sit next to him.

He patted the mattress again, refusing to take no for an answer. "Come on, I won't bite."

She sat, careful to avoid the tubing in his arm. She

stared down at the linoleum floor tiles, not brave enough yet to meet his gaze.

"So," he said softly, and something in his voice reached out to her.

She looked into his eyes, bracing herself for the kind of look you'd expect from someone who was about to walk away.

But she saw only tenderness. "You okay?"

She didn't deserve it. Tears sprang up inside her. She'd thought she had cried herself out, but she was wrong. After years of holding back all her emotions, now it seemed she couldn't stop crying.

Ken reached for her hand, the one without the cast, and held it. He did not try to silence her or say anything at all, a fact she appreciated.

After a minute or two she was done. She sniffed loudly, looking around for something to wipe her nose with.

He offered his arm with the tubes, grinning.

She couldn't hold back a giggle. She wiped her nose on her sleeve.

He repeated his question. "You okay?"

She sighed. "Yeah."

"Caroline," he said again, still smiling. "You know, I'm just crazy about that name."

She couldn't hold back a smile herself.

"So, what's up with your hair? I take it you're not a true blond?"

Now Caroline laughed harder. "My hair's brown. With really, really bad highlights, I guess."

"What a relief. I've never had much luck with blonds." Now Ken was laughing, too, the sound rumbling up deep inside his broad chest.

It was infectious. As crazy as it was to joke around about hair at a time like this, it felt good just to share a laugh with him.

He grew quiet. "Your hair is your business," he said.

And the way he said it, this simple fact, settled something between them. "Yes," she agreed, solemn now. "It is." Ken Kincaid was her . . . what, exactly? Companion?

Ken settled that question with a small movement of his arms, both the good one and the one with the IV tube taped to it. The gesture was small but there was no mistaking his intention.

Caroline gave in, leaning forward so those strong arms could close around her, gathering her up against his chest.

He was warm and solid.

She could hear his heart beating.

He planted a kiss on her hair and then another and held her even tighter, and Caroline knew in her heart she could stay this way for a long time.

But there were heavy footsteps in the hall, more than one pair, and so she pulled away.

The door opened and the sheriffs entered.

It was time for her to go. She told Ken she'd be back in the morning.

"I'm not going anywhere," he said. His tone was light but the expression in his eyes told her he meant it.

Something that had lain crushed inside her unfolded its wings and took flight.

Nan and Gus were in the waiting room. They had visited with Maebeth, and pronounced her on the road to recovery.

Nan gave Caroline an appraising look. "You could use a hot bath and a good night's sleep."

Gus pressed the keys to his pickup into her hand. "You go on. We'll get a ride with Ted."

Caroline accepted the keys gratefully.

"The dogs will be glad to see you," Nan said. "Pippin's in the truck and Scout's probably sleeping near a heat vent at home."

Caroline's heart leaped at the mention of her dog. She didn't remember much about the ride down the mountain in the Sky County SUV, except for Pippin whimpering in the back.

She searched for the right words now. "I don't know how to thank you."

Gus's voice was gruff. "You just run along and take care of yourself."

"He's right," Nan said, ruffling Caroline's hair before giving her a small push toward the door.

Caroline was too worn out to do anything but follow their advice.

A security guard brought Gus's pickup around to the ambulance bay, as promised, so she could avoid the small band of reporters waiting at the main entrance.

Steering with her good arm, she drove through Storm Pass to Nan's place. Everything gleamed silvery white under the full moon. Main Street was quiet, empty at this hour. The buildings, constructed for miners in search of fortunes long since found and spent, rested under a blanket of winter white. Tomorrow would bring another sunrise, and with it the fresh possibilities of a new day.

The following is a sneak peek at

RIPTIDE

MARGARET CARROLL's

next suspenseful romantic adventure
Coming October 2009
from Avon Books

rip•tide (rip/tîd/), *n.* a tide that opposes another or other tides, causing a violent disturbance in the sea.

Random House Webster's Unabridged Dictionary

I came to on a moonlit beach. I was running, or trying to. My bare feet made furrows in the cold night sand. My right hand was wrapped around the slim neck of a near-empty bottle of Jamesport Vineyards Chardonnay. An onshore breeze played havoc with the sheer voile of my wrap dress. The bow at my waist had come undone, so most of the dress billowed at my side like a sail. It felt like I had an imaginary invisible twin.

This struck me as hilarious. I stopped so I could laugh as hard as I wanted. I felt I should tell all this to Dan, explain to him about my imaginary twin, and how we could finally have that threesome he kept bugging me about.

But the wind tore away my words before I could say them. I hiccupped.

*I heard Dan's deep, booming laugh behind me. He
came up close, and I felt his breath on my shoulder that
was bare except for the silk strap of my bra. I got a whiff
of the hot cloud that was Daniel Cunningham, a thick
stew of Old Spice and cigarettes, and the fruity scent of
the wine we'd been drinking since lunch at Lenny's on
the dock in Montauk.*

*His bare arms came up sharp around my waist, warm
and muscled, marbled through with thick veins on
smooth skin, pulling me back against him. I lost my balance and fell against his chest, melting into that cloud of
his, slipping down and down and down . . .*

"Christina?"

Christina felt their eyes on her. The circle was quiet,
waiting.

Dan, his face, his scent, the knowing way of his hands
on her bare skin, filled her mind. He was always there
for her, the lover who lived in her head. Like a drug she
could always come back to and use again.

But not here. Not now.

The counselor's name was Peter, and he leaned forward until he was in danger of slipping off the edge of
his molded plastic chair. "Christina?" He said her name
again, coming down heavy on the next to last syllable so
it sounded like a question.

But it was not a question, not really, and Christina
knew it. It was a command to spill her guts.

The group watched, like so many hyenas in the veldt
waiting to pounce on a fresh kill.

Peter let a moment or two pass. He began to speak
when Christina did not. "There came a day, finally,
when I knew my number was up. I don't know why
that day was different, but it was. I had hit my bottom

and I knew it." Peter picked up the folded napkin from underneath his Styrofoam cup and used it to mop up the sheen along his upper lip.

Heat from outside seeped in around the edges of the heavy automatic doors and sealed windows of the rehab despite the A.C., which was kept in arctic blast mode to protect the patients from the merciless furnace that was Minnesota in July.

Beads of sweat poked through Peter's polo shirt, dotting his midsection like chicken pox. "The way I was drinking, I should have been dead ten times over." He used the flip side of the napkin to blot at his forehead.

Nods and murmurs of assent moved around the circle like a wave through the stands inside a football stadium.

"But the day I finally got it, I was done. My number had come up. I had taken my last drink. And I knew it." The counselor leaned back until the plastic chair creaked, his gaze never wavering from Christina's face. "That's what we call hitting bottom, Christina. Have you hit your bottom yet?"

She looked at him, taking stock of the pale blue eyes and thinning blond hair, the face that was arranged into a permanent frown of understanding. He was a third-generation Norwegian American whose drinking had taken him on a wild ride across the Midwest through two marriages, seven locked psych wards, and even a brief stint in prison. Until he had seen the light and found his way here, where he could dedicate all his time and energy to shining the beacon of recovery into the dark hearts of drunks like Christina.

"You don't need to hide anymore, Christina. You're in a safe place." Peter's blue eyes swam with compassion for her, so deep and so full, apparently, that he needed to press the napkin into service yet again to dab at them. He took a swig of coffee that went down with an audible gulp.

Signaling to Christina that it was okay, he had all the time in the world when it came to saving her soul.

God, she hated him.

She stared down at the carpet, a sculpted pattern in a drab mix of colors that was designed to handle high-volume traffic. She risked a glance at some of the faces she had gotten to know over the last six days, since she had stopped shaking and come off the IV, leaving the medical unit behind to join Peter and his motley crew. There was the bass player, HIV-positive, from the boy band Christina's son had once idolized. The wattle-faced CEO of the largest chain of dry cleaning stores in the Midwest, who was facing indictment for tax evasion. A saw-voiced woman from Montecito who debated hourly whether she should sell her share in the family vineyard in order to stay sober. And Sylphan, Christina's roommate, whose flowing goth attire could not hide her tortuous thinness. The name was a put-on like the black lipstick and spiky pink hair. The girl wept through the night even in her sleep. Yesterday in group she had hinted that her addiction had its roots in the bedtime routine at her stepfather's place in Bucks County.

No doubt about it, Christina thought, the carpet in this place was designed to take a beating. She cleared her throat, calculating whether she could get away with saying she preferred to listen instead of talk, just for today.

"Just for today" was Peter's mantra.

"It's okay, Christina," he said in a soft voice. "We're here for you, and we're not going anywhere."

That much was obvious. Most of her fellow recovering addicts had no choice but to stick it out, here by court order or the result of a workplace intervention. But Christina did not have a workplace, nor did she have any sheet from a judge. She doubted anyone from her life would even notice she was gone. Except Dan. He knew where she was. But he didn't count. He was not, strictly speaking, part of her world.

Christina's son Tyler was vacationing in Aix-en-Provence with her in-laws until the middle of August, when Christina and Jason would drive him down to the Hill School for opening weekend. And Jason? Her husband could be in the city, or in East Hampton, or who knew where. He hadn't offered to fly out here with her. She'd come on her own. The rehab would have provided an escort if she had wanted to pay for one, but that wasn't the point.

"Jesus Christ," Jason had said, wrinkling his nose at the sight of Christina lying on rumpled sheets in the guest bedroom.

She told him then what she was planning to do, her voice weak, her skull so heavy she was not able to lift it more than an inch, just enough to sip water from the glass she'd thought to leave out next to the bed the night before. A drunk's trick.

"Jesus Christ," he said again, shaking his head. He sneered. And then, of all things, he laughed.

Even with the blinds drawn tight against the glare from the beach and her eyes swollen almost shut, Christina saw a white flash of teeth against Jason's tanned skin. It had been a long, long time since she had heard him laugh. She noticed this despite her skull, which was throbbing like it was two sizes too tight. She couldn't sit up. She fell back against the pillows.

This, it turned out, would be the last time Christina saw her husband alive.

She would remember him this way, standing in the guest room doorway of their beach house on a summer afternoon (or possibly morning or early evening, Christina didn't know which), throwing his head back to laugh at her plan.

Truth be told, and the truth was not something either Christina or Jason was in the habit of telling, it was an outrageous plan. But she had run out of options.

Jason laughed hard with a sound that rolled up from deep inside. He took his time until he was good and finished. He looked at her, for probably the first time in ages.

Christina did not like the look in his eyes.

He shook his head, planting one hand high on the door frame. "Whatever." He turned to go.

Christina would always remember the squeaking sound his fingers made as he dragged them down the wall.

As though he was being tugged away by an unseen hand.

"Take a car service to JFK," he said over his shoulder. "Leave the Mercedes here."

Christina couldn't imagine how she was going to transport herself to Minnesota, a state she couldn't pinpoint on a map, when she wasn't able to sit up in bed without vomiting. But she had to. She had run out of ideas and couldn't think of anything else to do. Maybe commit suicide. But as the sun shone brightly down on the Cardiffs' oceanfront estate on Jonah's Path that day, Christina was too worn out even to kill herself.

So she had landed here just over a week ago, in a place more foreign to her than any of the capitals in Western Europe, to do the unthinkable.

Quit drinking.

The problem was, once the shaking stopped and she was transferred into the residential treatment program that had cured legendary sports figures, politicians, rock bands, a first lady, and, it was rumored, a certain individual who was less than tenth in line to the British throne, Christina Cardiff was caught off guard by something she never saw coming.

A wave of terror so big and so deep she nearly drowned in it.

If she stopped drinking, then what?

Christina's life stretched out before her like a vast uncharted wilderness, for which she had no map.

The fear was followed by a second wave of emotion, no less powerful than the first. Self-pity. It rose up and swamped her, flooding her, washing away her resolve.

Hot tears pulsed at the backs of her eyes. When had her life turned into this, drinking shitty coffee from a vat while perfect strangers took turns spilling their guts?

She tried to swallow around the lump that formed in her throat. To her horror a small sound escaped, one that was shapeless and feral. Like the sound made by the possum they'd caught in the attic last fall. The trap was supposed to be humane because the animal was simply cornered, not killed.

So much for Havahart traps, Christina thought,

clamping her teeth down tight to avoid making that sound again. She was pretty sure she knew just how that possum had felt.

"It's okay, Christina." Peter leaned forward, pressing his napkin into her hand.

Soggy as it was, she wiped her eyes, wet now with tears.

"This is a safe place," Peter said.

It was a weird place, Christina wanted to tell him, straight out of an old skit from *Saturday Night Live*.

Instead she hunched forward in her chair, pressing the limp napkin tightly to her face. In that moment she got a sense of herself floating high in an imaginary perch up near the acoustical ceiling tiles, looking down at the Christina below. And she glimpsed herself not as the person she had become, pouring her life out in the liquid measures of goblets and pints and liters required to get her through each day, but as she really was.

In the parlance of Alcoholics Anonymous, Christina Cardiff was a garden-variety drunk.

In that moment of mental clarity came an opening. Maybe, just maybe, she could do it.

Get sober.

Christina considered for the first time since she'd arrived here that she might succeed.

Which in turn meant she would have to begin the process of mental undressing that seemed to be at the core of what went on here. She would have to humble herself, ask for help. Take a chance that help would come from the random assortment of junkies and drunks, any one of whom the Cardiff fortune could have bought and sold ten times over, seated around her now in a semi-circle.

"Stay with us, Christina." Peter was using his best Dr. Phil therapy voice. But he sensed the tug on the line, she could tell. His plastic molded chair creaked, giving him away.

Murmurs rippled around the circle. The group wanted, more than anything, for her to seize this moment.

Carpe diem. Another AA slogan.

But it was so hard. She had never imagined it would be this hard, just to open her mouth and start. A surge of nausea, like the morning sickness she'd had with Tyler, sprang up inside her, and she hunched over with her head between her knees. The nausea was followed by something far worse.

A wave of panic that rolled in and crashed on top of her. Christina had not gone more than two days without a drink or a joint or a pill or *something* since high school.

Someone began to massage the back of her neck.

Christina practically hit the ceiling.

It was Sylphan, her roommate. "You can do this, Christina," Sylphan whispered. "I'll help you. We all will."

The simple act of kindness from frail little Sylphan proved Christina's undoing. Sobs rose up from deep within her, and Christina began to cry.

Christina never usually cried.

"It's okay," Sylphan murmured, patting Christina's shoulder. "We've all been there. We all know what it's like."

Christina marveled at the love that welled up inside her for a girl who up until one week ago would not have been allowed to escort Christina's son to a school dance. A girl who had been molested from when she

was eight years old, and who had needed to steal her
mother's prescription drugs just to get through a day
of junior high.

Correction, Christina thought. Sylphan didn't become
a drug addict because her stepfather had molested her.
Sylphan had been *born* a drug addict. It just didn't man-
ifest itself until Sylphan's life turned tough. That's when
she started stealing her mother's Vicodin. The setup was
there. Drug addiction was a genetic disease. Access to
painkillers had served to move the process along, like
pouring gasoline onto a fire.

Jesus, Christina thought, she could hear Peter's words
in her head even when he wasn't lecturing. As now.

Some of it was beginning to sink in. Maybe she was
getting the hang of this. She sat up, feeling brave enough
now to risk a look in Peter's direction.

He watched her, not moving a muscle, with a lopsided
sort of smile on his smooth round face. Not the kind of
come-on smile she'd been getting from men since she
was twelve, but a proud smile like a father watching his
little girl.

Their eyes met.

Christina managed a half smile of her own. Her nose
was hopelessly clogged but her tears were slowing down
a little. She pressed the soaked napkin into service one
more time, covered her nose, and blew hard.

A week ago it would have been unthinkable for Christina to leave the house without makeup and jewelry, and
now here she was honking away into somebody else's
used napkin in front of a room full of strangers.

God, she hoped this guy knew what he was doing.

Sylphan gave Christina's shoulder one last squeeze
and took her hand away.

As though she, too, sensed that Christina's moment had arrived.

Christina took a deep breath, shifted around on her molded plastic seat, and sat up.

The boy band bass player from Studio City stopped tapping his foot.

"Okay?" Peter's pale eyebrows rose on his forehead.

Christina nodded. She cleared her throat while about a million snapshots of her drinking career whirled through her mind. She tried to sort through them and pick one to start with.

And then, just as in the movies, she was saved by a knock on the door. Two sharp raps.

They sounded really loud.

The door opened before anyone said it was okay.

In walked the head honcho.

"Peter. I need a few minutes with you."

Christina blinked. She recognized the man in the doorway from the dust jacket photo of his book, which had been on the *New York Times* best-seller list for two years. Every nightstand in the place had a copy parked right next to Gideon's Bible and the blue book of Alcoholics Anonymous.

The room grew even quieter as everyone did the kind of double take they'd do if, say, Donald Trump popped his head in.

As rehab directors went, Christina thought, this guy was Elvis.

But he didn't look happy. He just stood there, gripping the doorknob with one hand.

Even Peter just stared.

Nobody interrupted Peter's group while it was in session. Nobody. The room always had gallons of coffee brewing, plus enough boxes of Kleenex to bail the *Titanic*. But how these things got there and when, Christina had no idea.

"Peter. Now, please." The director cocked his head in the direction of the hallway.

"I'm sorry." Peter's frown deepened, and he set his Styrofoam cup down so hard it landed with a splash. "We're in session." His warm, soft therapy tone was gone. His voice held a this-is-my-turf-get-out kind of edge, and for the first time Christina could see how Drinking Peter had a mouth that landed him in jail in his bad old days.

"Sorry." The director gave a quick nod of apology but pressed on. "I have something urgent to discuss with you. Now."

Peter looked really pissed off, like he was considering telling his big boss to get lost, but he must have thought better of it because he literally chewed his lip instead. "Take five, guys," he said to the room in general, and then, to Christina, "Hold that thought, Christina, okay? We'll pick it up in a minute."

Christina nodded, pretty certain they would not. Her moment had passed, or was passing before her eyes. She shrugged, became aware of the director's eyes on her, and glanced up.

Their gaze locked for a couple of seconds, no more. Long enough for her to read something there. Curiosity, and something else she couldn't put her finger on. Something that didn't match up with the I'm-okay-you're-okay therapy face that was a job requirement around here.

The moment passed. Peter was already on his feet, out the door.

The room let out its collective breath when they had gone. People stretched, made small talk, got up for another cup of coffee. Like a union shift on break.

Except it didn't last as long.

Peter was back in less than five minutes. "Christina? Will you come with me, please? Next door."

Everyone looked at Christina and got quiet again, even the loudmouthed bartender from Manhattan who dreamed of doing stand-up.

Christina was being called to the principal's office, and it didn't feel any better than she remembered from school.

Sylphan gave a thumbs-up.

Peter stood back to let Christina pass.

"This way, Christina." He motioned that she should go to where the director was waiting at the entrance to another, smaller conference room down the hall.

It had the feel of a Cold War prisoner exchange. Christina wondered what they'd do if she bolted for the exit sign at the end of the long hallway. Somehow, she couldn't imagine Elvis the Rehab King sprinting very far. But Peter the Ex-Con was coiled and ready to pounce. Christina did as she was told.

"I'll catch up with you in a minute," Peter said. He did not smile.

She wondered if they were kicking her out, if there was a problem with her health insurance. In which case Jason could wire the money, cover it till they worked it out. He'd be pissed, Christina thought. But too bad. He had paid cash at the Storm dealership in Southampton when he had his mind set on a brand new BMW roadster last fall, so he could wire money here to cover her treatment.

Christina wanted to stay for the full sixty days. This realization startled her. She hadn't admitted it even to herself till now. She couldn't go back to that life. She wanted a chance at a new start.

Elvis the Rehab King moved away, giving Christina plenty of space to pass through the doorway into a small conference room set up with a table and Aeron chairs.

Someone had thought to set the table with several tiny paper cups full of water and a box of Kleenex tissues.

"Have a seat." He did not meet her gaze.

Christina was getting a bad vibe.

She sat.

He pulled out one of the chairs near her but not directly next to her. "Christina Cardiff."

She nodded. This fact was well within his reach. They had all been photographed and fingerprinted at check-in. Not to mention he had obviously just sent Peter in to collect her.

"Your primary residence is in Manhattan, on Park Avenue, is that correct?"

She nodded.

"And you have a second home on Long Island?"

"Yes."

"And that would be?" He let his voice trail off so she could supply the information.

"East Hampton. Only during the summer." They had a place in Aspen, but that was in her in-laws' name.

"Right." He gave another quick nod but did not check her answers against the paperwork in his folder, nor did he jot anything down using his Montblanc pen.

The temperature in the room dropped a few degrees. Christina folded her arms across the thin silk mesh of her T-shirt. "Is there a problem with my health insurance?"

"No," he answered quickly. "No, your insurance has processed the claim and there is no problem with it. Everything is fine there."

He was stalling. He cleared his throat and reached for one of the tiny paper cups. He emptied it in a single gulp.

The Rehab King was nervous. The clarity of this realization caught Christina off guard. The fact that she noticed anything about him at all was out of character for her. Christina was not one to read other people's moods. Correction, she thought: Drunk Christina didn't notice other people's moods. Sober, Nervous, Jittery, Jumping-Out-of-Her-Skin Christina noticed lots of things about other people.

Such as the way Rehab King was unfurling the top of his Dixie cup and shredding it into tiny pieces.

And then she understood.

This man, who had amassed a fortune telling other people how to get through the worst moments of their lives, wished he were someplace else right now.

Because he knew something she didn't know.

Something bad. Something seriously awful, life-changing bad.

Christina felt the prick of a thousand tiny toothpicks on the move, fanning out across her shoulders, down her back, and along her arms.

A tiny marching Army of Doom.

Outside, the fescue lawn crisped under a blazing sun.

Inside, the room turned airless and cold, like the inside of a refrigerator.

Christina shivered.

The Rehab King saw it and leaped to his feet. "Let me lower the fan. Sometimes it's difficult to regulate the temperature in these smaller rooms."

She gripped the edge of the polished mahogany table so hard her hands hurt. "What's wrong?"

Careful not to look her way, he hunched low over the air-conditioning controls. "Some of these smaller rooms get way too cold in summer, and they overheat in winter."

"What is it?" Christina's voice rose.

Peter entered the room. He glanced from Christina to his boss and then back again, carefully closing the door behind him. "I'm sorry," he said, the expression on his face even more mournful than usual.

Rehab King shook his head, embarrassed. "She doesn't . . . I mean, I didn't . . ." His voice trailed off.

Men are cowards, Christina thought. She was on her feet without knowing how she got there. "What is it?" She directed her question at Peter.

He blinked. "Christina, I'm sorry. I have bad news. Please sit down."

"No." Edging back, Christina raised one hand in protest, as if she could stop whatever this was from happening if she could just keep the words from leaving Peter's mouth.

"Christina, I need you to stay calm now and be strong."

Something like the claw of a Tonka truck, but bigger, went to work on her insides, scraping out everything between her shoulders and knees.

Peter's words floated past her with no weight, as Christina's gut rearranged itself around the hole left behind by the claw.

"No, no." She stood not moving as a series of images, each more terrible than the last, flashed through her mind like static. "No." She was shrieking now.

The Rehab King flinched. He pressed himself as far back as he could against the console near the windows.

Peter, to his credit, held his ground. The look in his eyes, normally gooey with compassion, had solidified. "Sit down," he ordered.

Christina sat.

Lowering himself quickly into the chair next to hers, he cut right to the chase. "I'm sorry, we have received very bad news about your husband, Jason."

It wasn't Tyler. Her son. Tyler was okay. It wasn't Tyler, or he would have said Tyler's name. He was talking about Jason, not Tyler. They had not called her in here with news about Tyler.

"Tyler?" The act of speaking her son's name out loud took away whatever was holding her head up, and Christina fell forward on the chair.

The room went dim, buzzing with a crazy hum.

Peter's voice had an urgent tone that was too loud.

He was scared, too.

"Your son is fine." Peter grabbed Christina's hand. "Tyler is okay. He's fine, safe and sound."

"You're sure?" Her voice was reedy and tinny and far away, like an old phonograph recording. She was going into shock at this moment but, like everything else surrounding this event in her life, it was a label that would not come to her until much later.

"Tyler is fine," Peter repeated. "Safe with your in-laws in France."

Relief splashed through her veins like a neap tide in

spring, flooding her heart and filling her ears with sound. She barely heard what he said next.

"This is about your husband, Christina. Jason went for a swim in the pool of your East Hampton home sometime during the night. He experienced some difficulty swimming, and he drowned."

Jason never went in the pool at night. Christina frowned.

"Apparently your husband had been entertaining some guests in the home earlier in the night." Peter shifted in his seat, looked away.

That bitch. Christina nearly blurted the words out loud. Jason had a girlfriend. Lisa, from the Upper West Side. Christina had caught a glimpse of her once. She stared at the thin film of dust motes on the polished surface of the table. This room didn't get much use.

Peter met her gaze once more. "After the guests left, your husband went for a swim. The cleaning crew came in this morning . . ." His voice faded.

No doubt trying to spare Christina the images that were tumbling through her mind.

The counselor tightened his grip on Christina's hand. "The housekeepers noticed something was amiss shortly after they began work, and they immediately alerted the authorities."

The head housekeeper, Rosa, was in her sixties. Tight-lipped, with a ruby-encrusted crucifix on a thick chain of gold that she wore around her neck. Her niece, Marisol, wore her hair in a black braid and sent money back to Costa Rica to provide for a son with special needs. The pair worked in silence, mainly, and could be moved to tears on an average day.

The pool on Jonah's Path had just been redone, lined with tiles that had been hand-fired in Milan and shipped air freight. They had installed an underwater stereo system and state-of-the-art lighting system that was radio-controlled.

The lighting system used some kind of high-tech diodes that operated on a sensor. As soon as anyone jumped in the pool at night, lights would pop on in red, green, blue, or yellow.

Christina blinked.

Peter massaged her hand.

A warning flare fired down in the deepest dark core of Christina's being, emitting a flash of white heat.

Dan on a ladder, paintbrush in hand, stopping long enough to do something obscene with his tongue that only Christina could see. Jason, oblivious at her side, discussing options for a stucco finish with the contractor.

"Your husband doesn't have a clue," Dan whispered later, his breath tickling the place he had just licked inside Christina's ear. "He doesn't appreciate what he has."

The warning flare burned itself out, leaving only a trace of doubt behind in Christina's panicked mind, lingering no longer than a wisp of sulfur.

Sulfur.

Satan's calling card.

Christina sniffed. Her shoulders hunched and her neck muscles constricted in a small movement that was, in certain people, an involuntary reaction to guilt.

Peter patted her knee.

Across the table, the Rehab King finally pulled out an Aeron chair and sat.

Nobody said anything.

Christina's mind, greedy now for reassurance, raced to Dan. She pictured his face with its stubble of five o'clock shadow, his musky scent, and the bruising weight of his lips on hers. But the staff here would not have interrupted the residents' morning group therapy session to bring her news of Daniel Cunningham. Nobody knew of her connection to him. She was not Dan's next of kin. He was a paint and plaster guy who worked for a contractor who had been hired to renovate the pool area of the Cardiffs' summer home.

Nobody knew Daniel Cunningham was Christina's lover.

If something bad had happened to Dan somehow, she would hear of it only as an afterthought. It would be a footnote to the shitty news Peter was telling her, brought up only after Peter was certain she had absorbed the news about Jason.

Christina couldn't wait that long. "Was anyone else . . . ?" Christina allowed her voice to trail off, hoping it sounded like a random expression of concern.

"No. Your husband was alone in the house." Peter kept his gaze steady but his crow's-feet deepened.

She nodded, hugging her arms across her chest to try to stop shaking.

The Rehab King broke his silence at last. "We're all very sorry for your loss, Mrs. Cardiff."

Loss. *Her* loss. Except her husband hadn't belonged to her. The marriage had been a fake front for a long time, but the Rehab King's words placed a terrible burden of ownership on her.

Christina blinked.

Jason, her husband of nearly sixteen years who had cheated on her beginning with their first married Valentine's Day when she was pregnant with Tyler, was dead.

Which made her a widow.

A widow who stood to inherit approximately one million dollars for each and every year she had been married.

Her in-laws had stood guard over that trust fund like the marines posted at Fort Knox.

And now it belonged to her.

This fact danced along Christina's nerve endings, already stretched taut like tuning wire. The result was a sensation that tingled its way out to the surface, releasing energy in the form of a sound that was halfway between strangulation and a giggle.

The vibration made it difficult to focus on the words that were flowing, warm and smooth like hot coffee, from Peter's mouth.

"It's okay." Peter reached now for both Christina's hands, working them over inside his with his thumbs. "Whatever you're feeling now is okay. Just feel the feelings and move through them."

But the look in his eyes was not as open and supportive as it had been just a few minutes ago. Christina frowned, struggling mightily to wrap her mind around the fact that she had just become the wealthiest widow she knew.

Another sound zoomed up, unbidden like the first, through her mouth.

Both men looked away, grabbing at the same time for the last remaining Dixie cup. They fumbled and nearly spilled its contents.

This struck Christina as funny, and she tried to hold back a giggle but could not.

The Rehab King frowned.

"It's okay, Christina." Peter pressed the Dixie cup into her hands. "Everybody grieves in their own way."